His kisses are a
Christmas miracle…
D0172481

ACCLAIM FOR

***NEW YORK TIMES* AND**

***USA TODAY* BESTSELLER**

ELOISA JAMES

"One of the brightest lights in our genre.
Her writing is truly scrumptious."

Teresa Medeiros

"She writes with a captivating blend of charm, style, and grace that never fails to leave the reader sighing and smiling and falling in love."

Julia Quinn

"Call her 'the historical Jennifer Crusie' . . .
James gives readers plenty of reasons to laugh."

Publishers Weekly

"She's a gift every romance reader
should give herself."

Connie Brockway

"[James] forces the reader
into a delicious surrender."

USA Today

"Romance writing
does not get much better than this."

People

By Eloisa James

An Affair Before Christmas
Desperate Duchesses
Pleasure for Pleasure
The Taming of the Duke
Kiss Me, Annabel
Much Ado About You
Your Wicked Ways
A Wild Pursuit
Fool for Love
Duchess in Love

Coming Soon

Duchess By Night

ELOISA JAMES

An Affair Before Christmas

AVON

An Imprint of HarperCollins*Publishers*

This is a work of fiction. Names, characters, places, and incidents are products of the author's imagination or are used fictitiously and are not to be construed as real. Any resemblance to actual events, locales, organizations, or persons, living or dead, is entirely coincidental.

AVON BOOKS
An Imprint of HarperCollins*Publishers*
10 East 53rd Street
New York, New York 10022-5299

ISBN: 978-0-06-124554-1
ISBN-10: 0-06-124554-2
www.avonromance.com

First Avon Books paperback printing: December 2007

Printed in the U.S.A.

10 9 8 7 6 5 4 3 2 1

This book is dedicated to
Monsignor James Mahoney,
who always celebrates romance
as an expression of the deepest human love.
And what's more, he served as a model
for the cover of The Taming of the Duke.

Thanks

With a thank you, from the bottom of my heart, to the usual suspects: my brilliant editor, Carrie Feron; my organized and imaginative assistant, Kim Castillo; and my erudite research assistant, Franzeca Drouin. I couldn't do it without you all!

The character of Mrs. Patton was inspired by Ann Rosamond, who would have made a terrific Georgian lady!

Prologue

Saint Germain des Prés
Paris, 1778

Ice hung from windowsills with a glitter that rivaled glass, and new snow turned the sooty streets to rivers of milk. Looking at the city from the bell tower of Saint Germain, the Duke of Fletcher could see candles flaring in store windows, and though he couldn't smell roasting goose, holly leaves and gleaming berries over doors signaled that all of Paris had turned its mind toward a delicious banquet of gingerbread and spice, of rich wine and sugared cakes. An ancient joy shone in each passerby's eyes and spilled from children's laughter. Magic sang in the wild peals of church bells that kept breaking out first in one church and then another, in the way each sprig of mistletoe sheltered sweet kisses. It was Christmas . . . It was Christmas in Paris, and if there was ever a city made for love, and a season made to enjoy it in, the two of them together were as intoxicating as the strongest red wine.

In fact, philosophers have argued for years whether it is possible to be in Paris and not fall in love . . . if not with a ravishing woman, then with the bells, with the baguettes, with the gleam of the illicit that touches every heart, even those of proper English noblemen. The duke would have answered that question without hesitation. He had thrown away his heart after one glance at Notre Dame, had succumbed to the siren call of delicious food after one bite of French bread, and had finally—absolutely—irrevocably—fallen in love with a young and ravishingly beautiful member of the opposite sex.

From where Fletch stood in the bell tower, Ponte Neuf leapt the Seine in a voluptuous curve, and all Paris shimmered below him, a forest of spires and roofs, dusted with snow. Every gargoyle sported a long silver nose. Notre Dame floated queen-like above the other more narrow and anxious spires that seemed to beg for God's attention. The cathedral ignored such slender anxieties, counting herself more beautiful, more devoted, more luxurious than the others. Christmas, she seemed to say, is mine.

"It's almost miraculous, how we feel about each other."

Fletch blinked and looked down at his bride-to-be, Miss Perdita Selby. For a moment Notre Dame, Poppy and Christmas were confusingly mixed in his mind: as if a cathedral were more erotic than a woman; as if a woman were more sacred than the holiday.

She smiled up at him, her face framed by soft curls, the color of white gold streaked with sunlight, her mouth as sweet and ripe as any French plum. "You don't think it's too good to be true, Fletch? You don't, do you?"

"Of course not!" Fletch said promptly. "You're the most

beautiful woman in the country, Poppy. The only miracle is that you fell in love with me."

"That's no miracle," Poppy said, putting a slender finger squarely on the dimple in the middle of his chin. "The moment I saw you, I knew that you were everything I wanted in a husband."

"And that is?" He put his arms around her, regardless of who might be watching. It was *Paris,* after all, and while there were plenty of English gentlefolk here, standards weren't as rigid as they were back in London.

"Well, you are a duke," she said teasingly.

"You just love me for my title?" He bent his head to kiss her on the cheek. Her skin was inexpressibly creamy and soft. It drove him into an ecstasy of lust . . . a French-inflected lust, the kind that wanted to kiss a woman from the very tip of her toes to the top of her ears, that wanted to lick and snuffle and eat her, as if she were more delicious than a truffle (which she would be).

It was not the kind of lust he ever felt before he came to France. In England, men looked at women as vessels in which to plunge and buck. But Fletch could feel himself changing and growing, the power of Paris and love. He wanted to worship Poppy's body, taste the sweet salt of her sweat, kiss away her tears of joy after he brought her to the ultimate happiness.

"Exactly," Poppy said, laughing. "Your title is all important. I didn't even notice how handsome you are, or the way you treat ladies with so much respect, or the fact that you dance so beautifully, or—or this dimple."

"Dimple?" Fletch was bent on kissing her again, and he meant to distract her into talking as long as he could so she would relax into the intimacy of it. Little Poppy was the sweetest girl in the world, but she was devilishly hard to kiss. Every time he managed to get her alone, there was always some reason why he couldn't hold her, why he couldn't kiss her. At this rate, they would have to wait until their wedding night to indulge in any and all of the wanton things that paraded through his mind twenty-four hours a day.

"In your chin," she said, nodding her head. "The dimple was what really made up my mind."

He pulled back, a little disgruntled. "I hate this dimple. In fact, I may well grow a beard to cover it up."

"Oh, you couldn't do that!" she sighed, caressing his chin. "It's so adorable. You can tell just from looking at it what kind of man you are."

"And what kind of man is that?" he asked, bending his head again and never guessing how much her answer would resound in his mind in years to come.

"Honorable, and true, and—and everything a woman could possibly want in a husband. All the ladies agree; you should hear the Countess Pellonnière. She says you're *delicious*."

Fletch thought that Poppy might have missed the point of the countess's admiration. "They all say that?" He was close enough to her mouth that he made a sudden dive at it. For a second he thought she was yielding; those sweet rosy lips of hers that kept him up half the night in a fever of lust softened under his assault. But when he added a little tongue to the mix—

"Eeek! What are you doing!"

"Kissing you," he said, dropping his arms from around her shoulders because she was whacking him with her muff and it seemed the right thing to do.

"That is disgusting," she said, glaring at him. "Disgusting! You don't think that duchesses go around doing that sort of thing, do you?"

"Kissing?" he asked helplessly.

"Kissing like *that.* You put your—your saliva in my mouth!" She looked truly horrified. "How could you think that I would allow something like that? I'm disgusted!"

"But Poppy, that's what kissing is like," he protested, feeling a chill wisp of alarm down his backbone. "Haven't you seen people kissing under the mistletoe? You can ask anyone."

"How could I ask anyone," she said in a heated whisper. "To ask anyone would be to allow them to know of your perversion—and I would never do that. You are going to be my husband, after all!" A strange mixture of adoration and reprobation crossed her eyes.

"I know!" he exclaimed in relief. "Ask the Duchess of Beaumont. She knows exactly what I'm talking about."

Poppy frowned. "My mother says that the duchess is the most unprincipled Englishwoman in Paris. It's true that I am very fond of Jemma, but I'm not sure that—"

"Your mother's disapproval of the duchess," Fletch said, "makes her the very person to ask about a little question like this."

"But Jemma is not kissing anyone," Poppy objected. "Why, Mother says that the duke barely even visits her. He finally came last summer, when Parliament was out." She gazed up at him, her blue eyes impossibly innocent. "How could I ask her about kissing you? It would make her feel sad that her own marriage is so terribly empty, when ours will be so lovely." She put a hand on his cheek, and suddenly none of it mattered.

"I don't care if you ask or not," he said, pulling her into his arms again. At least she let him hold her. That would have to do until they wed. "We can work it all out on our wedding night." He was determined to bring his beloved Poppy the same pleasure that he would find in her body. He'd read all about it in a French book, stumbling along through the strange words. And he was astute enough to realize that none of the semi-professional encounters with women he'd had before coming to Paris had had anything to do with his partner's pleasure. In fact, thinking of their practiced moans made him shudder.

If Paris had taught him anything, it was this: he could sleep with Cleopatra herself, and if she wasn't enjoying the act, he didn't want anything to do with it. When a Parisian woman smiled, her smile was an invitation that had everything to do with *her* pleasure, and little to do with his. When a Parisian woman smiled at him, Fletch remembered Cécile, who told him that his lips were as beautiful as cherries, or Élise, who uttered little screams when she saw him unclothed. Of course, Élise and Cécile belonged to his first month in Paris, before he fell in love. Now his heart was full of Poppy . . . and his loins would love to follow his heart.

But Poppy, leaning against his broad shoulder, frowned to herself. What exactly did Fletch mean by saying that they would *work it out*? That sounded as if this type of kissing was something he had his heart set upon.

Poppy was a practical little soul, at the heart. She could see that her husband's easygoing manners and sweet eyes masked a sturdy determination to get his own way. One only had to look at his wind-swept locks to see that. Never a touch of powder! Her mother clucked, but Fletch refused . . . and Poppy had to admit that he looked well with raven locks tumbling around his neck.

"I'll ask Jemma," she promised. He was kissing her ear, and she liked that. In fact, she enjoyed many of the things Fletch did, like putting his arms around her (as long as he didn't disturb her hair), and kissing her ear and her cheek and her chin, and even her lips, except when he became a trifle too forceful in that respect.

Her mother had instructed her very firmly on that front.

"You must allow him to brush your lips with his," she had said. "After all, he is a duke. You will be a duchess. In order to catch a duke, one must allow certain indignities."

At the time, Poppy had laughed at the idea that Fletch's lips on hers could be seen as an indignity. Joy had flooded her soul that she was so lucky. She was in love with a duke, and that made her mother happy. A duke (darling Fletch) was in love with her . . . and that made her happy. In fact, the world was all sunshine and light, if she could just work out this kissing business.

"Let me show you how nice it is," Fletch said coaxingly. When his voice deepened like that, Poppy wanted to do anything he wished, though of course she would never have told him so. One mustn't let men know how much power they have, her mother often said. And she was right, of course.

But she obediently bent her head up towards his, and he brushed his lips across hers. "That's nice," she said encouragingly. "Why, I—"

The next moment he pulled her so sharply into his arms that she felt her stays poke directly into her breasts; her brooch unhooked and fell to the stone floor. "Fletch!" she cried. He took advantage of that, and stuck his tongue directly into her mouth. Directly! And—and swept it about, as if she were some sort of cupboard he were cleaning.

"Awk, urg, no!" she shrieked, shoving him away. For a small woman, Poppy had a lot of strength.

"But Poppy . . ."

Not even his sad eyes could make her change her mind about this. "I love you, Fletch, you know that." She narrowed her eyes and waited.

"You know how much I love you," he said, giving her a coaxing little smile.

She didn't smile back. "You simply have to learn that there are things that—that an English lady doesn't *do*."

"What do you mean?" He looked a bit confused, and Poppy had a flash of pride. For once, she knew something he didn't!

"Mama says that ladies have different rules for intimacy than—than, say, our *lavandière* does," she explained to him, carefully keeping even the slightest bit of condescension out of her voice.

"They don't kiss? Of course ladies kiss. And washerwomen too, no matter whether they're French or English!"

"They may kiss," she said, "but there are different kinds of intimacies practiced by the different classes, of course. Just as we wear different clothing, and eat different foods. And different nations too. We are fundamentally different. My mother says that English gentlewomen have very little in common with the French."

He stared down at her and Poppy nearly blinked. Could that look be, just a little, well, disappointed? She hated disappointing people. "Do you understand?" she asked, a catch of anxiety in her voice.

"I suppose," he said, rather slowly.

"You can see it yourself, Fletch, if you compare our monarchy to that of the French. The English court is virtuous, whereas the French court is riddled with scandal. My mother says—"

"Believe me, the English court is as rife with scandal as is the French. The distance of the Channel just makes it look cleaner. Their rumors don't make it across the water."

Poppy thought about that. "So you mean that last week, when there was all that fuss about Lady Serrard flirting with L'Anou . . ."

"They never heard about it in England, obviously, but it was all we talked of for days. Yet it came to nothing. We never hear English tittle-tattle, any more than they will hear of Lady Serrard's supposed indiscretion."

"That's a fair point," Poppy conceded.

He grinned down at her and her breath caught in her throat. She couldn't help thinking that Fletch was far too beautiful for her.

The eyes of all the French ladies followed him, even those of the Countess Pellonnière. He often didn't appear to notice, but Poppy did. Looking up at him now, she felt as if she could turn to stone, admiring his beautiful eyes (black in the center with a luminous gray rim), his lean body, the way he moved so gracefully, even when just walking. A lady had once sighed and said that to watch the Duke of Fletcher make his bow was to see the male body at its utter peak of grace. How on earth could such a nonpareil have fallen in love with her, Poppy, short for Perdita and just short in general?

She wasn't the only one with that question in mind. French ladies looked at her and tittered behind their fans. They drifted past, congratulating her on her cleverness or called her a *mignonne,* which was next thing to calling her an infant.

Last night Fletch wore a mantle of black Epingle velvet embroidered with black jet beads to a ball given by the Duchess of Orleans. With his hair in a simple queue at his neck, he combined a rakish care-for-nothing air with the garments of an *élégante*. French ladies dropped their fans to smile at him, with that special pout they kept for delicious men. She had watched him smile in return, and then bow before the Countess d'Argentau, dancing with her for the second time.

"Sit straight!" her mother had barked at her. "*You* are going to be his duchess, not that rag-tale piece of nobility. Don't peer like a lovesick nursling; you lower yourself by noticing her attentions to him."

"But Mama," Poppy had said, pushed into honesty by the

twist in her gut, "the countess is so much more beautiful than I. And her gown is so much more revealing."

"You are attired perfectly for a young girl making her debut," her mother had said, looking her over. "And if your face and figure are not the height of regularity and beauty, no one could say that I spared the least expense." That was true. Her mother favored two ruffles where one might do, and often decided on five instead. Poppy's skirts were festooned with strings of seed pearls, and her bodices were trimmed with ermine.

But Poppy thought (secretly) that something simple might suit her better. Her frame was so small that side panniers, a long train, and a markedly large hairstyle, no matter how fashionable, made her feel like a decorated child.

Fletch tipped a finger under her chin. "I didn't mean to send you into a daze, Poppy. I picked up your brooch, but I'm afraid the pin is bent. I'll have it fixed for you."

It was foolish to worry. Fletch was here—and he was hers. She smiled at him. "Thank you."

Fletch turned the brooch over in his hand. "What an odd cameo."

"It's the only cameo of a bird I've ever seen. The Wedgwood company made it in honor of Queen Charlotte."

"And just how is a flying crane with a crown on its head supposed to honor the queen?"

"Foolish, isn't it? But look here"—she pointed it out to him—"the craftsman was marvelous. You can see each feather in the wingspan."

"But the crown makes it look as if the bird has horns," he objected.

"I know. That's a small problem in the execution, though I still like it." She tucked her hand under his arm. "Shall we return? It's quite chilly, and I wouldn't want Mama to become concerned about me." And then, because he still looked a little distant in a way that she didn't like, she added: "I'll ask Jemma exactly what ladies do and don't when it comes to kissing, Fletch. I promise."

A few minutes later they walked out the door of the abbey. Paris lay on either side of them, dreaming in the chilly morning air until suddenly the air came alive again with a wild ringing of bells, liquid notes falling from the tower above them, echoing off snowy brick walls and steep cathedral spires.

"It's Christmas," Poppy said, feeling a sudden rush of joy. "It's my favorite day of the year. I adore Christmas."

"I adore you," Fletch said, stopping. "Do you see what I see, Poppy?"

"What?" she breathed, looking up at him and not wherever he was pointing.

"Mistletoe," he said, putting his arms around her. "Mistletoe hanging in thin air."

Poppy closed her eyes and tipped up her face. It was just the right sort of kiss: sweet, short and loving. Then they began to walk back, Poppy picking her way over cobblestones lined in a thin gleaming sheet of ice.

A young woman hurried toward them, head down, a long loaf of bread tucked under her arm. Fletch felt as if he could smell the warm, fresh bread, and then before he knew it, he was imagining the luxurious curve of her breast pressed against the warm crust. He would—

He wrenched his thoughts away. When he and Poppy were married, he would have fresh-baked bread delivered to their chambers, and he would break it apart and eat it from her body, as though she were a platter for the gods.

"You have such a curious smile on your face," Poppy said. "What are you thinking about?"

"You. Only you."

Poppy smiled to herself, and an old Parisian who passed

reflected that he, one of the world's connoisseurs of beauty, had never seen a lady quite so exquisite. In her face and figure were years of English and French ancestry, and having been raised mostly in France, every aspect of her figure and costume was *à la mode*. But it was her eyes, and the way she looked only at the tall Englishman striding beside her, that made her shine with that particular joy that makes even the plainest person beautiful.

"Ah," he sighed. *"L'amour!"*

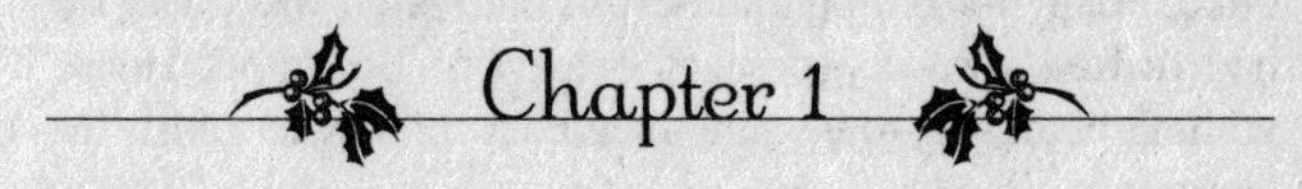

Chapter 1

Four years later

AN EXCERPT FROM THE MORNING POST,
APRIL 22, 1783

The buzz of the past few days amongst the *ton* has been the challenge that the Earl of Gryffyn offered the Duke of Villiers. It seems that the earl has stolen away the duke's fiancée. We cannot comment on the veracity of this report, but we would note that dueling has been strictly prohibited by our gracious sovereign . . .

Townhouse of the Duke and Duchess of Beaumont
A morning party in celebration
of the Earl of Gryffyn's victory in a duel

"The Duchess of Fletcher," the butler announced with a magnificent bellow. When he said nothing about the duke, Poppy looked behind her . . . but Fletch was gone. He had drifted away to some other part of Beaumont House without bothering to be announced. Or inform her of his intentions.

She could feel her smile turning rigid so she picked up her skirts and edged down the three marble steps into the ballroom. Side panniers made it difficult enough to negotiate doorways and stairs, but this morning her French maid had outdone herself. A veritable cascade of frills, curls and bows towered over Poppy's head, the whole of it draped with strings of small pear-shaped pearls. Walking was challenging; stairs were truly dangerous.

Not that it wasn't worth it. She was fiercely determined to achieve an elegance to match her husband's. Fletch and his costumes were the toast of London; she would *never* allow it to be said that his duchess shamed him. She didn't want anyone to be sorry for her. Ever.

Naturally Fletch hadn't said a word about her costume in the carriage, though he must have realized that her gown was new. Perhaps he thought its embroidery (in shades of gold and pearl) was too formal for a morning occasion. Poppy took a deep breath. If she'd learned anything from her four years of marriage, it was that one cannot guess what a man is thinking.

She revised that thought. Certain male thoughts were crystal clear.

"Your Grace," came a deep voice at her ear. "May I escort you to the other side of the ballroom, where there is less of a crush? The Duchess of Beaumont is to be found there."

"I'd be honored," Poppy said to her host, curtsying just deeply enough to acknowledge his rank without disbalancing her hair. The Duke of Beaumont was attired in a simple coat of dark green velvet with turned-back cuffs of sage green. Of course, men rarely dressed as formally as women. She placed her hand lightly on his arm and they strolled through the ballroom, nodding at acquaintances. "I hadn't thought to see you this morning," Poppy said, before she realized that was rather impolite.

The duke—a consummate politician known jointly for his disdain for infamy and his infamous duchess, Jemma—gave a rueful smile. "Undoubtedly this party will be the scandal of the week, since it is held to celebrate a duel. To be quite truthful, in the normal run of events I would likely avoid this particular gathering. But as it is my own duchess holding the party, and in my own house, more commotion would result if I did not attend."

Poppy felt a rush of sympathy for the poor duke. He was one of the most important men in the House of Lords, a man whose conviction, eloquence and power were known all over England. The last thing he needed in his life was scandal. And though she dearly loved Jemma from their days together in Paris, she had to admit that gossip-mongers adored the Duchess of Beaumont for good reason; everything Jemma did seemed to cause a sensation. It must be difficult to be married to her.

Almost as difficult as being married to Fletch.

She froze for a second. "Are you fatigued, Your Grace?" Beaumont asked, pausing. "Would you prefer to sit down?"

"Oh no," she said, pushing thoughts about her marriage away. "I am so looking forward to seeing Jemma. I haven't seen her since before I married, when we both lived in Paris. She must be happy to find that her brother won the duel."

"Naturally we are all relieved that the occasion ended

without undue bloodshed," Beaumont said evenly, his voice showing how much he disliked the idea of celebrating his brother-in-law's illegal foray into dueling. "And here is the duchess herself."

He bowed, and left. Jemma looked even more elegant than she had four years ago in Paris. Though she was wearing panniers too, her skirts weren't stiff like Poppy's but soft and flowing. And whereas Poppy's hair was curled into rigid little snail shells, Jemma's hair was shaped into soft curls, so lightly powdered that its natural gold color shone through. Her beauty had deepened; the sensual air that Poppy remembered was even more pronounced.

"Jemma," Poppy exclaimed. "How lovely you look!"

Jemma turned and gave a little shriek of welcome. "It's Poppy!" she cried, snatching her into a hug. Then she backed up and narrowed her eyes. "*What* has happened to the little mademoiselle I knew so well in Paris? You are exquisite! You put us all to shame. Look at us, three duchesses, and you are the only one who looks the part."

Poppy had already realized that she had grotesquely miscalculated the formality of the party. No wonder Fletch said nothing of her gown. Poppy smiled apologetically at the lady standing beside Jemma. "I'm sorry, but I don't think—"

"We've never met," she said, dropping a curtsy. "Jemma is engaging in hyperbole. I am no duchess. My name is Lady Isidore Del'Fino." Lady Isidore was wearing a gorgeous costume of soft rose-colored *crêpe-de-chine*. If Jemma was all sleek perfection, Lady Isidore looked like a ripe cherry, seductive and delicious. Poppy's heart sank even deeper.

"Isidore, this is the Duchess of Fletcher. Isidore is almost a duchess," Jemma said, giving Poppy's arm another affectionate squeeze. "She married by proxy and is just waiting for her duke to return from his travels."

"I might add that I've been waiting ten years," Isidore said, with such a funny wrinkle of her nose that Poppy started laughing. "I'm very happy to meet you, Lady Fletcher," she continued. "I've heard so much about your charitable endeavors."

"Which I shall not be joining," Jemma said. "I ought to make that clear to you now, darling, before I disappoint you. I'm no more charitable than I was when we knew each other in Paris. In fact, probably less so."

"How can you be less so?" Isidore demanded. "I've been living in Italy for the past three years, but I paid many a visit to Jemma," she explained to Poppy. "I can't say that I ever saw her exert herself to sew a charitable seam."

"I have my moments," Jemma said. And then added: "I consider charity to gentlemen my particular area of expertise."

Her look was so mischievous that Poppy broke out laughing.

"It's so strange to think of you married, darling," Jemma said. "You would hardly believe it, looking at her now, Isidore, but Poppy was the sweetest little poppet you ever saw. She used to wander around the French court with her eyes as round as—as plums."

"While everyone laughed at me," Poppy said to Isidore, snapping open her fan. "To call me naïve would have underestimated the truth. I was in a stupor of surprise most of the time."

"They never laughed!" Jemma cried, loyally. "They were too riveted with jealousy to laugh. You see," she told Isidore, "Poppy appeared in Paris with her mother and within a week—nay within the hour!—she snapped up the most eligible bachelor in the city, the Duke of Fletcher."

"I have seen him!" Isidore said, giving Poppy a smile. "In Italy we call such a man *bellissimo*."

Poppy gave her a tight smile. There was a limit to how

many times a woman wanted to be complimented for her husband's beauty. It always made Poppy feel like a bracket-faced harpy who had managed a miracle.

"Poppy seduced Fletch straight from the arms of the Parisian court. I think the Duchess of Guise has not yet forgiven you. She still mutters about English fledglings."

"Did you fall in love at first sight?" Isidore asked. "I would so like to do that, but it never seems to happen. Perhaps I could have fallen for your husband. Although," she added, "I wouldn't want you to think that I will look to your husband *now*."

Jemma broke in. "Don't be silly, Isidore. Poppy has Fletch at her feet. She's not one to become nervous about your charms. You see," she said, turning to Poppy, "Isidore's rather awkward position—"

"In fact, legally married though I haven't seen my husband since I was in leading strings," Isidore interrupted.

"Means that she tends to make married ladies nervous."

"I can't even *talk* to a married man," Isidore complained.

"You can certainly talk to mine if you wish," Poppy offered.

"There! I told you, Isidore. The two of you should become dear friends. Fletch is hopelessly in love, and so Poppy wouldn't blink even if you flirt with him. Isidore," Jemma said, turning to Poppy, "does have a disconcerting habit of making gentlemen fall in love with her, though I assure you that she does no more than talk to them."

"I promise not to flirt with your duke," Isidore said, giving Jemma a blinding smile. "But we shall be friends. The truth is that I find the Duke of Fletcher almost *troppo elegante* for me. I am greatly taken by men of a rougher cast."

"I know just what you mean," Poppy said. "A pirate!"

"Everyone loves a pirate," Jemma said sadly. "Sometimes it seems so cruel that I find myself married to a politician."

"There are no pirates in English society," Isidore observed. "Still, I would resign myself to a man without piratical attitudes if he would lavishly adore me as your husband does, Your Grace."

"Please call me Poppy." And, desperate to change the subject: "I'm sure that your husband will lavishly adore you."

"If he recognizes me," Isidore said with a little hiccup of laughter.

Chapter 2

THE MORNING POST (CONTINUED)

We do not comment on the veracity of this report, but we cannot help but wonder whether the Duke of Beaumont will be the next to challenge Villiers, given the rumor that the duchess, recently returned from Paris, is playing an intimate game of chess with the said duke . . .

"What you need is a mistress. For Christ's sake man, you're going to wither up and blow away. You'll be sprouting bubbies, if you don't watch out."

Fletch curled his lip. "I'll tell you what. If I grow breasts I'll let you have a look so you can finally see what a woman's chest looks like."

Frederick Augustus Gill, the future Earl of Glasse, responded with an amiable curse, and they went back to leaning against the wall and watching the exuberant, chaotic scene before them. The room was full of titled gentlemen, shouting about the Earl of Gryffyn's victory in a duel with the Duke of Villiers.

"Five minutes!" Fletch heard one red-faced man shout to another. "That's the way to do it!"

Gill shuddered and took a deep swallow of brandy. "Did you see the moment when Villiers brought out that *pass in tierce*? I thought Gryffyn was a croaker for sure."

"Gryffyn had Villiers from the beginning," Fletch stated. "It was all a matter of his deciding the moment to take the duke out."

"They're saying Villiers lost a lot of blood before the surgeon got himself together."

"He should be all right. It was a clean blow through the shoulder."

"Gryffyn is a lucky man," Gill said with a little sigh. "You should see the way his fiancée looks at him."

"What a romantic," Fletch sneered.

"You didn't used to be so hard-edged," his friend said, startled into a rebuttal. "You act as if you've got a stick up your ass. For God's sake, get yourself a mistress! So your wife's not interested in your bed. Practically every man in this room has experienced that. You could give the average English gentlewoman fifteen quinces, and they wouldn't strike up a flush."

"Back to the mistress you think I should take," Fletch said, with deadly boredom in his voice. "I had no idea you were so interested in my bedroom activities."

Gill's face flushed; he said something unrepeatable. And left.

Fletch sighed and drank from his glass again. He was a fool. It had been years. He needed a mistress. He needed to admit to himself that his marriage was a failure. He needed to . . .

Poppy floated by on the far side of the room. Her breasts swelled from the stiff little bodice of her gown. He hardened instantly. It was like the tortures of Tantalus to desire someone who never desired him. To be married to someone like that was like being tied to a well and never allowed to drink.

Yet the very idea of going to her chamber door made him wilt instantly. She would let him in, of course. Oh, her mother had tutored her in that. She would chatter and smile, but he was no fool. He could read the wary resignation in her eyes. Not to mention the way she would slip off her nightgown, lie down on the bed (his only triumph: she no longer insisted on being inside the covers) and suffer his attentions.

He drank again.

Suffer was the right word.

No matter what he did, she just lay there. In the beginning he had lavished time on her breasts, hoping that she would suddenly start panting and writhing beneath him, the way Élise had when he barely touched her. Élise had directed him about her body as if he were learning a new sport. "There," she said softly, and then, "harder," and then, "*oui!!*"

For God's sake, he was sick of thinking about Élise.

Poppy, on the other hand, sometimes stroked his head. She would kiss him, even allow him to put his tongue in her mouth occasionally, but she never responded to anything. In the beginning, he thought she was inexperienced.

Then a year passed, and another year, and she never grew any more interested, never raised a finger, never turned pink—let alone calling out "Yes, yes!" His thinking had changed.

Now he was pretty certain that it simply would never

work with Poppy. He stopped going to her chamber a few months ago. She said nothing; he said nothing. She was secretly relieved. She was probably celebrating it with all her friends.

And yet he still loved her.

Which was hell. She floated by again, laughing. Everyone loved Poppy. What was not to love, with the sweetness of her eyes, and the kind way she listened to every foolish complaint anyone told her? She never told her dragon of a mother to take herself to the devil, even when the woman ran Poppy from pillar to post, so pleased to have a duchess for a daughter that she showed her off like a trained monkey.

Poppy never rebuked her, never said a word.

In short, she was an angel.

Bloody hell, angels were boring to take to bed.

Still, his innards revolted at the idea of paying a woman to bed him. Take a mistress, take a mistress—that was Gill's advice. He'd be paying a woman to fake interest then. Paying her to pant and moan.

Yet there were other English gentlewomen . . . women who were interested in bedding and even, perhaps, in him. The Duchess of Beaumont had just returned from Paris, and the whole world knew that Jemma and Beaumont never slept together and hadn't in years. What's more, she had been playing a scandalous game of chess with the Duke of Villiers—and everyone knew that if Villiers won two out of three . . . the duchess herself was the prize.

Well, now Villiers was incapacitated. Lost a lot of blood, they said. Probably be in bed for weeks, if not a month.

Fletch pushed himself away from the wall and twitched up the high collar of his coat. The duchess had an eye for male finery; Villiers was the best-dressed man in London. But Fletch had brought over his own French *tailleur*; he thought he had a bit of an edge.

He stood up, and put down his empty glass. Walked forward. Very few would have recognized the fresh-faced young Englishman who walked the Pont Neuf only four years ago. Back then he had been sweet-faced, as Poppy had told him, with a dimple in the middle of his chin.

Now . . .

His hair was pulled back in a sleek tie that emphasized his cheekbones. In a fit of anger at Poppy he had grown a little, close-trimmed beard, covering the dimple she loved. And he walked with the controlled, hungry prowl of a man who hasn't had decent sex in years and is thinking of doing something about it.

He couldn't help but acknowledge how ridiculous it all was. As his marital life had dwindled to a visit a month and even less, he had fashioned himself ruthlessly into the kind of man who drew all women's eyes.

Except his wife's, of course.

He wore one color only—not for him the bright extravagances of the Duke of Villiers. For Fletch, clothing was not about making a statement about one's aggression, but about making clear his erotic appeal. His breeches were almost sewn on. They slipped, smooth as silk—and they often were silk—over thighs bulging with muscle from his daily pounding rides. His coats were designed to display his shoulders, to flaunt his chest, cut away from his flat stomach.

The only thing left from the unassuming duke who first arrived in Paris and fell in love with an English girl was his habit of wearing his hair unpowdered. He still did, but less from a dislike of the powder itself than from the realization that when he pulled his hair from its ribbon, unruly locks tumbling to his shoulders gave the impression that he just rose from a bed in which he had been well pleasured.

In short, Fletch knew perfectly well what an elaborate façade he had created. Only Gill knew he was a fraud. Only his old friend Gill knew how shocked the women who followed him with hot eyes, dreaming of his acrobatic stunts in the bedchamber, would be if they knew he was practically . . . practically a virgin, it felt sometimes.

Poppy played her part; he had to give her that. She even blushed in his presence sometimes. He had no idea how she held up the charade, and could only think that duplicity came naturally to her.

He could see her in the corner of his eye—to his disgust, he always seemed to know where his wife was—but he didn't walk in her direction. Instead, he started to move deliberately in the other direction.

In that moment, he gave up.

He needed a lover.

Now.

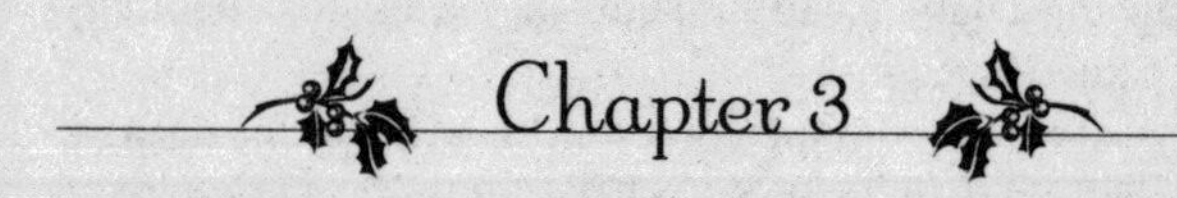

Chapter 3

<u>THE MORNING POST</u> (CONTINUED)

The Duchess of Beaumont, recently returned from Paris, is playing an intimate game of chess with Villiers . . . and reportedly with her husband as well. There has been some suggestion that these games are played in the bedchamber—even in the bed itself! This paper is moved to query the effect on the country's moral fiber of the host of female libertines recently returned from Paris . . .

"What's the matter with my party?" the Duchess of Beaumont demanded. "There are no naked singers, and I promise you I'm not planning to strip off my own clothing. Though if it wasn't such a cold morning I might consider it, just to vex Beaumont, since he has condescended to attend with all his parliamentary types."

"Well," her brother Damon said wryly, "let's just say that it's the first party I've ever attended in celebration of an illegal duel. I suspect there are those who might—just might—think it in rather poor taste."

If there was one thing Jemma was absolutely certain of, it was that she never displayed poor taste. Outrageous taste, yes. Occasionally vulgar taste, because there is nothing more delicious than an occasional dollop of vulgarity. But poor taste? Never!

"You are mistaken," she stated. "The people who decry this festivity will be only those whom I did not invite."

"Invite?" Damon said. "How could you invite anyone? I thought these people just followed us home from the duel."

"Quick," Jemma said, taking her brother's arm. "Let's move toward the other side of the room. Lady Chaussinand-Nogaret is approaching, and I can't bear the way she always chastises me for dressing in an overly Frenchified manner."

"She looks French to me," Damon said, with a characteristically ignorant view of clothing. Lady Chaussinand-Nogaret was wearing a dress of French violet, but it was trimmed with puckerings of blue satin that no Frenchwoman would tolerate, let alone paired with a hat ornamented with marabou plumes.

Jemma steered him to the right. "Of course these people didn't follow us home from the duel," she said. "I invited them all. I had my secretary up half the night writing out cards, and they were delivered an hour before your duel began."

"And what did those cards say?" Damon said, starting to laugh. Mr. Cachemire paused before him and congratulated him on an excellent bout.

"Did you note his wig?" Jemma said, after Mr. Cachemire drifted on, trailing perfume and hair powder behind him.

"Two pounds of false hair at the least," Damon said. "But really: what on earth did your invitation cards say?"

"They invited everyone to a festivity in honor of your success," Jemma replied, tapping him with her fan. "You see how much sisterly devotion I show you. I anticipated your win before you reached the field."

"There's your husband," Damon said. "I must remember to thank him for attending the party. Though perhaps I should apologize for issuing the challenge at all. I know how fiercely Beaumont feels about illegalities."

Jemma spied her husband in a huddle of men, and then noticed Miss Charlotte Tatlock in the midst, her thin hands flying in the air as she said something. She must have made a salient observation, because even Lord Manning was nodding with approval. Tatlock or Fetlock, Jemma thought to herself. The woman looks like a horse. I don't care how intelligent she is.

Deciding there was nothing more pretentious than a woman who claimed to love politics—or politicians—she moved in the opposite direction, dragging Damon with her.

"What are you scowling at?" he enquired.

"My husband's propensities."

Damon groaned. "There's nothing worse than the inner details of a marriage; please don't tell me."

"Only matched by brothers who engage in scandalous duels," she added. "Villiers is going to be all right, isn't he?"

"Of course he is," Damon said. "I was very careful; the blade went just where I planned and didn't touch the bone. The truth is that your party will likely cause more scandal than the duel itself. Poor Beaumont."

All morning the ducal butler, Fowle, had been opening the grand salon doors and droning out names of various peers. But at this name Jemma's and Damon's heads both swung around.

Fowle spoke rather louder than he needed to, and as the ballroom had gone suddenly silent, his voice boomed over the heads of the assembled.

"His Grace, the Duke of Villiers."

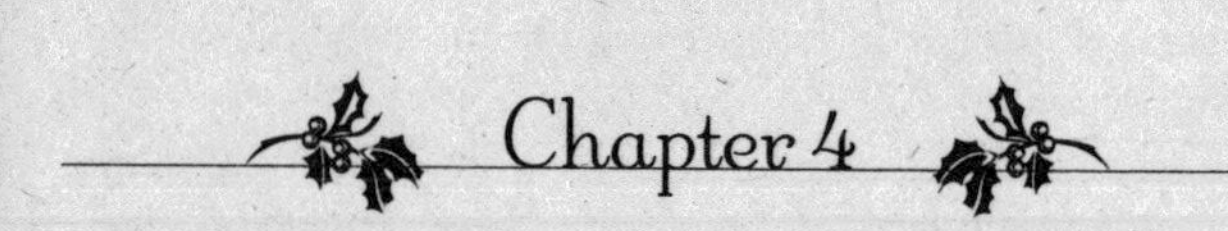

Chapter 4

THE MORNING POST (CONTINUED)

> The host of female libertines recently returning to London is not limited to the Duchess of Beaumont, though perhaps she carries with her the most notorious reputation . . . reportedly, the duchess's friends of the same rank are as untamed and unprincipled as she. In short, duchesses of a desperate disposition . . . wild to a fault and liable to obey no man's word.

Fletch knew exactly the type of woman he wanted to find. Someone who would be interested in pleasure, but not love, someone who would come with no emotional ties. Someone who would actually touch him.

The thought steeled his determination. Damn it, he'd spent enough nights lying in an empty bed, pleasuring himself by thinking—like a paltry, fourteen-year-old—about his wife's delectable little body. He had to get over that. He had to leave that behind.

What he needed was a bout of enthusiastic sex with someone. Anyone who desired him. He met Lord Randulf's eyes and changed that sentence. Any *woman* who desired him. His crafted eroticism, he had quickly discovered, pleased indiscriminately.

He saw the Duke of Beaumont in a cluster of politicians to the side, doubtless poring over tedious matters of state, as that type were always wont to do. Fletch had yet to take up his seat in the House of Lords. He was too busy riding off his sexual frustration.

And mooning over Poppy, he said to himself with a sickening jolt of self-hatred. Beaumont looked up and welcomed him with a smile. "Do you know Lord Holland?"

"I was a great supporter of your father's on the debating floor," Holland said. "It's a pleasure to meet you. Your dear wife and mine, Your Grace, serve on the Board of Directors of Queen Charlotte's Lying-In Hospital."

"Really," Fletch murmured. "My wife is remarkably devoted to her causes."

"So's my wife," Holland said with a twinkle. "Keeps 'em busy, what? Wish we could say the same about Beaumont's duchess here, but she dances to her own piper!"

Beaumont's face instantly became frigid. "Her Grace's charitable activities may not be well known, but they are no less bountiful. Not long ago I found my wife closeted with a young woman collecting for Chelsea pensioners, for example."

"I meant to imply nothing less," Holland said.

But it was obvious in his tone that he felt the Duchess of Beaumont was a liability. That was one good thing about Poppy, Fletch thought. She would never cuckold him.

Holland turned to Fletch. "Though I hate to say it in front of Beaumont here, since he's of the devil's party, we'd like to see you take your father's place in the House of Lords. He was a fine debater, never missed a point."

"A son needn't follow his father into the same party," Beaumont pointed out.

"Ah, but the smart ones do," Holland said, beaming at Fletch. "May I enquire whether you will take up your seat with us, Your Grace?"

"Naturally," Fletch said. He had no real idea what either party stood for, and at the moment he didn't give a rat's ass. His priorities were rapidly becoming clear: he was going to rut his brains out (to use the coarse country phrase) and then he would go to Lords and start being the sort of man his father was. He could figure out the actual politics of the thing later. "If you'll forgive me, gentlemen?" He swept a bow and wandered on.

Two rooms later, he found exactly what he was looking for.

Lady Nevill.

She was slightly older than he, with precisely the sort of French elegance that he remembered. And he'd heard about her. Her husband had been incapacitated in a carriage accident; who could deny her the pleasure of an *affaire* now and then? The *ton*'s pity was such that she was never denied an invitation to any event, although everyone knew perfectly well that she had thrown away her reputation long ago.

She was luscious, deeper-breasted than Poppy, with longer legs, and a loose-limbed air about her that suggested she would throw her legs around a man's neck and ride him for all he was worth.

The lady was talking to Lord Kendrick, who had to be old enough to be her father. He paused to watch and instantly knew that she was aware of him. He could see it in every lineament of her body, all those invisible, sweet ways that women had of registering interest in a man. He was probably one of the most observant men in the world when it came to that sort of thing, since he kept looking for signs of desire in Poppy—and not seeing any.

It was different with Lady Nevill. She turned her head and met his eyes straight on. No subterfuge, no silliness, no flirtation.

He didn't smile. He let his eyes smile instead.

She said something to Lord Kendrick, moved toward him. He walked a step or two, bowed before her.

"Do we know each other?" she said, laughing a little.

"I think not," he answered.

"It is much nicer this way," she said. "One can hardly ever endure the conversation of old friends, whereas that of new friends can be irresistible."

Her eyes were a strange dark golden color; she was as sensuous as a purring cat in the dark. "I shall do my best to be irresistible," he said, feeling as if he were grasping at sophisticated conversation. He and Poppy never had conversations laden with *double entendres.*

She tapped him on the arm with her fan. "There is nothing a woman desires more than . . ."

He leaned toward her. "Yes?"

"To be desired." Her voice was husky and suggestive. Maybe Poppy truly was unusual in that respect. She didn't want to be desired. He shook the thought off. Poppy was his wife. Lady Nevill was . . .

"How does the lady in question choose among all those who desire her? For their numbers must be legion."

"Like the maddened swine in the Bible?" She unfurled her fan; her eyes laughed over the edge. They were delicately marked with a sensual line of kohl. "The lady simply looks for the least pig-like, I assure you."

"And if they hide their curly little tails?" He laughed right back at her.

"Ladies are never interested in anything *little*," she said softly. Fletch let the corner of his mouth rise in brief appreciation of her jest. She was perfect: interested in his body for the pleasure it would bring her.

"I outgrew my short pants long ago."

"And yet you are still so young!" Her eyes raked his body from head to foot, lingering in places where Poppy never bothered to look. The Frenchwomen had exclaimed over his endowments. He wouldn't disappoint her.

"Not so young," he said, almost sadly.

"None of us can claim eternal youth." He could see in her eyes just a shadow of regret that echoed his.

"Yet you look as beautiful as a girl of eighteen," he said, taking her hand to his mouth.

"I shouldn't want to be that," she said. "If I were only eighteen, after all, I should be young and just married. Which is what you appear to be."

"Married four years," he said. "Believe me, that doesn't come within the purview of *just married.*"

"We must stop telling each other truths this very moment," she said, her eyes dancing. "There is nothing more disconcerting—or dreary—than a conversation laden with veracity."

But Fletch was enjoying a conversation in which the truth was desire, and the words were nothing. "The most dreary conversation," he said, "is one in which all the truths are unspoken."

"Now I can see that you are no newlywed. A wearisome topic, marriage," she said, tapping him again on the wrist with her fan. "Since there seems to be no one here to introduce us, sir, perhaps we should do the honors ourselves."

Fletch was suddenly overcome by a giddy delight, by the

pure pleasure of being in the company of a woman who wanted to touch him, who used her fan as an extension of her fingers. "But surely there is no need . . . I can guess who you are. A goddess?"

"Do not say Venus, if you please. I find that good lady remarkably tiresome, and so overused."

"I wasn't thinking mythologically. But if I were . . ."

"Helen of Troy?"

"I hope not. Poor Helen. Young Paris simply scooped her straight away from her older husband's bed."

"I didn't know that her husband's bed was involved," she said.

"I assure you that it was. Paris arrived on the shores of—the shores of—where the devil was that, anyway?"

"Greece," she said, giggling. Her laugh was a century away from a girl's excited giggle; it was a sultry chuckle that heated his groin. "I am fairly sure that we are talking about Homer's epic about the Trojan War, are we not? In which Paris left Troy and came to Greece to steal the queen."

"He didn't come to steal her," Fletch objected. "He was promised her, was he not?"

"Ah, men. They always think they have been promised some woman or another."

"Are we so demanding?"

"Without fail. In my experience, men live in a fever of expectations about promises they think they were given."

"For example?"

"Oh, that their wives will desire them forever . . . that they will *be* desirable forever . . . that their breath will always be sweet."

"But women are just the same. Oh, the promises men break without ever knowing that they made them! When all along women break *their* promises right and left."

"Now you must tell me." Her eyes were dancing in the

most delicious way. "What promise did I ever break to you?"

"You haven't broken any yet," he said, allowing his voice to drop a register into a deeper intimacy. "But you will."

"I will?" She raised a delicate eyebrow.

"Alas and alack," he said, sighing. "A man says he loves a woman, and she invariably believes that he worships her. Yet we men are so awkward at kneeling. We do it without much conviction."

She shook her head dolefully. "And still a man invariably expects that a woman will kneel in front of him with . . . utmost enthusiasm."

Fletch had a sudden, enlivening idea of precisely what she would do, kneeling before him. The smile lurking on the edge of her lush lips suggested she might even enjoy it.

"You haven't guessed my name yet," she prompted.

"I know you are Lady Nevill," he said. "But I don't know the most important thing of all."

"And that is?"

"Your proper name, of course." He picked up her hand. "One learns much from a woman's intimate name. I hope you aren't a Mary . . . so puritanical."

She giggled at that, and the sensual sound of it raced down his legs. "I'm not Mary."

He traced a small pattern on her wrist. "There are many English names that evoke a kind of sturdy Englishhood," he said. "I find it hard to put you together with a name like Lucy or Margaret."

"Surely I don't look like a sturdy Englishwoman!"

He took up her invitation and surveyed her from head to foot. Her eyes had a wicked slant, tipped up at the edges and emphasized by the kohl. Her lips were lushly red, crimson almost. Her bodice was stiffly laced and low; her breasts were much larger than Poppy's and plumped above their restraint, as if begging for a man's hand.

"No," he said slowly, feeling desire as a palpable ache. "No, you don't look sturdy to me."

"I'll give you a hint," she said. "It begins with an L."

"Lily," he said, "like a flower."

"Too wholesome." Her eyes danced again.

"Lettice."

She put up her nose. "I am not a garden vegetable."

"I'm sorry," he said. "I had a great-aunt named Lettice and I've always liked it. Laetitia?" She shook her head. "Lorelei?" A nice name, she declared, but not hers. "Liliane?"

Finally, she gave in and told him. "Louise."

"Louise . . ." He rolled the word on his tongue. "Very nice."

Her throaty giggle was reply enough.

Fletch laughed—they were both laughing—

When Poppy suddenly appeared with Gill and St. Albans beside her. "Hello," she said.

She wasn't smiling.

Chapter 5

THE MORNING POST (CONTINUED)

Such is our plight when duchesses of a desperate disposition—wild to a fault and liable to obey no man's word—are nurtured on the Continent, and return to our shores. One can only hope that such virtuous young duchesses as the esteemed Duchess of Fletcher, noted throughout the land for her charitable activities, will not find herself drawn into this circle of Amazons.

Jemma could feel a weight fall from her shoulders that she hadn't realized was there. Yes, her brother was fine. But her friend . . . her chess partner . . . Villiers?

The duke stood in the doorway, seemingly oblivious to the scrutiny of several hundred pairs of eyes. He looked, perhaps, a trifle white, but otherwise he was as extravagantly elegant as ever.

The word *cloak* brings to mind black velvet: but Villiers wore a sweep of rosy silk, edged in a stiff little ruffle of deep violet taffeta. The ruffle bore a gorgeous pattern of embroidery that resembled iron lattice work; in all Jemma's years in Paris, at the Court of Versailles, she had never seen such an exquisite costume. His black hair, streaked with white, was pulled back and tied with a velvet ribbon that perfectly matched his cape.

"The cape will protect his shoulder injury," Damon murmured as they both made their way toward the door. "Smart fellow."

"There is no one like him," Jemma said, finding herself smiling like an idiot. Villiers walked a dangerous boundary, between masculinity and its opposite and yet—as always—his flamboyant clothes managed to make him look more male. Of course, his features weren't in the least feminine: not that large nose and rough-hewn chin. Especially combined with his customary laconic, bored expression.

There wasn't another man in England who could have worn the cloak. Correction: there wasn't another man in England who would have dared to wear the cloak. But Villiers looked like a prince—the kind of prince who has a harem of dancing women, what's more.

Jemma turned sideways to slip her hoops between two gawking ladies and swept into a deep curtsy before Villiers. "Your Grace," she said, "you do us too much honor."

Villiers made her as deep a leg. "The day I miss one of the Duchess of Beaumont's entertainments will be the day you measure me for a coffin. And"—he turned to Damon—"though your brother has done his best to fit me for that uncomfortable bed, I find that I survive to fight another day."

Damon's bow would have honored an emperor. "But never with me again, Your Grace."

"I trust not indeed," Villiers said, walking forward and giving his surprisingly sweet, if rare, smile. "I find losing uncomfortable and should not wish to repeat the occasion, Gryffyn. You do realize that I lost to both brother and sister in only two days?"

Jemma smiled. "If you refer to the chess match between us, Your Grace, you have lost but the first game of our match."

Villiers glanced around at the hushed guests, who instantly turned away, ineffectually pretending that they weren't hanging on every word of their conversation. The smile playing around his mouth was devilish. "I thought perhaps we could begin that second game today, Your Grace. After all, as I understand it"—and he glanced about again—"some foolish men have bet over two thousand pounds on the outcome. It would be an unkindness to delay their curiosity as to the final winner."

There was a little murmur in the room, as if a sudden sweep of wind had blown over a field of wheat. In the last weeks, betting on the match between the Duchess of Beaumont and the Duke of Villiers had reached a frenzied pitch. Villiers was widely proclaimed to be the best chess player in England, and the fact that Jemma had beaten him in their first game would likely drive the betting to new heights. Not to mention the fact that—

The Duke of Beaumont appeared at Jemma's shoulder and swept a deep, diplomat's bow. "I am enchanted to see you," he said to Villiers, not even a shadow in his tone indicating that he was both estranged from Villiers and engaged in a parallel match of chess with his wife. Not to mention the fact that most of London believed that Jemma herself was the prize, to be given to the winner, whether it be her own husband or Villiers.

Naturally, Jemma fully intended to win both matches herself.

"I was sorry to hear that you suffered injury this morning," Beaumont said, acting as if his brother-in-law had nothing to do with that wound. "Should you be resting, Your Grace?"

"Ah, rest," Villiers said idly. "So often overrated, particularly when there is a chance that one might play a decent game of chess. Indeed, Beaumont, I had hoped that your duchess would open a new stage in our match. You see," he added, "I dearly hate to lose."

"We're only playing one move a day," Jemma said to him with mock severity. "You cannot hope to know whether you will win or lose based on today's move, Your Grace."

"I shall endeavor to frighten you with my brilliance," Villiers said, "blunting your intelligence so that you throw in the game."

"I tremble at the thought. But I agree with my husband that you must be in need of rest. If you would accompany me to the library, perhaps we might begin that game?"

"I would be honored," Villiers said. He made a leg to Beaumont, and Jemma noticed with a little pinch of anxiety that he seemed a bit unsteady. Villiers was never unsteady, for all he affected high red heels.

She took his arm. "The library?" he said to her, *sotto voce*, as they walked through the crowds. The chattering peers fell back on either side as if they were royalty progressing to the throne. "I so enjoyed the more intimate setting of our first game."

Jemma threw him a reproving glance. "If you insist on beginning play during a party, you must accept a public setting. I shall certainly not invite you to my bedchamber in the midst of one of my own events."

Villiers nodded to Lord Sosney and turned back to her. "I

realized something during that match with your brother."

"You plan to take lessons in swordfighting?" she asked with feigned innocence, smiling at Lady Rapsfellow, whose eyes were nearly bulging from her head with curiosity. "Yes, your ladyship, we go to play the first move in our second game. Would you like to join us?"

Lady Rapsfellow gibbered with enthusiasm and fell in behind them.

Villiers bent his head toward her ear and said, "Have you heard of that old legend about the Pied Piper who pipes the rats away from town?"

"It's all a plot to throw your concentration off," she said, laughing up at him. "But do tell me, what did you realize during the duel?"

"Since I am not stupid, I quickly understood that I was at your brother's mercy," Villiers said. "That gave my mind a peculiar clarity. I believe the experience is common to men tumbling down waterfalls and the like."

"Damon would never have killed you," Jemma said, nodding to two ladies whose names she really didn't know.

"I assumed that the good name of his fiancée was worth less to him than the life of an errant duke, but one never knows," Villiers responded. "At any rate, I wish that I could say that I had a change of heart that will send me to a monastery or some other place of good works, but alas, no."

"I can understand that," Jemma said. "I fell under a carriage in Paris once, and regrettably my first thoughts on waking up had to do with the condition of my pelisse rather than the state of my soul."

A footman stood at attention, holding open the library doors. They swept through, followed by some forty or so guests. Villiers seated himself opposite Jemma at the chess table with a magnificent sweep of his cloak.

Lord Randulf minced up behind Villiers. "I believe you

began your most recent game at Parsloe's with a pawn to Queen's Bishop Four," he said to Villiers. "Will you strike out in a new direction?"

"No," Villiers said, moving a pawn to just that place.

"Novelty is always risky," Jemma said, throwing Randulf a smile as she made her own move.

"Is that it?" Lady Rapsfellow said in a shrill undertone. "It's over?"

Lord Randulf took her arm. "When a game is played at one move a day, it's a tedious slow business, my lady."

"But don't they have to think about it more?" Lady Rapsfellow persisted as Randulf steered her toward the door.

Jemma met Villiers's eyes. There was a little smile there. "I do mean to think more," he told her. "Don't count yourself the winner yet."

"I never underestimate my opponents," Jemma replied.

Those who watched were flooding back out of the library as quickly as they arrived. "What did you realize during your duel with my brother, Your Grace?"

He slanted a look around the empty library and then leaned against his seat, heavy-lidded eyes watching her. "That I had made a mistake."

Jemma was conscious of a feeling of disappointment. "Only one? I've made so many."

"You have the advantage of me, then. I make few."

"One might add, in your own estimation," Jemma put in.

"Precisely. But when I make mistakes, I do it in a grand fashion," Villiers said. "I made a mistake with Benjamin . . . the Duke of Berrow." Jemma raised her eyes but he forestalled her. "I know that you know of Benjamin's suicide, and of my role in his death. You and I agreed to be friends; it may be that my friendship is a tainted thing."

"I would not agree. It is true that Benjamin chose to kill himself—"

"After losing a game of chess to me."

"That is no reflection on your friendship. Benjamin always rushed into actions that he later regretted."

"True . . . true."

He was looking down at his hands, his eyes shadowed by long eyelashes. Suddenly he looked up and she felt herself growing a bit pink at something in his eyes. "I have decided to make no more mistakes with friends," he said, his voice rough.

"*If* you win a game from me, you may feel free to point out my errors," she said. "I am so hideously competitive that I will certainly kill you rather than myself."

"Bitch," he said unemotionally.

She laughed. "But you see what good friends we can be? My passion for chess is equal to Benjamin's, but when I lose a match the only thing I want is to play again."

"And is chess your only passion?"

She sat for a moment, before deciding to answer truthfully. "I suppose it is. I hold my friends and husband in great esteem; I adore my brother. But my heart is in chess. I have observed that those who are masters at the game rarely find deep passion elsewhere."

"I would appear to confirm your theory, since I have no family to adore and thus my interests have lingered on the opposite sex in a fleeting way."

"As have mine," she acknowledged. "'Tis a grave fault that has resulted in a great deal of scandal."

"Yet I am not so dismissive of the possibility of love as you are. You made me an offer of companionship a few weeks ago," Villiers said. "I told you then that I would not cuckold my old friend Beaumont."

Jemma froze. She had offered an *affaire,* in a fit of rage at her husband, and Villiers had refused.

"I have changed my mind," he said. "In the five minutes I

was at the mercy of your brother's sword, I remembered that I have never loved a woman. And that it is one of the experiences that I dearly wished to have many years ago. I cannot explain how it has so unaccountably passed me by."

Jemma's lips felt stiff. "Surely you are not saying that you love me."

"No," he said consideringly, "but I could do so. I believe, in fact, that you are the only woman I have met whom I could love. Love is always a decision, you know. Though I love chess, I find the wish in me to love something else as well. Perhaps you and I, Jemma, could find love together."

"Unless we are incapable of true love."

"Do you believe that of yourself? I have loved, though not in a sexual way."

"Benjamin?" she asked.

"Indeed. And"—he raised his eyes again, and the shock of it went to the bottom of her spine—"and Elijah. Your husband."

"You and Beaumont were childhood friends," she said. "But?"

"He was golden, you know, even then."

"*My* husband?"

"He was full of plans, to change the world, to change the village. He talked of them constantly."

"He's still full of plans," Jemma said feelingly. "I do believe he thinks the House of Lords wouldn't function without him."

"He was always so," Villiers said. "To be fair, I believe he may be right. He is not only intelligent, but incorruptible, which is a rare value in a politician."

"What happened to your friendship?"

There was a queer lopsided smile on his lips. "What ever happens to men?"

"A woman."

"Her name was Bess. I wish I could speak rhapsodically about her, but the truth is that I hardly remember her face. Though I loved her dearly—or thought I did."

"And Beaumont did as well?" Jemma laughed a bit. "I can just imagine the two of you, sparring over Bess's attentions. From her name, I gather that she was not a marriageable young lady?"

"I have a cousin named Bess," Villiers said, standing and offering her his arm. "But of course you are right. Bess had an altogether worthy position drawing beer in the village."

"Where the two of you sat night after night, mooning over her blue eyes?"

"No, I sat alone. You have to understand that this nose of mine was even bigger in my youth."

"But you won Bess anyway," Jemma said, feeling quite sure she knew precisely how attractive a young Villiers would have been. She herself wouldn't have lasted a moment against those eyes with less cynicism, more eagerness, his bottom lip, his hair . . .

"I did. Until Beaumont decided that he wanted her instead."

"That sounds unfair—and quite unlike him."

"Ah, there were wheels within wheels, as there so often are," Villiers said, sighing as he opened the library door. "But all I meant to say, Jemma"—and his voice lingered on her name, turned it into a caress—"is that I was mistaken to refuse your generosity."

Jemma wasn't sure how to reply.

He turned to her and made, suddenly, a deep bow. "With fair warning, Your Grace. I shall do my very best to entice you." And then he turned with a swish of his magnificent rose cloak, and walked away.

Jemma stood like a clod in the corridor and watched him leave.

Chapter 6

THE MORNING POST (CONTINUED)

And should the circle of Amazons open its arms to our young, unmarried sprites, the chaste and virtuous children of our best nobility, one hates to think of the effect. Young ladies are vulnerable, yes, vulnerable—to the lure of sin, the sweet lure of sin!

All laughter disappeared, replaced by civil smiles and deep bows.

"Your Grace," said St. Albans, a sharp-tongued fellow with a lamentable fascination with gossip. Who happened to have Fletch's wife on his arm.

"Lady Nevill, your servant," said Gill.

Fletch contented himself with bowing. He should introduce Poppy to Lady Nevill. Poppy was as beribboned and decorated as a box of French sweets, her hair carefully arranged into a towering stack of bows and curls.

The worst possible thing happened, then.

"Why Your Darling Grace," Lady Nevill said. "How are you this morning?"

Poppy dimpled at her. "Lovely, thank you, Louise. I thought I'd be exhausted after all that sewing we did yesterday, but I'm fine."

"Sewing?" Fletch said hollowly.

"That's where I was yesterday morning," Poppy said to him. "The sewing circle for Queen Charlotte's hospital. Louise and I kept sewing and sewing, and drinking cups of tea, for *hours*."

"You should keep better track of your wife, Fletch," St. Albans said, obviously trying to turn the whole awkward mess into a light joke.

"I never know where she is," Fletch said. "It would be most tedious to track one's wife like a grouse in hunting season. I find it easier to proceed on the grounds of total ignorance of her whereabouts."

"I always tell you of my plans," Poppy said stiffly.

"You must all think I am very slow," Lady Nevill said, looking to Fletch. "I gather this gentleman is your charming husband, Poppy, about whom you've told me so much?"

"Oh, yes it is," Poppy said. "I'm so sorry; I thought you knew each other. May I present my husband, the Duke of Fletcher? Fletch, this is a very good friend of mine, Lady Nevill."

He made a leg. Lady Nevill dropped a deep curtsy. Her eyes were completely different now. She was friends with Poppy, damn it.

"Your Grace, it's a pleasure to meet you," she said. "And now you young children must forgive me. I see a dear friend on the other side of the room whom I must greet. *Au revoir!*"

Fletch bowed again. It was as if they had never flirted. As if he were no more than any other man. And he could tell from the delicious way she said *au revoir* that she even spoke French.

Dammit.

There was a moment of silence after she left.

"You were both laughing so hard," Poppy said. "Could you share the joke?"

"You wouldn't understand," he said. Anger was starting to burn in the back of his throat. Rage at her, rage at life . . .

She dimpled. "I take it you were telling each other naughty jokes? I'm certain that I could understand anything Louise enjoyed."

"I doubt it," Fletch said. The other men were absolutely silent. He knew his voice was laden with scorn and near disgust. He couldn't help it.

She blinked and then her sprightly smile popped out again. "Then I shall give you all the pleasure of explaining it to me!"

"You must be joking," he said. "There are some things that ladies of your type never understand."

She pulled herself taller. "Ladies of my type?"

"You know the type, St. Albans," he said. But St. Albans wouldn't meet his eyes. "Good to the bone. Practically achieving sainthood right here in London."

"Fletch," Poppy said. "Do not speak to me like this, I beg you."

"Why not?" For the first time he looked at her directly in the face. "We never say anything significant to each other any longer. In fact, I don't believe we've exchanged an interesting word in a year."

She was rather white. "That is not true."

"Name one interesting sentence," he said, jeering at her.

She raised her chin. "I told you last week that I loved you.

Under the circumstances, that was remarkably interesting." She spun on her heel and left.

"Dammit," Gill said. He forgot he was wearing a wig and tried to run a hand through his hair. His wig fell off and plopped on the floor. It looked like a dead hare, lying on the carpet.

Fletch's jaw tightened. "I'm sick of her childish views. I can't stand any more of her cheerful little comments about every damn thing. If I dropped dead in the street, she'd probably kneel down next to me and coo some platitude about how much I will enjoy heaven."

"She loves you, not that you deserve it," Gill said.

"Who cares if I deserve it? I don't want it," Fletch said. "Our marriage is a sham and a fraud. That being the case, I'd rather that we both understood precisely where we are, rather than my wife pretending that we're a normal couple. That we have"—he spat it—"any sort of life in the bed."

"Almost no one does have an intimate life with his wife," St. Albans said, apparently recovering his tongue after the shock. "Doesn't mean he has to shoot her down in cold blood like that."

"She sees the world in rose and gold," Fletch said flatly. "I believe she actually thinks we're happy."

"She doesn't now," Gill said.

Fletch hunched his shoulders. "Good."

Chapter 7

THE MORNING POST (CONTINUED)

> There can be nothing more dangerous to moral fiber than a circle of women bent on achieving their desires, living a life of pleasure, and paying heed to no admonishments. This paper fears for the souls of every duchess in London!

Poppy never used to cry before she became a duchess. Unfortunately, having a spouse had turned Poppy into a waterspout. She cried herself to sleep. She cried in the oddest moments, for example, in between meetings of the Charitable Society for the Reception of Repenting Prostitutes and the meetings of the board of Lady Charlotte's Lying-In Hospital. Now she ran down a long corridor of Beaumont House, wiping away the tears as they rolled off her chin.

How could he? How could he have said that, and in front of his friends? She knew they didn't talk very much. She knew—she knew there was something terribly wrong.

But try as she might, she couldn't make it work. She woke every morning determined to make Fletch love her again, the way he used to before they married. She never betrayed the faintest irritation at the way he stalked around the house. Never, ever, did she irritate him by pointing out that they would have no children, given that he visited her bed once a month, if that. She never commented when he grew a silly little pointed beard, though he knew well that she loved his dimple. In truth, the goatee was vastly becoming.

But it was like everything else in the past few years. Fletch had turned himself into a distinguished, incredibly beautiful stranger. He wore clothes of a kind that dazzled and frightened her. He wore that little beard. He hired a French valet and a French chef, and rattled away to both of them in the language.

While growing up, her mother had made her study pianoforte for hours a day, saying the skill was essential to marriage. But if she offered to play for Fletch after supper, he would get a look of grueling boredom on his face, cross his arms over his chest, and sit until she finished a piece. Then he would stand, bow politely enough, and say his good-night. Without kissing her.

She slowed to a walk. When had Fletch stopped kissing her? The very thought made her hiccup with tears, but after a bit she found a handkerchief and tried to think about it. She couldn't remember. The last kiss . . . she didn't realize it was the last kiss.

The last kiss he would ever give her, perhaps!

It wasn't until she discovered that someone was standing before her, touching her cheek and saying something that

Poppy realized that she was leaning against the wall and howling. Literally howling with sobs.

"I—I—I," she said, and peered through her swollen eyes. "Oh dear!" she wailed, collapsing into Jemma's arms. "I'm so—so—"

Jemma gave her a kiss and said, "Hush," and then said to someone over her shoulder, "You did precisely the right thing, Isidore."

Then Jemma gave her another kiss, as if she were a little girl, and said, "Darling, Isidore fetched me as soon as she realized you were in distress. Now, come in here, and Isidore will come too."

Poppy let herself be put on a sofa without saying a word and Lady Isidore Del'Fino sat opposite. Her mama had said that she should never share the particulars of her marriage, that it was disloyal. But every time that Poppy said anything about marriage to her mama, her mother would say that she had to train Fletch into a sense of his responsibilities and proper behavior.

"Does he respect you?" she would demand.

And Poppy would nod. She wasn't absolutely sure of the truth of that, because she had seen something very close to disgust in Fletch's eyes lately. But the alternative was so horrible that she couldn't bear it.

"If he respects you, there is nothing to worry about," her mother would pronounce. "Do not say a word to anyone about your disappointments in Fletcher, and he will pay you the same favor. This is the nature of marriage."

More tears welled in Poppy's eyes at the thought. She didn't feel like adhering to the nature of marriage anymore. Especially when Jemma sat down next to her (at least as close as they could be, given the size of Poppy's panniers, and said, "Now what on earth is going on, Poppy?"

"It's Fletch," she said, hiccupping. Her handkerchief was sodden with tears, so she accepted Jemma's. "My marriage—I can't say it!" She sobbed a bit more instead.

After a while Jemma said, "Marriages are like lap dogs. Everyone boasts about having a good one, but the only ones I ever see are devoted to scratching the paneling and jumping on people. Failures, in my eyes."

Poppy hiccupped again, loudly. "I'm sorry," she said, gasping a little. "I always—always hiccup when I'm upset and mama says it is a most disgusting habit, but I truly am not in control of it."

"It's not as bad as scratching the paneling with your claws," Jemma said reassuringly. "Now what's happening in your marriage? Or should I say, what can possibly be happening in your marriage that hasn't already happened in mine?"

"I am sure this is just the conversation to make me very glad not to be living with a husband yet," Isidore said, while Poppy tried to stop crying. "Has your husband taken to wearing rouge?"

"No!"

"I only asked because I'm certain that Viscount St. Albans put a little something on his cheeks, and he and Fletcher are close friends, aren't they?"

"They doesn't mean they share a pot of rouge," Jemma said. She squeezed Poppy's hand again. "You'll feel better after you tell us, darling."

"I think he's"—but Poppy couldn't say it. The enormity of her suspicion was just too cruel to contemplate. "He was abominably rude to me in front of his friends," she said. "He said—He made it clear that our marital activites are not all that—that he desires." Tears welled up again. "But since he never comes to my bedchamber, I don't see what I could do about that!"

"He said that *in front of his friends?*" Jemma said. Her voice rose about two octaves. It made Poppy feel better just to hear it.

"*Bastardo!*" Isidore hissed.

"Precisely," Jemma said. "What a bastard thing to do. What exactly did he say, Poppy?"

"Well, I walked up with—with"—Her voice faltered.

"With whom?" Jemma asked.

"Viscount St. Albans," Poppy said reluctantly, "and Gill. And . . ."

"He was talking to a woman?" Isidore guessed. "He didn't say this in front of a woman!"

"No, she left." But Poppy stopped.

"I see," Jemma said, giving Poppy's hand another squeeze. "I would guess that Fletch has a mistress."

At the word, tears started backing up in Poppy's throat again. "We were in love," she whispered. "He was in love with me just a few years ago. And then it all went wrong!"

"At least he had the decency to wait a year," Jemma said. "I was only married a few weeks when I walked into Beaumont's chambers in Westminster to find him tupping his mistress on the desk."

Poppy's gasp was matched by Isidore's.

"No!" Poppy cried.

"You never told me that," Isidore said, at the same moment.

Jemma smiled a bit tightly. "It's not the sort of information one offers to one's friends."

"Who was she?" Poppy asked.

"Her name was Sarah Cobbett," Jemma said. "Which is really irrelevant, because I gather he's pensioned her off, or whatever it is they do with women when they're done with them."

"At least you didn't know her," Poppy said.

"I suppose the good thing is that they can't pension *us* off," Isidore said thoughtfully.

"Yes, they're stuck with us for life," Poppy said. "Though Fletch would love to pension me off. He looks at me in such a way." Her voice trembled and she steadied it. "I just wish I knew what I did wrong! Something I said? Or did? Now he loathes me. He truly does."

"Beaumont was a *bastardo* as well," Isidore said.

"The problem is that I still love him," Poppy said. "I can't help it. Ever since I realized how much he dislikes me, I've tried and tried to just cast him out of my heart."

"Goodness," Jemma said. "Cast him out of your heart? You're a poet."

Poppy hiccupped loudly.

"Are you sure you can't do it?" Jemma continued. "I had a foolish fondness for Beaumont in the early weeks of our marriage, but after I found him with his mistress—and, I must admit, after he told me that he loved the woman—I did not find it overly difficult to excise him from my heart. At the moment, he appears to be flirting madly with Miss Charlotte Tatlock, and I find it merely irritating."

"Really?" Poppy asked damply. "I've tried and tried this year, but I can't help it. I still love him. If he's in the room, I'm happier. And if I don't know where he is"—her eyes filled with tears again—"I suppose he's been off consorting with other women. I didn't even think of that!"

"Who was the woman he was speaking to?" Isidore asked.

"Lady Nevill," Poppy said. "Lu—" The name was broken by a particularly loud hiccup. "Louise! But—but I can't believe that Louise . . . and yet they were smiling in such a way."

"Not Louise," Jemma said firmly. "I'm not saying that Louise respects her marriage vows, though with her poor husband incapacitated as he is, no one makes much of a fuss about it. But Louise has her own code of honor and she would never sleep with your husband." She reached out and pulled the bell cord.

A footman opened the door directly. "May I help you, Your Grace?" he said, staring at the far wall. "Fowle asked me to stand outside and ensure that you were not interrupted."

"Could you please ask Lady Nevill to join us, if she's still in the house?" Jemma asked. "We would like a tray with all sorts of comforting things on it like gingerbread and hot chocolate."

The moment the door closed again Poppy said urgently: "You cannot tell Louise of my suspicions, Jemma! She'll be mortified that I thought so poorly of her."

"No, she won't," Jemma said.

"I don't believe she will either," Isidore put in. "I don't know her as well as you do, since I cannot abide all those charitable organizations that you both toil in. But I've had several very interesting conversations with her. I like her."

Since Isidore was as opinionated and prickly as her Italian ancestry implied, this was high praise.

"It's just so mortifying," Poppy said in a low voice.

But Louise walked in that very moment, took one look at Poppy and, presumably, Poppy's swollen red eyes, and came straight to her side. She went down on her knees and took both of her hands. "It was merely a flirtation, darling. Nothing more. I had no idea that he was your husband."

Poppy smiled at her, trying to make the corners of her mouth turn up more joyfully. "I knew that, Louise. I—I'm afraid that—that Fletch was a bit abrupt with me after you left and so I indulged in a great weeping fit."

Louise rocked back and looked at Jemma. Jemma's eyebrow went up ruefully; Poppy caught it out of the corner of her eye.

"Please sit," Poppy said, sniffing.

Louise stood up and said to Jemma and Isidore, "Darlings, I would drop you a curtsy, but I'm used to Poppy telling me what to do in committee meetings." She sat.

Poppy folded her hands. "Louise, my husband was flirting with you."

"I would love to say no," Louise said, biting her lip. "Does it sound better if I say that I was flirting with him? But only because I had no idea who he was. He's terribly handsome. You're a fortunate woman!" She finished with such a celebratory smile that Poppy half expected her to cheer.

"Isidore," Poppy said, "has Fletch ever flirted with you?"

Isidore looked surprised. "No. But then I have hardly met him. Perhaps next time."

"You are terrifying," Louise told her.

"Jemma, has Fletch ever flirted with you?" And Poppy held her breath, because she knew how much Fletch admired Jemma.

"Never," Jemma said promptly. "He's perfectly friendly but not at all desirous."

"He was"—Poppy swallowed—"desirous of further acquaintance with you, wouldn't you say, Louise?"

Louise turned a little pink. "Only because I didn't know who he was," she said.

"He planned to be unfaithful with you," Poppy said flatly. "My marriage is over."

"You'd be surprised how much it takes to kill a marriage," Jemma put in. "Mine was over, in that sense, years ago. And yet here I am, returned to London and planning to create an heir."

Isidore raised an eyebrow. "An heir?"

"Would that be before or after you finish the chess matches with the Duke of Villiers *and* your own husband?" Louise asked.

"After," Jemma said. "My point was that your marriage is not over, Poppy. It's merely entered another phase." She sighed.

"Are you still making an heir if Villiers wins the chess match?" Isidore asked, looking even more curious.

"Of course I am!" Jemma said. "Not that Villiers will win. I'm just warming myself to the task of beating him resoundingly. But Beaumont and I haven't seen each other under intimate circumstances for eight years. It's not something I am looking forward to."

"My marriage as I thought of it is over," Poppy said, interrupting.

They were all silent, so she took that as agreement. "My husband is no longer in love with me. He plans to seduce another woman, and although Louise will not be the one, he is likely out there right now, finding a substitute."

"Much though I hate to malign my own reputation," Louise said, frowning a bit, "I don't think he'll have much luck. Unless he looks to Lady Rutledge, of course."

Poppy shuddered slightly. "Louise!" Jemma scolded. "You and I are much more battle-scarred than dear Poppy. We must protect her sensibilities."

"My husband just told anyone who cared to listen that our marriage was a sham," Poppy said. "I think my sensibilities had better adjust to the truth of it."

They all looked up with a certain amount of relief as Fowle entered carrying a tray. "Gingerbread, Your Grace," he said ponderously. "Hot tea, of course, and hot chocolate. Lemon squares, as Cook feels they are very comforting."

"This is lovely," Jemma said.

Poppy took a deep breath and accepted a muffin dripping with butter. "I shall have to make adjustments, that's all. Do you know, it's better to know the truth? I've felt terrible for the past year, trying and trying to make things better."

"It's not your fault, darling, when men stray," Jemma said.

"No, it's the fault of women like Louise!" Isidore said, giggling madly.

Louise raised an eyebrow and said, "Quiet, youngster, or I'll swat you with a lemon square."

"Who's calling whom a youngster?" Isidore asked indignantly. "I'm twenty-two years old, Louise Nevill, and you can't be more than three years over that."

"Five," Louise said, adding, "but I am extremely well-preserved."

Poppy finished her muffin, and let the conversation of her friends wash over her. It had seemed so stark and death-dealing to think that Fletch didn't love her anymore. As if she had nowhere to turn, and no one to love her. But now—

"I love you all," she said, sniffing a little.

"Are you going to cry again?" Isidore asked. "Because I love you too, at least as much as I know of you, but not if it's going to make you cry."

"We love you too, darling," Jemma said.

"Perhaps I should leave," Louise said, putting down her napkin. "I would truly not wish to intrude, and you have my every assurance, Poppy, that your husband will remain *terra incognita* as far as I'm concerned."

"Please stay," Poppy said. "After all, now that I'm leaving Fletch, I need to know what to do next."

She truly enjoyed the shocked silence that followed her statement.

Chapter 8

<u>THE MORNING POST</u> (CONTINUED)

If the soul of every duchess in London is at risk . . . let us not neglect the souls of their august partners, the dukes. While the gossip columns rage with stories of drunkenness and infidelity, there are those rare few, like the Duke of Beaumont, who seem to grace their high rank. Yet we have been credibly informed that even this most revered of politicians has shown untoward interest in a young lady, Miss T—. We protect her name in the hope that these reports are mere folly.

He interrupted her. "You used to call me Elijah in private. The party is over; you needn't address me as Beaumont."

Jemma almost pitied her husband, although the emotion was inconceivable. Yet he looked so confused—and stupid, in a manly sort of way. "I came back to London for you, Elijah." She hesitated. How to say the unspeakable?

"Because my heart may be giving out," he said, a line appearing between his brows.

"I'm also getting old," she said, trying to make him smile, God knows why. "I'd better have that child now or I'll find myself incapable."

"Hardly." His smile was no more than a twist of his lips.

"There's no real evidence that your heart is giving out, is there?" she asked.

"The doctors see none, but I have the feeling they have no idea what a failing heart would look like." He did smile at her now, a ruefulness in his eyes.

"They don't know," she said firmly. "You could have passed out that day in Lords because you drank too much at luncheon."

She saw the truth in his eyes.

"All right, you never drink to excess. Lord almighty, Elijah, is there anything you do wrong?"

A queer little silence greeted her.

"Besides marrying me, of course." She said it with dignity.

"That wasn't what I was thinking."

"Well," Jemma said, feeling a curious wish to make the bleak look in his eyes go away, "you'll be very happy to hear that my brother is taking his disreputable fiancée to the country. Your reputation is saved," she said, leaning forward and tapping his finger. His fingers looked strong and durable. Surely his heart was the same.

He shrugged. "My reputation appears to be intact; I just received a missive from Pitt asking me to address the House of Lords and prepare them for his enclosure tax. The more pressing question seems to me to be when we begin our next chess game. Tomorrow, perhaps?"

"It's very kind of you not to dwell on the fact that you just won the first one," she said.

"I see no reason to dwell on it," he said, smiling at her. "I fully intend to win this game as well."

"That would mean no third game," she said.

"True, and won't that make the *ton* irritable. They are so looking forward to hearing of our third game. Blindfolded and in bed, wasn't it?"

He was watching her closely, so she raised her eyes and met his. "Indeed, those were the terms of the match."

"You appear to have beaten Villiers in the first game," he said. He sounded casual, but she knew him better.

"We began our second this morning."

"A subject that fascinates everyone from the younger chambermaid to the highest duke in the land," Beaumont said.

There was a moment and Jemma realized what he had said. "You, my lord, are the highest duke in the land."

He rose and looked down at her. He had taken off his wig at some point. His hair was cut so short that it left his face unguarded, his beautiful cheekbones, tired eyes. "I would not wish you to think that I don't find the outcome fascinating," he said. And then swept her a bow.

Chapter 9

<u>THE MORNING POST</u> (CONTINUED)

We will close our report with an admonishment to these Desperate Duchesses . . . pleasure yourselves as you will, but remember that your dukes will do the same. And when a duke strays, he may well stray permanently and to the detriment of your welfare!

Nine in the evening
The same day

Fletch didn't come home for hours. Supper passed, but Poppy didn't allow herself to be dressed for the night. Instead she sat, bolt upright as her mother had always taught her, and stared at the wall. The only—only—good thing about the day was that her mother refused to go anywhere near the Duchess of Beaumont, so she had not been at the party. While she would undoubtedly hear of Fletch's insult by the next morning, that gave Poppy a very small window in which to think her own thoughts.

Not her mother's thoughts.

There was a great difference. Somehow she'd fallen into the habit of letting her mother command. It was easier to go along with her, to keep her happy. When she was unhappy . . .

Poppy shuddered a little. She had never liked screaming, not from the time she was a little girl. It wasn't that her mother didn't love her. She did. She really did. Sometimes Poppy had to remind herself of that, because being Lady Flora's daughter sometimes felt like being something that belonged *to* Lady Flora. A possession.

She still remembered sitting for hours as a little girl and pretending to be a hassock. A foot stool. Because if she could just stay very small, and very quiet, her mother would forget she was there, and then she wouldn't scream about people and places and things that had gone wrong.

The memory made Poppy feel guilty. It wasn't as if her mother screamed at her—at least, not most of the time. It was just that gales of anger would sweep around Poppy's head until she felt as if she were in the middle of a great thunderstorm. If Lady Flora noticed Poppy, she generally would scream. There were so many ways in which Poppy could improve.

What she felt was weary. Tired of people who disapproved, people who were impossible to please, people who made her feel inadequate. Stupid. That was the one clear thought she had in her head. She didn't want to be screamed at by her mother. And she didn't want to see that closed, disgusted look on Fletch's face ever again, even if that meant she never saw him again.

A tear fell on her hand, but the truth of it was clear.

Even if she never saw him again.

Fletch finally came home around ten in the evening. She heard the bustle that always accompanied Fletch, the footman taking his hat, his manservant fussing over his coat, his hair, his . . .

It felt quite good to curl her lip.

He came to her chamber as soon as Quince informed him of her request, of course. Until this evening she and Fletch had always been entirely courteous to each other. He stood in the door a moment, looking like a fashion illustration from *Journal de la Mode*. It made her tongue-tied, especially in this last year, as he grew more like a valet's dream, and thus she more inarticulate.

"Please come in," she said. "We need to speak."

"I'm sorry about this morning," he said. He stopped in front of her, his eyes serious for once. Not scornful. "I should never have spoken that way in front of my friends."

"I would prefer that you expressed yourself to me before others," Poppy said. "But I noticed Gill showed no surprise, so I gather you have already discussed our marriage with him. Perhaps you should tell me everything that you've told Gill."

"Gill is an old friend," he said, his eyes going opaque at once. "Men say things to each other in the heat of the moment that they don't mean. Gill was surprised; he gave me a proper scolding after you left."

"Do give him my gratitude," Poppy said, folding her hands. The conversation was veering toward hostility. She could feel herself curling into a little mouse, running away to some part of her head where she wouldn't be shouted at. She took a deep breath and told herself to be brave.

"Please sit down, Fletch."

He sat.

"I should like to know what you think of our marriage. Not because I want to argue with you, or . . ."

He sat down, looking so tired that her heart wrung and she almost jumped to her feet to ring for tea and a hot bath to be drawn. But she bit her lip and forced herself to stay put.

"I think we are probably doing as well as any other duke and duchess in England," he said, looking at her with a rueful twist of his lips. "Better than the Duke and Duchess of Beaumont, certainly. I've been acting like an ass, Poppy. I'm sorry."

He did sound sorry, not that it mattered much. "Still," she said, "what do you wish was different, Fletch?"

"We all fall into foolish ideas sometimes."

"I don't understand those ideas. I feel as if I'm always trying to be something that you want, but I don't know what it is."

"There's nothing," he said sharply. "You're perfect as you are, Poppy. I've been a fool. Let's say no more of it."

She swallowed. "You're not happy with our marital intimacies."

The silence grew like stale bread, with the stink of a rotting egg. Bravery seemed a very stupid concept.

"Did you think I was not aware of your unhappiness?" Poppy asked. "From the moment we fell in love, you've wanted me to be different. And yet I am precisely the kind of wife that I understand. I—I don't know how to be other than myself."

His jaw tightened. She saw it under her lashes. "No doubt I have made untoward demands on you."

"How would you like me to be?"

He didn't answer. She gathered her courage and kept blundering on because it all had to be said. She couldn't bear another conversation of this nature. "I'm really asking you, Fletch. I keep wondering how I disappoint you, and I don't know. What am I doing wrong? I have tried to do everything you asked of me, stayed quiet when I thought you wished me to, modeled my behavior on yours."

"You have not disappointed me."

Her stomach was so sour that she almost felt as if she might throw up right here, sitting in her own bedchamber. She clenched her hands instead, under a fold of her gown so that he couldn't see it. Her face was completely calm; she knew that. "What do you expect? Or perhaps I should ask, what do you wish I would do?"

"You told me once that ladies are different from washer-women, do you remember that?"

She smiled faintly. "I've done so much work in hospitals in the last two years that I can tell you that women are not really very different. I don't remember saying that. What was it in reference to?"

"You didn't want me to kiss you other than with a closed mouth."

Now he had that furious look again.

"But I allowed you to do so," she said, forcing all her fear into her stomach and not letting her voice wobble. "Once we were married, I have tried very hard never to say no to you, Fletch."

"We shouldn't have this conversation."

"Why not?"

"Because you have done your best, Poppy, I know that. And my hopes were naïve."

"But what did you expect me to *do*!"

His head jerked up at the sharpness in her tone.

"You always look disappointed. You demand, and demand, without saying what you want. What is it?"

"I would have wanted you to—to—"

"Well?" She hardly recognized the hardness in her own voice.

"Enjoy yourself," he said sadly. "Enjoy yourself, enjoy me, it's all the same."

She bit down so hard on her lip that she could taste blood, metallic and strange. "I do enjoy myself."

He rose at that and walked to the window. "I've been blaming you for something that is outside your control, and it's grossly unfair. I'm sorry."

She stared at his back and knew that her marriage was indeed over. She couldn't give him what he wanted. They would never be happy together, and she would always disappoint him.

She couldn't stand that anymore.

Chapter 10

Two days later
April 24

The Duke of Villiers lay in bed. His shoulder burned in the spot where the rapier thrust had gone through, with an intensity unabated by cold compresses. "The brandy makes it worse, dammit," he said through clenched teeth.

It was mortifying to discover just how much he did not like pain. At the moment, for example, he was pretending to be lying down simply due to surgeon's orders but in truth he wasn't sure he could rise. It must be blood loss.

"Brandy kills infection, Your Grace," his valet told him. As if he were some sort of idiot child.

"I'm not saying that it shouldn't be done; I'm just saying that it increases the—the discomfort." Surely men didn't suffer *pain*. Anyway, this didn't feel like pain. It felt like something on a much higher magnitude, like a red-hot poker straight to the gut.

"More barley water, Your Grace?" Finchley said.

Villiers narrowed his eyes and watched his valet sweep about the room. Finchley was the sort of valet who would have made a better duke than Villiers himself. Villiers knew it; Finchley knew it. Villiers had presence, arrogance and blood lines. Finchley had presence, arrogance, a ducal way of walking, a penchant for wigs and high heels, and—alas—no blood lines.

Finchley turned around and Villiers realized he had forgotten to answer. The odd thing was that Finchley's face looked exactly like his old nanny's. In fact, for a moment, he saw her broad disapproving face superimposed over Finchley's long-jawed one. He watched in fascination as Finchley and Nanny's nose wavered and seemed to come together.

"Your Grace?"

"Finchley, do you have any relatives in Somerset?" Villiers said, narrowing his eyes again to try to bring Finchley's noses down to one. Which—he was fairly certain—was the right number of noses for a face like Finchley's.

"None whatsoever, Your Grace. Why do you ask?"

"You share a great deal with my childhood nanny," Villiers muttered, not wanting to admit that what Finchley shared was a nose.

Finchley didn't like the idea of sharing anything with a nanny; Villiers could see that. His back became even more erect, and his chin went further into the air. In short, he looked even more ducal, barring the fact that he still had two noses.

"I'd forgotten Nanny's nose had that wart on it," Villiers said, almost dreamily. "I loved her anyway, you know. Perhaps that's why I've never married . . . do you think it was because I've not found a woman with a wart on her nose,

Finchley? Do you suppose that's the reason? If *you,* Finchley, were a lady with a wart on your nose, do you suppose I would marry you?"

Finchley's mouth fell open for a heartbeat and then he said: "Your Grace, I shall summon the surgeon."

"I would get that nose removed, if I were you," Villiers said, squinting at him. "After all, you had a fine nose before. A ducal nose, really."

"Yes, Your Grace. If Your Grace will excuse me." He moved toward the door.

"Not yet," Villiers said. "I'd like a glass, Finchley."

"Your Grace?"

"A glass! Bring me that small mirror. I need to see how many noses I have." That seemed to get Finchley moving. He plumped a small mirror into Villiers's hand and left the room as if the bats of hell were after him. In fact, Finchley looked rather like a gargoyle, not a bat. It was the two noses.

For a moment Villiers was almost afraid to look in the mirror. Would he too have grown an extra nose?

But no. There he was . . . big nose and all. He felt it cautiously. There was only one. He still didn't look like a duke. Dukes had pale complexions and long delicate features, like a superior kind of hunting dog. Or they were remarkably beautiful, like his old friend Elijah. But he'd grown practiced over the past few years at not thinking about Elijah, otherwise known as the Duke of Beaumont, and so he dropped that thought immediately.

In contrast, Villiers looked like a docksman. His hair was jet black—except where there were streaks of pure white. His hair would probably turn all white now. The shoulder didn't seem to be burning quite as much. In fact, he felt a floating sensation, which was a pleasant change.

At least his eyebrows were still black. A woman had told him once that he had the eyes of a snake. By closing one eye,

Villiers discovered that he could almost see what she meant. The one open eye was black as midnight. Peculiar, really.

He only had one nose, but he was a damned ugly specimen, anyway.

The door burst open as that hopeless fool of a surgeon, Banderspit, charged in, followed by Finchley. Finchley had lost a nose and looked entirely normal. Banderspit, on the other hand, was sprouting red feathers from the back of his head. It looked most peculiar.

"Your Grace," Banderspit said, moving over to the bed and pawing at Villiers's forehead in a distasteful way, "a fever is come upon you. We shall have to bleed you."

"Too late," Villiers said, laughing. "I was already bled. Fought a duel, didn't I? And lost. Damn it!" He sat up. "I have to get to Beaumont House. It's time for our next move!"

A few seconds later he found that he was struggling against Finchley and Banderspit, who were holding him down to the bed.

"What the hell do you think you're doing?" he roared. "Take your hands off me."

"Your Grace?" Finchley asked in a quavering voice that was unlike his usual ducal drawl. "Are you yourself again?"

"I am always myself," Villiers said promptly. "It may not be pleasant, but it's the only choice I have."

Banderspit wiped his forehead. "We'll have to do it immediately," he said to Finchley.

"Do what?"

"Bleed you, Your Grace," Banderspit replied.

"Like hell," Villiers said, suddenly remembering again that he had to go play chess with the duchess. "I must play my piece! I must play my piece." He started to rise, only to find that Finchley was practically throwing himself onto his uninjured side.

"Really," Villiers said, rather coldly. "I have always shown you a measured amount of affection, Finchley. Do you keep to the same boundaries. I have no wish to share a bed."

"What are these pieces he's talking about?" Banderspit asked Finchley.

"Surely you know that His Grace is playing a chess match with the Duchess of Beaumont?" Finchley said.

"I am," Villiers interjected. "And she won the first game, dammit."

Finchley ignored him. "His Grace is anxious to continue their current game."

"One move a day," Villiers said. "If we go to a third game, it's in bed and blindfolded. Surely you can understand that I must win this game." He grinned at the portly doctor. "If only to blindfold the duchess."

Banderspit looked appalled. "The Duchess of *Beaumont*? Are you talking about the Duke of Beaumont's wife?"

"Not the dowager duchess," Villiers put in. He was beginning to feel a most unpleasant spinning sensation. "I'd never bed *her*. Nor play her at chess either. Though the two activities aren't so far apart as you might think."

"I can see that," Banderspit said, snapping his mouth shut. "It is not for me to comment on the morality or immortality of your games, Your Grace. Though I cannot but comment that the Duke of Beaumont is a highly respected man in the Parliament, and one working night and day to bring about a change in government—to give England a government that will be respected and free of corruption!"

Villiers blinked at him. "I like those red feathers you have coming from the back of your wig," he said. "I've seen women doing that sort of thing with their wigs, but never a man."

Banderspit's hand touched his wig briefly, and then he straightened up. "Fetch me my assistant," he snapped at Finchley. "We must proceed at once."

Chapter 11

The Duke of Fletcher's townhouse
April 30

"I have listened to you for years, Mama," Poppy said calmly. "Luce, please be careful with my enameled brushes. I'm very fond of them."

"You stop packing those things this minute," Lady Flora snarled at Poppy's maid. Luce froze. When Lady Flora commanded, people around her tended to stop short, as if a celestial command had been visited on them. "*We* do not trot away from a husband, in some sort of ignominious retreat! I did not raise you for this!"

"I know that, Mama," Poppy said. "You raised me to be a duchess."

"A duchess is the wife to a duke," Lady Flora said with clipped logic.

"So I understand."

"I trust that is not an insolent tone I hear."

Poppy looked at her. From years of practice, she knew that her expression would appear open and inquiring, the epitome of innocence. "Of course not, Mama."

"A wife never leaves her husband. Not even if he's as much of a dunce as your own father. I never left him."

Poppy nodded obediently. From what she understood, her mother had discovered that marriage did not agree with her approximately one hour after the ceremony, and she had always freely imparted her wisdom in that arena to her only daughter. "There's no use marrying unless it's to a duke," she had repeatedly told Poppy when her daughter was just a mop-headed babe toddling through the nursery. "A *duke,* Poppy."

As was often the case for Lady Flora, events had aligned themselves precisely as she wished.

"I always wanted you to marry a duke," she said now. "And for once you did as I requested."

"Mother, I always do as you request," Poppy said, handing the prayerbook from her bedside to Luce.

"Not at the moment. Have you given any thought to this decision to leave your husband?"

"I have thought of nothing else for a week."

"You've always been a foolish little thing," her mother said dispassionately. "I thought you were a fool when you were burbling of love for Fletcher, but I shall think you worse than a fool if you leave him. Your role in life is to be a duchess. I did not raise you to be a disgrace."

That was true, Poppy thought. In fact, her role as a duchess was to be precisely what it was when she was a mere daughter: to support, compliment, adorn and otherwise support one Lady Flora, the mother of a duchess.

"I told you to stop packing," Lady Flora snapped at Luce. "Are you as deaf as you are ugly, girl?"

Poppy drew herself to her full height, which was a little higher than her mother. "Luce will continue packing, Mama, because she is my servant and I have instructed her to do so." She looked steadily into her mother's steely blue eyes. "And Luce is not ugly."

"How dare you contradict me!" Lady Flora's eyes had been compared to a soft summer sky and a delicate pansy; if her wooers could see how those eyes bulged they might have rethought their sonnets.

Poppy almost quailed, so she turned away to gather up her journal to give to Luce instead. Then she took a deep breath.

"Face me when I'm speaking to you," her mother shrilled. "For God's sakes," she turned on Luce. "Will you leave the room rather than lurking here like an untrained dog?"

Poor Luce turned a stricken face to Poppy, who nodded. The maid fled, closing the door behind her with a clap that made Poppy jump.

"Untrained," Lady Flora remarked. "I would have terminated her employment long ago, for all she's got a good hand with hair. She has an insolent look and she *is* ugly with that potato nose. I don't believe in lying to the lower classes. It isn't good for them. It would be better for her to understand her place in life."

"I'm leaving this house," Poppy stated. "I am leaving my husband. You can either accept that, or not accept that, Mama."

"I do not accept it, and I shall never accept it. You are a *duchess*."

"I'm still going to be a duchess. I'm just not going to be a duchess going through the sham of a marriage."

"A duchess belongs in her husband's townhouse. Do you think I ever contemplated leaving your father's house? Why should I? Because he was an idiot? Men are idiots; he was hardly alone in his shame. Because we disliked each other? A woman who doesn't grow to dislike her husband is a simpleton. How long do you think I *liked* your father?"

Poppy shook her head, wishing again that she remembered her father. Wishing that he had stayed alive long enough to know whether he liked his daughter: that would have meant one of her parents did.

"I thought he was a fool before I married him," her mother said. "I grew to dislike him after our first night together. I've told you about that, haven't I?"

"Yes, Mama."

"The man was a disgusting reprobate," Lady Flora said. "Disgusting. He smelled like a stoat and he acted like a bull. But I didn't let you go into that night unprepared, the way I had to, did I?"

The lurid shudder that accompanied her words had the same effect on Poppy as it had ever since her mother began talking of marital intimacies. She felt sick. "No, Mama," she said.

"I've always told you the worst, prepared you. I told you men were tedious, if useful. I prepared you for their revolting habits in bed. I would consider myself to have failed as a mother—yes, *failed*—if I had allowed you to marry anyone below a duke, or if I had sent you into marriage without knowing what lay ahead of you."

As Poppy watched, her mother caught sight of herself in the mirror and turned to the side for a better view. Because she couldn't see her entire hair style, she bent her knees; even then she couldn't see the whole of it, as it had three distinct stories, the first ornamented with blue bows, the second with loops of pearl and the third with a blue satin ribbon. She looked ready to be presented at court, and never mind the fact that it was a mere morning visit to her daughter.

Poppy sat down, even though it was a disgrace to do so in

the presence of her mother. But then, she thought wearily, duchesses can sit before mere ladies.

As if her mother heard her thoughts, she erupted into a tide of anger against her parents for handing her to Mr. Selby when she could have commanded the highest in the land, if only they'd had faith in her. "Look at me!" she demanded. "Just look at me!"

Poppy looked.

"I've never lied to you, daughter, and I won't lie now. You married a duke but I'm more beautiful than you ever were, even at this grotesquely advanced age of mine. If there was an appropriate duke, I could marry him now. *If* I wished, of course." She straightened up and patted one last blue ribbon in place.

"My point," she said, "is that you're a fool to even think of leaving your husband. What will you gain? You won't be free until he dies, and he doesn't show any sign of that."

Poppy thought it was most unbecoming of her mother to sound so disappointed at the prospect of Fletch's good health. But then her own father had given up and died fairly shortly after marriage, and her mother likely thought that was the natural way of things. "I don't want Fletch to die," she pointed out.

"Then why leave him? Explain that, Perdita. I see absolutely no reason for the two of you to part. You should simply allow him to go his way, and you go yours . . ." She paused, with a frown. "Is it a matter of the bed?"

Poppy had the oddest sensation that her mother had been struck by a moment of sympathy.

Sure enough, her mother made a grimace that might have been compassion on any other woman's face, and sat on the edge of the bed. "I know it's disgusting. I remember, Perdita. I do remember. A woman can never forget the pain and indignity of it."

"It wasn't—"

But her mother was properly in stride now. "His engorged instrument, so purple and revolting in every way . . . it made me vomit, you know. I vomited, right there in the room. That didn't even stop him. It didn't. No, he—he laughed and proceeded. It's hard to believe now, but it took me at least three months before I gathered enough strength to bar your father from my bedchamber."

Poppy had never heard that before. "You barred him? I thought you said Father visited you once a week."

"Oh, he did, after I readmitted him. In the beginning, though—he didn't take me seriously, can you imagine?"

Poppy shook her head. It was hard to imagine anyone not taking her mother seriously.

"I crowned him with a full chamber pot," her mother said.

"Ug!"

"And I had had my monthly," her mother said with satisfaction. "I planned it so."

Poppy felt as if she, too, were going to throw up.

"The point is that once I readmitted him to my presence, he was chastened and understood precisely what his role was in the bedroom," her mother said. "I allowed him to visit me once a week until you were conceived. Then since his land wasn't entailed, and you could inherit it all, I told him that I never wanted his disgusting male organ to touch my skin again."

Poppy organized her features into something like a smile.

"I can see that your husband would likely be not as easy to tame as mine," her mother said thoughtfully.

"I—"

"I have not been thinking enough of you, child."

Poppy just stopped her mouth from falling open. Her

mother patted her on the shoulder. "How often does he visit his mistress?"

Poppy shook her head. "I don't believe Fletch has a mistress."

"No mistress," her mother gasped. "Surely you don't mean that you've been forced to service him all these—how many years is it?—by yourself?"

"We've been married four years. But it's not—"

"Revolting!" her mother spat. "A sordid way for a duke to behave. One has to suppose that he's trying for an heir. Yet if he's been trying this long with no fruit, the man is almost certainly incapable." She patted her shoulder again.

"Perhaps I am," Poppy said wretchedly.

"Never," her mother said. "You're good strong stock, and you have my blood in you. Your father and I got the task done in a reasonable period of time. No, if need be, you'll just have to pick out someone else and provide the heir. It's a woman's job, unpleasant though it may be. When the time comes, I'll choose an appropriate consort for you, just as I did your husband."

"You didn't pick out Fletch, Mama," Poppy said. "We chose each other."

"Nonsense," her mother said briskly. "I selected him the moment he appeared in Paris. It was charming that the two of you played at love so prettily, though I dare say it did make it harder for you when the sordid truth finally dawned."

Poppy swallowed. "What is the sordid truth, Mama?"

"Marriage is a convenience," her mother said bluntly. "Women would never indulge men in their filthy habits otherwise; but by marriage, a man buys a woman and she agrees to bear him children. That's what your jointure paid for: you received one-third of the duchy on signing your marriage lines, after all. *And* that's why it makes it difficult that you want to leave him." She patted Poppy again. "Don't worry. I'm thinking about it. I would never want you to think that you couldn't tell your mother when you are at the end of your rope."

"It's not exactly—" But she didn't get to finish the sentence, of course. Sometimes Poppy thought she went for a week without finishing a sentence in her mother's company.

"I hadn't realized that you had endured *four years* of—of that," her mother said, staring into the distance. "I know you were prepared for the act; I made sure of that. But still, a mother's soul recoils at the idea of her daughter undergoing what you must have endured. I think you're right. You should leave."

"I should?"

"Leave. It will force Fletcher to find a mistress; men are at the mercy of their lusts, you know. They can't control their vices. It's unusual for a man to maintain interest in one woman over five years, so I'm sure he merely needs some encouragement. You mustn't hate him too much. At least he bathes."

"Yes," Poppy murmured.

"I'll move into this house," her mother said. "I'll soon bring him to a sense of the error of his ways. You're too young and too malleable, Poppy. You don't have the backbone I had when I crowned your father with that chamber pot. For goodness sake, you've suffered four years! I feel like a terrible mother for not guessing your pain."

To her astonishment, Poppy saw that her mother's blue eyes were actually a bit misty. "It's all right, Mama," she said. "It hasn't been so—"

"I care for you," her mother said. "I know that you probably find me overwhelming occasionally; we have different personalities, and I'm not good at concealing the truth when I see it. But I do care for you, Perdita, and I always have."

"I know that, Mama," Poppy said. "I've always known that."

Her mother's jaw set. "I'll show that husband of yours the proper way to act toward his duchess."

"Oh—"

"Don't worry." Her mother raised a hand; just so a general might stop an entire army in its tracks. "I shall not be as blunt as is my natural wont. I shall use cunning. I shall be subtle. I will let the poor young fool draw his own conclusions. Then, when I judge that he has a better understanding of his rights and responsibilities, you shall return and the two of you can live in harmony."

"But if you stay here, Mama—"

Her mother frowned. "I see what you mean. Where will you go? It would seem a bit odd if you returned to my house by yourself."

Then like a miracle, Poppy's lips opened and she said: "I'm going to stay with a dear friend."

"Who?"

"The Duchess of Beaumont."

"Beaumont?" Lady Flora said. "That trollop? Why on earth would you wish to stay with her?"

"I like her."

"Could you not stay with Lady Wartley? She's such a wonderful presence on the hospital board, and I know she has a sincere affection for you."

"I would feel more comfortable with Jemma."

"I should never have allowed that acquaintance," her mother said. "It was all very well in Paris, but who would have thought such a light-skirt would find her way back to England?"

"She's my friend, mother. I wish you wouldn't be—"

"I call a spade a spade," her mother said. "I always have. The woman's a light-skirt, and that's all there is to it. I pity her husband, Beaumont, that I do. On the other hand, she is a duchess. You have my permission to pay her a visit."

"If you'll excuse me, Mother," Poppy said, standing up and dropping a curtsy that was just a shade disrespectful, "I have an appointment. Do request any refreshments you may desire."

"Do you know," her mother said thoughtfully, "this might be enjoyable? I always thought that if circumstances were different I would do well on the stage."

Poppy almost felt a pang of sympathy for Fletch.

"I shall begin with a fit of hysteria. I have observed that men dislike hysteria above all else. That will put his household in a proper frame of mind." Her mother took her face in her hands; to Poppy's alarm her mother's eyes were misty again. "I have been a terrible mother, to thoughtlessly leave you in this house for years," she said.

"Really, I—"

"Hush." Lady Flora ceremoniously kissed Poppy on the forehead. "Mother is in charge now. By the time I signal for your return, Perdita, your husband will be a new man. I promise you that. He will beg you to return home, and you can set your own terms. Just think of me"—and there was a rare gleam of humor in her eyes—"as the chamber pot that Fletcher has yet to encounter."

Poppy got as far as the bottom of the stair and then leaned against the banister, hand on her heart. Could she really leave Fletch to whatever punishment her mother had in mind? When she thought about his behavior, flirting with Louise—yes, she could.

He deserved her mother.

One problem was that while she was certainly friends with Jemma, there were far more women she knew better, women whom she joined on committees, women with charitable ambitions. Women whose reputations were snowy white compared to Jemma's.

All of London knew that Jemma had had *affaires* in those

years she lived in Paris, apart from her husband. All of London was watching the chess matches Jemma was playing with her husband—and the Duke of Villiers. Jemma was a *bad woman.*

Which was precisely why Jemma was just the right person. She wouldn't condemn her. Or try to talk her into returning.

And her mother would never darken the door of a strumpet like Jemma, duchess or no. If Lady Flora thought men were fools, she thought that women who voluntarily dabbled with them worse than fools. *Slut*, she would hiss, on hearing the least bit of gossip about a woman. She had only allowed Poppy to be friends with Jemma, all those years ago in Paris, because her disdain warred with her snobbism. After all, Jemma was a duchess.

Poppy finally let go of the banister, realizing that her hands were damp with sweat. She straightened up and asked the butler for her pelisse. Then she said, "I shall trust you, Quince, to tell the duke that I am leaving the house to him."

The butler's eyes bulged. "Your Grace?"

"I've decided to live elsewhere," she said, buttoning her pelisse under her chin. It was quite chilly for the end of April. "I doubt he will mind much. If he has anything to say about it, I expect I'll see him at Lady Vesey's ball later this week."

The butler's mouth snapped shut and he bowed. "May I offer the household's regrets, Your Grace?"

Poppy's head was spinning with the freedom of speaking her mind. "Why should you? It will be much easier without a duchess in residence, you know. I expect that the duke will be out most of the time, just as he is now, and you won't have much work at all."

Quince seemed to be flummoxed, so she patted him on

the arm. "If you wouldn't mind calling the carriage for me?"

"Your Grace," he said with a gulp, and bowed.

Poppy sat down on a chair in the antechamber and hummed a little to herself. The anteroom was large and austere and it made her very happy to think how much she disliked it. It was cold. Forbidding.

The thought wandered through her mind that Jemma might be surprised by her visit, but she dismissed it. The important thing was that she felt quite happy. Relieved, really.

Fowle, Jemma's butler, had such a kind face that Poppy almost grew tearful when he asked if she would remove her cloak. And a few minutes later, Jemma entered the sitting room.

Poppy stood but no words came to her mouth.

Jemma paused in the doorway, the very picture of French elegance, from the tip of her curled hair to the pink silk toes of her slippers.

"What a pleasure to see you," she said.

Poppy gulped. "I thought that I would return home to Mama. But in fact she is going to stay in my house and—and mother Fletch."

Jemma blinked. "Did you say that Lady Flora is going to *mother* Fletch?"

"Yes indeed," Poppy said, nodding.

"I can't imagine anyone mothering Fletch, let alone your mother!"

"May I pay you a visit?" Poppy asked.

"I would love that above all things," Jemma said, dropping a kiss on Poppy's cheek. "It must be providence, given that my brother dragged my beloved ward off to the country and left me all alone."

"Is it true that they will marry by special license?" Poppy asked.

Jemma sighed. The truth of it was that her ward had been caught practically in the very act of intimacy with her brother—and in an *open boat!*—so a hasty marriage was prudent for all concerned. "I believe that my brother is so consumed with passion for his new wife that he cannot wait," she said.

"I'm afraid I won't be very good company," Poppy said, feeling tears welling up again. "I just—I don't feel like being—"

"When I left Beaumont I cried for weeks," Jemma said, her eyes looking a little haunted. "Weeks."

"I could do that," Poppy said, choking a bit. "I mean, I think I might do that."

"Then you're in just the right place," Jemma said. "I shan't bother you, but if you wish for company all you have to do is ask. Cry away!"

Poppy couldn't help smiling, even through her tears.

Chapter 12

"The only way to abate the fever is to bleed him," Banderspit said. "That or to cup him. He's had this fever for over a week now."

Finchley looked down at the duke. He seemed peaceful, but even as he watched, Villiers opened his eyes and began to struggle up again. Finchley jumped forward and held him down.

"I must play!" the duke bellowed.

"Even then, his mind may be permanently disordered," Banderspit said, his mouth curving downwards in a disapproving sniff. "A man with his moral tendencies is obviously already on the very edge of derangement. A wound of this sort is enough to put his mind into a permanent state of restlessness."

"No!" Finchley cried, relaxing his grip on Villiers's arm, since the duke had relapsed again into a semi-dreaming state. "The duke is perfectly sane in mind and body. He simply has a fever."

"The piece! I must make my move!" Villiers whispered. His voice was a little hoarse, so Finchley put a glass of water to his mouth. Some of it spilled down his throat. He'd never seen his master so vulnerable, not even once.

"We should get a priest to him," Banderspit said briskly. "As I said, a man of such moral turpitude will likely die of it. He has no reason to live other than degenerate desires, and that's no inspiration."

"That is not the case!" Finchley cried.

"Has he family?"

"No."

"Obviously he's not married," Banderspit said with a sniff. "Though it appears that he's working to ruin other people's marriages."

Villiers was tossing again. He opened his eyes and fixed them on Finchley's face. "Finchley?"

"Yes, Your Grace," Finchley said, bending over.

"I have to play the piece, Finchley. You know that. She'll have to come here to me because I shan't rise today. Send her a message." His hand loosened and his head dropped back to the pillow.

"Raving," Banderspit said. "I doubt that bleeding him will do any good. You've waited too long."

Finchley had his doubts about bleeding. Hadn't the surgeon bled the second footman, and the man languished in the attics for a month before he died? Finchley always thought that he would have gotten better on his own, if they hadn't taken blood from him.

"I agree with you," he said to Banderspit. "Bleeding is unlikely to help."

Banderspit cast him a suspicious glance. "I am His Grace's

chosen surgeon," he said. "You've no right to call anyone else."

"I won't," Finchley said, automatically pressing down on the duke as he tried again to rise and go play his chess piece.

"I shall return this afternoon," Banderspit announced. "If His Grace is no better, and I have no expectation that he will be, I will bleed him no matter what you say. Though his morals are not to my liking, I have taken my oath under God to do all I can for sinners as well as the blessed."

Right, Finchley thought. Especially when the sinners of this world pay you so well. He got Banderspit out of the room and then turned around. Villiers was tossing from side to side.

There was no help for it. The duchess had to play her piece.

He went to the door and called for the butler.

Chapter 13

Fletch emerged from his carriage after spending a tedious afternoon with Gill feeling rather thoughtful. He had all the slightly resentful shame of a schoolboy who'd broken a window. Of course he would make it all better with Poppy. It had been a week and surely she had calmed down by now. He had a diamond necklace snug in his pocket. Maybe he'd just leave it in her bedchamber and let that be his apology.

But no: thinking of the shock in her eyes, he knew that he had to do the thing properly. The thought made him recoil. There was nothing *fun* about Poppy anymore. The only fun was in flirtation.

He handed his cloak to Quince.

"If you please, Your Grace," the butler said with an unusual tone to his voice.

Fletch paused.

"If I might speak to you in private."

Fletch ground his teeth. He wanted to get it over with Poppy and then have a strong drink. "Can't it wait, Quince? I have something to say to the duchess and then—"

A voice interrupted him from the top of the stairs. "Your Grace!"

He looked up and felt a perfectly horrible day grow more awful. He bowed smartly. "I shall greet you in a moment, Lady Flora. Quince has something urgent to tell me." And without waiting for an answer he walked into the west drawing room.

"We probably have five minutes before she hounds me here," he told the butler. "Did the chef dismiss all the kitchen staff again?" He answered himself. "If he had, you'd be telling the duchess. So what can I do for you, Quince?"

"This concerns the duchess," Quince said.

Fletch raised an eyebrow. "Yes?"

"She asked me to give you a message."

"She did?"

Quince didn't hand him a slip of foolscap. "I believe her to have indicated, Your Grace, that she will be residing elsewhere."

"Residing—what the devil are you talking about? Isn't she upstairs with that harridan of a mother of hers?"

"No," Quince said. "Lady Flora is here quite alone, and has been engaged in hysterics for the past hour or so. Perhaps longer. It seems longer," he added with feeling.

Fletch felt an icy calm. Poppy was clearly kicking up her heels. But how could she storm out of the house and leave her mother behind?

"Your Grace?" Quince bleated.

"Yes," Fletch said, heading toward the door.

Quince spoke in a low voice. "Lady Flora instructed her maid to go to Selby House and return with her clothing."

Fletch stopped, his hand falling from the door. "Quince," he said. "Tell me you are joking and I'll double your wages."

"Your Grace," Quince said, "Should this event come to pass, I envision doubling most of the staff's wages in order to keep them."

Fletch reached the hallway just as Poppy's mother descended the last step. He saw her with the clear eyes of shock. Poppy had run off and it was going to cause him serious annoyance to bring her back. And whose fault was it? Poppy's mother. And whose fault was it that his bride loathed the bedchamber? Her mother. And whose fault was it that Poppy spent most of her time in hospitals and charities? Her mother.

There wasn't much about Lady Flora that revealed her true nature. She dressed with all the formality of a queen and generally commanded that sort of attention. In truth, she was beautiful. Her figure was alluring, which was unusual in a woman in her forties. But it was her face that made her truly dangerous. Fletch admitted, from the depths of his rage, that it was a bewitching face, more so even than her daughter's. It was the face of a woman who was accustomed to doing exactly as she liked, when she liked and how she liked. It was the face of a woman who rarely encountered opposition to her commands: in short, she had come to regard herself as something akin to the Queen of England. Or perhaps, given that Lady Flora scorned those who spent their lives in one small island, the female equivalent of the Tsar of Russia.

Fletch bowed so abruptly that his chin might have cut the air if such a thing were possible. "Lady Flora. I regret to say that you seem to have caught us at an unfortunate moment."

She glided up to him and put a hand on his arm. "You poor dear," she said.

Fletch blinked. To this point, his mother-in-law had always treated him with the same regard with which she regarded every gentleman: as if he were a slightly more gilded version of a manservant.

"I feel responsible," she cooed. Yes! It was a coo. Fletch ground his back teeth and didn't shift backwards, as was his instinct. "I obviously failed in raising my daughter, and through that, I failed you. I have been in the greatest agony of mind for an hour; you must understand, the agony of a mother's heart is like no other."

Fletch opened his mouth but her lovely lips just kept moving.

"Then I realized that there is only one person in the world who can solve this dilemma, who can make up for the extraordinary behavior of my daughter"—and for a moment Fletch saw her blue eyes harden into something like glass—"and assuage my own *overwhelming* sense of guilt. I shall stand by your side, Your Grace, I shall not desert you, even though my daughter has done so. I—"

Fletch cleared his throat. "Lady Flora, I have every confidence that my wife will return to the house by nightfall; there is no need to put yourself into such anxiety."

"I only wish that were the case," she cried, her voice rising a little. "Yet I must admit that I know Perdita better than you do. She is nothing if not amenable—until she—"

Fletch caught the flash of Lady Flora's white teeth. "She had it from my late husband, may God rest his soul," Lady Flora said. "I very much doubt that Poppy will return to your house, Your Grace."

"Of course she will!" Fletch growled, moving backwards so that her hand fell from his sleeve. "Now if you will allow me, madam, I will ask Quince to accompany you to your house himself, since you are distressed."

She smiled at him as if she hadn't heard him. "Don't

worry," she said. "I'll speak to the housekeeper and get everything under control immediately. I won't have you discomforted in the slightest by this absurd flight on the part of my daughter!"

There wasn't even a twitch in her eye to admit that there was something incongruous about a mother offering to replace a daughter. The only thing Fletch could imagine was that Lady Flora, like her daughter, was the sort of person who never thought of bedroom matters.

Fletch's only thought was of flight. "I do apologize, Lady Flora. I am due at an urgent appointment."

She smiled at him with all the warmth of a ravening tiger. "Do make yourself comfortable wherever you wish to go. Everything will be in order for you in this house."

Sure enough, she turned away and began barking at Quince about housekeeping and menus and her maid and sheets. It was amazing how quickly her smooth tone peeled away when she addressed a servant.

"Oh, Your Grace!" she carrolled, as a footman was opening the door.

He turned back to her once more.

"Do give my best to my daughter, should you happen to speak to her."

Fletch bowed. The funny thing was that Lady Flora's hair was a still vibrant golden color; it didn't look as if it were made of snakes. But surely . . .

His butler bowed by the door, holding out the coat he had just taken off. "Quince," he said, pausing, "who was that goddess whose hair was made of snakes?"

"Medusa, Your Grace," Quince said. "One glimpse at her hair and a man was struck to stone."

"Just so," Fletch said thoughtfully, heading toward his carriage. Poppy would understand that she had to come home.

Chapter 14

May 1

The wig was damnably heavy, but no itchier than the one he wore every day. The hooped petticoat was more of a problem. "How do you sit down in this?" he asked Mrs. Ferrers, the housekeeper.

"You've nothing but small side panniers," she observed. "Now those of twenty years ago were something terrible, they were. This will do little more than give you a woman's shape."

Finchley glanced down at the bodice of his sky-blue gown and snorted. "My hips aren't the only part in need of padding, Mrs. Ferrers."

"It would be much easier if you'd allow one of the housemaids to do it for you," she said. "Betty, now. She has a properly dramatic way with her."

He shook his head. "The duke would never forgive me for allowing a woman to see him in his current state. Never."

Mrs. Ferrers pursed her lips. "Betty can't afford to lose her place. She's got those three sisters of hers."

"There you are, then."

"Your arms look terribly hairy, Mr. Finchley, if you don't mind my saying so."

"Perhaps a shawl? I tried to get into that red gown with the long sleeves, but it didn't fit."

"Well, you look as best a man can look in a woman's costume. I'll give you a shawl, and we'll tuck a lace fichu into the bodice; you've a bit of hair showing there as well."

"I suppose I could shave it off," Finchley said doubtfully.

Mrs. Ferrers backed up and eyed him.

"His Grace is dreadfully feverish. He hardly opens his eyes."

"All he'd have to do was squint to see those arms of yours, and he'll think he's having a nightmare."

With a groan, Finchley went off to do the necessary.

"I'm ready," he said grimly, some time later. Mrs. Ferrers wrapped a length of cloth around him. "There's not a shawl large enough, Mr. Finchley; this is the Easter cloth from the small dining room, and I think it looks quite pretty."

Finchley didn't look in the glass, just turned to go.

"Walk lightly now," Mrs. Ferrers reminded him. "You don't want to stamp in there and have His Grace open his eyes from surprise. You'll need to talk soft and high."

Finchley paused in the doorway of the bedchamber and said in his normal voice, "Your Grace, may I present the Duchess of Beaumont, who has come to play a chess move in her game with you?"

"Good!" the duke said, sitting up and tumbling off his nightcap. "Dammit, it's as dark as a wolf's mouth in here.

How are we to play in the dark, Finchley? Bring us a lamp."

Finchley tucked himself down by the bed and cooed in a high voice, "But Your Grace, I can see perfectly well. Surely we can simply continue?"

Villiers blinked at Finchley, who pulled back nervously. But Villiers was apparently fooled, because he said: "You look like a white ghost, Jemma. All wrapped in white like that. It's not a look that will set London on fire, in my opinion."

Finchley took the chess board handed to him by the footman. "Now I shall move my pawn *so*, Your Grace," he chirped. "Do you make your move, and I'll leave you to take a good night's rest."

The duke seemed to be having trouble staying awake so Finchley nudged the chessboard a little closer to him. Villiers opened his eyes and stared at the pieces. "Jemma," he said finally, "does the rook ever stand up on his hind legs and buck when you look at him?"

"Never," Finchley squeaked. He exchanged looks with the footman.

Villiers reached out a hand and then paused. His hand froze in the air above the pieces.

"Your Grace?" Finchley quavered.

Slowly, slowly Villiers turned his head. His eyes narrowed, and he looked from the very tip of Finchley's wig, over his cleanly shaven chin, paused for a moment on the reddened skin that showed above his bodice.

"Finchley," he said, sounding clear-headed and utterly sane, "I think I may be losing my mind. Would you be contributing to that situation for some reason?"

"I'm not Finchley," Finchley said.

"No? Then the Duchess of Beaumont has truly changed

her spots. I can only assume that some distress has led to this change in your apparel."

Finchley swallowed. "Your Grace has been quite worried that you would miss your move with the duchess," he ventured.

"I am disagreeably sweaty," the duke said. "I should like a bath immediately. I certainly couldn't entertain a duchess in this condition."

"So I thought." He had to ask. "Your Grace, why?"

"Why did I regain my wits? The Duchess of Beaumont opened this game with a pawn to Queen's Four, Finchley. The idea that she would then take a knight to King's Rook Three was enough to shock me out of a fever dream. She would never move a knight to the edge of the board in the opening moves. I gather that I have not been in my proper head."

"No, Your Grace."

He peered around the room. "What day is it?"

"Saturday," Finchley said, and then added, reluctantly: "You've been ill for well nigh ten days, Your Grace."

The duke's eyelids closed. "What do they say?"

"Who say?"

"The doctors, fool."

"You could be ill for quite some time," Finchley said. "Banderspit has seen cases linger for months with this sort of fever."

"Linger? Linger and then—"

"Recover!" Finchley said, cursing his choice of words.

"Write a note to the duchess and call off our match for the time being," Villiers said, ignoring him. "And you'd better call my solicitor here as well. Now, while I'm still in my right head."

"Yes, Your Grace," Finchley said. "You do come out of the fever in the mornings, Your Grace."

"I've no memory of that." He rubbed his head. "I feel as if that benighted duel took place yesterday."

To Finchley's practiced eye, the fever was already coming back again. "I'll summon your solicitor tomorrow morning."

His master's eyes focused on him. "You'd better remind me that I'm dying before he comes, Finchley. I won't have the faintest idea why he's there."

It broke his heart, but he bowed his head and said: "Yes, Your Grace."

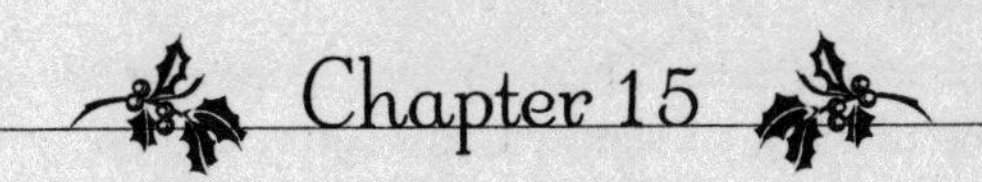

Chapter 15

Two weeks later
May 15

Jemma was rereading *The Noble Game of Chess* when her maid Brigitte scratched on the door and told her that the Duchess of Fletcher was asking to see her. She leapt to her feet. "Poppy, darling, how lovely you look!"

"I'm afraid I'm the worst of house guests."

Poppy certainly was an unusual house guest. She stayed in her room and, by account of the maids, did nothing but read. And cry, Jemma thought. "There's nothing better than an invisible house guest," she said reassuringly.

Poppy reached out and touched her book. "I wouldn't have thought there were books written just about chess."

"In fact, there are many."

"You must forgive my innocence. I do know that you are very, very good at the game . . . And that you are playing matches both with the Duke of Villiers and with your husband."

Jemma looked at her guest from under her lashes and gave a mental shrug. Poppy might as well know the worst. "One move a day," she said. "In each match. If either match goes to a third game, the third will be played blindfolded—and in bed."

There was silence. Then: "Why?" Poppy finally asked. She didn't look a bit shocked, just surprised. "Why would you want to play in bed? Won't the pieces tip to the side and you'll lose your spot?"

"Perhaps."

Another moment's silence. "I suppose it was your husband who came up with that idea."

"Actually, it was the Duke of Villiers."

"Will you win?"

"Both matches? I grow frightened that this might be a case of pride goeth before a fall," Jemma said. "I was rather shocked when I lost the first game to my husband. At the moment both games are postponed until Villiers recovers."

"Why not lose this game as well? Then you avoid the whole third game business," Poppy asked.

Jemma blinked. "Are you suggesting that I deliberately lose a game?"

"Why not?"

The question was inconceivable, but there was a more interesting point behind it. "Would you deliberately lose the game to avoid an encounter in bed?"

Poppy turned a little pink. "Playing chess in bed sounds quite uncomfortable."

Jemma leaned back in her chair. Her guest was perched upright, her back as straight as if it were soldered with iron. Poppy was exquisite although—now that Jemma looked more closely—rather brittle-looking, as if she might burst into tears.

"I gather the bedchamber is not a place where you and your husband are in accord," Jemma said.

"I always did my best. But Fletch is not happy with me. And yet, I have tried! If—if my mother only knew the things I did with him, and yet it wasn't enough!"

Disturbing possibilities raced through Jemma's mind. She hadn't lived in Paris for eight years without hearing a great deal about human depravity. And Poppy's sweet little face and yellow curls looked . . . young. She felt a little sick. "Perhaps it is better that the duke meandered off to greener pastures?" she asked.

There was a strangled silence on the other side of the table, a silence that did not seem entirely to agree. Yet if Poppy were being veritably abused, she would presumably long to see the back of her husband.

"Exactly what does Fletch request of you, Poppy?" Jemma asked.

"Nothing," she said wretchedly. "I suppose I am a prude. He said as much once. And after that I tried—I really tried."

"To do what?"

"I take off my nightgown," Poppy said.

Jemma nodded. "And?"

"I take it off *before* getting into bed."

"Yes?"

"And then I lie down on the bed and I never make a fuss about anything he might do."

Jemma didn't have a patient nature. "And what exactly *is* that, Poppy?"

"He rootles about," Poppy said. "He—he—does what he came to my chambers for. I never make any fuss," she added. "I hope that he knows that he's welcome to take as long as he possibly could wish. I—"

"Oh dear."

Poppy burst into tears. "There's something wrong with me, isn't there? I've been thinking about it. Other women are different. Except my mother, of course. I must take after her. There's Louise, flirting with Fletch and it wasn't a matter of falling in love with him."

Jemma didn't answer immediately, so she demanded: "Louise wasn't thinking of love, was she?"

"Absolutely not!" Jemma replied.

"And if you—if you play this third game in bed with the Duke of Villiers, not to mention your husband—you wouldn't be entirely dismayed to find yourself there, would you?" Poppy demanded.

"I suppose not."

"He will sweep the board to the side and—and then you will enjoy it, won't you?"

"Which man are we talking about?" Jemma asked cautiously.

"Either of them," Poppy said, catching a sob.

"I think I shall be able to beat my husband," Jemma said, thinking about it. "And Villiers—" But then she broke off, realizing that the point was not whether she could win the games, but what would happen if she didn't. "Bed with my husband will happen sometime, of course, because I returned from Paris just so that we could make an heir. One must go to bed in order to create children. Poppy, did you know that?"

"Of course I did!" Poppy wailed. Her little face was all blotched with tears now, and she looked red and angry and grieved all at the same time. "I went so far as to tell Fletch that! How can we have children if he never visits my bed? He should make it his duty! My mother said that father visited her punctiliously until that event occurred, but Fletch—Fletch is only interested in—well . . ." Whatever she said disappeared into a mumble of sobs.

"I expect that Fletch is interested in pleasure," Jemma said.

"If that's what you call it!"

"What would you call it?"

"I don't know." Poppy's tear-streaked face contorted. "I just don't know. I tried . . . I did everything he wanted. I let him do anything he wanted, kiss me all over even though it was—was *wrong.*"

Jemma was beginning to wonder whether Poppy's marital problems might be more than she could reasonably hope to help her with. "Why wrong?" she asked cautiously.

"My mother . . ." but whatever it was Poppy meant to say, she was sobbing too hard.

"We need a cup of tea," Jemma said. "Then I will tell you exactly what I have ever done—or allowed a man to do—in bed. So prepare to be shocked."

It took two cups of tea, but finally Jemma and Poppy were seated on the little sofa before the window and Poppy was looking at Jemma expectantly.

"It's not a matter of what one allows a man to do *to* one," Jemma said. "Take an apple puff, Poppy; they're delicious. It's a matter of what one requires a man to do."

"To darken the room," Poppy said nodding. "I told Fletch that."

"Nothing to do with lights. The crucial thing to remember is that men find it very easy to please themselves and women don't. Therefore, your pleasure should be foremost."

"Oh." Poppy's face drooped. "Believe me, Fletch knows that. He's asked me so many times whether I like this or that, that I felt as if I could scream if he asked another question. No answer satisfies him. I can say no, and he doesn't stop. If I say yes, he doesn't stop either. Or if he does, he's angry at me."

"It's nice that Fletch shows interest in your pleasure."

"Too much," Poppy said with feeling.

To Jemma's mind, they had reached the heart of it. "Are you saying that nothing Fletch does feels good?"

Poppy bit her lip. "There's something wrong with me, isn't there? One night Fletch told me that I should be instructing *him* in what to do. I should tell *him* exactly what I wanted."

"That's easier than relying on a man," Jemma said encouragingly.

"I just—I just want to do it right," Poppy said despairingly. "Ever since the first night after we married, I've never been right. He wanted me to do this, or do that, and I didn't even know what he was talking about. And then everything he did was so embarrassing. I don't think he has any idea what well-bred women are supposed to be like!"

"Undoubtedly true. I have to say, Poppy, that Fletch sounds much more interesting than most English men."

"Oh, he's interesting," Poppy said morosely. "He's so beautiful now. I—I keep looking at him, and I can't believe that I'm lucky enough to be married to him. And then he looks at me with such scorn and I remember how much of a failure I am, and I just wish he were married to someone else. That way I could love him from afar—and I would. I can't imagine loving anyone but Fletch. If we weren't married, he wouldn't hate me so."

"It seems to me that Fletch's standards are entirely too high," Jemma said. "Beaumont and I never showed any sort of ability in bed together, but that certainly wasn't a source of concern to him." She stopped short, remembering that their marriage had fallen apart when she discovered her husband making vigorous love to his mistress in his chambers at Westminster. "Or perhaps I just didn't see it that way. After all, Beaumont had his mistress, though I didn't realize it."

"Before I married, Mama told me that Fletch would have

a mistress," Popppy said. Her voice wavered a little but she raised her chin. "I didn't think he would because—because he loved me so much. But I expect I can get accustomed to the situation. I can become accustomed to *anything*. I have, after all, lived with my mother for years."

"Listening to you, I could almost be grateful for my mother's early demise," Jemma said. "I never really knew her."

"My mother loves me. She really does. And she sees in me all the possibilities that she lost when she was forced to marry my father. She says he was never clever, and of course, he wasn't titled."

"A distasteful comment to make about one's husband," Jemma said bluntly.

"She told me once that the cleverest thing my father ever did was die young."

"Substitute cruel for distasteful."

"But when she took over the estates, she made them quite enormously profitable."

"How did she do that?"

"She enclosed all the land and put sheep in the fields where the tenants used to farm."

The fate of the tenants hung in the air between Jemma and Poppy.

"I am not very good at rebelling," Poppy said with a helpless little shrug. "I am not a strong sort of person."

"You might surprise yourself," Jemma said. "You are certainly surprising me. And I have no doubt but that your mama is surprised as well."

Poppy smiled for the first time. "Horrified."

"Good," Jemma said. "Good."

Chapter 16

June 5

It was the beginning of June; the Duke of Villiers had been ill over a month. Yet still he tossed on the pillow, his cheeks stained cherry red, words tumbling from his lips like leaves from a tree in autumn. Finchley found himself terrified. He scared off Banderspit, who still wanted to bleed him. He shouted at Mrs. Ferrers when she wanted to give the duke sips of fresh cock's blood.

"If he doesn't come out of this by morning," the doctor said as he departed, "he won't come out of it at all. Mark my words. A patient can't survive with that fever if he doesn't drink."

No one could get the duke to take more than the smallest sip of water. The last real drink he'd had had been during that brief period of sanity when Finchley tried the chess gambit.

"It's chess," Finchley said to Mrs. Ferrers. "It's the only thing that speaks to him. Listen!"

Sure enough, the duke, voice cracked and hoarse from talking all night, said, "That's two pawns in return for the sacrifice . . ." His hands waved pieces in the air: they had to give him chess pieces or he plucked them from the thin air, and that was so ghoulish that Mrs. Ferrers said it quite gave her a turn.

"I'm going to fetch the duchess," Finchley stated.

"The Duchess of Beaumont? I thought as how you said that the master would never forgive you for letting the duchess see him in this condition."

"No more he will," Finchley said, looking at his master. Villiers's hair was all sweaty again, his face red and pinched. "But he'll die soon. I have to try it."

He took the duke's own carriage, and stamped up the steps to the town residence of the Duke of Beaumont. But it wasn't all clear sailing. "I won't have that," the Beaumont butler, Mr. Fowle, said, on hearing his request. "The duke has enough to plague him without his duchess calling on Villiers at his home. Half of London is already thinking that they're on their way to a tryst."

"He's sick unto death," Finchley said desperately. "No one could think that."

"Don't be a fool," the butler replied. "You know perfectly well Villiers could be a corpse in that bed, and the stories will have him doing a lively dance in the sheets. The only thing is to speak to Beaumont himself. Because if the duke accompanies the duchess, why then there's nothing to it."

"Do you think he would?" Finchley said. "You know that Villiers and Beaumont aren't the best of friends."

Mr. Fowle drew himself up. "His Grace may not approve of Villiers's actions, but he would never desert a man in need."

No more would he. A moment later Finchley's story was tumbling out before the duke.

"Damn these duels," Beaumont said. "And damn Gryffyn for challenging Villiers in the first place. Bring me my greatcoat, Fowle."

"The duchess?" Finchley asked.

"The duchess has retired to bed," Beaumont said. "If Villiers needs to play a game of chess, I'll play with him."

"He must drink water," Finchley said, feeling desperate. "I tried to play chess with him, Your Grace. It's not just that he needs to play chess; I'm afraid that no one but the duchess will do. Please, could we rouse her? Please?"

Beaumont looked at him for moment. "You're a good man," he said. "If I don't have Villiers drinking within the hour, I'll drive back here myself and cart my wife over to the house. Will that be sufficient?"

Finchley bowed. "Yes, Your Grace."

It was only a few weeks since Elijah had watched Villiers's grand entrance to Jemma's party. But now Villiers's eyes seemed to have sunk into his head. There was a horrible lividity around his forehead that made the red spots in his cheeks burn brightly.

The duke walked forward, pulling off his greatcoat and throwing it behind him. Villiers was holding a rook in the air and as Elijah cocked his ear, he heard him mumble something about a backward queen's pawn.

"I'll try," he had told Finchley. But he couldn't talk to Villiers, not with a footman bathing Villiers's forehead, and Finchley breathing heavily to his right, and the housekeeper peering in from the stairs. "I'll ask you all to leave."

Finchley started to say something, so Elijah hit him with the look he gave recalcitrant legislators in the House of Lords.

Once the room was quiet, Elijah pulled the chair closer. "Villiers," he said.

There was no appreciable response. "Your Grace!" he said more loudly. "Villiers!"

"His white queen is being smothered," Villiers said. He didn't even glance in Elijah's direction, just waved the rook in the air.

Elijah picked up a glass of water and tried to bring it to Villiers's lips, but the rook struck the glass and he almost dropped it onto the covers.

"Smothered," Villiers said hoarsely. "It's being . . ." His voice died into a cracked mumble.

He's going to die, Elijah thought. Villiers—Villiers, who's that? They hadn't really spoken in years, but this was no Villiers. This was Leopold, his oldest, dearest friend. Somewhere under that mop of sweaty hair and reddened eyes was Leo, the first person he had ever loved in the world.

He put down the glass and snatched Villiers's rook. That got a response. Leopold's reddened eyes swung about and he said, "Black is desperate. He has no more checks."

"Leopold," Elijah said, using his most forceful voice. "Leopold, I've come to play a game of chess with you."

Villiers tried to pull the rook away.

"That's *my* rook," Elijah said. "I always play white, don't you remember?"

For the first time, Villiers's eyes fixed on him. "Who are you?" he said.

"Elijah," he said. "I'm Elijah."

"Elijah," Villiers said dreamily. And then: "Oh no, Elijah's a duke now. He's married to a duchess."

"You are a duke too," Elijah said firmly. "I'm come to play chess with you."

Villiers struggled to sit up, so Elijah hauled him up on his pillows. "First you must drink some water. Then you may make a move."

There was something different about Villiers now; he was inhabiting his own body again. Elijah avoided his eyes and picked up the chess board, swiftly putting the pieces in their places. Then he picked up the glass of water and put it to his lips. Villiers was staring at him over the glass, but he opened his cracked lips—and drank.

"Who are you?" he said suddenly.

"Elijah. The Duke of Beaumont." Elijah smiled a little. "Jemma's husband."

"Jemma doesn't have a husband," Villiers said.

"She doesn't?"

Elijah moved a pawn to Queen's Four.

Villiers reached out his hand but Elijah stopped him. "Not unless you drink."

Villiers took a gulp and then picked up a black pawn. His hand trembled, but he managed to move his pawn to Queen's Four as well.

Elijah took out a knight. Once prompted, Villiers drank and then, his hand shaking terribly, managed to move a pawn to Queen's Bishop Four.

"Jemma is not married," Villiers said, when the glass of water was almost gone. "I know she's not married because she doesn't look married."

"How does she look?" Elijah asked with interest.

Villiers gulped the last of his water and held out his glass. "I seem to be unaccountably thirsty." He moved his queen forward.

Elijah found it rather vexing to realize that he was playing a man who was verifiably out of his mind, and yet that madman was spinning a pretty web around his queen. "Why do you say that Jemma doesn't look married?" he asked again.

"She looks like a woman who's never been properly

loved," Villiers said. "*You* wouldn't know this, but she's actually married to a fellow I used to know."

Elijah cast him a quick look, but Villiers was frowning at the board.

"We're no longer friends," he said, making his move and taking an unprompted drink of water.

"Perhaps the fellow loves her," Elijah said.

"Oh no," Villiers said. "She told me that he loves his mistress, which is a bloody strange thing under the circumstances, but apparently he told her so himself."

Elijah ground his teeth. Of course, he had said such a bloody foolish thing but it was years ago. Could it be that Jemma remembered? One had to suppose . . .

"I should like to be married to her myself," Villiers said, sounding quite chatty now that his voice wasn't so hoarse. He had almost finished the second glass of water, so Elijah poured more into his glass.

"Would you?" His own voice sounded like two pieces of iron rubbing together.

"She knows her way around a bed," Villiers said. "Did you really move your rook to King's Seven? That was remarkably foolish." He promptly took the piece. "She knows her way around a bed, and yet she's remarkably intelligent. I would bed her, but I'm afraid I would lose her. Stupid, isn't it?"

"No, why?" Elijah managed. His queen was in danger; he saw his queen was in danger and he could do nothing. Even in a fit of fever and madness, when Villiers couldn't seem to recognize who he was, he had spun a web of black pawns around him and now a black rook was looming.

"I want her, but I want her friendship more," Villiers said. "I'm afraid you've lost this game. What did you say your name was? The doctor, aren't you? I do feel better." He picked up Elijah's queen and lay back against his pillows. His eyes drooped closed but he said something.

"What is it?" Elijah said, bending over.

"Lord, what fools these mortals be," Villiers said.

Could he be quoting from Shakespeare in the midst of a fever? Elijah ventured to put the back of his hand against his forehead and he seemed cool enough. It was Elijah who felt as if he had a fever. A fever of rage.

Villiers opened his eyes again. "Just be sure to take Betsy out before you leave, would you?" he said.

"Betsy? *Betsy*?"

"My dog," Villiers said. "She'll need to go out. She's been keeping me company."

"She's not your dog," Elijah managed. "She was *my* dog, though she died many years ago!"

For a moment Villiers's eyes opened all the way and he looked at him. "Why, so she did," he said, sounding surprised. "Is that Beaumont? Did you keep the dog and the woman as well? Are you married to the barmaid now? Lucky sod."

"No, I'm not," Elijah said. "Drink some more water." There was something in his voice that seemed to snap into Villiers's consciousness because he frowned. But he drank the entire glass Elijah handed him.

Elijah took the glass back, then picked up his greatcoat.

"If you have Betsy," came the voice from behind him, "and you have Jemma too, then . . . then you have everything, don't you?"

It was not the first time in Elijah's life that he realized how unimportant "everything" can feel.

Finchley was outside the door. "He drank five glasses of water," Elijah said. "I expect he needs to piss. I'm not prepared to hand him a chamber pot; I'll leave that up to you."

"Your Grace," Finchley said, and there were tears in his eyes. "Will you come again?"

Elijah tightened his lips. "If you need me, I'll come," he

said. "Send me word in my chambers. You say he doesn't have the fever in the mornings?"

Finchley nodded.

"Make him drink five to six glasses of water. Not just sips. He has to drink enough for the whole day."

Finchley clasped his hands. "I will, Your Grace. I will. And you'll—"

"If you need me, I'll come."

Chapter 17

July 13

Poppy wasn't used to being angry. Now she had a little coal of rage under her breastbone. She'd been nurturing it ever since Fletch sent a note indicating that he intended to pay her a call.

A call! It had been over two months and her husband had decided to pay her a call.

What had she done to Fletch that he should be so rude to her? Loved him, that was all. Loved him even when he grew that little beard, and became so bewilderingly elegant, and stopped breakfasting with her.

There were limits to any woman's patience. Although patience didn't seem to be the word for the twist of poker-hot anger she felt on remembering how Fletch smiled at Louise. He smiled at Louise the way he used to smile at her. And then it all dropped away when he saw her, and there was nothing but scorn and dislike in his eyes.

"He used to love me," she told her reflection in the glass. It looked back at her, precisely the same face that Fletch first fell in love with. She wore the same clothes—or near enough as made no matter. She maintained appropriate standards when they were married. She tinted her lips before coming to breakfast, and was never seen in *dishabille*.

But the weight of Fletch's silent demands was always with her. More French, she thought. He wanted her to be French, even though she wasn't French.

Her marriage had turned out to be just like her relationship with her mother. Her mother's demands were different. Be beautiful. Be powerful. Be obedient. But the important ones were the ones Poppy could never achieve: you'll never be as beautiful as I am, her mother had remarked many a time. You'll never charm men the way I do. I would have married a duke . . .

An awful thought struck Poppy: what if she had never been in love with Fletch? What if she had simply obeyed her mother's command to marry a duke . . . and he was an available duke? Now she thought of it, Fletch was the only unmarried duke she met in Paris after her debut.

She didn't understand Fletch. She didn't even feel as if she knew who Fletch was—so how could she be in love with him? The awful pressure in her chest eased a little. She had only thought she loved him.

She had no choice but to love her mother, no matter how badly she disappointed her. But she could choose not to love Fletch, and she could choose to make his disappointment irrelevant to her.

I need to make my own choices, Poppy thought. Decide for myself. What do I want to do with my days? Never go back to that house, said her heart. Stop trying to please my husband. Stop trying to love him.

What she really wanted was time to be Poppy, rather than the Duchess of Fletcher. With a sudden rush, ideas crowded into her head: things she wanted to do, books she wanted to read, places she wanted to see. She almost felt giddy with the joy of it. She didn't need to be a duchess. She could be just herself. Poppy.

She could live alone. Look at Jemma. Jemma had left her husband and set up her own house. She could do that as well. And she could travel! Giddy images of Paris, the Nile, the wild Americas, came to mind.

There was a little tap at the door, and her maid said, "His Grace requests your presence."

She turned toward her lip color, and dropped her hand. She didn't love Fletch. She had never loved Fletch. Why should she make herself beautiful for him?

She walked down the stairs and found she was actually smiling. How long had it been since she genuinely smiled in Fletch's presence? Probably over a year. She had spent all that time wound tight as a top, trying desperately to figure out how to please him, how to make him love her.

Walking into the drawing room was a bit difficult because—though it was unimportant, she quickly reminded herself—Fletch was so beautiful. His hair was like ebony, with a sheen like midnight. His nose was straight and his eyes slanted under his eyebrows, making him look just faintly exotic. If he wasn't so infernally beautiful, he wouldn't be so demanding.

"Poppy!" he said, turning around with a frown. That made it easier. He was always frowning at her, and she was sick of it.

She smiled at him, a different smile than the one she normally gave him. It wasn't a cringing puppy smile, begging for love. "Yes, Fletch?"

"I need you to come home now."

"I won't be coming home," she said, seating herself. "I'm staying with Jemma for the foreseeable future. She won't retire to the country until December because of Beaumont's involvement in the House of Lords; I shall stay with her."

"Couldn't we just skip all the fuss, please, Poppy? Surely we've known each other long enough so that you could simply forgive me and come home."

"I do forgive you."

"Oh good," he said, looking as if he'd never had a doubt of it.

"Although you were abysmally rude to me in public."

"I did apologize. I will never do such a thing again."

"And you were flirting with one of my friends."

"I hadn't the faintest idea—" he said, and stopped.

"Yes," she said thoughtfully, tapping her finger on the chair, "that one is a bit more difficult to explain away, isn't it? It *is* true that Louise is one of my friends. A dear friend, unfortunately for you. But of course there are many women in London with whom I am positively unacquainted."

"Yes," he said, looking uneasy for the first time.

"So I think we can both agree that you should simply look farther afield," she said gently.

His mouth actually fell open a bit, which was very pleasant to observe.

"We should make some plans," Poppy said. "Obviously, we shall have to co-habit again at some point in the future . . . shall we say five years or so? When you feel that the question of an heir becomes pressing, I assure you that I will be compliant. I had felt that I wanted a child early in our marriage, but now I realize that it would be far, far wiser to wait. I have things to do."

"You do?" He sounded stunned.

"Yes. You and I have separated in an amicable way, and so we can plan everything without acrimony. I would suggest five years and then we shall have to live in the same household again."

"You what?"

"We could plan for more than five years, but we run the risk of childlessness. After all, we have been married four years with no issue."

He just stared at her.

"We can discuss these arrangements later," she said with another encouraging smile. "Fletch, was there something you wished to say at this point?"

Though she was being tremendously cheerful, the hot little coal of rage was still under her breastbone. She paused, but he seemed to have been struck dumb.

"Jemma assures me that she would love me to retire with them to the country for the Christmas season. She will be bringing a large party with her. After that, I thought I might return to France for a few years, but I'm not certain of my plans yet. I hope to travel widely." The little coal of rage prompted her to say, very sweetly, "But never fear, Fletch, I will be certain to give you my direction. I know it would be most incommodious if you had no idea where your wife was. No one wants to have to track his wife like a grouse in hunting season."

He finally opened his mouth. "I didn't mean the comment in this light."

"I will tell you where I am going, and you won't have to worry about me. Oh! I forgot. You never do worry, do you?"

His brows knit. "You sound most unlike yourself, Poppy. I am truly sorry that I have made you angry."

He looked so perplexed that she actually laughed, a genuine little laugh. "I'm angry, Fletch, but I'm as angry at myself as you. I should never have married you."

"You shouldn't?"

"I think I married you because my mother told me to do so."

"You—you married me because you were in love with me!"

She smiled again because it felt good to tell him the truth. "No, I wasn't, Fletch. My mother told me from the moment I was seven years old that I was to marry a duke. You were the first English duke who arrived in Paris, and so I married you. Yes, I thought myself in love with you, but now I've discovered that I made a mistake. Which is"—she pointed out—"a very good thing, as you clearly made the same discovery some time ago."

He opened his mouth.

"Didn't you?" she prompted. "Because it seems to me that you not only realized you were not in love but you decided to seek companionship elsewhere."

The silence grew between them until she couldn't stand it. For all she wasn't in love with him, it was terribly humiliating to have one's husband be so uncaring. "I really don't see any point in our discussion continuing."

"We haven't discussed anything yet!" Fletch protested.

"There's not much to discuss."

"You need to come home now," he said, exhibiting the kind of stubbornness that characterized little boys in the orphanage.

"I'm not coming home."

"You must."

"Why?" For a moment, the world froze on its spiral. Because, despite herself, despite her talk and her bravery and her lack of love, there was a little part of her heart—

"Your mother," he said.

"My mother." The aching part of her heart closed its doors. For a second she thought she might cry and then she grabbed control. "What about my mother?"

"You knew quite well that your mother has moved into our house," he said, glaring. "It's been two months, and she shows no sign of leaving."

Poppy was very pleased to discover that Fletch's glare didn't bother her in the least. "I'm certain that you can handle her."

Fletch's eyes narrowed. "What are you up to, Poppy? Where is all this wild talk coming from? Did the Duchess of Beaumont put you up to this?"

"I haven't spoken to Jemma about my plans," Poppy said truthfully. "Beyond asking her if I could stay with her through Christmas. And I certainly haven't told her the conclusions I've drawn about our marriage. Naturally, she knows what *you* think of our marriage. Most of London has heard it by now."

"You sound spiteful," Fletch said.

"Oh dear," Poppy said. "I'm sure I didn't mean to. I've spent so much time trying to charm you that I suppose it was bound to wear thin."

"Your mother—" he said, helplessly.

The coal of rage got a little larger as she realized that the only thing he really gave a damn about was the fact that her mother was living with him. Poppy knew perfectly well that her mother was a rather unpleasant person to live with.

"I'll speak to my mother," she said, resolving to do just that. She would thank her for staying with Fletch.

"Poppy!" he said, sounding urgent, for once.

But Poppy was done. He could go to hell, him and his black clothes and the pure beauty of him. She turned her back to him without even saying goodbye and walked to the door.

"Poppy!"

She left.

Chapter 18

Beaumont House
That evening

Jemma was setting up the pieces, Beaumont opposite her. "I'm happy to hear that Villiers is better."

"I wouldn't describe it as better. He's still in the grip of a fever most of the day, according to a note I had from his valet this morning. He may be out of immediate danger, but he still has to beat the fever. Shall we begin our second game of the match?"

"I don't think we should start a second game until Villiers is capable once again."

"Why not? Simply because the first two games played in tandem doesn't mean that the others have to. It was proximity that lent itself to the distasteful supposition that you were choosing between myself and Villiers."

She glanced at him, but he was studying the black queen.

His eyelashes cast a shadow on his cheek. "You challenged me to a match only on hearing of my match with Villiers," she said. "That parallel was in your mind, and thereafter in the minds of Londoners."

"If we play our game now, while Villiers is incapacitated, it will quell the feverish interest in the next occupant of your bed."

It must be the politician in him; he was utterly dispassionate in discussing his wife's bed. Of course, his reputation was all-important. "Is there a chance that Villiers will not survive?" she asked, fiddling with a bishop.

"The fever has a grip on him. I would think him a lucky man if he lives."

Jemma felt sick at the thought. "Oh God . . ." she whispered.

He still didn't look at her. "Will it break your heart, Jemma? Because if so, I'm truly sorry for it."

"Break my heart? No. I haven't known him long. We were getting to be friends, though, and I enjoyed that. I am so sad to hear that he is dying."

"Perhaps more than friends," he said. His voice was wooden.

"My heart is a singularly strong instrument," she said, resenting the conversation, resenting the way he was prying into her feelings. "You broke it long ago, Elijah, and I've never given it away since."

He looked up. "I?"

"Did you not think so?"

"No. You—we shared little, I thought."

"That's the worst of it, perhaps," she said sadly. "We shared little and yet I built a castle out of it. I suppose the word *marriage* has that nonsensical effect on women sometimes. But it was a salutary lesson."

"I apologize."

Jemma studied her husband from under her eyelashes. He didn't have that whip-thin exhausted look tonight, the one where his eyes turned shadowed and his cheekbones stood out. He looked a bit tired, but not sick to the bone. "What's happening in the House of Lords these days?" she ventured.

"Scots and brandy."

"Scots? Oh, because of the Scottish representation in Lords?"

He raised an eyebrow. "You've been reading about that tangle? I thought you weren't interested in politics."

"I am as interested as any sensible person," Jemma said, startled. "I haven't a great deal of time to study all the newspapers, but I do my best." She couldn't stop herself. "Though I'm sure I have less understanding than your Miss Tatlock."

"She is an extraordinary woman," Elijah said, with a hint of pride in his voice. "For someone of her sex and age, she really has an intuitive understanding of politics. She made a suggestion at the Royal Society today that made Lord Rollins take notice."

"Oh?" Jemma decided she quite disliked Miss Tatlock. "How did that come about?"

"I gave a lecture there today," Beaumont said. "That's why I'm not in parliament. Miss Tatlock runs the Ladies' Membership. Most lectures are reserved for regular members, but the ladies are invited to join us on occasion."

Jemma thought about whether she was supposed to know about her husband's lecture and decided not, since no one had bothered to tell her. "How enterprising of her to attend your lecture. Dare I wonder whether she had a hand in your invitation?"

He looked at her. "Enterprising?"

"Is it too harsh a word? The two of you were linked again in last week's *Morning Post,* you know. Apparently you drew eyes by having an intimate conversation at Lord Rochester's *musicale.* I wonder what she thinks will happen to me if she manages to impress you with her manifold virtues?"

He surprised her by not pretending to obtuseness. "Perhaps she thinks you might be fading due to a wasting illness. I notice that young women in the grip of love have no difficulty thinking that miracles will happen."

"I feel perfectly healthy," she said lightly. "Shall we play chess?"

"If you would prefer not to resume our match," Elijah suggested, "perhaps we might play a game on the side."

Neither one of them said the obvious: if Villiers could not play out his match, the appetite for their parallel match would die with him.

"A sound idea. We'll play a game or two for the pleasure of it, and wait for Leopold to improve."

"Leopold?" He raised an eyebrow.

"Villiers's given name . . . surely you knew it?" Jemma asked, her face carefully innocent. "I thought you two were the best of boyhood friends."

"I had not realized that you were quite as intimate as that."

Jemma moved a pawn forward, the lovely rhythm of pawn to king, queen and castle swelling into her heart and soul and stealing away all those elusive worries about Beaumont's health and Miss Tatlock, and Villiers's fever.

An hour later she grinned at her husband. "Now I feel better," she observed.

"I don't," he said sourly.

"You won our first game," Jemma said, "the one that counted. This is a game which naught sees but us, and yet I am very pleased to have won."

"Let's begin our second game in the match," Elijah said.

"Please. I don't want to wait for Villiers to die. It's too ghoulish."

She nodded, set up the board quickly, and moved a pawn to Queen's Four.

He moved his pawn to the same position and that was that. For today.

He uncoiled himself from the chair, and stood up, all six feet plus of him. Jemma stayed where she was. Her husband was a tremendously handsome man. It was no wonder, really, that he cut such a wide swath through the Parliament.

"I came here to ask you a question, Jemma."

She raised an eyebrow.

"You returned from France so that we can create an heir. I wondered if you had any schedule in mind for that?"

In other words, when would they go to bed together? Despite herself, Jemma felt a little prickle of interest.

But he kept talking. "I ask because if Villiers were to win his match, Jemma, I think it should alter our plans."

She stiffened. "You assume that I am the prize for the match, and I assure you that I do not wager myself nor my body on the chessboard."

She couldn't read his eyes at all, and cursed silently at his politician's face.

"Our problem is not whether or with whom you share your favors," he said evenly, "but the fact that should Villiers win this chess game, all of London will *think* you are bedding him. Whether you do so or not is irrelevant."

"I hardly think it's irrelevant," she answered, stung. "You're suggesting that your heir might end up being of Villiers's blood."

"You misunderstand me," he said, patient as always. "I am well aware that you are not the sort to accidentally grow large with child."

It was a notable insult, delivered with all the calm precision of an arrow to the heart. And yet Jemma always found herself warring between truth and logic. The truth was that she had been unfaithful to him while living in Paris. And of course she had no children of those unions. The fact that he had been blatantly unfaithful to her—and presumably was to this day, with one mistress or another—didn't carry the same weight.

"If you and I were to conceive a child during this period of intense interest in Villiers," he continued, "I fear that most people would consider that child a cuckoo. At the very least, they would show an unbecoming interest in the child's heritage that could damage his or her future happiness."

She nodded. "I can see that."

"I thought of asking you to give up the match, but I have made a practice of never asking politicians for the one thing I know they will not give, and I am holding to that policy in the home."

"If you are feeling unwell," she said, "I will resign from the match. Have you fainted again, Beaumont?"

"Thankfully, no."

"In that case, I believe you are right and it would be best to wait until the match is over before we engage in . . . intimacies."

He bowed. "In that case—"

"That does not mean," Jemma said, looking at the chessboard, "that you are free to engage in a flirtation with the estimable Miss Tatlock. I am not like to die of a wasting disease; I feel entirely healthy."

"I am enchanted to hear it."

"Somehow I feel that the young woman will not share your pleasure."

His chuckle was rare and all the more welcome for that. "The Duchess of Beaumont jealous! I never thought to see the day. I must say that this makes me feel even kinder toward Miss Tatlock."

She rose to her feet. "I've never been any good at sharing, Elijah. Surely you noticed that from our early marriage?"

He opened his mouth, but she didn't want his politician's words, his apologies. She gave him the smoky kind of look one gave a lover, reached up and pulled his head toward hers.

He tasted wonderful, like blackberries and spice. She meant to kiss him as a warning, as a promise, as a way to control him. But the moment after her hand curled around his neck, and their kiss deepened, she remembered the one important fact she'd managed to forget while living in Paris: Elijah's kisses weren't like other men's. They did something to her. Melted her defenses, remade her into a foolish, vulnerable girl who cried for months after they separated.

She jumped back so quickly that she almost knocked over the chess table, then made sure her face reflected nothing of the utter panic she felt.

"A warning?" he asked, eyebrow quizzical, eyes dark.

He always knew . . . he always knew what she was thinking. For a moment the pain revisited her like a slim shaft to the heart. Then she smiled. "Precisely, Elijah. Precisely."

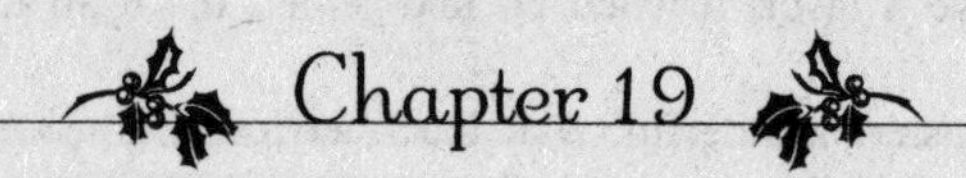

Chapter 19

The same evening, in a far less fashionable part of London . . .

When Miss Charlotte Tatlock stopped to think about the last few weeks, she got such a giddy feeling that her head spun. Giddiness was *not* her sister May's reaction, alas. May was in a frenzy of doubt and apprehension; she couldn't countenance the fact that Charlotte's name was being linked with the Duke of Beaumont. "I just can't believe it!" she had squealed, over and over in the past fortnight. "As if you ever would . . . thank goodness, Mama is dead. Oh, thank goodness, Mama is *dead!*"

After the fourteenth reiteration of May's gratitude in their parent's demise, Charlotte almost started wishing the same about the rest of her family: that is, May herself.

"You simply must stay away from him, away, away, away

from him!" May screeched many a time. And Charlotte had agreed, of course. May's ponderous fiancé, Mr. Muddle, had even taken it upon himself to inform Charlotte that a woman's reputation was her most golden possession. Charlotte had swallowed an angry retort and nodded soberly.

No one seemed to believe that the Duke of Beaumont had, in fact, made no moves to tarnish her reputation in the slightest.

All in all, she thought she behaved admirably—except when she actually ended up in the same room with the Duke of Beaumont, of course. As soon as she saw his face, her heart would start to pound. And then she couldn't help it; she would tell him what she thought of the *Gazette*'s report of his last speech in Parliament. He would bend his head just so, a bit to the side, and listen so gravely. And he heard her! He really heard her. They . . .

They . . .

They talked far too much, and she knew it.

And she knew, even if no one else did, that the duke didn't have the faintest interest in her as a woman. He never looked at her that way. Charlotte had never been one to fool herself. Her nose was too long and her fortune was too small to allow her to indulge in fantasies of her own beauty. Or her desirability, financial or otherwise.

"Don't you see," she finally snapped at May, "what you're implying is horribly painful to me. You're implying that the duke would actually like to—to kiss me. And we both know that dukes simply don't kiss women who look like me. Not single women, not women with disagreeably small fortunes. Dukes *never* kiss spinsters!"

"You're not that," May had said.

"I am. You know I am. I'm an old maid," Charlotte said, hating the world. "I'm an ape-leader. And a tabby, and all those other horrible words. The truth is that no one wanted me, May, and when you make play as if a duke would actually desire me, you just rub salt into the wound!" Her voice rose in a way that had a dangerous little wobble to it.

May was never one for physical demonstrations of affection, but she gave her sister a prompt hug and said that if *she* were a duke, she couldn't think of a better thing to do than kiss Miss Charlotte Tatlock.

Charlotte smiled a bit mistily and said, "And May, if you happened to have one of the most beautiful women in the *ton* waiting for you at home . . . to wit, Jemma, the Duchess of Beaumont, would you still want to kiss an old maid named Charlotte Tatlock?"

"Of course!" May said stoutly, but Charlotte knew her point had gone home.

The duchess, after all, was exquisite from the top of her head to the tip of her toes. Charlotte had actually amused herself one day trying to ascertain the color of the duchess's hair. She decided it was like an egg yolk. That didn't sound very complimentary, but Charlotte meant one of the eggs that are delivered straight from the country. And when they crack open in your egg cup, the yolk is a deep rich gold, a kind of burnished brandy color, and yet there's the shine of good health, a sort of deep, natural beauty that was a year and a day from Charlotte's drab locks.

Put the duchess's hair together with a lush figure and the unmistakable intelligence in her face—"She is," Charlotte reminded her sister, "the best chess player in all France, or that's what they say"—and her argument was finished.

The husband of such a paragon . . . and Miss Charlotte Tatlock? Never.

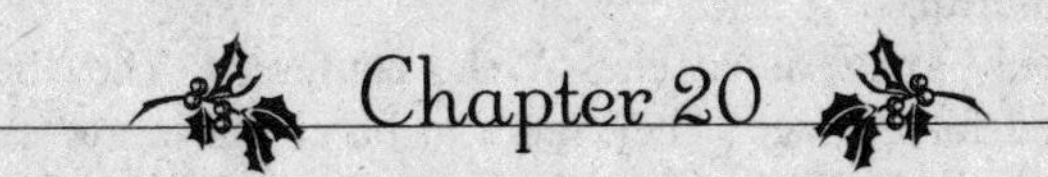

Chapter 20

August 1

Poppy didn't really expect Fletch to visit again, and he didn't.

She cried herself to sleep every night for another few weeks, dressing in the morning to look her very best, in case Fletch paid her a call. After all, her mother was still living with him. How could he survive?

Clearly, he survived. One morning Poppy dismissed her maid before her hair was curled and powdered, put on a dressing gown, curled up next to the window and watched the birds in Jemma's garden. Starlings hopped from branch to branch, took sudden flight and spilled up into the sky like gravy thrown into the air, settled back down on the branches to chat. She stayed there all day, wondering about starlings' nests and their conversations.

It was the kind of question her mother loathed. "Why

waste your time?" she would demand whenever Poppy ventured such a question. "Why waste *my* time?" she would continue, leaving the room.

Jemma seemed to find it perfectly sensible that Poppy had stopped dressing formally. "I often don't dress myself until the late afternoon," she said. Not that she knew anything about starlings.

"I only know about chess," she confessed. They both watched for a time. "They seem to be chattering to each other, don't they?" Jemma asked, rather startled. "I expect they're friends."

"I've never had a real friend before you," Poppy said.

"A pretty compliment but untrue! There's a salver stuffed with cards downstairs to attest that you have many friends, and not all of them are merely curious about your current situation. The ladies from your sewing circle for the penitent poor, for instance—"

"The sewing circle is for indigent mothers," Poppy said. "The reception of penitent poor meets at Lady Cleland's house, and we don't sew. In truth," she added gloomily, "we just talk about the immorality of prostitutes."

"The seamstresses and gossipers have all paid you calls, though most of them have now retreated to the country," Jemma said. "Every charitable lady in the city has summoned up her courage and crossed my threshold. No! That's not quite true."

"Someone faltered?"

"Could one picture Lady Langhorne faltering?"

"No," Jemma said, picturing that stout and invincible woman.

"She sent her card from the carriage, because presumably she could not bring herself to enter such a den of iniquity as Beaumont House when the duchess is in residence," Jemma said. "So tell me no more fibs about your lack of friends."

"It's not that," Poppy said, feeling weary. "They are friends of a kind. They wouldn't approve of my lying about in my nightgown all day long."

"That's due to their virtue," Jemma said. "Having been born with a complete lack of virtue myself, I never worry about the harsh standards the rest of you put to yourselves."

"Born with a complete lack of virtue?" Poppy said, laughing a little.

"The curse of the Reeves," Jemma said. "That's my maiden name, you know. We're a scurrilous lot. I have an uncle who is stark raving mad. And my brother is hardly a model of sober behavior. The duel with Villiers was his fourth, you know. Is there anything I can get you, Poppy?"

"Books," Poppy said. "I stupidly forgot my books at home and I have now read every volume on nature in your library."

"Nature? You mean about trees and such? I'm surprised there are any."

"I prefer to read about animal life," Poppy said, "though I was in the middle of a very interesting treatise on the nature of air as contained in water, which I left at home."

"We definitely don't have anything like that. How peculiar and interesting of you, Poppy. Why on earth haven't you sent a footman for your books?"

"I shall send a list to Lackington's Bookshop." Then she added, rather slowly, "I've decided to read all the books I never had time to tackle. And I mean to take notes on them, Jemma, though there's no point to that, as my mother would say. I shall do so for the pleasure of it."

"You'll be buried in three volume sets," Jemma said, hopping out of her chair. "Do you know, I've discovered that women can join the London Chess Club because they forgot to preclude the possibility in their rules? I'm thinking of becoming a member just because everyone thinks that only men can be chess masters."

"You must," Poppy said. "Only men are supposed to become naturalists."

"Then you must become a naturalist," Jemma said. "You must."

A month later
September 1

"Do you know what your husband is doing?" Jemma asked, looking up from the breakfast table.

"What?" Poppy asked warily. Given that Fletch wasn't wasting his time visiting his estranged wife, she wasn't sure she wanted to know his other activities.

"It says here that he made a lively speech in the House of Lords that was well received by both sides. How odd. Generally one side at least pretends to detest the speech. What do you think of going to Lady Wigstead's party this evening?"

"Perhaps," Poppy said.

Jemma narrowed her eyes. "I know just what you're thinking, Poppy, and it won't do. I've given you a decent mourning period, because it's called for when a marriage expires. It's September. That's five months, long enough to recover. I took about that long, and I fancied myself in love with my husband. Though it was no love match, the way you had."

"I thought I had," Poppy corrected her.

"But there's something bewitching about waking up next to a man."

"You slept together all night?" Poppy asked, startled.

"We did. Frankly, what we did in that bed was never very

interesting, in retrospect. But I used to like waking up when the morning light was just a faint yellow and asking him about what lay ahead of him. I was such an innocent that it's hard to imagine."

"How so?" Poppy asked.

"I thought that he enjoyed our conversations, that I might make a difference to his day in the House. That he listened to me."

"He didn't?"

"Of course he did. But he had no real interest in my advice; he listened courteously because courtesy is in his bones and his breeding. Beaumont is one of the most well-bred persons I've ever met. The only time I saw him be truly rude was when I discovered him with his mistress."

"Dreadful," Poppy said, shuddering. "Of course Fletch has a mistress by now. But every time I think about it, I feel sick."

"I *was* sick. I was sick in the carriage on the way home. Even now if I think about the way her hair fell over the edge of the desk, I feel a twinge of nausea."

"Did you leave for Paris immediately?"

"No. I was eager for explanations, for excuses, for anything. But along with his other faults, Beaumont is honest. He had told me he would leave his mistress, and apologized for what I'd seen—but then I asked him if he loved her. He hesitated for a moment and declined to answer, but it was too late. And he finally admitted the truth."

"He *loved* his mistress? My mother said that men form those relationships in a purely practical fashion."

"Your mother's axioms should be taken with a grain of salt," Jemma said. "Sarah was very beautiful. By the time we married, they'd been together, if you can use that term, for three years. He says she's no longer his mistress now, but I don't know how their relationship ended. I do know that he had an attachment to her that was far greater than his attachment to me, with our stilted intimacies and my foolish comments in bed."

Poppy swallowed. "It sounds as if you and I are in similar marriages."

"You saw Fletch flirting with someone," Jemma corrected her. "Beaumont left my bed, after making love to me, and proceeded to his office, where he made love to Miss Cobbett. There is a world of difference there, Poppy."

"Not really," Poppy said. "You know there isn't. If Louise hadn't happened to be my friend, he'd be making love to her on a desk right now. Is that—is that a common place for such activities?" she burst out.

"No," Jemma said. Then she grinned. "We shouldn't be so gloom-filled, Poppy. Not that many marriages survive, for one reason or another. I waited in Paris for three years, thinking that Beaumont would bring me back, but he didn't. And by the time he finally deigned to pay me a visit, I had discovered some pleasures of my own—if not on a table top."

"I see," Poppy said. "You're suggesting that Fletch will wait three years before paying me another call?"

Jemma leaned over and gave her a squeeze, but said nothing.

"He isn't going to come, is he?" It was a relief to say it out loud.

"I'm not sure how parallel our situations are," Jemma said, "but my guess is that he's rather surprised he hasn't encountered you at a party."

"He's going to parties?" Poppy asked.

Jemma turned back the newspaper and pointed to a column entitled "Taradiddle about the *Ton.*" Just above Jemma's pink-tipped finger was a sentence that made Poppy's heart drop into her slippers.

The Duke of F—found himself at the du Maurier ball last night without his duchess. The tiddle is that the said duchess may have departed for Venice. The Duke appeared unmoved by the buzz of interest and spent most of the evening in colloquy with Pitt's lords, who seemed overjoyed to welcome the sprig of fashion to their ranks.

"How Fletch must hate being called *a sprig of fashion*," Poppy said. And: "I'm in Venice?"

"They always get those things wrong," Jemma said. "If they're not sure where you are, they make something up."

"I should go to a meeting of Lady Cleland's sewing circle," Poppy said, after a bit.

"I wouldn't," Jemma said.

"Why not?"

"It sounds boring."

"It's our duty," Poppy said. "Caring for the poor and succouring the afflicted."

"I don't do it well," Jemma said. "I do give a great deal of money away. Beaumont's money, but believe me, an impoverished person far prefers the solid clink of coin to a poorly stitched sheet, which is about all that I can sew."

"I was wondering about money . . . What am I to do about money?"

"What do you mean? Fletcher certainly has plenty of money. I've never heard otherwise."

"But I don't have any," Poppy said. "I haven't even tuppence."

"Don't you have an allowance?"

Poppy shook her head. "Fletch offered one, but Mother said that I should simply send him all my bills and leave the financial details to him. She gave me lots of advice about how I should react if he questioned my bills, but Fletch has never said a word, not even when I bought two hats—and they were scandalously expensive—in the same month."

"Why did your mother believe you shouldn't have an allowance?"

"I don't know." But she did know. "She thinks I'm not intelligent enough to handle money," Poppy said, controlling her voice. "She doesn't say it cruelly, but she believes that very few women handle money well."

"She says that to you, the woman immersed in studies of water and air and starlings? And are you saying that you haven't bought a thing in the years you've been married without thinking about your husband's reaction?"

"Yes."

"And before that, I suppose your mother—"

"Of course," Poppy said, feeling like the fool she was. "I shall stay with you through Christmas, Jemma, but then I want to set up my own establishment. And I intend to travel a great deal."

Jemma raised an eyebrow. "Let me guess . . . to the wild African plains?"

Poppy grinned. "Actually, I was thinking of the Nile River to start."

"The Nile will only be comfortable if you are veritably swimming in money," Jemma said firmly. "I assume that your husband banks at Hoare's Bank, along with every other sprig of fashion in the capital?"

"You mustn't call him that. He would hate it so!"

"But he *is* a sprig," Jemma said. "For one thing, he's so young."

"He's older than I am."

"But younger than I, and worse, he makes me *feel* old with that little beard of his, and the way he slouches through a room, burning with something or other."

"It is tiresome, isn't it?" Poppy said, starting to laugh.

"And he's tediously beautiful," Jemma said. "*Tediously* so."

"Yes!"

"It's not manly to be so perfect in every way."

Poppy was laughing delightedly.

"What you need," Jemma said, "is to withdraw a great deal of money and spend it however you like, without thinking twice about whether you're buying two hats or forty hats. And then we'll send Fletch a letter and tell him that you'd like your allowance deposited into your own account at Hoare's Bank. It will be much easier for both of you that way. You can set up your own household, and travel wherever you like, and he won't have to worry about it."

It was all delightfully simple.

Faced with the smiling, confident faces of the Duchesses of Beaumont and Fletcher, Mr. Pisner of Hoare's Bank handed over the truly outrageous sum the duchess demanded without a quibble. "After all," he told his manager, Mr. Fiddler, later, "I knew who she was and it was her." That wasn't grammatical, but it was clear enough. "And it were the Duchess of Beaumont as well, and the two of them as thick as thieves, you could tell. And then she told me, the Duchess of Fletcher that is, that she would like her own account at the bank, and that her husband will be depositing her allowance there."

"The world is going to hell in a handbasket," Mr. Fiddler observed. "Not a man has control of his wife anymore. I mean, if a duke doesn't, what's the hope for us?"

Since Mr. Pisner privately thought that he would rather drink poison than be married to Mrs. Fiddler, there wasn't much else to be said about it, so they went back to adding up last month's receipts.

Out in the carriage, Poppy looked disbelievingly at the

thick sheaf of banknotes in her hand. "Jemma," she said, "Fletch is going to be *furious*."

"Really?" Jemma said, powdering her nose in a small glass she took from her bag. "Shall we go back tomorrow and get some more?"

Poppy thought about that.

"Why will he be furious? He doesn't look stingy."

"He's not," Poppy said.

"Likely he won't even notice."

Poppy doubted that. But what did she know? She was slowly coming to understand that she knew almost nothing about her husband.

"Now, let's buy something you always wanted but didn't buy."

But Poppy couldn't think of anything.

"A new gown?"

"I always bought them when I felt I had a need."

"What we're doing," Jemma said, "is buying something for which you *have no need*. For the pure pleasure of it. Not because there's a hole in your stockings, but because you love stockings." Then she started laughing.

"What is it?" Poppy said, smiling along with her.

"Your expression," Jemma said. "You look like a kitten with your first mouse."

"Well, there is something," Poppy said shyly.

"What?"

"Promise you won't laugh?"

"I can't promise that," Jemma said. "But I promise not to hoot, will that do?"

Poppy unfolded a small advertisement cut neatly from the newspaper.

"What on earth?" Jemma said, taking the scrap of paper. It was an advertisement. "*For Sale: The horn of a strange beast recovered in Sisfreyan Babylon.* What?"

"Did you hear about that beast?" Poppy asked. "It was written up in the *Gazette* last year. They said that it had two horns above its nose and two twisting horns above each ear. The article said that it was as large as a horse and might easily have carried two men. And its fur was blue."

Jemma had a look on her face that was something akin to that of Poppy's mother whenever Poppy showed her interesting snippets from the papers. "Why on earth are you carrying that about in your pocket?"

"I should like to buy it," Poppy said.

"*Buy* it?"

Poppy leaned forward and rapped on the roof. "Yer Grace," came back the booming voice of the coachman.

"We'd like to go to Grudner's Curiosity Shop."

"What?"

"Grudner's Curiosity Shop in Whitefriars," she shrieked. "Now, please."

The carriage pulled ponderously to the right. "Grudner's Curiosity Shop?" Jemma asked.

"I've read his advertisements," Poppy explained. "He's got all kinds of wonderful things . . . once he had a cherry stone with one hundred heads carved on it. And an ostrich egg. Do you know what an ostrich is, Jemma?"

"Absolutely not," Jemma said, leaning back and grinning at her.

"It's a very large, fat bird," Poppy said. "My father had a book of natural curiosities, and I kept it under my bed for years. All the maids knew, of course, but they never told my mother. Why are you smiling at me so?"

"Because your eyes are shining," Jemma said. "Your eyes are shining and your cheeks are pink, and you look—interested, Poppy. Really interested."

"Well, who wouldn't be? Did you know that Lord Prestle has a stuffed alligator? I would love to see that!"

"A stuffed alligator? What is an alligator?"

"A monster," Poppy said. "A veritable monster with huge huge teeth and tusks the size of a man's leg. That's how they described it in the *Rambler's Magazine*. It roams the wilderness in America and snaps up a whole man in one mouthful."

"Goodness sakes," Jemma said. "You seem to be reading different articles than I do."

"The first thing I'm going to do is buy a cabinet."

"For a stuffed alligator?"

"I'm not interested in stuffed animals, particularly," Poppy said. "Well, I am interested, but I think I'm more interested in curiosities. There was an advertisement a few months ago for a clear crystal pebble with water trapped inside it, for instance. I almost asked Mother if I could buy that."

"Why didn't you?"

"My mother doesn't feel that curiosity is an appropriate emotion for a duchess."

"I must be a duchess in your mother's mold," Jemma said comfortably. "I've never had the faintest curiosity unless it was about discovering a new way to solve a chess problem. But I do have a question, Poppy. Why on earth were you asking your mother for permission about how to spend Fletch's money?"

Poppy frowned. "I'm not sure."

"I never ask anyone's permission for anything," Jemma said frankly. "It is a far more entertaining way to live."

"I see what you mean. I suppose I was just in the habit of asking Mama about things. Though I knew she would say no."

"Then you must stop asking her questions. I loathe people who say no."

Poppy started laughing. "Who says no to you, Jemma?"

"Not very many people, which is just as it should be. Beaumont and I have a wrangle now and then."

"I am beginning to realize that my mother says no about a great many things."

"Few of which are her prerogative," Jemma said. "The more I hear about your mother, the more grateful I am for my paucity of relatives. I wouldn't trade my mad uncle for your mad mother any day of the week!"

"Do you know, we haven't even written each other a letter in the last month? I expect she's furious at me."

"She's duchessing it in your place," Jemma said, with a distinct edge in her voice. "She held a soirée last week, according to the gossip columns."

"She always wanted to be a duchess," Poppy said, feeling a stab of loyalty. "And she would have made a much better one than I."

"Now she is one," Jemma pointed out. "We dissolute duchesses live in Beaumont House, and all the proper ones can pay visits to your mother, and we're all comfortable."

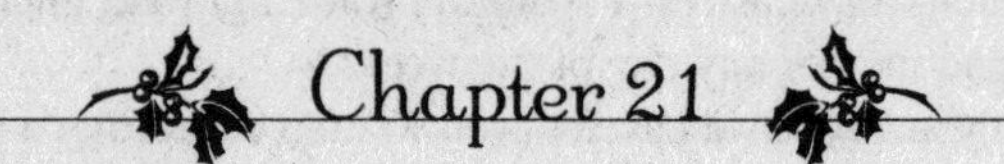

Chapter 21

Still September 1

The Duke of Villiers opened the elegant piece of embossed stationery, scanned it and let it fall from his hand. He was so terribly tired that he couldn't bring himself to care that one of his friends had sent him a long page of gossip. Apparently the Duke of Beaumont was indulging in a flirtation with Miss Charlotte Tatlock. They were seen speaking together at all events.

Elijah must be insane, to flirt with an old maid like Charlotte Tatlock, when he could be talking to Jemma. Though now he thought about it, he had the idea that Elijah had talked to Miss Tatlock through most of Jemma's last dinner party.

Villiers didn't even have the strength to read the rest of the letter, which was galling.

He had his chess board by the bed, but he couldn't seem

to keep his mind on a good chess problem, even though Finchley set it up from *Chess Analyzed*, by Philidor, just as he had asked him to do.

His eyes kept slipping around his room, his empty, tedious room. He had redone it two years ago in a pale gray, the color of an early sky over the ocean, of a day when autumn is just turning into winter. He still liked the color. But it was empty . . . empty . . . terribly empty.

He could even find it in himself to regret the fact that his fiancée had left him for Jemma's brother, though he didn't give a damn about that when it happened.

"May I bring you some barley soup, Your Grace?" Finchley said, hovering in the doorway like some sort of specter of death.

"No," Villiers said. And then: "No, thank you, Finchley."

"A number of visitors called this morning," Finchley announced with some pride. He took a tray from a waiting footman and displayed it as if it were a baby. Sure enough there was a little heap of cardboard bits, embossed with the names of nobility, acquaintances, friends and the purely curious.

"No, thank you," Villiers said. There was no one he cared to see among the heaps of cardboard. The truth was that he was depressed. He would have liked to see Benjamin. Benjamin would have rushed into the room like a breath of chill water, and Villiers would have had to say something sharp to him, and would have thought about clumsy-footed puppies and the like.

It was something, to come so close to death. And then to remember that his friend Benjamin had already died.

"I don't suppose," he said, just as Finchley was about to leave, "that the Duchess of Beaumont paid a call? Or the Duchess of Berrow?" That would be Benjamin's widow.

Finchley bowed. "No ladies were among your visitors,

Your Grace." He said it patiently, as though Villiers had forgotten all the social etiquette. Of course no ladies came. Why on earth would Benjamin's widow pay him a call? Doubtless she blamed him for Benjamin's suicide.

He would have thought that Jemma might have come. She had said they were friends, after all. One had to suppose that they weren't as good friends as that. It was hard to remember . . . his brain was all foggy.

"The Duchess of Beaumont didn't call, did she?" he asked again, just to make sure.

Finchley got an odd expression on his face, but he shook his head. "No, Your Grace."

"Raved about her, did I?" Villiers guessed. "I suspect I said all sorts of things, Finchley. I have the oddest memories. Did the solicitor ever come?"

"Yes, Your Grace," Finchley said. "Do you not remember creating your will?"

"Of course," Villiers said, lying through his teeth. Then he took pity on the uncomfortable manservant. "You may go."

Finchley disappeared and Villiers stared at his fingers in the light. They had grown thinner, almost transparent, really. Of course Jemma hadn't visited. She couldn't visit him. That would be tantamount to telling all London that they were having an *affaire*—and the worst of it was that they weren't. In fact, Villiers had been stupid enough, as he recalled it, to turn down what might have been an invitation.

"Fool, fool," he whispered under his breath.

And then, thinking of Benjamin, "*Fool.*" The fever was coming back, making his head reel. It lapsed in the mornings, but he felt it coming back now that luncheon was over, approaching like a dark velvet tide that would pull him under.

And for the first time, he thought: I might die. I really

might die. And what a fool way to die, dueling over a fiancée for whom he didn't give a fig. A life thrown away for a careless word, for a twist of steel.

Not that there was much to give up but a tangle of regrets and some lost friends. Benjamin . . . dead. Elijah. Elijah, married to Jemma. His life made his head ache.

There was one thing, though . . .

One thing that had to be done.

Already his eyesight was wavering. "Finchley," he called, hearing his voice crack.

His manservant appeared instantly. "I've got the fever again," he said, to forestall the patient hand on his forehead. "I'll have some water please, and I need to write a note. Quickly, before it comes on."

But by the time Finchley came back with a sheet of foolscap, the fever had come, and Villiers couldn't remember what he meant to say.

"That woman," he managed. "Address it to her."

Finchley sat beside the bed and said, "What woman?"

To Villiers, his valet's lean figure grew longer, grew horns, swayed against the wall. He closed his eyes. "We were all friends, of course. What is her name? Charlotte, I think. Perhaps Charlotte. From His Grace, the Duke of Villiers. Greetings."

He forgot what he wanted to say and that he wanted to say anything, and fell into a pool of warm water that was inexplicably waiting behind his closed lids. He was floating in it, flying really, when Finchley's persistent voice came through the water, dimly, watery. "Your Grace. Can you tell me this woman's last name?"

"Whose?"

"Charlotte," Finchley said. "A woman named Charlotte. You are writing her a missive, Your Grace."

"I am? Charlotte? Do you mean Charlotte Tatlock?" he

said, knowing he sounded irritable. "A rather odd young woman, long in the tooth."

Saying all that exhausted him and he fell back. A missive? What the hell is that? "No, no, I mean to say, tell her—tell her—" The pool yawned at his feet again, welcoming, warm. Perhaps there were mermaids there with bright eyes who would make him feel warm and loved. Nourished. Perhaps . . . Surely Benjamin's widow's name wasn't Tatlock. Because Benjamin's last name . . . what was Benjamin's last name? "Tell her to visit me," he said. "Tell her that—tell her that I miss Benjamin."

He could hear Finchley's quill scratching and it made his head throb. "Now go away, do," he said. "Deliver it by messenger."

When the door closed, he closed his eyes and fell into the pool but there were no bright-eyed mermaids with sleek green tails, merely shifting shadows and heat. It was so hot that the pool must be heated by volcanos.

And so it went, until another dawn.

Chapter 22

Grudner's Curiosity Shop was set well back from the street, its gabled windows crowded with a variety of what looked like rubbish.

Poppy sprang out of the carriage. She'd wanted to visit Grudner's for years, ever since she learned of its existence, but her mother had said no. Grudner's was located in one of the liberties of London, Whitefriars, which was an area without rule or law, according to her mother. To Poppy, the street looked as dingy and crowded as any street and showed no obvious sign that it was located in a hub for criminal activity.

Jemma followed in a more leisurely fashion, making sure that her side bustles didn't touch the carriage door. "I suspect that Mr. Grudner doesn't believe in cleaning," she said, looking in the window.

"Look at that," Poppy said, pointing.

Jemma peered closer. "An old riding glove? What does it do, fly by itself?"

"It belonged to King Henry VIII. See? It says so on the card."

"And what's the proof of that," Jemma said, snorting. "You could take any old glove and put a card next to it saying it belonged to King Solomon himself. Besides, Poppy, did you know that Henry VIII never bathed? He didn't like water next to his skin, apparently. My uncle told me that the king's skin was as smooth as a baby's behind. But imagine . . ." She shuddered. "Imagine the inside of that glove!"

It was a small store, painted a pleasing cherry red. Everywhere Poppy looked were boxes topped with glass, glass shelves, even glass pedestals with precious objects on top.

"Ladies," a man said, coming forward. "You do me too much honor." He was tall and thin with a wild shock of white hair that made his head appear too large for his body, like a puppet at Barthlomew Fair. "I am Ludwig Grudner. May I show you something? Perhaps the glove of Henry VIII that you admired in the window?"

"No," Poppy said, smiling at him. "I'm interested in scientific curiosities, if you please."

"I have a lanhado from Africa," Mr. Grudner said. "Ten foot wing span, of course, and beautifully stuffed. I have to keep it in another location, but I could have it delivered to you tomorrow morning."

"Not stuffed animals, but curiosities," Poppy explained. "I intend to develop my own curiosity cabinet. I saw your advertisement for the horn of a Sisfreyan beast."

"A notable piece," Mr. Grudner said. "A true miracle, that. I sold it for three hundred pounds."

"Three hundred pounds!" Jemma interjected. "That's an outrage!"

"The only one of its kind," Mr. Grudner retorted. "It was

worth far more than that, and I did it only because Lord Strange is one of my best customers."

"He is?" Jemma asked.

"Lord Strange is a great naturalist," Mr. Grudner reported. "And, of course, he is able to indulge his curiosity. He has one of the best collections in England, and most of it purchased from this very shop."

"Oh," Poppy said, obviously entranced. "I'm so sorry that I didn't get to see the horn of the beast before it was purchased."

"The store is full of wonderful objects . . . Every lady should have her own curiosity cabinet. Can I show you the hand of a mermaid, perhaps?"

Jemma wandered away once Poppy was happily occupied in poring over Mr. Grudner's unsavory collection. She found a small picture made entirely of feathers and was trying to decide whether it depicted a monkey climbing up the back of a man—or possibly a person climbing a flight of stairs or perhaps a cow next to a tree, when she saw a chess piece, sitting by itself on a small pedestal.

It was the white queen, carved from ivory. She stood with a regal frown, her body shadowed by the enormous crown that bloomed on her head. The crown was a hollow sphere, exquisitely carved with open work, and when Jemma peered inside she saw inside another sphere, also open, and inside that, yet another.

"Exquisite, is it not?" Mr. Grudner said, popping up at her shoulder. "I'm afraid that I have only the one piece. The entire set belongs to Lord Strange and I have not been able to convince him to part with it."

"Then why on earth did he part with the queen?"

"I'm sure I couldn't say for certain," Mr. Grudner said.

"A chess set," Jemma said, "is nothing without its queen.

Useless. Why on earth would Strange give you the queen?"

"He sold it to me, ha ha," Mr. Grudner said. "Didn't get to be the richest man in England by giving away pieces of artwork like this."

"Why would he sell it to you?"

"I suppose he must have given up chess," Mr. Grudner said. "However it may be, Your Grace, I assure you that this piece is quite lovely on its own. There are five nested spheres inside the crown, ending with the smallest ivory marble I've ever seen."

Poppy called from the other side of the store. "Jemma, do look at this!"

Jemma walked over, bringing the queen with her. For some reason she was reluctant to put down her fiendishly frowning little face, so obstinate even in the face of losing her king and the rest of her court.

"I found a marvelous statue of a boy and a butterfly," Poppy said, holding it out.

"A copy of an ancient Greek statue," Mr. Grudner said, "and a very fine one, if I say so myself."

"Just look at the detail on the butterfly!" Poppy exclaimed.

Jemma looked, but it wasn't the butterfly but the naked youth kneeling before it that struck her as interesting. "Who does the piece represent?" she asked Grudner.

"Eros, or Cupid, in love with Psyche," he said. "Psyche means butterfly in Greek, of course."

"And what is that?" Jemma asked, peering at the odd rock in Poppy's other hand.

"It's a geode," Poppy said. She put down the statue of Cupid. "Look. You open it like this." The two rough bits of rock fell open to reveal a gorgeous amethyst interior. "It's like a wild little cave that you can hold in your hand," she said. "A fairy grotto."

"I couldn't have put it better myself," Mr. Grudner said promptly, looking like a man who had no idea what a fairy grotto might be but knew that the phrase suggested pure profit.

"I found this as well," Poppy said, ignoring him. She held out the pit of a fruit, a small one, perhaps an apricot. Delicately she pulled at it until it fell apart. Inside was a mess of the tiniest spoons Jemma had ever seen.

"That's darling!" Jemma said, suddenly remembering a little serving set she'd had for a long-lost doll.

"Twenty-four spoons inside a cherry pit," Poppy said.

"The smallest such in the world," Mr. Grudner put in.

"That's no cherry pit," Jemma stated. "It's a peach at least."

"Cherry, Your Grace," Mr. Grudner said stubbornly.

Jemma sighed. Clearly, Poppy was about to be fleeced of all the money she had taken from her husband's bank account and yet . . . why shouldn't she be fleeced if she wanted to? It was not a Reeve family habit to shelter people from making errors. Cherries, peaches, who cared?

But Poppy surprised her. She dimpled at Mr. Grudner and asked for a chair, and then charmed him into dusting it, and by the time she sat down and took off her gloves, and accepted a cup of tea, Jemma could see exactly where this was going. Sure enough, forty minutes later they walked out of the store leaving a bewildered owner, who had half convinced himself that he had practically given away the cherry stone to the duchess because she was . . . because she was . . .

Charming. He sighed and shook his head, thinking about what Mrs. Grudner, God rest her soul, would have said. It wouldn't have been pretty.

"The worst of it is that I had to pay full price for my chess queen," Jemma said. "And you bought everything for about half what he first requested. That's unfair!"

Poppy dimpled at her in complete unrepentance. "My mother says that a lady never bargains for anything."

"Then what do you call the exchange that just went on there? That poor man asked for fifty pounds for the cherry stone, and you paid him, what, four?"

Poppy grinned. "I call it—I call it—"

"Let's just call it rebellion," Jemma said dryly. "Would it be fair to say, Poppy, that in the process of leaving your husband, you have also left your mother?"

"That's just how I see it," Poppy said, leaning back and opening the sack containing her cherry stone. "Tomorrow I intend to visit France & Banting. By all accounts they make delightful curiosity cabinets."

"There are cabinets built for cherry pits?" Jemma asked incredulously.

"Haven't you ever seen a curiosity cabinet? The King of Sweden's was displayed at the Leverian Museum last year, and I told my mother I was visiting the poor but I went to the museum instead."

"Quite a mutiny," Jemma said dryly. "I trust she didn't discover your perfidy?"

"Thankfully no. And you may be as sharp as you please, Jemma, but I assure you that it is hard to withstand my mother's will."

"I can only imagine," Jemma said. "Luckily, she's never shown me the faintest interest."

"That," Poppy said candidly, "is one of the reasons why I am so grateful that you took me in. My mother's concern for her reputation is such that she cannot visit me, no matter how she may wish to do so."

"I knew that my reputation would come in handy for something. You should hear Beaumont complain about how that same reputation is ruining his chances for this and that in Parliament. I shall have to inform him that it is actually of service in keeping away mothers and other marauding armies."

"I think I shall request a cabinet of oak and ebony. I love the combination of black and brown woods."

"Hmmm," Jemma said. She had taken out her Queen and was examining her again. In truth, she was a delicious chess piece. Her gown frothed in the back like the curve of an ocean wave crashing on the shore.

"Mr. Grudner said that your piece came from Lord Strange, didn't he? His is one of the curiosity collections that I would love to see."

"It's such a shame about Strange," Jemma said. "Even I couldn't visit Fonthill, his estate, of course. Why, why do you suppose that he broke up the set and sold the Queen? It's such a cruel thing to do."

"Why couldn't you visit Fonthill? I mean to."

"His reputation is ten times blacker than mine. The man has scandalized people who think of me as angelic."

Poppy leaned back. "I mean to see his collection. And I want to go to the Ashmoleon Museum as well. And to the Royal Society. Mother never allowed me to go to their meetings, even though they regularly allow ladies to attend."

Jemma blinked at her. Poppy's face was as charming as ever, but Jemma suddenly realized that there was nothing soft about Poppy's jaw, and that her smile was as determined as it was sweet.

"Miss Tatlock is the secretary of the Ladies' Auxiliary of the Royal Society," she offered.

"You mean that young woman who flirts with your husband?"

"I think of her as Miss Fetlock," Jemma said. "It is an affectionate name, you understand."

Poppy smiled at her. "I wish I could think up a mean name for Louise, but I'm too fond of her."

"There we differ. I have no liking whatsoever for Miss Fetlock, though I am the first to admit that my dislike is extremely unfair. As far as I know, she adores Beaumont from afar and he certainly would never risk his precious reputation to do more than converse with the poor woman."

"Then we must direct her attentions in some other direction," Poppy said firmly. "As it happens, I know a delightful young scientist, Dr. Loudan."

"She couldn't marry just any young man from Oxford, no matter how intelligent he was," Jemma said. "She's caught in the bounds of propriety, you know. One of those. Poor but a peer."

"He's the Honorable George Loudan," Poppy said. "And he stands to be Viscount Howitt someday."

Jemma raised an eyebrow. "What a splendid idea, Poppy!"

"I shall go to the next Royal Society meeting. At least, the next one to which they invite women. And I'll introduce the two of them."

"How on earth did you meet this scientist, Poppy?"

To Jemma's amusement, Poppy got a little pink.

"Poppy!"

"I wrote him a letter," Poppy confessed. "You see, he wrote a treatise on the three-toed sloth in *Transactions of the Royal Society,* and while I felt he made some astute comments, he overlooked an important point that Dr. Hembleton made in a previous article, having to do with their back claws."

"You wrote him a letter? About a three-toed sloth?" Whatever Jemma was expecting, it wasn't missives to do with sloths.

Poppy nodded.

"Illicit correspondence with a gorgeous young man." Jemma leaned back, grinning. "You did say that he was gorgeous, didn't you, Poppy?"

Poppy looked even more flustered. "Well, of course, I wasn't thinking of his person when I wrote him a letter—"

"Of course you weren't," Jemma said, chortling. "Not a thought. Never. Of course not. Did he write back?"

"It isn't like that," she protested.

"He wrote back, did he? Probably thought you were brilliant, didn't he? And—just how many letters have ensued, Miss Holier-than-Thou Duchess?"

Poppy looked a little faint. "Do you really think—see it—do you think that he—"

"Who knows how he thinks? Men are a mystery to me. I love the idea that you're engaged in conversation, albeit epistolary, with one of the world's great scientists!"

"I hardly think he's one of the world's great scientists," Poppy said. "He may be an expert on the three-toed sloth, but he makes frequent errors in his assessments of research. I suspect him of sloppy note-keeping."

And then, when Jemma kept giggling, she said: "Truly, this is not an illicit flirtation."

"No? I suppose you showed all your letters to Fletch?"

"He wouldn't be interested. Fletch doesn't care about sloths."

"I suppose if the sloths were wearing little ermine-lined cloaks, it might be different," Jemma said mischievously.

"You shouldn't—" Poppy said, and then started laughing. "Fletch is rather ridiculous, isn't he?"

"Delicious," Jemma said. "But ridiculous."

"He never used to be like that," Poppy said a little sadly. "In the last year, he just became more and more polished."

"No wonder you turned to the purveyor of two-toed sloths. I would have done the same. Well, if I had the faintest inclination to discuss such a topic."

"Three-toed, not two-toed. You would be interested,"

Poppy said. "Really, you would! Dr. Loudan can be quite fascinating."

"I suppose he thinks you're fascinating as well?" Jemma asked mischievously.

"No," Poppy said.

"No?"

"You see, I have the sort of brain that simply can't forget a tiny detail I read somewhere. I'm just like that."

"I forget everything," Jemma observed.

"But you remember every chess game you ever played. My brain works that way when it comes to articles about sloths and French marmoses. It's terribly inconvenient," she said feelingly.

"Why?"

"Unladylike," Poppy said, wrinkling her nose. "I can't help it, though. I see a new book or an article on a subject that interests me and I become simply feverish to read it. My mother loathes that propensity."

"How strange," Jemma said. "I don't mean you, but the very idea of feeling feverish about a sloth, three-toed or not, is peculiar. You must know that."

"I never tell anyone. And you must promise to do the same."

"Why doesn't this Oxford fellow simply embrace you and your detailed brain, then?"

"I find that scientists are not always excited to be reminded about details," Poppy said, looking rather surprised. "Surely accuracy is of the utmost importance when it comes to natural study, but you would be surprised, Jemma, at how inexact some people can be. Dr. Loudan is occasionally quite reluctant to drop an idea, even when the evidence is against him."

"I don't think I've ever spoken to a naturalist. There are very few of them wandering around Paris. So do you really think we could interest the inexact but Honorable George Loudan in Miss Fetlock?"

"The curious thing to me, Jemma, is why you are so interested in removing Miss Tatlock from your husband's company. You acknowledge that he would never endanger his reputation. And she is a gently bred young lady. Your marriage is in no danger."

"I already saw my husband in love with another woman," Jemma said. "I left for Paris because I couldn't bear to be around him in that circumstance. That's one thing that Beaumont has never understood: marriage and reputation are not the most important things."

"It's a common problem," Poppy said thoughtfully. "My mother would agree with Beaumont."

Chapter 23

September 2

Charlotte didn't know what to make of the letter when it arrived. She saw the ducal seal and snatched it from the housemaid as if it might burn her fingers. And then she ran upstairs where May couldn't see it.

Only to find to her disappointment that the seal was that of the Villiers family, and not that of the Beaumonts. Of course not. The Duke of Beaumont wouldn't write to her. He would never do that. He was solid, respectable, honorable . . .

She came back to herself with a start and stared down at the note. It was obviously written by a servant, and it stated that the Duke of Villiers would like her to pay a call. The Duke of Villiers? An unmarried man? How on earth could she do that? Why would he even expect that she would consider it?

And why would he want her to visit? He barely exchanged two words with her at the dinner party given by the Duchess of Beaumont, which was the only time they'd met. And finally, who was Benjamin, the name mentioned in the letter?

The problem, Charlotte thought, was that her life was boring. She'd been on the shelf more years than she cared to count. Her mother had always said that she had an intelligent countenance, and she knew that she was honest, fairly virtuous and chaste. Not that she'd ever had a chance to be less than chaste, but a virtue is still a virtue, even if untested. But none of those qualities made life interesting.

May entered the room. "Is that a letter from Beaumont?" her sister demanded.

"How did you know that I received a letter?"

"The maid told me, of course," May said impatiently. "I see that Mr. Muddle shall indeed have to have a word with His Grace. He is toying with your reputation in a most unkind fashion, sending you private letters."

"Mr. Muddle will have nothing to do with the Duke of Beaumont!" Charlotte cried, horrified at the thought of her sister's fiancé muddling his way through a conversation with the duke. "You couldn't possibly ask it of him, May!"

"I most certainly could," May said, drawing herself up. "Mother would not have permitted the visit. And no one could have your welfare more at heart than my future husband, Mr. Muddle!"

Charlotte hated the way that May's voice dropped when she said the word *husband.* And it wasn't just jealousy either. It wasn't.

"It's not a letter from Beaumont," she said flatly.

"Oh." May sat down. "Well."

"Beaumont has never written me and he won't. You just don't understand, May. He's not interested in flirting with me."

"But you are interested in flirting with him," May said, with a sister's shrewish perception. "And sometimes that's even more dangerous to a woman's reputation, Charlotte."

Charlotte was too depressed to answer, so they just sat for a moment until May said, "Who's the letter from, then?"

"It's from the Duke of Villiers."

"Oh!" May said. "Is it a deathbed confession?"

"Confession? Confession to what?"

"I don't know!" May cried, clasping her hands together. "I believe he is already dead. Maybe it's"—her voice lowered to a curdled whisper—"a letter from a dead man!"

"Villiers is dead?"

"So I heard this morning," May said. "Dead. The coal man had it on the best authority from the fishmonger in Gatrell Street."

"That's awful," Charlotte said, letting the letter fall from her fingers.

"But what did he want from you? I didn't think you even knew him." She reached for the foolscap.

"He attended the dinner party given by the Duchess of Beaumont that I was at last spring, but we hardly spoke. I think a mistake was made in the address."

"No," May said, with her usual brand of tiresome logic. "It's plainly addressed to you, both on the overleaf and the letter itself." She read the note. "How peculiar. Of course, I know what he's talking about. And so do you, Charlotte. So do you."

"I do?"

"Of course you do! It's that mad Reeve whom you danced with all those years ago. The one you thought would offer you marriage and instead he hived off to the country, mad as a march hare."

"You needn't make me sound like such a fool!" Charlotte snapped.

"Be that as it may," her sister said, "obviously His Grace is referring to Reeve. They must have been friends, and he wanted you to know that on his deathbed."

"Except," Charlotte said, "that Reeve's given name is Barnabe, not Benjamin."

"Close enough," May said. "It's obvious."

"Well, it hardly matters if the duke is dead," Charlotte said.

"You should drop off your card," May said. "The duke was thinking of you—of *you*, Charlotte—practically on his deathbed. It's the least you can do."

"I've never understood that custom," Charlotte said. "What service does it do the dead person when I drop my card at his house? What good is that, pray? Suddenly all the carriages line up outside a house and small bits of paper fly back and forth, but does the dead person sit up in his coffin and count his visitors? No, he does not!"

"You are unaccountably strange," May said. She'd said it many times before, so the sentence flowed with practiced ease. "All I can say is, thank goodness it isn't the Duke of Beaumont thinking of you with his last breath. You'd never live that one down!"

"How many times must I tell you," Charlotte said between clenched teeth.

"I know," May said, "but you must admit that it's all rather strange. Here you are, practically a spinster, Charlotte, if you don't mind my saying so. Neither of us ever had a shard of interest from, well, the nobility. And suddenly you're being chased around by dukes. It's—it's *odd*."

Charlotte folded up the letter. "I'll drop my card at Villiers's house on my way to buy some physic for the downstairs maid. Her face is swollen again, and Cook wants mustard to make up a poultice."

"You could send Roberts," May observed. "It isn't ladylike for you to traipse off to the market for herbs."

"I'm an old maid, remember," Charlotte said, with an edge. "And I need some fresh air. It's quite odd to receive a letter from someone who just died."

"I can't imagine what everyone will think of it! I just hope they don't think that you were as close to Villiers as you supposedly are to Beaumont!" She laughed shrilly at the very idea and trotted off.

Charlotte didn't bother to change her dress. She was neatly attired in a simple blue sacque gown. It was neither particularly flattering nor particularly fashionable, but it served. She stared down at it for a moment, remembering how resplendent the Duke of Villiers always appeared, clothed in fantastically embroidered costumes. When he appeared at the party following that fatal duel, he looked white, but gorgeous.

It was so sad. And now she thought of it, sad for the Earl of Gryffyn as well. One had to suppose that he would have to flee the country now that his opponent had died.

Stupid men and their stupid duels. The butler was nowhere to be seen, so she had Roberts hail her a hackney. She wasn't in a mood to wait for their ancient black carriage to be brought around from the mews so she could shamble down the street, all their genteel poverty revealed in every rusty spot on that carriage.

"Fifteen, Picadilly," she told the driver. When they pulled up in front of Villiers's townhouse she realized for the first time the problem with a hackney. There wasn't a footman to deliver her card. "Here, driver!" she called. "Will you be so good as to deliver my card?"

He tugged his cap and took the card obediently enough. She watched through the window as he trundled up to the door, his driver's cape blowing in a stiff wind. It wasn't proper; one's card should be delivered by a footman, but she couldn't get over the fact that Villiers was dead. Dead men presumably didn't care for niceties.

A butler answered the door and took the card, but when Charlotte expected the driver to trundle directly back to the carriage, he didn't do so. Instead a footman slipped past the butler and came down the path. He opened the door of the carriage.

"If you please," he said, bowing.

"I'm afraid you've misunderstood," Charlotte said, feeling horribly embarrassed. Who knows what that foolish driver had told them? "I didn't come to pay a call; I would never do that at this moment of turmoil. I didn't mean to disturb the household, so we'll be on our way."

The footman bowed again. "Your presence is requested, madam."

Charlotte pursed her lips. But who could see anything untoward in visiting the house of a *dead* unmarried man, after all? A man who wasn't breathing could hardly be viewed as likely to steal one's virtue.

So she climbed out of the carriage and marched up to the house. The wind was unseasonably nipping and cold, and she arrived feeling as if her cheeks were red and her clothes all in a twist.

"We are very grateful for your call," a butler said, bowing.

"I'm not visiting—" she began, but before she quite knew what was happening, her pelisse was gone and she was being bundled up the stairs. "I don't wish to view the body!" she said. And then, thinking the butler hadn't heard her, she stopped on the stair and said, "I am not here for a viewing, if you please."

The butler turned at the head of the stairs and peered down at her. "You wish a viewing? A viewing of what?"

"I *don't* wish for a viewing," Charlotte said loudly.

"A viewing?"

Charlotte sighed and climbed the rest of the stairs. The butler was obviously deaf, and likely under a great deal of pressure. She noticed, for example, that he hadn't managed to swath the house in black, which surely needed to be done as soon as possible. "I'm not interested in viewing the dead body," she said as loudly as she could, once she reached the top. "The duke's body. I'm not here to view it."

The butler's mouth fell open, and through an open door at the right, she heard a low laugh. "I haven't been put up for viewing yet, have I?" It was unmistakably the Duke of Villiers's voice.

Charlotte clapped a hand to her mouth.

"If you please, Miss Tatlock," the butler said, seemingly unperturbed. "His Grace is receiving visitors."

She backed up a step. "No," she whispered in a horrified voice.

A man with an anxious rabbity face popped out of the bedchamber and grabbed her by the elbow as she was about to retreat down the stairs. "Miss Tatlock, I really must insist. His Grace has been so very ill, you see, and he expressed a wish to see you."

"I don't know him!" she said, in a low voice, keeping an eye on the door. "I thought he was dead!"

"I'm not," the duke said from inside. "So you might as well come in, whoever you are. I'm having a sane moment, thank God."

"No!" Charlotte said.

But the rabbity man leaned close and said, "Please, Miss Tatlock, as an act of charity. He hasn't requested a visitor in over a fortnight."

And then Charlotte realized that of course the poor duke must be just on the verge of expiring. She had never been one for succoring the sick and dying. But obviously one could not refuse the opportunity when offered.

"I'll send your carriage around the park," the valet said, at least acknowledging the social rules that Charlotte was about to break by entering the duke's bedchamber.

"It's a hackney," she said. "Just send it away, if you please."

And she walked past him.

Chapter 24

Fletch couldn't go home. In fact, he could never go home. Lady Flora was there; she was always there. His drawing room was filled with scented ladies and their delicate laughter. If he ventured home for dinner, the meal would be fraught with unfamiliar foods and servants he'd never seen before. He had the impression that most of his household had left. The house smelled different: scented.

"Candles," Quince told him when he asked. "Lady Flora feels that every room should have its own ambiance."

One had to suppose that was what made thresholds so unpleasant; one exited one ambiance only to be greeted by something quite different and yet equally sweet.

Equally unpleasant was the fact that Lady Flora always seemed to know where he had been. He went to Pitt's quarters in the Inns of Court, and she was ready with a comment about Pitt's Indian policy. He went for a ride with Gill, and that evening she commented that Gill was getting a bit old for his short pants.

"Gill doesn't wear short pants!" he snapped, wondering if she'd gone mad.

She smiled. "It's merely a gentle comment about the earl's need to grow up," she told him. "I hear he tries to draw portraits, like a veritable maiden. One has to wonder whether he's even had a woman, if you will excuse the indelicacy."

He did mind the indelicacy, though there was no way to say such a thing. He didn't want an indelicacy from his mother-in-law. In fact, he didn't want to see her ever, not at breakfast, nor at luncheon, nor waiting up when he returned, breathing concern. But not curiosity—never curiosity, because she always seemed to know what he was doing.

Occasionally she would inform him, in passing, where she was going or the changes she had made to this or that room.

"Did you ask Poppy?" he asked once, when she informed him that she was changing the hangings in the east parlor to a rich persimmon.

"Poppy?" she said, looking as startled as if he'd mentioned King George himself. "Poppy? Of course not." And she walked away, looking as if the ghost of a daughter fled before her.

Fletch couldn't help thinking it was peculiar.

It had been months since he'd even seen Poppy. Though of course he wasn't really looking for her, because he was establishing—*trying* to establish—himself in the House of Lords. But he had been to every party worth noting and she was never there. Yet she was still living with Jemma. Or perhaps not. No one would tell him.

He had received a discreet note from his banker, informing him of Her Grace's private account; of course he dispatched a large sum of money immediately. One did, when one's wife left. That is, none of his friends' wives had actually left, but he felt the etiquette of the situation was obvious.

The question—the real question—was what he should be doing with himself.

He knew what Poppy thought he was doing. He was supposed to be indulging himself in the company of women.

In reality, he was spending most of every day in the House of Lords. He was bent on making a name for himself, making a difference in government. Making a difference to his country.

His wife thought he was simply frolicking with courtesans. And she didn't care.

The thought was searing.

Why should Poppy care? She never liked making love to him. And now she said she never loved him at all.

So why should that bother him?

He was due to luncheon with Fox, at Mrs. Armistead's house. And he'd heard rumors of lovely women and intimacies . . .

It shouldn't bother him.

Chapter 25

The Duke of Villiers's bedchamber looked like the back of a waterfall to Charlotte: all dim and silvery with just a few candles strewn about. In the middle of the room was a resplendent bed, hung with watered gray silk embroidered with bluebells.

Villiers was lying against the pillows, looking very white and stark. His cheekbones were always pronounced; May had once proclaimed him alarmingly handsome, and Charlotte had thought it a fair comment. But now his skin seemed translucent. He waved a hand in greeting, and Charlotte saw it was painfully thin, his knuckles sharp-cut. A rush of pity gripped her.

"Please do me the honor of sitting," he said. "Thank you for paying me a call."

The manservant rushed forward with a chair and she sat.

Villiers didn't say another word, just looked at her. Charlotte was suddenly aware of every aspect of herself, of her windblown brown hair, her reddened cheeks, the unexciting ruffle at the bottom of her prim gown. The room smelled like peppermint and lime-water.

"What may I do for you, Your Grace?" she asked, trying to keep her voice low and calm, as befitted a deathbed.

"Nothing, I expect," he said.

Funny: he didn't sound as if he were dying. He sounded faintly amused and just a bit tired. Charlotte risked another look at him.

He had closed his eyes. Oddly enough, he was even more beautiful when ill. His skin was so white that his lashes looked fantastically long and dark against his cheeks. "Surely there must be something I can do, since you wrote me a letter," she said, finally.

"Did I?" There was a faint tone of surprise in his voice that nettled her and she started to rise.

"Please forgive me. I must have received the letter in error."

"Please," he said. "Please stay. I'm sure I did write to you. I remember it now."

She subsided, wondering what one said to a dying man.

"What are you thinking?" he asked.

"Well, if you did write me, I am wondering why you told me that you missed Benjamin, and whether you meant Barnabe."

"Barnabe?" he asked. "I don't know a Barnabe. I meant Benjamin, the Duke of Berrow. In truth I believed I was sending a note to his widow, but somehow the letter went astray. My fever recurs in the afternoons, and my mind becomes horribly confused. There are too many B's involved here, Barnabe, Benjamin and Berrow. Not to mention Beaumont. We met at the Duchess of Beaumont's dinner party, did we not?"

"Yes, we did. And I would be glad to contact the duchess

for you, Your Grace," Charlotte said. "I could do it immediately. Shall I ask your man for some writing paper?"

"You're that young woman Beaumont has set up a flirtation with," Villiers said suddenly. "Lord Thrush wrote and said that you revised one of Beaumont's speeches to Parliament and he thought you made it better."

Charlotte felt a blush edging up her neck. "I didn't revise it," she said. "I merely gave His Grace an idea of how to structure it."

"You needn't do that Your Grace and His Grace business here," Villiers said. "Surely my man told you that I'm dying?"

Charlotte's mouth fell open.

"You look like a dying fish yourself," he said. "I wonder that being on my deathbed hasn't made me any more charitable. I don't feel in the least like consigning myself to almighty powers and turning myself over to good works, you know. Not in the least. My doctors have been telling me that I'm dying for weeks now, and I haven't heard even a single note of the heavenly choir in my ear."

"You show a great deal of confidence in the opinion of your doctors," Charlotte observed.

He smiled faintly. "My doctor would be much affronted if I decided to live. I have the distinct impression that he thinks one should only act under proper medical advice."

"May I suggest that you live just to affront them?"

"An excellent suggestion. If I weren't so tired, I would take it seriously. I'm not used to visitors, you know. You're the first person I've seen in months, other than my valet."

"Your family?" she ventured.

"I don't have one. I expect it would be even more tiring to die while people weep around you. You, on the other hand, show a refreshing lack of sentiment."

"I assure you that I would be tearful if I knew you a bit

better," Charlotte said, smiling. It was hard not to like the phlegmatic way he was approaching the whole subject.

"We must remain strangers then. Tell me something interesting, please."

"As a stranger?"

"Yes. The best strangers are the ones who tell you intimate truths about themselves and then are never met again."

"I don't think I've ever met that sort of stranger," Charlotte said.

"That's because you're a woman and so they never let you alone. I spent a number of years on the continent. It's amazing what strangers will tell you if you're trapped together in a sandstorm, for example."

"You've been in a sandstorm?"

"No, but if I were I would babble all my most intimate secrets, I assure you."

"I don't have any intimate secrets," Charlotte said, a little sadly. "I wish I had, if only to enliven the conversation."

"Well, you're flirting with Beaumont, for one. Are you in love with him?"

Charlotte didn't think his eyes were condemning, just tired and curious. "A bit," she said. "But really only because there's no one else to be in love with. He listens to me."

"He's a politician. If he's listening to you, it's because you're useful to him."

"I know that. But I'd rather be useful to him than useful to no one."

"Whereas I quite like being useful to no one. Of course, that does lead to disconcertingly empty bedchambers. I suppose if I'd made myself useful to a woman I'd have a flock of children in here now."

Charlotte glanced around. The room was exquisitely

elegant and thoroughly male. The only accoutrement was a hairbrush, its handle covered in the same color as the walls.

"I agree with your tactful silence," his deep voice said from the bed. He had his eyes closed again. "It's hard to imagine children with me or me with children. What about you? Did you want children?"

"I'm not dead yet!" she exclaimed.

"Well, in terms of the *ton* I expect you practically are," Villiers said. "You're all of, what, twenty-six?"

"Yes," she whispered.

"Twenty-six and you're engaged in a very public flirtation with a very married man . . . unless you'd like to have an illegitimate son to a duke . . ."

"I don't suppose you're offering," she snapped. She was stinging all over from his matter-of-fact assessment.

"Alas, my candle is quite limp. Even your manifest charms couldn't light it at this moment."

"There's no need to be rude. Just because you're dying doesn't mean that you must indulge yourself at my expense."

He opened his eyes very wide. "In truth, I didn't mean to do so."

"Yes, you did. I know perfectly well that my nose is too long, and my face undistinguished. And my clothing is all very well, but hardly of the latest *mode*. I look like what I am: an old maid with a paltry dowry who will never have children." And with that she burst into tears.

"Oh, bloody hell," came from the bed.

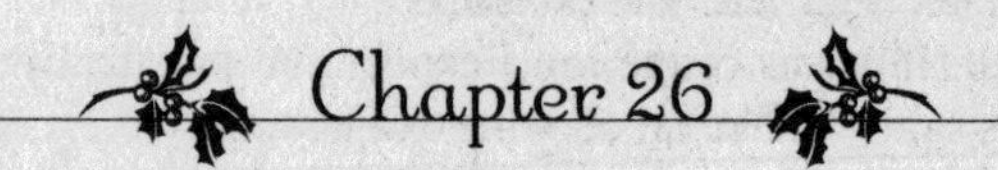

Chapter 26

She was a lovely woman. She was plumply curvy, with a dimple in the middle of her right cheek that drew a man's eyes like a magnet. Her figure bounced in the right places.

And she didn't have blond hair. Fletch couldn't have an *affaire* with a woman with Poppy's hair color. It wouldn't be right. This woman was a brown-haired cousin of Elizabeth Armistead, who was Fox's consort.

Consort: it was a kinder word than prostitute. Mrs. Armistead was beautiful, but more stately than her cousin.

Fox was across the room, discussing strategy. Fletch hardly knew any of the men in the room, which made it easier. The wine was deep and rich and burned its way to his stomach. It was dark and intense, like Cressida's eyes.

"I'm married, you know," she said, after they'd been talking for a while.

"As am I," he said.

"I know that," she laughed. "Everyone knows the marital circumstances of dukes. I know all about you. And your duchess."

"What about her?" he asked, suddenly protective.

"She's a most estimable lady," Cressida said. "Actually my husband isn't bad either. He's a tailor. He lives in Suffolk and pretends that he doesn't know what I'm up to. And I always go home for Christmas, and sometimes in the summer, if I can bear to do it."

"How long have you been away?"

"We've been married for nine years," she said, finishing her drink. "I was married out of the cradle, of course. But since the moment when I decided that I couldn't abide another conversation about satin or thread, I came to live here at St. Anne's Hill. A lady-in-waiting, I suppose you could call me."

"It's a beautiful place to live," Fletch said, glancing at the damasked walls.

"Fox treats her very well," Cressida said. "But in case you're wondering, I'm not available for this sort of arrangement. I'm a lady-in-waiting, and not in waiting for a protector, not matter how noble."

Fletch laughed. He couldn't help liking her, with her odd flaring black brows. She wasn't entirely beautiful, but she was frank and very funny.

"Would you like a tour of the house?" she asked.

For a moment it felt as if the world held its breath. And then Fletch's mouth opened, and he heard himself say, "Yes, of course. Of all things," and then she took his hand, and she was smiling at him and they left the room.

It was that easy.

And it was easy enough to find themselves in a bedchamber too, a beautiful one all hung with rose and pale green. Cressida kept laughing, and saying sarcastic funny little things, and somehow Fletch found he was kissing her.

It was all different from kissing Poppy. Of course. Her mouth was—well, bigger and wet and—

Fletch knew it wasn't going right. But of course, she didn't know that. And somehow it grew imperative to him that she not guess. So every time she reached out toward his breeches, he pulled back. He kept kissing her, though, and caressing her.

Somehow she had only her chemise on a short time later, and he was still kissing her, and caressing her.

He was miserable.

Sick feeling, really. Poppy had left him months ago.

By all rights, he should have been congratulating himself. All those nights when he'd worried that he'd never be able to satisfy a woman again were proven wrong. But finally Cressida reached out and he didn't roll to the side fast enough and her body stilled because she knew exactly what she was feeling. Or wasn't feeling, as the case may be.

"Odds bucket," she said, pulling her hands back. "What are you doing, then?"

"I don't know."

"Well, I wish you wouldn't play your games with me," she said, staring up at the ceiling. "I was having fun with you, and now you've made me feel shabby. What's the matter with you?"

"It's nothing to do with you."

"I suppose you're one of those that prefer men," she said gloomily, sitting up and pulling her stays toward her.

"No."

The twist in her mouth showed that denial was a common event.

"I—I'm married," he said.

"You're a fool."

"That too."

"And I suppose this is the first time that you've considered being unfaithful." Cressida was pinning up her hair now, sounding more resigned than angry.

"Practically."

"Amazing. Most of the gentlemen I've met are unfaithful before the ink's dry on their marriage lines. What's gone wrong, then?"

"Wrong?"

"You must have been in love," she said, looking at him with a strange combination of pity and sharpness in her eyes.

"She doesn't like bedding me." It actually felt good to say it out loud. "She doesn't say no, but she only suffers it."

"Some women are like that. Mind you, every woman feels like that sometimes. Touch me and I'll scream."

"She never says that."

Cressida took the pins out of her mouth and said, "Some women never like the act. We had one girl here like that. She just couldn't tolerate it after a while and then one day she ran away."

"But this isn't a brothel," Fletch said. "Why did she have to run away?"

She didn't answer that. "If you change your mind and decide that you would like a woman in your bed who can really pleasure you, you know how to find me. And I'm a bargain compared to some of those trollops out there."

"But you said—"

She turned around and laughed at him. "You believed me?"

He saw her with different eyes.

"Duke," she said to him, "how would a woman like me support myself in my old age? Do you think I can just traipse back to my husband any day of the week and he'll take me in? Oh, I go there for Christmas because he has to let me in as it would disappoint the boys too much."

"Boy—"

"Two of them. Smart little poppets." Her smile faded. "They're starting to ask questions, though. I need to find a protector, one like Fox. One who will support me and buy me a house. Then maybe the boys could come to me, or I could visit them in a carriage. My husband would respect that."

Fletch thought it was unlikely that her husband would ever let his sons visit their fallen mother.

Perhaps she read it in his eyes; she turned away and poked the last pins in her hair. "You're not the one, I can see that." She was gone before he could craft an offer. Did one give guineas? Or send jewelry later, by messenger?

He sat in the bedchamber and thought about jewelry. One sent jewelry, and had it arrive the next day, he decided. Even, or perhaps especially, when intimacies were disrupted.

He went home before he remembered that Lady Flora would be waiting. She rustled forward to greet him. "Your Grace," she said, holding out her hand. He bent to kiss it.

"Hmmm," she said. "You smell like roses, a woman's scent."

He straightened hastily. But she was smiling at him as if he'd achieved something. Fletch cautiously moved backward.

"I hope I do not insult by my candor," she told him, her blue eyes glinting in the candlelight. "It is my opinion that every young gentleman should find a female libertine who will entertain him. Some gentlemen seem to take longer to come to this realization than others."

Fletch gulped. Could she possibly be saying what she appeared to be saying? She was wearing a grotesquely high headdress, with ostrich feathers stretching feet above her head and brushing the candlelabra hanging from the ceiling. Alas, the candles were only lighted for formal occasions because otherwise she might have caught on fire.

An unkind thought, he told himself, and bared his teeth in an approximation of a smile.

"I am glad to see some evidence that you're not one of our"—she tittered—"less than *virile* men. Every gentleman should have an Amazon of his own."

He clenched his jaw.

"You do understand me, don't you, Your Grace?" she smiled at him and Fletch thought he'd never seen a woman who more resembled a wolf. "My daughter should not have to bear the burden of your dissolute desires. Perhaps the lady who scented her person and thus yours can become a regular habit for you. That might be enough to persuade my daughter to return to your side."

Fletch swallowed his rage and bowed again. "I had no idea that my wife was quite so anxious for me to find female company."

"Ah, but men are so selfish, are they not?"

She paused, which seemed to imply he was supposed to answer. "Not to my knowledge."

"No?" She raised a delicately arched eyebrow. "Of course, those who are most selfish generally do not see themselves as such, do they?"

"I couldn't say, madam. Would you consider yourself to be selfish, for example?"

She smiled at him. "In every sense of the word. To be selfish is to be self-interested. There is only one area in which I would not consider it a weakness and a distraction to think of another above myself: and that is where my daughter is concerned. For her sake, and only for her sake, do I put myself to such discomfort as to reside with you." She paused, and added, "Your Grace."

She hates me, Fletch thought. Well, the feeling is mutual. "I presume that your Herculean sacrifice is not intended to last forever?"

"For my daughter, I put my own comforts to the side." She dropped into a chair, giving an excellent imitation of a lady overcome by cruel exigencies that had her living in a ducal mansion with some fifty-four servants at her beck and call.

"Then do allow me to know how I could persuade you to return you to your former comforts," he said.

"Why, is it not obvious?" she said, smiling at him as genially as if they were at a tea party. "Your marital intimacies are distasteful to my daughter. You appear to be incapable of producing an heir, but I strongly suggest that you leave that little problem to the side for a year or so. Poor Perdita has done such an excellent job of servicing your disordered desires. It's too much to ask her to pick out a suitable gentleman to play your part in the marital saddle at this point. Goodness," she said, looking rather pleased with herself, "that *was* harsh, wasn't it? I find that I am divided between the strongest pity for poor Perdita and the naturally homicidal feelings that any mother must feel in this situation."

"Homicidal?" Fletch said, sitting down and crossing his legs. "Dear me, I see that the situation is rather more urgent than I thought. I gather that my embracing of a courtesan would be a positive interest to my wife. I wonder that she didn't tell me this herself."

"Perdita?" Lady Flora said, raising an eyebrow. "You think that dearest Perdita could bring herself to tell you? I call a spade a spade, Your Grace. My daughter is a weak-kneed fool, with a soft heart. She could not bear to tell you how disgusting you are to her. I consider it my prerogative as her mother to tell you of her feelings. I told her that you simply didn't realize the truth."

Fletch couldn't bring himself to reply. All those nights . . . he knew Poppy wasn't enjoying herself, but he never thought she was discussing things with her mother. The very idea made his skin crawl.

Lady Flora was not one to allow silence to grow. "Men

rarely understand these things," she said. "Of course your bodies disgust those of the delicate sex. Our sensibilities are sweetly tuned; our bodies beautifully curved, as all the poets celebrate. How could you think that a lady would honestly desire intimacy with a hairy . . . Well. I leave Poppy's feelings to your imagination."

Fletch rose and bowed. "If you'll forgive me, Lady Flora, I find that—"

She was looking at him with amusement. "You'll have to beg her."

"I—"

"Beg her to come back. Tell her you finally found yourself a courtesan and you won't use her like a common washerwoman any more."

"I shall certainly speak to my wife," Fletch said, resisting the impulse to commit homicide. Though who he wanted to kill—his mother-in-law or his wife—he didn't know.

"When Perdita agrees to return to your house, I shall naturally return to my own," she said sweetly. "That should provide you with some impetus, should it not? I expect you wonder why I am so active in Perdita's behalf?"

"In fact," he ground out, "given your self-proclaimed selfishness—"

She didn't let him finish, of course. "I don't believe Perdita should reside much longer with the Duchess of Beaumont. You do remember how my poor daughter fancied herself in love with you, don't you?"

He didn't move a muscle.

"Don't you?" she said impatiently. "It wasn't that long ago. At any rate, she's a trifle weak in the head, my daughter, though it pains me to say it. If I leave her with that light-heeled duchess in Beaumont House, she'll fall in love again—and it won't be with you, Duke. Do you understand me?"

He nodded.

"She's a romantic. Forever thinking that men are more interesting than they could possibly be. You know that strange hankering she has to attend meetings at the Royal Society?"

"She has?"

Lady Flora smirked at him. "I gather you aren't spending much time talking to Perdita? You didn't know of her utter fascination with naturalists? Why do I even ask?"

Fletch shook his head. He felt cold from head to foot. "Are you implying—"

"Not yet. But there's no saying now that she's moved out of your house into Beaumont House where God knows adultery is merely a fashionable vice, and one much indulged in."

"I shall speak to Poppy."

"As soon as she moves back into this house, I shall return to my establishment," Lady Flora said brightly. "Although I might point out that the dearth of children produced by you in the past four years implies that the offspring of a young scientist might be just the thing to revitalize the family tree!"

Fletch had never hated anyone so much in his entire life. The feeling went through his head like a wildfire. His fingers shook slightly with the wish to—to—

She rose and walked rather quickly to the door. "I wish you good night, Your Grace," she said. And paused, turning her head in such a way that one of her ostrich plumes bent against the doorframe. "I trust that you will not inform Perdita of our conversation. She, poor angel, hopes to drift through life without talking about unpleasantries. But relations between men and women are always unpleasant, don't you think? I find that candor is a healthy way to cope."

She walked through the door, finally, and from where he stood Fletch could see two feathers proudly rearing to the ceiling and one hanging drunkenly over one ear. Which served her right.

Chapter 27

Back at the Duke of Villiers's townhouse

"You *ought* to be sorry," Charlotte said, hiccupping. "You are unkind, and the fact that you're dying is no excuse. I don't believe that you are, anyway. Dying people think of their immortal souls and speak kindly."

"I told you," he said, "my brain has turned to rubbish. Likely my soul has given up, knowing that I'll be shoveling coal down in Beelzebub's furnaces."

She sniffed and wiped her nose with her handkerchief. "Well, I must be leaving," she said. "This has been utterly charming, and I'm so grateful that I was able to succor you in your last hours."

"Here," he said, "you can't go yet." He actually started to struggle up in bed.

"Stop that," she snapped. "You're too weak to sit up. I certainly shall leave. I don't know you very well. I am sorry you're dying, but you obviously don't want me to read you Bible verses—"

"You haven't offered," he put in.

"Well, that is the comfort generally offered to patients in your condition." She stood up. "I wish you the very best, Your Grace."

"No, you must stop."

"I made a huge mistake coming here, and you never wanted to see me anyway. Then I made a greater fool of myself and I think that I really have had enough humiliation for the day. Goodbye."

Charlotte got herself out the door and down the stairs before he could say another word. "A hackney," she told one of the four footmen in the hallway.

She occupied herself until the footman returned by staring at the marble statues strewn around the entryway.

Villiers was strangely appealing. Perhaps all dying people were. But appealing or not, he had no call to make her feel so wretched.

Though he said nothing that wasn't the truth.

She almost turned to go back and tell him so when the front door opened and she left. It was better anyway.

Chapter 28

September 20

The Royal Society met at Somerset House. Jemma and Poppy arrived before its welter of brick archways and white marble walls, Jemma still protesting.

"You're going to find it fascinating," Poppy told her. "I've read about Mr. Moorehead for years. He's travelled to the very edges of the world."

Jemma groaned. She groaned even louder when the first person they saw was Miss Tatlock, who was greeting people at the entrance to the society's chambers. Miss Tatlock smiled at them quite as if she wasn't notoriously in love with Jemma's husband.

"This is such a pleasure, Your Graces," she said. "I am certain that you will find Mr. Belsize's talk incantatory."

"*Incantatory?*" Jemma whispered as they made their way

into a large room, already crowded with people. "What a jackass she is."

"Jemma!" Poppy exclaimed.

"Honestly, Poppy, didn't you think that she's revolting?"

"No," Poppy said. "She looks like a most intelligent young woman to me."

"Revolting," Jemma said with a shudder. She sat down and unfolded the paper Miss Tatlock had handed them. "The evening opens with a discussion of male tamarin monkeys. Excellent. I've always been fascinated by short, hairy males."

"Hush," Poppy said, elbowing her.

"And then a lively debate between Mr. Brownrigg and Mr. Pringle regarding the question of whether Adam and Eve had bellybuttons. Poppy!"

"Well, it's an interesting question," Poppy said. "But look, after that Mr. Moorehead will talk about his recent travels in Africa. That will be fascinating."

"Humph," Jemma said. "Goodness, there are a lot of people here. There's Lord Strange. Do you think I ought to ask him to sell me the rest of the chess set?"

"Where?"

"By the window. Talking to that exquisite young woman."

Sure enough, leaning against a beautifully arched stone window was a hawk-faced man, lean and excitable looking. He was talking to a young woman whose hair was more gold than Poppy's and whose lips were definitely redder.

"Hmmm," Poppy said.

"I did warn you," Jemma said cheerfully. "So, do you think that he would sell me the rest of the chess set?"

Just then Strange turned away and looked over the room. His eyes slid over Poppy and Jemma without hesitating, as if they were no more than potatoes waiting to be planted.

Poppy turned to Jemma. "No."

"No, he wouldn't sell them to me?"

"Not unless you are prepared to bargain intimacies."

"Poppy, you surprise me! I thought you were such an innocent."

"I am not blind to the fact that some men are uninterested in respectable women."

"By all accounts he loved his wife dearly. She died after the birth of their child."

"He had a wife?"

Jemma nodded and turned away to greet a friend, so Poppy sat there and thought about the fact that a nobleman notorious for his illicit liaisons had apparently desired *his* wife and loved *his* wife. But she was learning that this wasn't a fruitful way to think—so she banished all thought of Fletch, at least until he bowed before her.

For a moment she just gaped up at him. "What on earth are you doing here?"

"I could say the same for you," he said. "I had no idea you were interested in scientific matters, Poppy."

She rose, finally, and dropped a curtsy, wishing that Jemma would return, but Jemma had drifted away into a cloud of chattering noblemen. "This is my first visit," she said. And then: "Could you leave, Fletch. Please?"

"Leave?" he said. "Why would I do that?"

"Because this is very awkward," she hissed, sitting down.

He promptly sat down beside her.

"Jemma is sitting there."

"Why should I leave?"

"You cannot possibly be interested in things of this nature," Poppy said. "And I am."

"You are?"

"Yes, and I would feel awkward if you were here. Please, may I ask you as a favor to leave?"

"You may ask but I'm not leaving." He scowled at her and folded his arms. "After all, you said we were to be friends."

Poppy felt a pulse of anxiety that he was irritated. She gave herself a mental shake and said brightly, "Then of course you're welcome to stay. Surely your friend Gill must be here? Isn't he coming to greet me?"

"He is not here. Why do you ask?"

"Because you never do anything without Gill?" she suggested. "Because if you're at an intellectual pursuit, it must be an interest of Gill's?"

"That's quite an insult," he said in a very even tone.

"I don't mean it to be. Look, there's Dr. Loudan, and since I explicitly asked him to come, I must greet him. If you'll excuse me, Fletch."

She was gone.

Fletch stared after her in dumbfounded surprise. When he pictured meeting Poppy, he didn't imagine her prancing away from him. Or smiling up at a young man with a long nose and . . . Fletch felt his fists curl and he was on his feet before he realized it.

He walked through the crowd and eased behind Poppy where she couldn't see him. For some reason he was quite certain that she wouldn't welcome his presence.

"I found the notes you sent me on the sloth's hind feet fascinating," she was telling this Dr. Loudan. He was short. Well, perhaps he wasn't short but he was shorter than Fletch. I could take him, Fletch thought contemptuously. Then, eyeing his shoulders, it would be a fair fight too.

But I could take him.

I *will* take him, said a thrumming beat in his head as he watched the scientist beam at Jemma. They appeared to be talking about sea otters. What did Poppy know of otters? Oddly, she seemed to know quite a lot, given that she was comparing the beasts to common English river otters.

Five minutes later, Poppy hadn't looked up from Dr. Loudan's face as he droned on and on about otters.

Fletch fell back a pace. As far as he could tell, she hadn't even glanced at him. He sat down, folded his arms, and waited.

Sure enough, as the audience began to tumble into their places, she made her way back to him, fussing a bit about where Jemma would sit.

"Jemma," he said, "has made a new friend in Lord Strange. Wait until Beaumont hears that!"

"Lord Strange has an astounding collection of curiosities," Poppy told him. "I understand that he mostly collects art, but he has a number of fascinating scientific relics as well. I would give anything to see his collection."

"I wouldn't let you within a furlong of his estate," Fletch hissed. "You don't know what goes on there, Poppy."

"I believe the word for it is *orgies*. I read all about them in a history of ancient Rome."

"Poppy!"

"Surely you don't think that I'd be tempted to join the festival?" she asked him. The edges of her lips tipped up but there was no humor there.

Fletch opened his mouth but no words came out.

"I didn't think so," Poppy said coolly. "That's one thing you should be celebrating, Fletch. I'm unlikely to cuckold you, after all." There was something so bleak in her eyes that Fletch's heart dropped in his chest.

"You—"

She turned her head away and waved at Jemma, who had seated herself on the other side of the room.

"It's not a question of cuckoldry," Fletch said, fumbling for words. "But Strange is a dissolute man."

"Oh, dissolute," Poppy said. "I used to think that any man who took a mistress was dissolute. My sort of rank naïveté exists only to be dispelled, don't you think?"

At the front of the room, Mr. Moorehead was starting a discussion of a tribe called the Karamojong, who lived in Africa. Poppy and Fletch sat silently beside each other.

"That was appallingly boring," Fletch said when it was over.

"I don't agree," Poppy said coolly. "I intend to buy his *No Room in the Ark* at my first opportunity."

"It sounds like a nursery rhyme."

"I have initiated a standing subscription for all travel and nature titles at Lackington's. You pay for them."

"We never discussed books like that."

"What on earth would we have to discuss? Unless you've been hiding an interest in natural discoveries?"

He opened his mouth but she wasn't done.

"I assure you that if I read an article about new designs for clocks on stockings or a revolution in satin embroidery, I will be sure to draw it to your attention."

"You rarely remind me of your mother," Fletch said, "but all of a sudden I see a resemblance."

"I imagine that sort of event must be rather frequent, since you are living with her. How is everything with my dearest mama? I knew we'd get around to speaking of her. There had to be some reason you were here."

"I didn't come here to talk about your mother!" He almost bellowed it.

"You surprise me," she said. But the so-called "lively debate" on the stage was quickly degenerating into a mud-slinging match between two bearded antiquarians.

Since Poppy didn't look any more interested in Eve's

bellybutton than he was—although who knew, given all the secrets she'd kept—Fletch felt free to continue their conversation under cover of the choleric debate.

"God would never have placed false evidence on Adam's body," Mr. Brownrigg stated, looking as if he'd addressed the point with the Almighty just last week.

"Your mother seems fine," he hissed at Poppy. "But how are you?"

She listened intently to Mr. Pringle's infuriated response to Brownrigg and turned to Fletch with a brilliant smile. "I'm having a *marvelous* time," she said. "I can't remember being so happy in my life. I trust you are just as happy?"

"Of course," he muttered.

"God has no need for false history," Mr. Brownrigg said, going head to head and jowl to jowl with his opponent.

"Jemma says that you gave a speech in the House of Lords," Poppy said. "What was it about?"

"It was about Pitt's fitness for the position of First Lord of the Treasury."

"I didn't know you were interested."

"It was an utter disaster."

She finally turned her head to look at him. "What do you mean? The paper reported that your speech was extremely lively."

"Lively, it was. And well received by the opposition," Fletch said. "Halfway through I began arguing for my opponent's viewpoint."

Poppy gasped and—to do her credit—managed not to smile. "How on earth did you do that, Fletch?"

"Lord Temple asked me to present his point of view, and I thought it would be easy. Then halfway through my speech I realized that I didn't quite agree with the line of argument I was making—so I turned it around."

"You can't do that!"

"I did." He grinned a little, remembering. "I thought wigs were going to start steaming."

"I would have never thought it of you," Poppy said, staring at him.

"What part of it? Making a hash of the speech? From what you said earlier, I'd think that was a natural for me."

"Speaking in Parliament. I never thought you cared about that sort of thing."

"Nothing but the color of my coat?"

She was starting to look a bit guilty. "I know that you take excellent care of the estate, of course."

"I enjoyed it," he told her. "It became a farce, of course, when I realized that I was arguing the wrong side, but my fault: I should have taken the time to think it through."

"Well, I'm sure that took courage," Poppy said, touching him on the arm. "Admitting you were wrong, I mean."

"I didn't admit it," Fletch said. "I just talked so much that no one had the faintest idea what precisely I said until I rounded into my conclusion."

"Adam was formed from dust with no scars!" one of the antiquarians said with huge emphasis.

"I think they're almost finished," Poppy whispered.

"How do you know? My guess is that they could go all night. They really hate each other, don't they?"

"Oh no, I don't think so. I believe it's staged. Why, in the last issue of *Philosophical Transactions,* Mr. Brownrigg quoted Mr. Pringle and said that his treatise on the trochus shell was one of the best of its kind."

"On the trochus shell?" Fletch asked.

"Yes, I ordered the treatise on that basis, but I didn't find it very interesting. Pringle argued that the concentric rings on the shell indicated the number of seasons a clam had lived."

Fletch just blinked at her.

"That suggests that a clam grows a new ring every year," Poppy explained to him.

"Why not?"

"It could be," she said.

On the stage Brownrigg and Pringle were glaring at each other in one final burst of scientific fury before they stamped off. Watching them, Fletch guessed that Poppy was right and they were about to retreat into some back room to swig a glass of brandy together. The whole event was like an odd shadow of debates in the House of Lords.

"Why didn't you tell me you were interested in shells and slothes and that sort of thing?"

She frowned at him, obviously puzzled. "You aren't interested in the concentric rings on shells, are you, Fletch?"

"No."

"Well, then."

"But you—you were in love with me!" For some reason, Fletch had the strongest desire to say it. To tell her again. To make her take back what she said before.

Her eyes were clear and blue. "I wasn't really, Fletch. We already discussed that. Neither of us was really in love. And anyway, this is—this is different from all of that life."

"*What* life?" Fletch felt as if he were desperately grasping at straws, trying to understand a foreign language.

"This—this is my pleasure," Poppy said, looking around. "Don't you see how interesting it is?"

Fletch looked around. The room was shabby and crowded, mostly with men but with a fair sprinkling of ladies. To the right several people were having a spirited discussion of flying squirrels.

"They don't really fly," a short plump man said, jutting his round plump chin forward. He had rusty colored hair that began somewhere around the middle of his head. If Fletch had ever seen a man in need of a wig, it was he.

"Yes, they do," a big-boned man replied.

"That's a *professor*," Poppy whispered, nodding toward the second speaker.

Fletch noticed her eyes were shining and grunted.

"Dr. Fibbin proved without a shadow of a doubt that squirrels can fly a distance of forty to fifty feet."

"Fibbin is a fool," the half-bald one said.

Though he hated to admit it, Fletch agreed with him.

"They have a stuffed flying squirrel at the Ashmoleon Museum in Oxford," Poppy said, settling back beside Fletch. "I have written for an appointment, and I'm going to the museum in December."

"Is that what you've been doing?" Fletch said, dumbfounded. "I haven't seen you at any parties. You've been going to museums?"

"Oh no," Poppy said. "That is, I haven't yet. But I mean to. You know, the only time my mother allowed me to visit Somerset House was for a lecture on the customs of polite society, even though the Royal Society was meeting here at precisely the same time!"

"You're married," Fletch said. "You could have visited a museum any damn day you please, Poppy."

"Now I can," she said. "Hush, Fletch. Mr. Belsize is going to speak."

Mr. Belsize did speak. And speak. But Fletch just sat there, staring at the worn carpet and wondering why Poppy never felt free to go to a museum, and why he never knew that she wanted to go to a museum. A tiny thread in the back of his mind was also thinking about the upcoming debate in the House over Fox's East India bill.

"You're not traveling to Oxford with Jemma," he said, as Mr. Belsize gulped a little water.

"Of course I am," Poppy said.

"I'm not having my wife trot around outside London without me," he said.

She looked at him with clear amusement in her eyes. "Fletch, if I want to go to Paris by myself, I will do so. Tomorrow."

"I'll take you to Oxford," he said, folding his arms.

"No."

"Poppy, if you don't let me escort you to Oxford, I'll tell your mother that you're suffering from a rare blood disorder and you need her by your side."

She narrowed her eyes at him. "I should have known this would all come back to my mother."

"In more ways than one," he muttered, and settled back into his chair. Mr. Belsize, refreshed, had launched into another lengthy tirade.

Chapter 29

On close observation, Jemma discovered that Lord Strange was as sleekly dressed as Fletch, and perhaps even more elegant.

"Your Grace," he said, sweeping her a bow.

"Lord Strange," she said, curtsying.

"What an honor that you came to speak to me," Strange said. "I see so little of proper women these days."

"I knew your wife," Jemma said. "Sally was a dear friend."

His eyes changed instantly. "Surely you were not sent to school?"

"No, but Sally's godmother, Lady Fibblesworth, was a great friend of my family, and we happily visited as children."

"Lady Fibblesworth was an admirable woman."

"Yes," Jemma agreed. "Sally used to visit us regularly until I married and then left for Paris. I wasn't in England when she made her debut."

"She never really debuted. I was too wild, so they married me off. It was the luckiest day of my life."

"I am so sorry that she is no longer alive."

He hunched a little. "I share your feelings."

They appeared to have finished that conversation, so Jemma tried a different tack. "Do you play chess, Lord Strange?"

"Yes."

She liked his brevity. Good chess players rarely squealed about their abilities.

"But"—he added—"when I last played Philidor, he told me that you were the only person who has beaten him three games in a row. I have only beaten him once or twice, so you might not wish to waste your time with me."

"You played against Philidor?"

He nodded. "Last year in Paris."

"We must have a game."

"I only play when I'm at Fonthill or in Paris."

Fonthill was famous for its beauty, three hundred acres that had been decorated at ruinous expense. Except that for a man with Strange's fortune, nothing is ruinous. But she said: "Fonthill? You must forgive me; I've lived out of the country for the past eight years. Is that your residence?"

"It is. You know, you're quite interesting, for one of your sex."

"I make a habit of never returning compliments of that nature. Men are so prone to thinking they are more interesting than the common run of their sex, when invariably they are nothing out of the ordinary."

His eyebrow raised in appreciation. "I suppose I deserved that."

"I expect we all deserve a great deal that we are not served."

"I would like to play chess with you. A shame. But it is

one of my foibles: I don't play a game of chess that doesn't occur at Fonthill or Paris."

"I shall have to live without the experience then," she murmured, letting a little edge tell him what she thought of his foibles and his vanity.

But he surprised her and laughed. "I could invite you to Fonthill, of course."

"A lovely prospect."

"Virtuous married women never visit me. Let me see. Could it be that I've heard rumors implying that you are not quite so . . . virtuous?"

"Rumors," she said sweetly, letting her eyes slide to the golden-haired lady standing to his right like a clothes-peg waiting to be animated. "They can be so imprecise."

"And yet often so accurate," he said, grinning at her. He was truly charming when he chose to be. "I leave for Fonthill tomorrow. Perhaps you'd like to pay a visit, Your Grace? I can promise you a great deal of entertainment, especially during the Christmas season."

Poor Beaumont's political reputation would never survive such a visit on her part. "While I'd never discount the pleasure of playing chess with you, I would like to discuss another matter. I bought a chess piece from Mr. Grudner."

"You bought the queen, did you? The African Queen, I call her."

"I should dearly love to buy her counterparts."

He laughed and then swept a grand bow. "Has no one told you how remarkably obstinate I am? One doesn't reach my place in life without nurturing stubbornness. When you visit Fonthill, Your Grace, they will be a gift from your host. In the meantime, I would suggest that you make the acquaintance of Mrs. Patton." He nodded toward a tall woman standing in the middle of a group. "She is the only woman admitted to the London Chess Club. Presumably you could join her in those august ranks, and play chess whenever you wish."

"I shall certainly introduce myself," Jemma said.

"You do know what they say about reputation, don't you?"

"They say so much. One can hardly catalog it."

"A fair hit! I like to think of reputation as nothing more than a second maidenhead."

Jemma smiled faintly. "As with virginity . . . the loss quickly suffered and the fruits enjoyed thereafter?"

"Precisely! I lost my reputation years ago. 'Twas naught but a word; the word is gone; the pleasure lingers." He bowed.

He was devilishly charming. If it weren't for her husband's reputation and the promises she'd made, she'd go to Fonthill in a minute. Strange had thrown down the gauntlet and it nettled her not to take it up.

He didn't think she'd visit Fonthill. She saw it in his eyes, the faint disparagement, the unnecessary compliment.

It fired her with the wish to throw societal rules to the wind and pay him a visit. But how could she possibly go to that estate, with its scandals and daily parties, if the stories were true? She couldn't. She couldn't do that to Beaumont.

Her French friends would have shrieked with laughter at her concern. They viewed husbands and honor subjects of interest to wives of the bourgeois. Somehow life was much more complicated in London than when she was gadding about the French court.

Jemma had lost the ability to be intimidated years ago. She had arrived in Paris as a young duchess without a husband, made her way to Versailles and began winning chess matches against Frenchmen. Any one of these three circumstances would be enough to daunt most ladies. But not, she was proud to think, a member of the Reeve family.

Thus it was quite interesting to discover that she felt just the slightest bit intimidated by Mrs. Patton. There was no obvious reason for it. Mrs. Patton was a slender woman with brown hair, rather eccentrically dressed, which fact alone ought to give Jemma a sense of superiority.

Most of the ladies in the room were wearing gowns with short ruffles and side bustles of one size or another, but Mrs. Patton had no curls, no ruffles and no bustles. Instead she was wearing a thigh-length jacket, shaped to her figure. Underneath the jacket was a periwinkle blue skirt that flared into long folds in the back. The final touch was the opening at the front of the jacket . . . which parted to reveal a waistcoat. A waistcoat! Jemma suddenly felt entirely too ruffled and be-laced and beribboned.

The group surrounding Mrs. Patton turned out to be discussing bookplates and typefaces, none of which Jemma knew the faintest thing about. Finally the discussion of barthcast fonts (whatever they were) ended, and Mrs. Patton turned to Jemma. "Your Grace, I have been longing to meet you," she said with a roguish smile. "I have heard so much of your prowess at chess."

"And I the same of you," Jemma said, bowing slightly.

"I doubt I'm at your level. I was roundly beaten by Philidor last year when he visited London. But he told me of you, and fired my wish to have you be my compatriot at Parsloe's. Rather than cede my place in the London Chess Club to you, I am hopeful that we could be the only two of our sex in the chosen one hundred."

"Is it awkward being the only woman?"

"I don't find it uncomfortable. Occasionally a topic is broached that I find tedious, such as the relative merits of a given opera dancer. I find that a quick comment about the difficulties of swollen breasts while nursing children will return gentlemen to awareness of my presence."

"Since I have nursed no children," Jemma said, "I shall have to echo you."

"I am certain that you can come up with your own topics by which to distress their sensibilities," Mrs. Patton said. "Men are so hideously sensitive, you know. It's easy to throw them off their stride. I try not to do it while playing chess, of course, though sometimes one cannot help taking the advantage."

"I would relish seeing you discomfit my husband. In fact, I would love to see you play him."

"Ah, but the Duke of Beaumont is a politician. That's another breed altogether." Mrs. Patton's smile was wry. "I doubt that he plays chess with mere mortals. If he is half as busy as the papers make him out to be, he has little time for games."

"I am thinking of gathering a house party at Christmas time," Jemma said. "I should dearly love to both play you at chess and watch you vanquish my husband. I believe I would bet on you over a politician."

"I am honored by your invitation," Mrs. Patton said, looking ready to refuse.

"Oh please," Jemma broke in. "It is months away; you can hardly do me the discourtesy to cry an earlier invitation. I have just returned from eight years in Paris, you know, and I have discovered few people with whom to play chess."

"Dear me," Mrs. Patton said, "and here I was under the impression that you had monopolized the market when it came to chess masters. Your paired matches with your husband and Villiers are being rather widely celebrated."

"I have never played a woman with ability at chess, and I must confess to an unbearable curiosity."

"I fancy I shall find myself matched in cunning," Mrs. Patton said.

"Then?"

"I travel with children. Children and—how could I forget—a husband as well."

"You would all be welcome. One must have children about to truly enjoy Christmas, so yours will fill a need. We shall have a magnificent Twelfth Night party and put a bean in everyone's slice."

"There you show yourself to be no mother," Mrs. Patton observed cheerfully. "It would be the Slaughter of the Innocents as they fought over who got the largest bean and thus got to be King for the Day."

"In that case," Jemma said, "I shall promise to manipulate things so that you, dear Mrs. Patton, are Queen of the Pea, if you will come."

Mrs. Patton laughed. "The chance to play chess *and* be queen, if illicitly gained? It's hard to resist. I expect my husband will be agreeable, but if he is not, I shall send you my regrets on the morrow."

Jemma adored her utter lack of fawning attention. She swept a deep curtsy, a duchess-to-duchess curtsy. "It will be my pleasure."

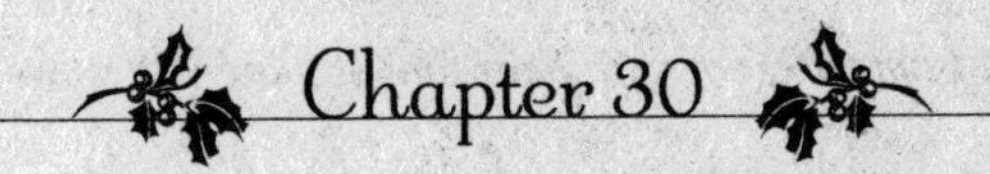

Chapter 30

The Duke of Villiers to Miss Charlotte Tatlock
November 20, 10 of the clock

Are you still angry at my rudeness? It has been months and I find myself still tied to this bed. In desperation I write to ask if you would read me Bible verses. Such wit and beauty as you have should apply itself to doing miracles, and I'm sure such an influx of heavenly influence would be miraculous. My footman will wait for your answer.

Miss Charlotte Tatlock to the Duke of Villiers
By Return

You are the most fantastical and unkind man to make fun of me. I leave it to you to judge what our heavenly Savior would think of your behavior.

P.S. I am truly sorry to hear that you are still unwell.

The Duke of Villiers to Miss Charlotte Tatlock
11:30 of the clock

I meant no unkindness. Please come talk to me. I am here with no one but the butler and the servants and some mice who squeak mightily in the night.

Miss Charlotte Tatlock to the Duke of Villiers
By Return

Your solitude is obviously the reward for a life ill-spent.

The Duke of Villiers to Miss Charlotte Tatlock
1:00 of the clock

You are far too kind to be as priggish as you sound. I am like to die of the tedium. And I have to add that there is many a hanger-on feverish to be admitted to my bedchamber.

Miss Charlotte Tatlock to the Duke of Villiers
By Return

Admit them. You have nothing to lose, and I have much to gain.

The Duke of Villiers to Miss Charlotte Tatlock
2:30 of the clock

Cruelty, thy name is Charlotte. Don't leave me to the ill entertainment of such as choose to visit. They come mawkishly only so they can describe my dying sighs, and the pitiful things I spoke, and how white in the face I am. I am persuaded that none of them will tell me I'm a pestilent knave, as you did.

Miss Charlotte Tatlock to the Duke of Villiers
By Return

Their ignorance is no reason for my discomfort, not to mention the loss of my reputation.

Miss Charlotte Tatlock to the Duke of Villiers
November 29 [nine days later], 10 of the clock

I venture this letter because I received the unhappy news of your death this morning. I am surprised to discover that I much hope that the tidings are untrue. I cannot help but write to inquire.

The Duke of Villiers to Miss Charlotte Tatlock
By Return

I live chiefly out of spite. My man tells me that I have been credibly announced to be dead three times, and once buried. I thought you wanted no more of me?

Miss Charlotte Tatlock to the Duke of Villiers
11 of the clock

I want nothing of you, but it would sit ill on my soul if I scorned the opportunity to read you a Bible verse.

The Duke of Villiers to Miss Charlotte Tatlock
November 30, 10 of the clock

My fever came on yesterday afternoon and prevented my reply. My coach waits, but please do not delay, as I'm afraid the fever is my constant companion. Could you possibly pay me a visit now?

Chapter 31

November 30

Fletch had taken a carriage into Hyde Park because he didn't want to go home. Lady Flora was always there, springing to meet him. Even the way she said "Your Grace" spoke of withering dislike. Though the worst was when she called him Duke, as if they were intimates. It was wearying. One had to suppose that Poppy—who had never said a word of reproach to him about her mother—encouraged her prolonged visit as some sort of revenge. It was a damned successful one.

Once in the park, he couldn't stand the small confines of the carriage and took himself out for a walk, though it was gray and drizzling.

He strolled along the Serpentine and watched gray water drops dimple the surface of the water. The rain was cold on his cheeks.

Poppy didn't love him.

She had never loved him. Her dragonish mother had coerced her into the marriage. The emotion at their wedding had been all his, which laid painfully bare the reasons for their pitiful intimacies. She didn't love him; of course she didn't desire him.

The rain was suddenly hot on his face, a hot drop here, a cold drizzle there.

"But I loved her." Fletch said it out loud, into the silence of the gray rain. "I was in love with her." That Christmas years ago in Paris was emblazoned in his memory. "I loved her. I—I—" But he stopped before he said that he still loved her.

She didn't want him in the most fundamental way. She told him to find a mistress.

He walked until his heart was as dreary as the sky, until some sort of truth came to him.

He must be cursed, because he still loved her. He loved his wife. Even so.

And that meant that he couldn't survive alone for five years as Poppy suggested. He couldn't lie awake in the middle of the night and wonder what she was doing, with whom was she dancing. Naturalists, for God's sake. Out of all the things her mother said, that stung the most.

Poppy was infatuated with that Dr. Loudan, for example. A skinny, weedy thing with a propensity for cutting up dead rodents for examination.

He'd spent years fashioning himself into someone he wasn't, all to catch her eye. But she wanted spectacles. He pulled off his hat, raised his head and the rain sluiced over his face, over his carefully tumbled locks, spotting his shirt, chilling his fingers.

He had to do something with his life, make himself into the kind of man whom she would admire. She would never desire him; he accepted that. The scorn he saw in her eyes as she compared him to the professor . . . that was a scorn he felt for himself.

Their awkward couplings would surely improve slightly with further practice, but they had little to do with the fierce desire he felt, with the way his body longed to make love to her.

Yet he wasn't the sort of man to be unfaithful. He couldn't take a courtesan, or even a lady, to bed. The truth was that he didn't want a mistress. He started walking again, letting the rain beat into the back of his neck.

He could survive without Poppy in his bed.

But he couldn't survive without her in his life. She had to come home. He would promise that he'd never visit her room until they decided to have children. And he would promise to stop sulking.

He'd spent the last few years sulking. He had to give Lady Flora credit for that observation. He'd sulked because life hadn't turned out the way he thought it should. Enough. Enough thinking about French women, and women's desire in general. In fact, the hell with desire.

Monks did it, didn't they? He didn't need sex in order to be a man. What he needed—what he needed was Poppy. Because for some strange, stupid reason, she felt like the coffee he drank in the morning.

He needed her.

He turned around and started back for the carriage. He would make himself into someone she would be proud of, someone who wasn't interested only in the cut of his coat and the sheen of his hair.

If he admitted the truth to himself, he wanted to be one of the most important men in the House of Lords. He wanted to make a difference to the country, to be a man whose words were feared and welcomed, like his father's had been.

Then he would dispense with Lady Flora, which would be his gift to Poppy.

And finally he would lure her back to the house, before Christmas came again.

And then somehow, someday, he would woo his wife into loving him the way she used to. The way she loved him that Christmas in Paris, when she looked at him as if he were the world to her.

When she loved him.

Chapter 32

The Rose Salon, Beaumont House
December 6

"I shall not go to Oxford," Jemma explained, "because you have a perfectly good husband who has offered to accompany you, Poppy. I don't wish to be unkind, but I haven't the faintest interest in three-toed rats or whatever it is you are going to see."

"I know," Poppy said. "I've been a frightful beast, taking you around to all these boring events."

"I wouldn't do it if I didn't enjoy being with you. But the truth is that I don't want to go all the way to Oxford. I really don't. Mrs. Patton is taking me to the London Chess Club tomorrow and I have every intention of joining, if they'll have me."

"Oh, you should. Then you can shame the men by beating them."

"You are turning into a bloodthirsty little thing."

"I have always been a bloodthirsty little thing," Poppy retorted. "I have a perfect model in my mother. That's why Fletch wants to accompany me to Oxford. So he can get away from my mother."

"Look at this," Jemma said, holding up a piece of foolscap. "I've had a letter from Roberta, my sister-in-law; she says that a bear went amok on her father's estate and ate a couple of rare ducks. I must answer this. Darling, you will be all right without me, won't you?"

"It's just that it's *Fletch!*"

"Your husband," Jemma prompted. "You've been married for years, remember?"

"It's all different now. I don't feel in the least comfortable with him. We may well argue. And what—what if he—"

"He won't," Jemma said comfortably. "And if he does, you can boot him out of the carriage. You're a bloodthirsty woman, remember? Think of your mother."

Poppy thought of her mother. If Fletch misbehaved in her presence, her mother would likely toss him from the carriage and send a chamber pot flying after him. "True."

"Men are very useful on these little trips," Jemma said, drifting out the door with a final blown kiss. "In case a wheel breaks or some such."

Poppy marched out to Fletch's carriage, trying hard to pretend she was her mother.

He looked up from the papers he was reading and gave her a careless smile, and it took all her strength to nip off her welcoming grin. She was not—*not*—going to smile at him like a lovesick puppy.

He peered at her. "Are you all right, Poppy? You look stiff as a poker."

"I just want to say again that you needn't accompany me, Fletch. I'm sure you have a lot to do."

"Actually, I do."

"Well, then, I'll just drop you off at the house," she said.

"With your mother? Not on your life. I brought my work with me." He rustled his documents.

Poppy subsided onto the opposite seat and eyed Fletch. He was already deep into the sheaf of papers. It was infuriating that he was so appealing. Deliberately, she made herself think about Dr. Loudan. Loudan listened to her. He thought she was intelligent. She thought about the letter she'd written Loudan that very morning, suggesting that his claim about the so-called muskrat found in Ceylon might have been incorrect, if one took into account the study published three years ago by Dr. Farthing. The animal couldn't be a muskrat, as Loudan maintained. Her mouth curved up.

Fletch didn't look up, but he said, "So what are you grinning about, then?"

"Nothing."

"What are you thinking about?"

"Dr. Loudan."

He grunted but didn't say anything to that. Still, it gave Poppy a little jolt of satisfaction. His Grace Beautiful Fletcher had to understand that there were men in the world who cared more about muskrats than they did about gorgeous clothing.

"What are you reading?" she asked. "I can't read in the carriage as I grow quite nauseated."

"An excruciatingly foolish treatise on the trade bill with France. The off-repeated point of twelve pages is that French brandy costs too much."

"What does the author intend to do about that?"

"Whine and complain," Fletch said. "It's a shock to see

how much paper is wasted by fellows in Lords, nattering on and on about inconsequentials. Now if I was going to argue this bill, I'd focus on the situation of English farmers. I have to give extra payments every year to the men working around my estate; it's impossible to survive with the price of wheat being what it is. This trade bill should ignore the brandy and bar French wheat from our shores."

"Why don't you do so?" Poppy said.

He didn't answer, just flipped to the next page.

"Well?" Poppy asked. "Didn't you hear me?" It felt good to ask a belligerent question. It was so un-Poppy-like.

"I made a fool of myself in the House in case you don't remember." He didn't look at her.

Poppy laughed. She couldn't help it. He looked so adorably disgruntled. "But you turned the speech around, didn't you?"

"No one understood my speech. My party, that is, Fox's party, thinks I did a fine job. They seemed to have no idea that I changed my mind halfway through."

"Oh."

"My language was a bit convoluted. Only Beaumont seems to have grasped it."

"Jemma's husband? Yes, he's very smart, isn't he?"

"He thanked me for striking a blow for his side," Fletch said morosely. "What's the point if people don't listen?"

"It's hard to follow long speeches. I find that they're much more intelligible if someone makes a fairly simple point and repeats it at least twice, like the author of your paper on brandy. I don't suppose your speech was simple, Fletch?"

"How could it be simple? It's a complicated topic. This idiot"—he shook the papers in his lap—"boiled the trade bill down to one idea."

"Yes, but you understood it immediately, didn't you?"

"Well—"

"I rest my case," Poppy said.

He eyed her. "You know, you never used to disagree with me."

"We were married then."

"We are still married!"

There was a flash of real anger in his eyes that she enjoyed. But she shrugged. "It's different now."

He waited until they were at supper at the Fox and Hummingbird, and Poppy had stated her intention to retire to her chamber.

Then he just blurted it out, with no preparation. "The truth of it is that whether your mother arranged our marriage, or whether it was all an illusion, I must be horribly obtuse, because I can't talk myself out of being in love with you."

Poppy had risen; she plumped back into her seat knowing that the look of surprise on her face must be almost comic.

"I know this sounds stupid, given the way you feel." He looked grumpy, the way men do when they're talking about emotions. "But I can't have you thinking that I don't love you. Because I do."

"Ump," she said.

He raised his hand. "I need to finish. I love you and so I want you to know that I understand. I don't think you're ever going to like physical intimacy, at least not with me, Poppy. I can accept that."

"Oh," she whispered. Her heart felt as if it had fallen into a black well. Her whole life she'd tried not to disappoint people. And now she'd disappointed Fletch. It made her want to fling herself from the window.

He reached out and pried her fingers apart. "It's not your fault. And it's not my fault. It's just the hand of cards we were dealt. Don't you see, Poppy?"

"I see that I should—I should have tried harder," she said

in a little wooden voice that disguised how much she wanted to cry.

"You did try, didn't you?" His eyes were so kind that she felt tears swell up in hers.

"Yes."

He shrugged. "So we give that up."

"You can't give it up!"

"Why not?"

"Men just can't."

"You think that men can't give it up, but women can?" He was smiling at her a little now, tugging at her hand to make her smile at him.

"It's so kind of you to say so, Fletch. But I think we would really do better if you just went off by yourself for a while. Then when we decide to have an heir we'll come back together and do that."

He sighed. "You didn't hear me."

"Yes, I did."

"I'm in love with you, Poppy."

She swallowed.

"I don't want to go off with some light-heeled woman who would pretend to like me and pretend to desire me. And I don't want to have an *affaire* with a woman like your friend Louise either."

"Yes you do."

"I did think of it. But if I imagine myself in bed with her—or any other woman—it doesn't work for me. Damn it, Poppy, don't you think it would be easier for me if it did work? I could skip out to Fonthill for the Christmas season and frolic with half the trollops in the kingdom."

"Yes, it would be easier for you," she said baldly. "And easier for me as well. Why don't you?"

His eyes darkened and for a moment she thought she'd hurt him, but then he just turned her hand over and said,

"We're both spoiled goods. Because unfortunately when I asked you to marry me, it seems to have been a long-term proposition."

Poppy's mind reeled. Part of her was screaming silently with the joy of it, dancing a hornpipe at the back of her brain. But part of her was terrified. Now they were back where they were before, back in the bed where she would just disappoint him again because she couldn't be—

He looked at her eyes and he must have seen exactly what she was thinking, because he shook his head. "I'm not asking for that, Poppy. We'll do it exactly as you wish. No bed. None of that. I don't need it and you don't want it."

"You don't need it?" This went against everything her mother had ever told her.

"I'm discovering that bedroom activity isn't terribly important to me. You've been gone for months and I haven't broken my wedding vows."

His eyes looked as if he were serious. Could it be? She herself was fine without marital intimacies. Why shouldn't Fletch be the same?

"We'll just skip that aspect until we decide that we want children," he added.

"I'm not sure we can have children, Fletch. We tried for four years."

He shrugged. "My father and mother were married for ten years before they had me. And then it was another eight before my brother happened along, and then finally the twins followed. So in the end they had four."

"Would it bother you if we don't have children?"

"Not particularly. One of my brothers will do the deed. So: I've thought it out, Poppy, and the only thing we can do is just pretend that all this bedding business doesn't exist. We haven't made love for months now and I've been doing just fine."

Poppy didn't really think he was fine. There was a tightness about him, the sense of a taut wire singing in the wind . . . but she didn't want to think about that. What she wanted more than anything was to believe him.

"Unless, of course, you just don't like having me around," he said, rather awkwardly, as the silence grew.

She let it grow some more. She didn't want him to think that she was going to be his willing little acolyte, slavishly grateful for his every glance. He was staring at the floor, looking rather miserable. Good.

"I wouldn't want you to do this just because of my mother's presence in your house," she said. "Though I know well that my mother has a great deal to do with your plea for my return."

"Your mother has no part in my request."

She didn't believe that for a moment, but she let it go. There was something more important that had to be said.

"You'd have to understand that I don't feel the same way as you do. I'm not in love, though I am very fond of you, Fletch."

He nodded. A lock of hair fell over his eyes and he looked so delicious that she almost jumped up to put her arms around him and make him foolish promises. Maybe she *could* try harder . . .

No.

She had felt free in the last months, living at Jemma's, not worrying about her dress, and how she looked, and whether her husband would think she was stupid for buying curiosities, or whether he was coming to her bedchamber that night.

"I'm not moving back home," she added. "Not yet."

He looked stunned. "Why not?"

"Because I don't want to."

"Is this because of that Loudan fellow?" When Fletch frowned he looked thrillingly pirate-like, Poppy thought.

"In a way it is. I always thought it would be improper of me to go to the meetings of the Royal Society. I hid my books. I tried so hard to be a proper duchess and make you happy. I've acquired a cabinet for my curiosities. I might as well warn you, Fletch, that it was quite expensive, as it's modeled on the cabinet owned by the King of Sweden. The other day I bought an ancient Greek coin for it. And I saw an advertisement for a string of Virginia wampum."

"But I never said you couldn't buy anything! You can have all the wampum you want, whatever that is."

"I don't feel like being a duchess at the moment."

"You *are* a duchess," he said stubbornly. "I'm your duke and you should be at home with me."

"This is about my mother, isn't it?"

"No. It's about you. And me. I don't like finding you're not there for breakfast. And I don't like going to parties without you. I miss talking to you."

"I can't imagine why. We haven't talked about anything particularly interesting in years."

"I thought it was interesting. Perhaps I like talking about boring things with you."

"I don't want to go back to your house."

"It's your mother's house," he said gloomily. "Wait until you see how she's changed the drapery."

"Very formal?"

"I feel as if I'm living in Versailles."

"How could I take the pleasure away from her?" Poppy said, grinning. "She always wanted to be a duchess."

He groaned. "Then can I live with you and Jemma?"

"You're not invited."

"Even for Christmas? What about Jemma's house party? Half of London is discussing it. You wouldn't leave me with your mother for the holiday, would you?"

"I'll see how I feel," Poppy said loftily. "It's to be a very intimate party. Surely you'd be happier retiring to the country with Pitt, or some friend from the government?"

"No," he said. "I'd be happier with you. Christmas always reminds me of being on the tower of Saint Germain des Près with you, Poppy. Do you remember that?"

"Yes," she said. "Of course I do." Her heart was beating very quickly.

"Now I think about it, I should have known from that absurd pin you were wearing that I'd find myself talking to you about river otters. I was so fevered with love that I couldn't think straight."

"We were dazed by the season," she said firmly. "Christmas can be like that."

He met her eyes. "The season had nothing to do with it, Poppy. Not for me."

She couldn't think what to say, and somehow the moment was lost. So she pretended he had said nothing. He looked at her, eyes serious, brow furrowed.

She didn't want him to be alone on Christmas.

"I'll ask Jemma," she said.

"What?"

"I'll ask Jemma to send you an invitation."

His smile made her feel very peculiar, so she retired to her bedchamber.

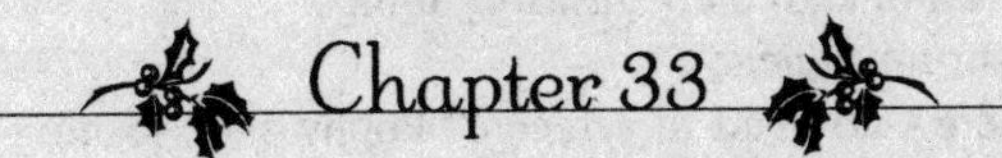

Chapter 33

The next day
December 7

The Ashmolean Museum was a bloody boring place full of stuffed mice. Poppy got excited over a poor flying squirrel, but Fletch thought it looked pitiful, pinned to a wall with its tiny claws extended.

"Look at that," he pointed out, "it's pleading for its life. Begging. Set me free!"

Poppy didn't pay any attention. "Look at its fifth claw," she said. "It's bent backward, almost as if it had a thumb. Isn't that interesting?"

Fletch thought the little squirrel was going to haunt him in his dreams. "It's supposed to be flying through the trees, though I don't believe it really can fly without wings," he said disgustedly. "Not pinned to a board. It smells in here."

"Taxidermy is not a perfect science," Poppy said. But she obviously didn't give a damn about the odor.

Naturally the curator of the Ashmoleon was so overwhelmed by her blue eyes that he started opening all sorts of cabinets marked "Not for Display." And then he started rootling around in the basement and coming up with dusty boxes full of extremely unsavory things.

"A shrunken head?"

"There's no need to screech," Poppy said, leaning over the disgusting little object as if it were made of gold.

The curator gave Fletch a scornful look, so he retreated to the entryway where the odor was less offensive and took out that blasted report of Linchberry's. It was bad. Twisted, even, in the way it thought only about French products and not English farmers.

He read it again and then got a bottle of ink and a quill off the curator; the man barely registered his request, he was so enthralled by Poppy. Fletch rolled up his cuffs and started writing. The trick was to keep it simple, the way Poppy suggested.

He'd noticed during the last months of haunting the House of Lords, listening to every speech, that not a single man talked about himself. Everything they said was couched in so much fancy language that the forest couldn't be seen for the trees. Hell, that's what he had done himself when he decided to make a speech of his own—which likely explained why no one had the faintest idea what he said.

If there was going to be a treaty with France, it had to take into account the way that treaty would affect English farmers. Not English noblemen, and their penchant for French brandy and French silk—he cast an affectionate glance at the ribbed twill of his coat—but English farmers. Men like Higgle, who farmed part of the Fletcher duchy. Higgle had the devil of a time making ends meet, what with his eight children and the price of bread.

Fletch thought about it, started a paragraph, threw it away.

The Duke of Beaumont had given him a bit of advice one day: that if he truly wanted to obliterate an opponent, the key was to create a story that would catch everyone's attention. Higgle could be his story.

He started again, crumpled up the page when he was nearly to the end, threw it away.

Finally he started over again, just talking about Higgle. The way the man worked from dawn til dusk, tilling the ground. The way he had all his children working in the fields with him, until Fletch made him stop and let the children go to the village school. The fact that he received less than a penny for ten pounds of wheat, but then had to pay seven pence for a loaf of bread.

By the time shadows started to grow in the museum entryway, he had five credible pages. And what's more, he knew that he could give the speech without looking at the paper, though it helped to write it down. It was simple, it was clear, and by God, it was powerful.

Just then Poppy came around the corner. He leapt to his feet. His wife looked as if she'd been in a fight. Her pink polonaise gown was streaked with brown smudges, and the lace hem was torn. "What the hell happened?" His voice echoed around the marble entry.

She blinked up at him, and he realized instantly that she was unharmed. Curls had fallen out of her elaborate arrangement; he'd never seen her so disheveled. Even when they'd made love she'd kept her head still so her curls weren't rumpled.

Museums seemed to be the exception to that rule.

"Mr. Munson let me see the collections that Captain Cook sent back from his second voyage. Even the ones in the basement that are uncatalogued."

"More flying squirrels?" Fletch tried to brush a black smear from Poppy's shoulder.

"There's an animal that's about twice the size of a large rat," she told him.

Fletch handed Mr. Munson a purse while Poppy wasn't looking. He'd never seen her so excited. Her excitement had a terrible effect on his body; he was about to burst out of his breeches. Luckily, Poppy never paid the faintest attention to his body. It was just that her hair was flying, and her eyes were bubbling with excitement. Her cheeks were pink, just a soft rosy color on top of her cheekbones that made him want to kiss her there, and maybe bite her ear . . .

He realized she was staring at him. "Are you quite all right, Fletch?"

"Your maid will have an apoplectic fit when she sees you. I was just thinking about that."

"The odd thing," Poppy said, ignoring the question of maids, "is that this animal carries its young in a pouch."

"What?"

"It's called a possum, though Captain Cook apparently decided it was in the family of dogs."

"Ah," Fletch said intelligently.

"I don't agree," Poppy said. "I shall write Dr. Loudan immediately and tell him so. Even though its head resembled a dog's, the pouch puts it in an entirely different species. Do you see my point, Fletch?"

"Of course," he said, handing her into the carriage.

"The Dog and the Partridge," he told his coachman, James. The name of the inn had an odd rightness about it, given Poppy's subject of conversation.

When he got inside the carriage, Poppy was still talking

about the dog. In fact, he didn't think she'd stopped for a moment.

"The curator said that Captain Cook suggested that the animal liked fruit. He gave one an orange. No dog would eat an orange."

"Definitely not," Fletch said.

They pulled up at the Dog and the Partridge, and Fletch stepped out into the damp twilight. The air smelled chill and raw, as if snow was on the way. Poppy still didn't seem to have realized how awful she looked, so Fletch just took her arm as if there were nothing untoward about her appearance.

Given the raucous noises pouring out of the public room, not to mention the fellow sleeping at the end of the corridor, the Dog and the Partridge was overrun by customers. The innkeeper came forward to meet them smiling the peculiarly tight grimace of a man with one too many guests in his inn.

"My lord," the man said, bowing nervously. "I'm not sure that we're able to accommodate you . . ."

"We reserved the rooms," Fletch said. "My man should have been here hours ago. I am the Duke of Fletcher."

"I'm afraid your man hasn't arrived yet," the innkeeper said. "I have Andrew Whiston here, Your Grace, and he's attracted quite a lot of attention, as you can see." He didn't even jump when a sodden heap of a man reeled out of a door and crashed into the wall.

"Hasn't arrived," Fletch said. "How can that be? The second carriage left Chalgrove when we did, early this morning."

"Do you think there was an accident?" Poppy asked, knitting her brow.

"It's possible," the innkeeper asked. He snapped his fingers and two postilions leapt to their feet. "Accompany His Grace's men; search the Chalgrove Road." He turned back to Fletch. "It may be that they're stuck in the mud. Unfortunately, there isn't another inn for at least an hour's drive. But I will do my best to accommodate you."

"Naturally I will reimburse anyone who is inconvenienced by our arrival," Fletch said.

Another man crashed out of the door and noisily began throwing up just outside the door. Poppy shuddered. "Who is Andrew Whiston?" she asked.

"The King of Beggars," the innkeeper said. "Only twenty-eight inches high, he is, and he's quite a curiosity in these parts. Comes out from London once a year and sings us a few songs."

"He's a drunkard, but a very short one," Fletch said. "Spends every night drinking in Surr's wine vaults when he's in London."

"He do love his liquor," the innkeeper said, turning about. "And the lads love to share it with him, if you take my meaning. I'll do everything I can to make you comfortable. I can put you in a good chamber now, but I'll have to see about a private dining room for yourself and your lady."

"We need two chambers," Poppy chirped up, "plus accommodations for my maid, of course."

A look of panic crossed the innkeeper's face. "I gave away my rooms already, Your Grace. I can likely put two of my guests together, but I'm afraid I can't turn people out altogether."

Fletch took his wife's arm. "We aren't going to turn anyone out into the cold and dark, are we, Poppy?"

She looked up at him and said, "Absolutely, we are. If you pay them double, Fletch, they'll probably be quite grateful."

He always knew that women were the crueler sex. But there was something slightly unnerved in her voice that he found interesting. "Unkind wench. I don't turn people out into the dark. It's coming on to snow. That isn't right."

She pursed her lips but he turned away. "Her Grace has kindly agreed to these uncomfortable arrangements," he said to the innkeeper, who bowed so low that his nose surely touched his knees.

"I'll prepare a private parlor," the man said, leading the way to the stairs, "and the very best meal that you've ever had in Oxford, that I can promise you. Just give me an hour to prepare the parlor, Your Graces, and you'll be completely comfortable, I assure you."

"You can sleep in the parlor," Poppy murmured to him, on the way up on the dark little stairs.

"I certainly will not," Fletch said. "I'm covered with dust and you are covered with worse. We are both going to have baths, supper, and then go to sleep. Remember, Poppy, I've put bedtime activities out of my mind. And I'm a man of my word."

She nodded. And if she believed that, Fletch had a whole army of flying squirrels that he could sell her. For some reason, his desire was utterly in flames again. It was as bad as when they first met.

He took his wife's arm and the only thing he wanted to do was spin her against the wall and kiss her so hard that her knees would buckle. It had to be because she looked disheveled. He never managed to get her in disarray; even when she was naked she always looked as if she were wearing an invisible corset.

The bedchamber was large with a sloping roof that slanted down over the bed. "It's cosy," the innkeeper said nervously. "Our best room, Your Graces."

The sheets were snowy white and the room looked clean. That and a drink were all Fletch really cared about. "We shall require hot baths, both of us," he said, "and meanwhile bring me a brandy, if you would. And a glass of wine for Her Grace."

"Wine?" Poppy said, looking up from the notes she had taken in the museum.

"Wine," he said firmly. "And a bath."

The innkeeper left and Poppy focused on him. "Hadn't you better leave? That is, if you'll allow me to have the first bath."

Fletch had just managed to wrench off his boots and in reply he walked over to the bed and fell onto it like timber crashing in the forest. "You're joking," he said from among the mounds of featherbed that popped around his face. "I'm exhausted, Poppy. We've been in the carriage for two days, and then spent seven hours in a bloody museum. I'm trying to get the sour taste of dust out of my mouth."

Poppy wandered over to the glass. When she saw herself she gave a little scream and started poking ineffectually at her hair.

"It's a mess," Fletch said, having managed to beat back the pillows and sit up. "You look awful."

"You never said such a thing before," she said, scowling at him. She'd managed to make things worse; there was a bit of that black furry stuff on her hair now.

"Ah, but we were properly married then. Now it's all different. It's as if we've been married for forty years. No interest in each other in bed. We can tell each other the truth and not worry about hurt feelings."

She turned back to the mirror and started poking around again.

"You're getting black all over your hair," he said a while later.

She shrieked again.

"Couldn't you brush it out?"

"Of course not. I'm sure you haven't arranged your own hair."

"I certainly have. I don't like men touching my body," he

said. "I've always dressed myself, perhaps just a little help with my boots."

"Well, women can't do that," she said flatly. "I can't even tie my own side bustles."

"I don't know if you've noticed, but your maid is not here. Can you get your own clothing off?" he said, thanking God that the quilt was concealing the rise in his breeches.

"Of course," she said firmly.

"Well, then, why don't you?" Fletch was starting to enjoy himself. "Because," he added in his most reasonable voice, "this room really isn't large enough for those baskets you're wearing on your hips. And frankly, I don't think the innkeeper is going to be happy with the way you're spreading that furry stuff on everything you touch."

"Furry stuff?" She twisted around to look over her shoulder and started screaming again. In truth, it was rather disgusting. Lord knows where those smudges came from, probably down in the basement.

"If you take off the bustles, you'll deflate," he said, grinning. He sat up just long enough to strip off his coat and waistcoat, and pull open his cuffs.

She eyed him and then said, "Don't watch."

He leaned back and closed his eyes. "I put all that behind me, remember? Besides, I have never had fantasies about women covered with dirt."

Then he watched her from under his lashes because frankly, he was having his first fantasy about a woman covered with dirt. Poppy's skirts were huge; she kept pulling them up and losing track of her underskirts. Finally she managed to get all the material bunched up in her fists.

Fletch had to take a deep breath when she pulled up her skirts. She had the sweetest turn of ankle he'd ever seen. He couldn't see much higher than the back of her knee because she was wearing so much wire bracketry around her body.

She was feeling around like a blind possum in the night, to use one of her own nature metaphors. She was never going to get that thing untied.

"Do you need some help?" he asked finally.

She whipped her head around and he grinned at her.

"You had your eyes open!" she accused.

He swung his legs out of bed and she let her skirts fall again. "You're never going to get all that clothing undone, Poppy. I've seen you naked, remember? What's the difference?"

She muttered something about privacy.

"You've taken off your clothes and laid down entirely naked on the bed in front of me," he said, pulling up her skirts. "What are you afraid of? We're an old married couple, remember? I'll probably start breaking wind in front of you after every meal."

"You wouldn't dare!"

"Yes, and if we're at a formal supper, I'll blame you," Fletch said, struggling with the tapes holding up her side bustle. "I'll jog you on the elbow and say very loudly, *Don't worry, darling, I'll say it was I.*"

"I'll kill you," Poppy said with certain resolution in her voice.

"Just how would you do that?" He turned her to the other side so he could untie the other string. He had to keep her talking because otherwise she might notice how his fingers were trembling. It was utterly ludicrous that he was so wild with lust now, when she was clothed, when he could have had her anytime in the year before she moved out, and had declined to do so.

"I'll give you a purge."

She was grinning at him with a wicked twinkle in her eye. Instead of untying, he managed to yank the knot tight.

"I'll give you a purge," she continued gleefully, "and then I'll drill a hole in your chamber pot."

"Loathsome wrench. How the hell does your maid usually get this off you?"

She craned a glance over her shoulder. "They untie, obviously. You got the other one off easily enough."

"Well, this one is stuck." He thought of asking her to bend over a chair so he could reach the knot better and bit his own tongue. He'd likely run stark raving mad if she did that, and lunge at her. Instead he threw her skirts over his left arm and started wrenching the string apart.

"That's a disgusting little idea you had about my chamber pot," he said, trying not to look at the curve of her bottom, perfectly visible through her sheer chemise.

"My mother—" she said and suddenly stopped.

"I find it hard to imagine your mother attacking a chamber pot."

"She might surprise you."

The second bustle fell to the floor in a jostling of wires. He kicked it out of the way to Poppy's little shriek. "Be careful with that! It's delicate."

"I like your own hips better," he said, going back to the bed and lying down quickly so that she didn't see the front of his breeches.

"I'm surprised to hear that from you of all people. After all, panniers are in fashion and surely that is of foremost concern for the Duke of Fletcher."

"I've gone a bit far in that direction," he said, propping himself up against the wall. "I was trying to get you to notice me, you know."

She turned away from the window, her mouth open. "What?"

"I wanted you to notice me. But now I've accepted that you'll never desire me, so I don't have to try so hard."

Instead of looking gratified, she suddenly looked as if she were going to cry. "That's so *sad*, Fletch."

"I've gone past that," he said. "It's not a problem."

She turned back to the mirror and started fussing with her hair again, but whatever she was doing just made it worse.

"You know, is there any chance that black stuff is tar?" he said, after a while. "Because it's spread over quite a bit of your hair in back now."

"Tar? What's tar?"

"Black, sticky stuff that doesn't come off," he said, getting out of bed again.

She had started out the day with a delightful hair arrangement involving one long feather, three shorter feathers, and a bunch of ribbons in the back. Plus a huge amount of curled, looped hair, naturally, a frizzed part on the top, and what must have been a full box of hair powder.

Now the feathers were bent and her hair . . . He put a finger to the black stuff. "Definitely tar," he said.

"Can you brush it off?" Poppy asked. She tried to look over her shoulder at the glass again. "I can see there's something black there, but—"

"First we have to get all these feathers and bows out of your hair."

There was a moment's silence. "Do you think Luce will be found soon?"

"Surely you know how to take down your own hair."

"It's different for men than women, you know!" She turned around and snapped at him, hands on her hips, and she looked so adorable he almost lost his head and kissed her. "All a man has to do is swat on a bit of powder—"

"Not me."

"And tie your hair back. I could do *that*."

"Why don't you, sometimes?"

She started laughing. "Go outside with my hair tied back like a five-year-old girl?"

"Surely you could do it in the house?"

"It's not done."

"I would do it, if I were you. This looks heavy and it smells awful."

"My hair doesn't smell!"

"I didn't mean it smelled dirty. It's just that there's so much lavender powder in here that I can't smell *you* at all."

"I don't have a smell," she said, setting that little jaw of hers and glaring at him.

"I do." He sniffed his own armpit. "I wonder when that bath is coming."

"You are disgusting!"

"I am not," he protested. "I rather like the smell of my sweat. I'd like yours, too."

A knock on the door signaled the entry of the innkeeper carrying a tin bathtub, followed by three men carrying buckets of hot water. He plunked it down by the window and turned to face them. "We've located your servants, Your Graces."

"Oh, lovely!" Poppy said. "Is my maid on the way?"

"Unfortunately, their carriage turned over in a ditch. As I understand it, the men outside jumped clear. But Your Graces' manservant and maid were inside the coach. Your valet was knocked clean out and only came to himself an hour or so ago. And your maid has broken her arm."

"Oh no! Poor Luce!" Poppy cried. "I must go to her!"

"She's right and tight back at the Fox and Hummingbird, Your Grace. My man said that she had a posset to take off the pain, and she was sleeping as sweetly as a babe."

"Is my valet there as well?" Fletch put in.

"They're both safe as bugs in a bed," the innkeeper said.

"Now I've thought about the duchess's situation, and I thought that Elsie here, from the kitchen, would be able to help you with your women's things." He moved to the side, and a great, strapping lass with hairier arms than Fletch entered. She grinned, showing that she had only three teeth to her name.

Fletch cast a look at Poppy and said, "My wife and I will quite relish the rustic pleasures of being without personal help for the night. Don't think about it twice; I wouldn't want to take Elsie away from her work in the kitchen."

Poppy opened her mouth, but Fletch had the innkeeper and his men out of that room before she could do more than splutter at him.

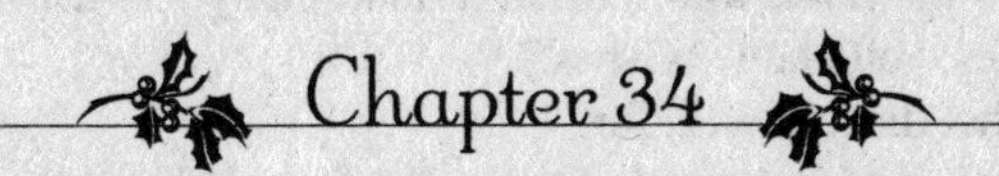

Chapter 34

Charlotte pulled out her Bible and sat down, trying to conceal the fact that she was rather anxiously trying to figure out whether Villiers looked closer to death than he had when she last saw him. The very thought made her heart knock against her chest, which was stupid because she hardly knew the man. She had only paid him a matter of four visits.

"I'm unchanged," he said, guessing her thoughts. "Just as pestilent, as resistant to Christian advice, and generally ill-tempered."

"I brought my Bible again," she said primly. "I'm sure it will be a great consolation to you."

"Will you read me the bits about David watching Bathsheba? That was always my favorite when I was a boy."

"Absolutely not. I'm going to read you from *Luke*." And she began to read the lovely old story of Christ's birth. He surprised her and didn't complain as she began, "There was in the days of Herod, King of Judea . . ."

At some point his man brought in a glass of water and Villiers sipped at it. "The Christmas story," he said, his voice as wry as ever. "Do you think I need to hear of miracles?"

"It wouldn't hurt you. Christmas is coming."

"I used to love the holiday," he said, handing the glass back to his man, who refilled it and quietly left the room. "Wishes, you know. Wishes."

"What did you wish for?"

"To fly. I always wanted to fly. But I would have accepted the gift of speaking with animals. What about you?"

"We were never encouraged to wish, at least not in connection with Christmas. But I have very fond memories of the holiday."

"You seem more starchy today."

"This is the way I always am. Would you like me to continue reading, Your Grace?"

"Don't Your Grace me, if you please."

"And the child grew, and waxed strong in spirit," she said, starting to read again. "He was filled with wisdom: and the grace of God was upon him."

But she didn't think about the words she was reading; she thought about the way Villiers's skin was drawn so tightly over his cheekbones. He was dying. She knew it in the pit of her stomach. So why was she being so prudish with him, when she could tell that it made him miserable?

She put the book down again. After a bit he opened his eyes—he really did have the longest eyelashes—and said, "Well, do keep going."

"I thought you'd heard enough."

"I want to know how the story ends." And then he started laughing at the expression on her face.

"You ought to drink the rest of your water."

He picked up the glass and she cudgeled her brains for

something to say that would make the spark come back into his eyes. "Why did you want to fly?" she asked.

"Who wouldn't? To have wings at your back, and the sky at your mercy . . . to drift on the belly of the wind the way hawks do, and perch on a tree to chatter to friends. I am persuaded that conversations that take place on the branches of a tree are far more interesting than those that take place in London townhouses."

"That's lovely!"

"You must have wished for something," he said. "There's not a true Englishman in the world who hasn't wished that he won the bean in his slice of cake and became King of the Bean, or wished that his horrid little sister would lose at snapdragon, and perhaps even singe a finger on a burning raisin."

Charlotte thought of meaningless answers and then said the truth. "I never wished for much until I turned sixteen."

He raised his heavy eyes. "You fell in love?"

"No. I just wanted a man to fall in love with me. I was sure I could adapt my emotions to whomever presented himself."

"Poor Charlotte," he said, and his voice sounded less bored. She was right; he needed to think of someone other than himself. "Did no man ever fall in love with you?"

"I thought one did, once. Lord Barnabe Reeve."

"Reeve was the Barnabe who brought you to my side? I never knew his first name."

"We danced all night long once," she said. "I thought . . . but he left London within days and went mad, or so they say."

"I hate to dispel your sweet memories of first love, but in my view it's better to have no spouse than one who's cracked. And I know many who would agree with me."

His hands lay on the counterpane, looking strangely still.

The sight of them made her hurry into speech. "Doubtless, you're right. After a while I stopped wishing for someone to fall in love with me and just wished for someone blind enough to mistake me for someone he might fall in love with."

He smiled faintly. "You're not an antidote. Particularly when you flare up and snap at me. I imagine that's what Elijah sees in you."

"Elijah?"

"Duke of Beaumont. I suppose I could marry you."

She looked at him with some horror. "You—" She stopped. He was dying, but how to say so?

"Dying, dying, dying, how it gets in the way of my social life," he said lightly. "To be but half-dead is as bad as being half-witted, like Reeve. Neither makes a man fit company for his betters nor a good consort for a woman."

"You don't want to marry me," Charlotte said, recovering herself. "Besides, you're far too high in the instep and grand for me to marry. I wouldn't have dared wish for you."

"I thought women liked to marry their betters. It does such nice things for one's offspring."

"As you pointed out, I have no offspring," Charlotte pointed out. "Why should I worry about their future titles under those circumstances?"

"I suppose this will shock you, but I was thinking last night that I should have bothered to create a few children, and then I remembered that I had already."

"You *did?*"

"Illegitimate ones," he said. "As sometimes happens."

"Not to me," she said tartly.

"Women on the whole are better at keeping track of their children."

He looked rather feverish again, so she said, "I think I'd better go back to the Bible, though it's likely too late for your soul."

"Do you think I might redeem my soul if I found a husband for you?"

"You would do better to see to the welfare of your poor children," she said. And then, hearing the fascinated horror in her own voice: "How many are there?"

"Not as many as would fill a choir," he said, "nor yet as few as to sing a solo. Can you sing, by the way?"

"No."

"I know a very nice lad in need of a wife but he loves song."

"I'm not very good at things of that nature," Charlotte said.

"What about horses?"

"They exist."

"Not an enthusiast. But you like to talk. We know that. And you have good ideas for Beaumont's speech . . . what about a promising young politician? Plenty of those about."

"They want someone with a large dowry," she said dispassionately.

"You could have that."

"As it happens, I don't."

"I could give it to you." He opened his eyes very wide and looked at her. They were a deep black.

"Why would you do that?"

"I like you. And dying men have their foibles, their foolishnesses . . ."

"I thank you for it." But she added, a little sadly: "It would be distasteful, don't you think, to buy a husband, even with a duke's largesse?"

"Oh, he wouldn't know that. A better dress and you must put a bit of color on your cheeks now and then. And your hair!" He peered at her. "Worse than I remembered."

She didn't tell him that she had dressed her own hair with trembling fingers that morning, afraid he was dead, or nearly so, and then rushed out of the house with May calling behind her. "I will still be just me."

"Not once I've transformed you. But I don't think that a politician would be right. Too hard, too grasping. You're correct: there's a chance the man would marry you thinking of money and political influence. They all have those distasteful propensities. I think you need an intellectual."

"A what?"

"A philosopher. Reeve was a thinker. I remember him madly talking about this and that. He was never boring."

"No," Charlotte agreed.

"Is it almost Christmas?"

"Tomorrow is St. Nicholas's day."

"God." He whispered it. "It seems like yesterday that I fought that duel and it's—it can't have been months."

"It has been."

"I really won't survive then, will I?"

"You're too unpleasant to die," she said sharply. "If you're not careful, I'll marry you while you're in a fever and then take all your money."

He stopped looking so dismal and laughed a bit, though it made him wheeze. "What the hell would you do with money? Buy some clothing?"

"Give it to your children," she said.

"They're set for money. No father, but money. I made a will. Seeing as I'm no father, they'll be better without me."

"Poppycock. You are a father. You're just a bad one."

"I'll have to find you a deaf husband," he said, eyes narrowed. "But I demand that you keep visiting me until I do."

"Why should I risk my reputation on your implausible matchmaking abilities?"

"That's something you don't know about me. I never fail at what I put my hand to. I'll find the perfect man. I'd like to see you refuse him."

"If I take him, you'll have to do something for me in return."

"What? In return for finding you your heart's desire, I have to do you a favor?"

"It'll keep you alive long enough to do it," she pointed out. "Otherwise you're like to tumble into the grave merely because your doctor told you to do it. I don't think anyone in London realizes how malleable you are."

"*You* are a hellcat. What's your favor, then?"

"If you find me a husband—one that I like, I'll turn wife and you turn father."

"I'm as much a father as my father ever was. Better, because I don't ever shout at them."

"You might, if you knew their names."

"Worse than a hellcat," he observed. "It's going to take a miracle to marry you off."

"And you're going to have to sit up," she retorted. "Just how do you expect to find me a husband while you're malingering in bed?"

He eyed her. "When the fever comes on I don't have much choice."

"Well, I can't ruin my reputation in your house. What decent man would want to marry a woman he met in your presence—in your bedchamber?"

"Good point," he murmured. "I suppose you're saying that I should get up."

"Well . . ." she hesitated.

"I always thought that generals should be female." He seemed to go to sleep, and she put her Bible back in her knotting bag, thinking to steal out. But he opened his eyes again and said, "A Christmas house party, that's what we need."

"Go to sleep," she said. "You're looking all weedy again."

"If we were invited to a house party you could read me the entire Old Testament and no one would have the faintest idea that we were in such promiscuous contact. I'll deal with it tomorrow," he said, his eyes closing again. "Do you know, I'm tired. But it's not the fever-tired. Maybe you're the miracle, Miss Charlotte Whatever your name is."

"Humph," she said, just to leave him with something to think about.

Finchley was hovering in the hallway and she smiled at him. "I think that's a healthy sleep," she whispered. "He doesn't have that feverish look."

"The Lord be praised," Finchley said, and looked as if he might cry. "Your hackney is waiting, Miss Charlotte."

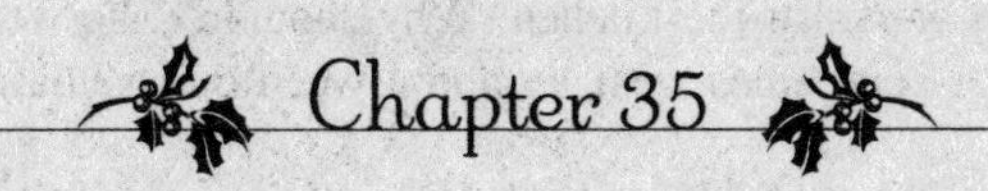

Chapter 35

"Just what do you intend to do now?" Poppy was incensed as she watched the door shut behind Elsie. "How am I supposed to ready myself for bed, let alone bathe? I can't sleep with all this powder in my hair!"

"Do you wash the powder out every night?"

"Of course!"

"I thought women slept with their heads upright so as not to disturb their curls. You never took your hair down when I visited your bedchamber."

"Certainly not."

"Well, why not?" He came up behind her and started tweaking her hair. "Even when I saw you in a nightgown your hair was always up; I thought you always left it so."

"I took another bath after your visits, naturally, so my maid would take down my hair then. What are you doing?" Poppy asked. She was starting to feel very peculiar. Even though Fletch wasn't interested in bedding her anymore . . . well, they were *alone*. Really alone. No maid waiting to bathe her. No maid at all.

"I'm taking all the pins out of your hair, of course."

"That young woman would have done perfectly well!"

"She was wearing an apron, Poppy. Did you see that apron?"

"She works in the kitchen. Why shouldn't she wear an apron? I sometimes wear an apron when doing household things."

"You didn't notice that the apron was bloody?" he enquired. "Because I did. It looked as if gentle Elsie had been twisting the heads off chickens with her bare hands."

Poppy had to admit that she was somewhat reluctant to be bathed by a chicken killer. "Ow!"

"I can't get this feather to come out. The long one in the back."

"Well, don't just pull!" But when Poppy put her hands up and tried to help out, he batted her away.

"I've got quite a few pins out," he said a minute later. "But this black stuff isn't coming out, Poppy. And the feather doesn't budge."

"It will wash out," she said. "If you leave now I'll wash it out in the tub."

"And just how are you going to do that yourself?"

She turned around and glared at him. A feather thwacked her in the eye and she brushed it out of the way.

"Those feathers are glued into your hair. Did you know that, Poppy? Your maid must be gluing them in and then cutting them out later."

She hadn't known that, but there was a great deal she didn't know about hair dressing. That's why she paid Luce so much.

"The problem is that we don't have a pair of scissors around here," he said. "I suppose I can ask the innkeeper."

He opened the door and bellowed down the hall before she thought to answer.

A moment later he waved a pair of scissors at her. "I'm going to have to cut out all that black stuff and the feathers. You'd better stay very still."

She backed away. "Are you jesting? You're not cutting my hair. I'll wash out the tar. And the glue."

"Right," he said, folding his arms. Poppy really hated the fact that he looked . . . well . . . so male. That was it. He was a big male, with a lot of muscles, and it naturally made her nervous. Actually, it made her want to run her hand up his arm, the part where the muscle was straining against the linen of his shirt.

"I'll scrub it out," she repeated. "So if you wouldn't mind leaving, Fletch, I'll get it done in a jiffy."

"Where am I to go? You want me to go down and ogle the King of Beggars?"

"I certainly don't care where you go but you can't stay here while I bathe."

"Why not? I've seen you naked, Poppy. Hell, I've kissed you all over naked. We've been married four years, remember? That side of our marital life is over. I think you need help." He picked up a strand of Poppy's hair and looked at it with a distasteful expression on his face. "Have you ever bathed yourself?"

There was something in his voice that sounded critical. "No, I have not," she said fiercely. "But neither has any other woman of my acquaintance."

"I was just offering to help."

Now he'd made her feel guilty for snapping at him. After all, what difference did it make? He'd seen her naked more times than she could count. And she could see tar clumping her hair powder. The itch was beginning to drive her mad. "All right. But I'm going to bathe in my chemise."

He shrugged. "I like to be really clean myself but I know many ladies aren't like that. One only has to walk into a ballroom in July to realize it."

"I *am* clean!" she snapped.

"Your choice," he said kindly. "It certainly doesn't matter to me what you wear in the bath. I might as well say it again, but that part of our marriage is over."

It was all quite embarrassing. Poppy started trying to untie her gown and realized that she couldn't unhook her sash by herself so it was just as well Fletch was there. He was working at the little hooks when she remembered what Jemma had said and started giggling.

"Thinking happy thoughts about Loudan again?"

He sounded rather unfriendly. "Jemma told me that men could come in quite handy on carriage trips," she said, feeling the laughter bubble up inside her again. "She was right."

He pulled her dress backward, off her shoulders and arms, and she stepped out of it. This particular dress had three separate petticoats sewn into it and it weighed quite a lot. Her stays laced behind, so Fletch started working on them and cursing a little under his breath. He certainly wasn't very handy. Poppy started thinking about the possum in the Ashmolean again.

"Those opposable thumbs are very important," she told him.

There was a ripping noise and her stays fell away. She spun around to find him holding up bits of lacing.

"They wouldn't come apart," he said with a silly grin.

Poppy put her hands on her hips. "Now what am I going to do without laces?"

"Well, you can't wear that gown again anyway." He turned it over with his toe and Poppy could see black marks on the sides. When she raised her eyes, Fletch was staring right at her chest. She looked down too and realized that she was wearing a chemise so light that the line of her breast could be seen through it. She even saw the pink tip of one of her nipples.

But before she could wrap her arms around her chest, his eyes slid away as if there was nothing interesting there and he said, "You get in the bath, and I'll try to wash out that tar."

Of course he wasn't attracted to her body anymore. After all, he'd had four years to sate himself on her, and that was more than enough. Plus, Poppy knew quite well that many women had really large bosoms compared to hers.

She lifted the hem of her chemise and stepped into the bath. She cast a quick glance at Fletch, but he was over on the other side of the room, looking out the window.

"It's snowing," he said. "A proper snowfall."

She could just see a blur of white over his shoulder. It made the room seem even smaller and more private.

"I'd like snow for Christmas," she said. She sat down in the water, thinking about what would happen to her chemise when it got wet.

Not that it would matter to him, anyway.

The wet cloth looked as fine as netting where it clung to her legs. She tugged it over her knees, but where it fell between her legs she could even see golden hair through the tissue-thin cloth. Quickly she brought her knees up to her chest, splashing water on the floor.

"Are you ready?" he said from the window.

"No!" If she wrapped her arms around her chest and kept her knees up, she was covered. Not decent, but covered.

"Yes," she said. "I'm ready."

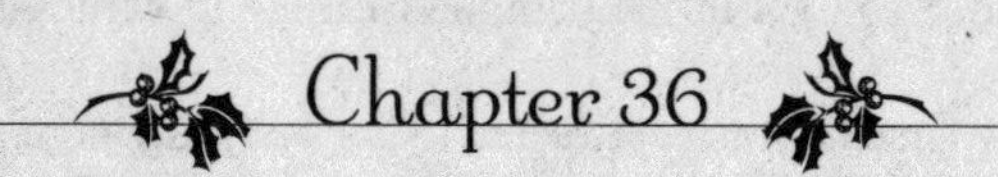

Chapter 36

Jemma and her husband were nearing the end of their game. If Jemma had to bet on it, she would say that she was winning, hands down. Beaumont had played the first game in this match with a fiery intensity, as if every move would determine the change of government.

But this game he kept moving carelessly and then talking of Fox's India bill, the French trade treaty, the brandy tax, the situation of Scottish peers in the House of Lords. Almost as if he wanted her opinion. And she would lay out the board for another game (for they had fallen into the habit of playing a side game, as they called it), and if she felt he was truly spouting nonsense, she would point it out.

She'd actually started reading the *Morning Chronicle* and the *Morning Post*, though she was careful not to let him know. There was no point in letting one's husband think that he was interesting; it would only end in disaster.

This night Jemma looked at the board and knew she had

him. There would be three more days, because of the one-move-a-day rule, but the game was over. "You didn't play this game seriously," she said, moving her queen to King's Four and taking his only remaining castle.

He moved a pawn in a hopeless gesture of solidarity toward his threatened queen. "True," he said. "But I wouldn't want you to think that I want any less to win."

"I believe it's competition that spurs you to play," she said. "Last game, Villiers was your competition, not myself. Without Villiers playing a parallel game, you can't bring yourself to play your best."

She didn't say the obvious: that if her assessment were correct, he didn't really care to win. And given that she herself was the purported prize for winning the match . . . well, there was nothing there that she hadn't known for years, was there?

"Fox's India Bill will be voted on any day," he said. "Shall we go to the country soon? My mother writes that she will remain in Scotland." There was no need to explain that comment: the dowager duchess was known far and wide as a harridan.

"We are having a house party," Jemma said. "I've just sent out invitations."

He was putting the pieces back in place and his hands paused for a moment and then continued. "Of course," he said. "A excellent idea."

Jemma felt nettled that he didn't show more reaction. "Shall I invite Miss Tatlock?"

The question hung in the air. She was deliberately baiting him, and why? Why?

"I would enjoy that."

So there was the answer to that question.

"Not her sister, though. I can't stand her sister."

"She dithers," he said, agreeing with her.

"Poppy and Fletch, of course."

"But not her mother," he said this time. "I can't stand her mother."

"Lady Flora is not fluffy," Jemma said feelingly.

"She's feral."

She laughed a little. "I'll invite that nice Dr. Loudan from the Royal Society," she said. "That will keep Fletch on his toes." Elijah looked amused once she explained. "Jemma the Matchmaker," he said. "It boggles the mind."

"Their marriage doesn't have to be over. They love each other."

"But if their intimate life is as terrible as you say—"

She shrugged. "Ours wasn't much better."

Too late she realized that she'd walked into a trap. "Our marriage," he said thoughtfully.

Jemma leaped from her chair. "Time to dress!"

He rose. "Perhaps . . . we could invite Villiers?"

"Villiers? But he's—"

"Alone. Servants, but—"

The Elijah she fell in love with all those years ago, appearing in such an unexpected way. "If we invite Villiers, the gossips will be overjoyed," she observed. "No one will believe he's dying. They will think I'm having an *affaire* with him under your very nose."

"When I think of him dying, I almost wish you were."

For a moment Jemma couldn't breathe. Then: "That certainly establishes my place in your life."

He was pushing in his chair and looked up. "Whaa—" And realized. "I didn't mean it that way."

But Jemma had had enough heart-wringing for the day. "It will serve you right," she said. "I'll nurse him back to health and then slip in his bed and prove all the gossips right."

There was something in his eyes—of course it wasn't

misery, though it looked . . . "I shall stoop to looking in key-holes," he said gravely.

"And why would you do that?"

He took a step toward her. "You are my duchess, Jemma."

"I have been so for years."

He tipped up her chin. "You kissed me the other night."

"A moment's aberration," she said, the words coming in a whisper.

"Kisses are like a claim of possession, don't you think?"

They were so close that she could feel the warmth of his body and suddenly remembered how large he was compared to her. How different his body was from hers. He didn't wait for her to come up with a clever riposte. He simply bent his head and kissed her breathless.

"Possession," he repeated, his voice a little deeper than normal.

And left the room.

Chapter 37

Fletch was afraid to turn around. It felt as if a spell had been cast over the room, a sweet, sleepy spell of privacy. The snow was like the brambles that grew around the princess's palace—the one who slept for one hundred years. If only they had one hundred years, without servants, without Poppy's mother, without all the Your Gracing and My Gracing.

The windows were steaming over as snow began to twirl and fly on the other side of the window. Perhaps the storm would prove bramble-like and keep them trapped in a snug bed together.

He could just see the gold of Poppy's hair reflected in the window, and the curve of one shoulder. She'd sat down with her back to him, of course. Her hair fell in lumpy coils, black mixed with the gold, and two feathers jutting out behind. It fell below her waist in the back.

The innkeeper had left some liquid soap, but Fletch couldn't imagine that it would work on that tar. Still, he picked up a basin and scooped some water out of the remaining bucket.

"I'm going to pour this over your head."

Poppy clasped her arms tighter around her chest and nodded.

He let it fall down slowly. Artistically. He poured a little to the right so that her chemise flattened against her shoulder blade, and then ran down her back. Moved to the left so that he could see the delicate pink of her skin through her chemise. She started shivering.

"The chemise will make you colder," he said. "And it's not clear to me how you can *wash* through cloth."

She just bent her head and said, "Will you wash my hair now, please?"

He got some more water but there was a lot of hair. The smell of lavender powder was starting to nauseate him so he sloshed on more water. Then he poured out the liquid soap and began rubbing it into her hair. She stayed quiet for a moment, but then she started protesting, and giving advice, and directions.

"Poppy!"

She shut up for a moment.

"Have you ever washed anyone's hair?"

"No."

"Well, I've washed my own, and I'm doing yours exactly the same way."

"But it hurts," Poppy said. She had stopped covering her breasts and was holding onto the sides of the tub instead. "This tub is going to tip!"

"I have to put some muscle into it," he said. "Your hair is a mess." He picked up a part that seemed all matted together. "Ug! Should I just cut it off?"

"No!" she squealed. "Don't! I can get out the snarl. I'm sure I can get it out."

"You could always wear a wig while it grew out," Fletch said. "I think it would be easier to wear a wig. You can't tell me that your maid bathes all of this out of your hair every night."

"Yes, she does. Sometimes it takes some time."

"How much time?"

"Usually not over a couple of hours," Poppy said. "Ow!"

"A couple of hours!" Fletch stopped trying to get his fingers through snarls of hair. "You're wasting a couple of hours every night on this? And what about the nights when I came to your bed—you would stay up for *two more hours* washing your hair?"

Poppy blinked up at him. Wet rat tails hung over her eyes. "Sometimes when I'm very tired, I almost fall asleep, but I cannot sleep with powder in my hair. It starts to itch horribly after a day. On a bad day I can be absolutely crazed by supper time. It's hard to sit still."

Fletch stared down at her. "Poppy," he said slowly, "would you say that your head was itching when we were making love?"

She went still for a second and then, "Only sometimes." She sounded like a guilty little girl. He stared down at her head feeling as if dawn had just broken over his head. Maybe . . . "You're shivering. You need to take that wet chemise off. You're liable to freeze." He walked over to the fireplace and put on another log. "I'm not watching. Take it off, Poppy."

He heard the sound of a wet cloth slap the ground. He poked at the fire again, thinking hard. He had to go slow. Very slow. Pray for snow. Tell her that he had no interest in her body. Make her trust him.

Which meant no sex tonight. Every muscle in his body, including his favorite, protested.

He had to make this work, because it had to be permanent. He was slowly starting to realize that he didn't even know his wife. How could he not have known that she was waiting through those hours he lavished on her body, desperate to wash her hair?

He remembered trying to touch her hair and she always protested. He had given in, of course, because everyone knew that ladies' hair took hours to arrange. The bucket of water next to the fire was still warm; he picked up the dipper and poured it over her again. She squealed. He saw her peeking to see whether he was looking at her naked self.

He wasn't. He wasn't, because if he actually looked at all that pink skin sitting before him like the most delectable sugarplum of his life, he'd fall on her like a ravening animal.

Instead he walked behind her, like a man who has no interest in marital beds. He poured more soap into her hair, grabbed the comb, and started trying to get out the tar in earnest. Fifteen minutes later he was getting worried. "It won't come out. I'm going to have to cut some of it, Poppy. Especially this long part." He picked up a long rat tail that fell down her back. It was tangled up with the feather and the tar and God knows what else.

Poppy looked up at him and to his horror, he saw a tear slide down her cheek. "Are you sure?"

"I'm sorry. Look."

She looked at the matted snarl and a few more tears fell down.

"It doesn't matter. You can wear a wig. Why do you need all this hair anyway? It makes you itch. You're better off without it."

"But then—" she sniffed adorably, so he got her his handkerchief. She buried her face and said something.

"What?"

"I'll be so ugly," she burst out, looking up at him with her bottom lip quivering. "And unfashionable. You hate unfashionable women!"

If only she knew. If only—he kept his eyes above her collarbone. "That's irrelevant, Poppy." He said it in his most friendly voice. "Your mother told you the truth about men: we don't stay attracted to one woman very long. I love you, and I want you to be comfortable. I don't care about your hair!"

She sniffed again and wiped away a few more tears.

"That doesn't sound as if you love me."

"Well, I do." He grabbed the scissors. "I would love you even if your hair was as short as that possum's."

He could see a few more tears on her cheeks, but she bent her head and didn't say anything, so he started cutting.

After a bit he said, "Poppy?"

"Yes." Her voice was muffled because she'd drawn up her knees and hidden her face in them.

"Did you know that there are snarls in your hair, next to your scalp?"

"What?"

He cut one out and showed it to her. "See? It's all matted up in there. I don't think your maid was actually combing your hair all the way through in the back."

She shuddered and started to cry again, loudly this time. "Just cut it off," she cried. "Go ahead. It doesn't matter."

So Fletch did. He clipped here and snipped there. He tried to save the parts that he could get a comb through, but all the tar had to go.

"I think the problem is that she's been gluing feathers into your hair in back. And then I suppose she would cut them out if they wouldn't wash out."

"That is so disgusting," Poppy said.

"I'm finding the tips of quills," he said. "It's a menagerie in here."

"More like an aviary," she said sourly.

"I'm surprised. I always wondered how women managed to get their hair up in the air and have it be three times their height. Now I know."

"Sometimes Luce puts a cushion inside," Poppy said. "How else can she make the plumes stay up? The plumes I wear for formal occasions are sixteen inches long. And I've been thinking that it's not really her fault. Most women leave their hair up between stylings, even with the feathers attached, but I always insisted on washing it, every night."

"I found a hair pin," Fletch said. "Look—it has a diamond head."

"It's only from yesterday," Poppy said crossly. "You're making me feel hideously unclean."

"If the shoe fits," Fletch retorted. But she looked so mortified that he relented and said, "At least you never smell, Poppy. I can't bear the way women smell like hog's grease."

"The powder sticks to grease too much and make me itch; I use tallow instead."

"Tallow!" That explained a lot. Fletch ruthlessly cut out a few more pieces of hair matted with candle wax.

"I'm going to find another maid," Poppy said. "I never liked Luce."

"Then why on earth did you keep her?"

"My mother found her. She's French. And she does the most wonderful frizzes on my hair. Remember Lady Salisbury's ball?"

"Your hair was as high as a Babylonian tower."

"It was beautiful."

Fletch cut out a few more chunks and they fell over Poppy's shoulder. She picked them up with a shudder and dropped them on the floor.

"What I don't understand is why you never noticed what your maid was doing. Or not doing, to be more exact."

Poppy sounded cross as the dickens. "Ladies don't brush their own hair."

"Ladies don't do this, ladies don't do that. I'm glad I'm a man."

"If I were a man," Poppy said, "I would go to Cambridge University and became a famous naturalist."

"Dr. Poppy, the world's expert on dog possums," Fletch said. "There, I think I'm finished." He pulled a comb through the hair that was left.

"I still need to take a bath," Poppy said. "This water has grown quite unpleasant."

Fletch picked up her gown and threw it strategically over the mirror in the corner. Then he grabbed a toweling cloth and handed it to her.

She looked at the small cloth and then at him.

"I'm not interested, remember?"

Her eyes were asking a question, but he forced himself to smile. "I'll go downstairs and tell the innkeeper that we need this bath emptied and fresh hot water."

He was so hard it actually hurt to go down the stairs. That had to be a first.

Chapter 38

Fletch stayed downstairs while Poppy took her second bath, which gave her time to pull her gown off the mirror, burst into tears again at the sight of her shorn, hacked-off locks, then climb into a steaming tub of fresh water and get clean. Really clean because she washed her hair herself: ran her fingers through every strand, rather than sitting there passively while her maid did it for her.

Never again, she vowed to herself.

It wasn't until she was toweling herself by the fire that she realized that *never* applied to lavender hair powder as well. There was no point in making herself look perfect every day. Her husband didn't desire her.

Oddly enough, the knowledge stung. "Dog in the manger," she muttered to herself, shaking out her hair and throwing it back over her shoulders. It weighed almost nothing, which was a delicious feeling. The steely truth was that she may not want him—at least to make love to her—but she wanted him to desire her.

Her heart ached, which was idiotic. She had lain there for years suffering agonies of embarrassment—and yes, itching—and generally just waiting for it to be over. Why, why, why would she want him to do that again?

She didn't, of course.

It was just that this room was so small, and he seemed so large. She hadn't been able to stop looking at his chest. He'd got wet washing her hair, and his shirt had clung to him. He was warm and hard and muscled in all the places where she had no muscles.

That was probably it. After all, she was a naturalist. His body was as different from hers as if he were a flying squirrel. His hair was silky and glossy whereas hers—she shuddered. How could she not know the state of her hair?

No wonder he didn't desire her.

She would never desire anyone who had disgusting matted bits in his hair. Of course, Fletch's hair was the kind of hair you could brush against your body and it would feel like satin.

Her skin was red from the scrubbing she'd given it, and her scalp felt clean and free. No more powder. No more tallow. No more feathers. No more frizzed hair. No more French maid.

There was a noise at the door and she hastily leaped under the covers. Fletch poked his head around, raised an eyebrow, and then ushered in a footman with an empty bathtub.

"They're in shock down below," he said, once the old tub had been removed by weary men. "I don't think the kitchen has ever heated this much water, not if it was bath day for the whole parish. They'll be sending up a few covered plates for our supper, since our trunks are back at the Fox and Hummingbird, and we can't dress for the meal."

"I'm clean," Poppy said. She should feel humiliated but she didn't.

Fletch started to pull his shirt out of his breeches. "It won't bother you if I bathe, will it?" he asked.

She shook her head as he undid the buckles at his knees.

"You've seen me naked enough and you never turned a hair."

"That's not true," Poppy said, averting her eyes as he pulled his shirt over his head. "When we first married, I thought I would throw up from pure nervousness every time you came to my room."

He blinked at her, his hands caught in his waistband about to pull down his breeches. Poppy felt herself redden. This was all so intimate. She'd never seen him undress. He came to her room sedately clothed in a dressing gown, ushered through the door by her maid. Somehow it felt different when she saw the way his chest expanded from the waist of his breeches. And he had a dusting of black hair on his chest, but it didn't hide the muscles. They bulged under his skin in . . .

"You felt as if you were going to throw up?"

"My mother threw up the first time," Poppy said. "Goodness, it's hot in here, isn't it?" She flapped her hand in front of her face.

"Your mother vomited?"

"Oh yes. Many women do, you know," Poppy said, chattering to cover up the fact that it was—he was making her feel quite peculiar.

"They vomit?"

"It's just such a shock. And so—well—"

"Unpleasant," he said, his mouth tight now. He pulled off his breeches in one smooth gesture.

Poppy felt the most peculiar sensation in her stomach. Fletch's legs were long and golden-colored. His flank was a smooth curve. Everything about Fletch was beautiful. He had his side to her so she couldn't see his privates. *That* wasn't beautiful, of course, as her mother had pointed out long ago.

Fletch lowered himself into the bath and threw his head back. His hair slid backwards like black embroidery floss, just the way that Poppy's was going to do from now on. He was so beautiful that she felt her mouth go dry. The sweep of muscle, golden skin, and there—between his legs—

She couldn't imagine how he kept it from being visible all the time, the way it stood out from his body like that. He must have to keep it penned in, the way her stays trapped her breasts. He had his eyes closed, so she leaned back against the pillows and looked.

He looked, well, elegant. Powerful.

The whole sight made Poppy start shivering a little, because it made her think about how he used to come over her and say, "Poppy, are you ready?" And she always nodded because she was desperate to get it over with. And then he would rub there, against her, and sometimes . . .

The memory of it made her feel feverish between her legs and she turned her head away.

Fletch, meanwhile, closed his eyes more tightly and smiled to himself. Things were going along quite well. A tiny sprig of hope was blossoming in his chest.

"Will you wash my hair?" he said, leaning his knees against the sides of the tub so that his wife could have her fill of looking, if she wanted. "You could pull on my shirt."

She could hardly say no, so she came behind him and started washing. He arched his back into her hands, and gave a little stifled groan.

Her hands froze. "Are you all right?"

He thought she sounded breathless. "It feels so good," he said hoarsely, laying it on as thick as he dared.

"Oh, good," she said, rubbing his head harder.

By the time she had finished, he'd thought up another scheme. "Poppy, would you mind washing my legs? I'm so large that I'm afraid I'll turn this tub over." He rocked it a little to illustrate and water splashed onto the floor.

"Don't do that!" she said. "I don't want those footmen up here again. They already think that we're half-cracked."

He reached out a long leg. "Would you mind?" If he said so himself, his legs were fine, though his crown jewels were what he really wanted her to inspect. She looked as pink as an Easter cake as she rubbed a cloth over his ankles. He bent his knee so that she could reach his thighs more easily.

She kept stealing looks at him, so finally he did her a favor and threw back his head (he was starting to get a neck cramp) and closed his eyes again. "Thanks, sugarplum," he murmured.

The cloth was inching up his thigh. He didn't dare even take a peek from under his lashes because if she looked interested he would have to throw the tub to the side and leap on her. That wasn't in his plan.

He let her get close to the crown jewels, but not close enough to touch. "Would you mind doing the other one?" he murmured, pulling his right leg back.

But instead of a slow caress of his ankle, a cloth rubbed him so fast and hard that he probably lost half his leg hair. Two seconds later she was tossing a towel in his direction and he was wondering what went wrong.

Probably it had to do with the jewels themselves.

Damn it, if most women threw up—and he'd never heard that before, but what did he know?—perhaps she was feeling a little nauseated. He knew damn well that he was a lot bigger than most men.

Not that it had ever done him any good, he thought morosely.

"What do we wear for nightclothes?" Poppy asked.

While he was standing in front of the fire, drying himself, she had tucked herself into the bed. She had her eyes rigidly on the far wall, the better not to see him, he supposed.

Damn.

"I'll get something," he said, pulling on his breeches and shirt. It took some rearranging to fit everything into its proper place, since certain parts of his body didn't seem to have recognized that the game was up, for the night at least.

All the way down the stairs he told himself that he didn't desire her. OK, that he did desire her, but that nothing was going to happen. Nothing. Nothing. He was as neutered . . . as neutered. Think St. Albans, he told himself. You think St. Albans walks around in this state?

The thought was certainly dampening, though his body paid no attention.

What was a bit more dampening was the vision of himself and Poppy dressed in the landlord's night clothing. The man had offered a nightrail owned by Elsie, but Fletch thought cleanliness might be an issue. So when the landlord offered two clean nightshirts, he grabbed them.

In the end it wasn't so hard to rein in his inner devil. Once they had eaten, and were back in bed, Poppy told him the idea she'd had about the possum and its strange thumb. And then he started to tell her about his talk, and she liked it so much that he actually got up and gave it. Without notes. Striding back and forth in front of the fire, the landlord's nightshirt flapping around his knees.

At first Poppy kept breaking into giggles, but he saw exactly when she started listening. And he saw when the spell was broken and mentally dropped the next two paragraphs and swept into a conclusion.

She clapped and he felt so proud that he was grinning like a maniac. "There can't be a lord in the house to disagree with you!" she cried.

"It's just because of some advice from Beaumont," he said. "You see, it's all about telling a story, rather than actually parsing out the arguments. And then you pointed out that it would be better to be clear and simple—"

But she was giggling again.

"What?"

"It's your—your *thing*," she said, covering up her mouth, "when you don't have it trapped in your breeches, it's so hopelessly odd-looking, Fletch! You have to forgive me, but—" and she broke into peals of laughter.

Fletch looked down and there it was, proudly tenting the front of the blasted nightshirt. Well, he couldn't expect any different. Poppy was drowned in acres of fabric, but her hair was curling in adorable ringlets, and she was the prettiest, sweetest, most delicious thing he'd ever seen.

He sighed.

"It's a man's curse."

"I know," Poppy said, sobering. "I shouldn't laugh. After all, you never laugh at my breasts, do you?"

"Never," he said with absolute truth.

"And yet they're just as odd in their own way. I mean, if I ever have children they'll leak milk and even now they bobble all around, and once in a while they actually fall out of my dress."

"Very odd," Fletch said. "Odd. Very odd." And then because he couldn't think of another thing to say that didn't involve close contact with those breasts, he suggested they go to sleep.

So he snuffed the candle and climbed back into the featherbed. The snow had stopped a while ago; to Fletch's regret it seemed likely that they would be able to leave in the morning. This storm wouldn't keep them in the bed for a hundred years.

He was lying on his back, staring up into the darkness of

the rafters when a small hand crept into his. "I'm so happy that you came to Oxford with me," Poppy whispered.

He was too. But he was afraid to tell her why in case he ruined it all.

"You're my responsibility," he said, a bit roughly. "I'll always look out for you, Poppy."

"Thank you," she whispered back.

He thought she sounded a little disappointed, but maybe it was just wishful thinking.

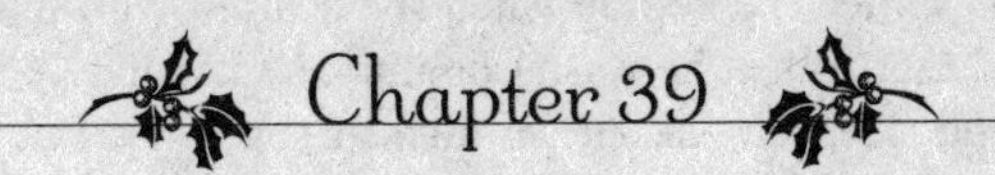

Chapter 39

It was only as Charlotte climbed out of the hackney the next day that she realized that she'd forgotten to put her Bible in her bag. Not that it really mattered, but she had convinced May (who thought her visits were scandalous) that she was succoring the dying by reading biblical passages.

"He's worried his immortal soul is lost," she had explained.

May dithered, torn between distrust and an innate wish to help. "I just wish there was someone else who could do the succoring," she had said over and over, wringing her hands. "Why must *you* be the one to read aloud the Bible?"

"No one will think anything of it, if they learn of it."

"They certainly will!"

"Not if he dies," Charlotte had said.

"Oh!" May had said. "It seems so . . ."

But Charlotte had stayed up half the night thinking about it. "I don't see how Villiers can possibly survive. He's had a fever for months now. He's thin as a rail and stretched . . . you can see it. It's a terribly cruel way to die."

"Oh, dear," May said.

"If there's anything I can do, I shall."

May wrung her hands again but they both knew Charlotte had no choice. Yet for all Charlotte talked of death, she had a plan. Villiers perked up when she sparred with him. He needed that. When he wasn't fighting, he lay quietly in his gray and sleepy room. He let himself slip away. But when she insulted him and fought with him, he woke up.

It probably wouldn't work. But it was the only thing she could think of.

She walked into his bedchamber, ready to insult him, and stopped. Villiers wasn't alone.

Propped against the window on the far side of the bed was a lean man with a rugged face. His eyes were black as midnight, with great circles under them, as if he'd had no sleep. Even tired, there was no mistaking those sharp-cut cheekbones; she looked from Villiers to the stranger and back again.

"Look at that," the man drawled, not bothering to come to a standing position. "Your churchifier has shown up and damned if she doesn't see a resemblance between the fanciest man in the *ton* and myself."

Villiers had been lying with his eyes shut. His skin looked translucent to Charlotte, drawn tightly over his cheekbones. He opened them now and looked—with the same eyes as his relative—at Charlotte. "There you are, Miss Tatlock," he said. He smiled too, that sweet smile that came so rarely.

She walked over to the bed and looked down at him. "I came to read you the rest of that story I began, but I forgot my Bible."

"Do tell," the man by the window said. " 'The Song of Songs,' Villiers?"

She would have thought he was horrible except there was

something strained in his voice, as if he too were trying to wake Villiers up, make him answer by taunting him.

"The story of Jesus's birth," she said. "His Grace was quite curious to find out how it ended."

"Badly," came the voice from the bed. "It ends badly, like so much else in life. My dear Miss Tatlock, I find I am hideously tired today."

She tried to think of something to say.

A thin hand waved. "My cousin. You see, I *do* have family. Someone has to be duke after me. It's taken months, but my solicitor just managed to track down the man himself."

The future duke grinned at Charlotte, his teeth white against his bronzed skin. "It's killing him to admit that such a shaggy type as I will take over the title." It was true that he wasn't very elegant. His coat was rumpled and hung open. He was wearing a cravat, of a sort, but it looked nothing like the gorgeous pieces of linen that dukes tied around their necks.

"Cruel," Villiers said. "Handing over my exquisite house, not to mention my collection of walking sticks, to this sad excuse for a gentleman."

"Your name, sir?" Charlotte asked.

"Miles Dautry. I wouldn't want to be rude, Miss Tatlock, but I think that the duke should preserve his strength at the moment."

He was evicting her. But she couldn't do that before she tried to rouse Villiers. "How can His Grace possibly relax when the dukedom is going to one such as you?" she asked, sitting down as if Dautry hadn't spoken. "The very name Villiers is known for exquisite judgment, style, taste . . . no wonder the duke cannot rest."

There was a moment of stunned silence in the room. Then Villiers started chuckling. It was weak, but a chuckle. And he opened his eyes and and peered at his cousin.

"A mess, isn't he? I'm so pleased that you agree with me, Miss Tatlock. I should have taken him on while I was still on my feet."

"It's not too late," Charlotte said quickly. "You could teach him all the ways of being a duke. How to dress."

Dautry snorted but he didn't say anything, which meant that he saw her plan. He raised an eyebrow at her and she gave him a quick frown, willing him to fall in.

Villiers waved his hand again. "Too late. I think the man has never polished his nails. He probably only owns one pair of stockings—"

"Not true," Dautry said. "I have several."

"Undoubtedly all worsted," Villiers said with a sigh. "And his coat . . . just look at his coat, Miss Tatlock. I may be sick unto death, but even I noticed when that coat entered the room. My only pleasure is that I get to flee this cruel world before a man wearing that coat becomes duke."

Charlotte looked. Dautry was singularly broad in the shoulders, wearing a black coat that had nothing to distinguish it but the fact it was made of linsey-woolsey. And it was rumpled.

"I rode all night after I got the message," he said.

"I see just what you mean, Your Grace," Charlotte said. "It's a disgrace. A disgrace to the name."

Dautry's eyes narrowed. "What about you, Miss Tatlock? After all, you are surely here hoping to become a duchess?"

She blinked at him.

"I know your type," he said. "You're hanging out for a title and merely pretending to do a bit of good works. I expect you hoped Villiers would rally."

"No," Charlotte said. "I was planning to snare the heir. That means you . . . if I hadn't had a *look* at you first! Now I shall have to reformulate all my plans."

Villiers started laughing weakly. "Help me up, Dautry.

She's got you there. No decent woman will marry you when you look more like a dock-worker than a duke. And then what will happen to my poor estate? Handed from man to man without a woman's intervention?"

Dautry looked around the bedroom and curled his lip. He still hadn't unfolded his arms. "I don't want to insult you, but the house shows signs of a woman's hand, though you never bothered to marry one."

"There's nothing manly about being a sartorial disgrace," Villiers said, looking truly awake now. "Dautry, you'll have to submit to my tailor. Dying man's last wish."

Charlotte couldn't grinning. "Don't forget the barber," she said, her voice as sweet as syrup. "No woman would marry a man who looked like a shag-bag."

"I think you should do the same for Miss Tatlock," the future duke said, his eyes narrowed. "Look at her gown. I'm surprised that you can tolerate being in the same room with it. Plain serge and tucked in the style of two years ago."

"I almost forgot," Villiers said. "I'm planning to find her a husband. What Miss Tatlock needs is a philosopher. I don't suppose you know any?"

"What a lucky little hymn-singer," Dautry said, his eyes flicking over her plain gown. "I'm afraid that philosophers rarely venture to sea. We prefer men who *do* rather than just think about it."

"She must wear colors," Villiers said dreamily. "Brilliant colors, jewel colors." He seemed to be turning a little pink and the words tumbled out in a manner that Charlotte recognized.

She bit her lip and looked to Dautry. He came over to put a hand on Villiers's forehead. "A cool cloth, if you please," he called to the footman outside the door.

Villiers's eyes closed again.

"Miss Tatlock," Dautry said.

It was time for her to leave.

"Strawberries . . . embroidered taffeta," Villiers murmured.

She could feel Dautry's eyes on her as she picked up her knotting bag. Then, just as she was leaving, he said: "I trust that you were not indeed hoping to make yourself a duchess, Miss Tatlock?"

She didn't pretend to misunderstand him. She didn't want to turn around, because her eyes were shining with tears, but she did. "I don't even know him, sir. He gave my name to the valet by accident whilst in a fever, I believe. So, no. But I wished that reading the Bible would keep him alive."

"I would agree with you there," he said with a rueful twist of his lips.

"He's been ill for months," she said. "Why weren't you here? He's so alone."

"I had no idea he was indisposed. I met him once, at seven years of age. I scarcely recall the event, and I certainly had no idea he'd fought a duel. Fool, at his age."

"He's not so old!"

"Cut velvet," the duke suddenly said. "With roses." His cheeks were stained with color.

"Too old to be fighting duels," Dautry said.

"I've never seen you before at any event."

He leaned back against the window and crossed his arms again. "So you're not just a good Samaritan happened off the street, but a member of the so-called *ton*?"

"It happens by birth and you, sir, are in the same dire predicament," she snapped.

"Actually, no."

"You are a future duke."

"An unlikely duke, and I never spent much time thinking about it. I only inherit due to a younger son two generations back who fell in love with the daughter of a sailor and went to sea."

"A sailor!" Of course it all made sense now. He had a windswept look about him, and there were crinkles at the corners of his eyes, for all he couldn't be more than thirty. A duke's son turning sailor. What a scandal that must have been! Charlotte couldn't help grinning. "Did she run away to sea with him?"

He raised an eyebrow. "Celebration from a dulcet young lady of the *ton*?"

She picked up her knotting bag again and slipped through the door. He followed, but stopped in the doorway.

"Don't you ever stand straight up?" she demanded.

"I like to know where the nearest solid support is."

"You're not on board ship now."

"I wish I was."

"Don't let him turn you into a duke too easily. You have to fight every inch of the way, do you hear?"

"Damned if you don't sound like my mother," he drawled.

The words thumped to the bottom of her stomach and she felt the old maid she was. "Well, goodbye."

"Wait a minute!" he said. "He's going to remake you as well."

"You need to get to know him," she said, halfway down the stair and not turning around. "He'll forget me. He doesn't remember things well. You can take care of him now."

"He's going to put me in cut velvet with roses." The future duke's voice was so disgusted that she couldn't help smiling.

"It will suit you," she said. She couldn't say what she really thought: that there probably wasn't enough time for a tailor to fashion a whole costume before Villiers slipped away. Charlotte went out the door.

May sighed with relief when she heard that a member of Villiers's family had appeared. "Well, of course there had to be an heir!" she trilled. "Trust the man to show up only at the deathbed."

"It didn't seem to be like that," Charlotte said. "I didn't get the impression that he cared much for the dukedom. I think he's a sailor and had no idea of the duke's infirmity. He only met the duke once."

May's rounded mouth was as circular as her cheeks. "A sailor! A sailor as the next Duke of Villiers. That's—that's—*awful.*"

"Yes." A tear rolled down her cheek.

May gave her a sharp glance. "You have to put Villiers out of your mind, Lottie." May only called her by her childhood nickname in moments of the greatest distress. "I know it's difficult, but life is like that. Here! Here's something that will help." With all the éclat of a conjurer with a rabbit, she pulled a franked letter from her pocket. "You remember how we thought that the Duke of Villiers's letter was from Beaumont?"

"Beaumont wrote to me?" Charlotte said, more puzzled than anything.

"No, the duchess did! Perhaps she's having another dinner!"

Charlotte tore open the sheet. "She's invited me to her estate for a Christmas house party."

May gasped. "Christmas at the duchy! You must go. Though it only begins just before the twenty-fifth."

"It isn't clear that the Parliament will adjourn until the last minute," Charlotte explained. "I thought you wanted me to stay away from the duke."

"A house party is different."

"How so?"

May bit her lip. "It's what you said."

"Beaumont isn't attracted to me?"

"And this proves it, don't you see? The letter is from the

duchess. She would never invite you if the reverse were true."

"I did tell you so," Charlotte said wearily.

"You must go." May came over and sat down next to Charlotte. "Villiers is going to die soon, isn't he?"

Charlotte nodded miserably.

"Go," May said. "Go."

Chapter 40

Poppy came back from Oxford looking as odd as a shorn sheep and without a maid, so Jemma sent a messenger to a brilliant young hair cutter she'd heard talk of, Monsieur Olivier.

A day later Poppy looked as pretty as a peach, with soft, short curls around a bandeau. "You'll set a new style," Jemma told her.

"I don't care, as long as I don't have to wear that horrid powder anymore."

"I've heard of people being sensitive to powder and coming out in red blotches," Jemma said. "Villiers never touches it."

"I shall be judged horribly unfashionable, but it doesn't matter," Poppy said. "I'm married."

"True," Jemma replied, somewhat startled. "Though I never considered dress to be relevant to marital status."

"I've always dressed with the wish to impress Fletch."

"I dress for myself," Jemma said. "Sometimes I spend all day in my dressing gown. But if I do dress, I make myself ravishing because then I feel ravishing."

"I never feel ravishing."

"You are ravishing, so why ignore the evidence? Here." She handed over a piece of foolscap. "What do you think of my house party? These are the people who've accepted my invitation. I'm composing a plan of battle for the estate butler. It's all very annoying that I've never met the staff; I hate relying on unfamiliar help."

"My goodness," Poppy said, eyeing the list. "How many people did you invite?"

"Not many," Jemma said. "I want this to be an intimate party. And besides, with Villiers ill upstairs, we can't be too celebratory. It wouldn't be proper."

"Proper? It's scandalous."

"I never worry about scandalous," Jemma said. "I just worry we will all become sunk in gloom. If he is doing well, we'll have a huge Twelfth Night party."

"Did Villiers agree to come?"

"He did. The only thing that makes me sanguine about his improvement is that he sent me a great many detailed instructions. For one thing, he requested that Miss Tatlock be invited. Isn't that peculiar?"

"You mean Miss Fetlock?"

"Yes."

Poppy scowled.

"I see you've reached the same conclusion I have," Jemma said, adding a note to her list. "Beaumont asked Villiers to make sure his *inamorata* would attend. But the curious thing is that I told Beaumont myself that I would invite her."

"Why on earth did you do that?"

"I was testing him. Or myself," she added wryly. "At any

rate, he said he would be very pleased if I would invite La Fetlock, so I would judge the testing a failure, wouldn't you?"

"Very foolish on both your parts," Poppy observed. "Especially yours."

Jemma smiled at her. "A few months ago you wouldn't have said that."

"What else did Villiers request?"

"He said that he was worried about the state of his soul—which doesn't bode well for his health, I have to admit—and he wants a few philosophers from Oxford to come to the party. To debate with him."

"How odd!"

"He can't possibly be as ill as is reported if he wishes to hold debates in his bedchamber. What's more, he wants unmarried philosophers. Most peculiar. And he's bringing a tailor and a mantua-maker and may bring a bonnet-maker as well. A bonnet-maker, Poppy! Do you think that he's utterly cracked?"

Poppy didn't know and she couldn't stop herself from asking the only question that really interested her. "Do you think I should send a note to Fletch? I haven't seen him for two days and while, naturally, I don't really care what he is doing for Christmas, I thought he might be interested in my curiosities. Perhaps I'll bring them with me."

"It's better for him not to know where you are. And that goes double for your mother. She is not invited, by the way."

"My mother," Poppy said gloomily, "wishes me to pay her a visit at my earliest convenience."

"Let me say again," Jemma said, looking alarmed, "that I may well cancel the house party rather than have your mother, myself and Villiers under one roof. The last time I met your mother in Paris, she told me that I was a daughter of the game. I don't think that was a compliment, do you?"

"My mother never compliments," Poppy observed. "I can translate the phrase for you, if you wish."

"No, don't. I prefer to think of it as referring to chess. I find it so wearying to be insulted."

Poppy leaned over and gave her a quick hug. "You are not nearly as degenerate as you pretend, do you realize that?"

"Actually, I'm twice as much," Jemma said promptly. "You're just too innocent to see the truth of it. Speak to my long-suffering husband on the subject."

"Husbands live to be thwarted," Poppy said mischievously. "Or so a very wise woman told me once."

Poppy stepped out of the carriage before the Duke of Fletcher's townhouse—her own residence—with a surprising little fillip of homesickness. There was no particular reason for that; Poppy had lately realized that she had only resided in the house. She had never really made it her own.

The house was, in a strange way, like her life. Sometimes she felt as if she'd never lived at all, just let her mother be the puppet master.

That thought had her walking through the front door with her jaw set. As Quince ushered her into the drawing room, she saw in a moment that her mother had not merely lived in the house: she had transformed it.

The walls were covered with red-flecked brocade. Huge sconces sprouted from the wall beside the fireplace, gleaming with a combination of brass and gold, candles thrusting in all directions. The fireplace itself could hardly be seen due to a screen set with an embroidery of cabbage roses and edged in a confection of frothing gold scrolls. The furniture had all been gilded to match.

"Mother?" Poppy asked, smiling at the butler to dismiss him.

Her mother rose from the depths of a brocaded sofa with all the elegance of Marie Antoinette herself on a Court Reception day. A positive forest of feathers bristled above her towering hair; her shoulders were bare though it was morning, and her dress was as formal as the rest of the room. In short, she looked like the portrait of a duchess.

"My daughter," Lady Flora said, holding out her hand.

Poppy curtsied and kissed it.

Lady Flora backed onto the sofa and sat down. In truth, she would probably only fit on the sofa, given the size of her side-panniers. Poppy sat across from her and waited.

Sure enough, there was a shriek. It wasn't a trilled exclamation of female alarm either. It was something like the full-throated bellow of alarm that Poppy had read certain monkeys uttered.

"Your hair!"

"I cut it."

Her mother touched her own hair, the horror on her face transferring perhaps into some sort of dread that someone had taken a scissors to her without her notice. "Why—why—you stupid girl, why would you do such a thing? You look like a common shrimp seller! Don't tell me that Luce had a hand in this!"

"I terminated Luce's employment."

"You terminated Luce! Luce! One of the finest French maids in England?"

She actually gaped. Poppy suppressed a smile. "She had been gluing feathers into my hair, Mama, and then cutting them out. I couldn't allow that to continue."

"How she achieved her effects is none of your concern! You should merely admire the effects. And Luce would faint to see you now; at least you were *à la mode* when she was with you!"

"My hair had to be cut off to remove the snarls." Poppy

eyed the towering series of curls atop her mother's head. "Do you have any idea how many snarls might be inside your hair, Mama?"

"You sound like a common street girl," her mother said, ignoring the question. "And you look like one too. A good French hairdresser isn't found on the street corner. You're going to have to find one immediately, before anyone sees you. I did want to tell you that I am gratified by the way that you have not advertised your stay with the Duchess of Beaumont. I have managed to keep it from the majority of my acquaintances."

Obviously, her mother was not acquainted with the sort of person who attended the Royal Society lectures. "You said you wished to speak to me, Mama?"

"It is time for you to come home. I am holding a *soirée* tomorrow to celebrate your return to your rightful position. I have reformed your house—and your husband. The young fool has a mistress now and should bother you no further."

The odd pinch at Poppy's heart only lasted a moment. He wouldn't lie to her. "Fletch doesn't have a mistress, Mama."

"For God's sake, don't insult both of us by lowering your speech to your hair," her mother said. "Fletch! Fletch! He sounds like the unfledged baby that he is. I have addressed him as Your Grace, and I'll warrant you that he liked it. Men always do. I summoned you, Poppy, because it is time to stop being so foolish and take over your rightful place as the Duchess of Fletcher."

"But I thought you were enjoying it," Poppy said.

The words fell into the drawing room like small stones.

Lady Flora narrowed her eyes and for the first time she actually looked at Poppy. "So that's it, is it?" she said softly. "You're jealous of your mother?"

"I am not jealous of you," Poppy said. She hated that tone

of voice. Any moment her mother was going to start screaming. Her brain was telling her to rush into speech, to patch over the wrong, to apologize, grovel . . .

Lady Flora rose to her feet. Feathers swayed above her head like a crowd of gossiping ladies. "Just what did you mean by that comment?"

Poppy rose as well, taking time to shake out her skirts. Then she met her mother's eyes. "I thought you were enjoying living in this house. You have certainly made it more ducal."

"I merely brought it to the correct standard."

Poppy said nothing.

Lady Flora took a step toward her. "You don't like it? After I spent months of my life, decorating the house that you were too stupid and timid to change into the appropriate dwelling for a duchess, you don't like it?"

Poppy wanted to step backwards, if only because spittle hit her cheek, but she merely wiped it off.

Her mother's voice rose. "You are jealous of my beauty and my refinement! You take after your father and it is *not my fault* that you are such a pitiful substitute for a duchess. I did my best! I raised you to your station in life!"

And then her hand flashed and she slapped Poppy across the face.

It was such a blow that Poppy's head whipped backward and she fell back a step. But in some odd way, it wasn't very painful. Since she had expected it.

Lady Flora threw herself back onto the couch and began to sob in a fashion that indicated to all who knew her—and Poppy had no doubt that Fletch's staff knew her well by now—that a full-fledged fit of hysterics was about to erupt.

Poppy stooped and picked up her brocaded bag. Then she said, "Mama."

Her mother raised her head and glared. "You are too much for me. What did I do to deserve such a fate?"

"I am leaving," Poppy told her. "I love you. But I don't wish to see you again. You may stay with Fletch for a period of time, if you wish. Certainly hold your *soirée* tomorrow. But then I must ask you to return to your own establishment."

"I forbid you to go back to that house of sin!" her mother shrilled, suddenly forgetting her tears. "The Duchess of Beaumont is as much a disgrace to her title as you are. She's a trull, who should be walking the streets in the dark instead of poisoning the very title she holds. I heard it on the best of authority that she is paying Lord Strange a visit this Christmas—at *Fonthill*! No one frequents that house but fornicators!"

"Goodbye," Poppy said.

Her hands were trembling, but she didn't stop, not even when her mother bellowed her name. She just reached out and pushed open the door to the corridor. She felt oddly detached and yet calmly triumphant.

She had done all that she could.

Quince took one look at her and began to stammer. Poppy put a hand to her cheek. It stung and was likely quite red. An appalling noise was beginning in the drawing room. "Do you help my mother—" she began.

But the front door swung open and a footman ushered in Fletch and his friend Gill.

Poppy's hand flew back to her cheek but the moment their eyes met, she knew it was foolish to try to conceal it. In one stride he was pulling away her hand.

Then it was as if all the footmen and the butler faded away, leaving no one but the two of them in the antechamber. Fletch's hair fell over his eyes and he put one arm around her and pulled her close. Without saying a word he bent to kiss her bruised cheek.

"It's all right," she whispered to his chest.

He put her from him, just enough so he could look down in her face and said, "No, it's not all right."

Gill was sending the butler and the footmen scurrying in all directions. Then he whisked himself away into the library.

"I knew what she would do," Poppy told him.

"You *knew*?"

"My mother has a temper. I knew that if she were pressed, she would strike me. She's never been able to resist it in moments of greatest fury. I said something that made her furious."

"I'm going to kill her." Fletch's face had utterly transformed. He didn't look pretty, as her mother called him, now. He looked violent, like flame and gunpowder mixed, like a man who would take on a mob with his bare fists.

"No," Poppy said, smiling at him although the motion made her wince as her cheek was starting to swell. "I caused it to happen, Fletch."

"That's absurd!"

"I've thought about it quite a bit in the past few months. I decided that I would be her daughter only if she never struck me again. Until I went to Jemma's house, you see, I never had a chance to think about it."

"How could you not tell me!" His voice was tight with rage. But not at her.

"Oh, she hasn't struck me since our marriage began," Jemma said. "And not for a considerable time before that. I'd become very good at appeasing her, you see. As long I had behaved well—"

"By marrying a duke." His hands fell from her shoulders.

She nodded. "True. I married a duke. But I really thought I was in love with you, Fletch."

"I can hardly believe that you were thinking clearly on the subject."

"Perhaps not."

Something came between them, the cold ugly truth of it. And still her mother's grating sobs echoed through the door beside them.

"Your mother must leave my house," Fletch said, and the level of barely controlled violence in his voice made Poppy shiver.

"She will. I humiliated her, you see. And I told her she had to leave. I've never given her instructions before."

"I'll see to it. I suppose—I suppose you don't wish to stay?" And without giving her a chance to answer. "Why would you?" He lifted his head and bellowed, "Quince!"

"Your Grace," the butler said, popping back out of the green baize door with an alacrity that suggested his ear had been pasted to the door.

"My coach waits outside. Her Grace will return to the Duchess of Beaumont's house. And for God's sake, could you send someone in there to stop that caterwauling?" He jerked his head toward the drawing room.

Poppy swallowed. "I would think that Mother will stay two or three days, just enough to show me that my command was not important. She holds a *soirée* tomorrow, and then she will leave shortly after that. I know her quite well, you see."

"So do I," Fletch said grimly. "Go home, Poppy. I am—" for a moment the rage dropped from his face and he looked starkly anguished. "I am just so damned sorry that my house wasn't a safe place for you."

"It hasn't always been like this, Fletch. You are seeing my mother at her very worst."

His mouth tightened again. "I don't wish to see her again in any form, ever, Poppy. Is that all right with you?"

Guilt almost sapped her strength, but then she said, "Yes." And then, "Yes." It helped to say it twice. To live her own life, to cut free the puppet strings.

She turned and allowed the butler to wrap her in her pelisse and then walked to the carriage.

In Poppy's mind, she turned her back on her mother. She walked proudly, without a backward look.

But to any story, there's always another side. Had she looked backward, she would have seen her husband, standing with a look of absolute despair on his face. In Fletch's mind, she had forgotten to say goodbye to him, but then, why would she?

The ugliness behind their marriage had solidified into something much worse than mere lack of desire on her part.

She walked away from him as if she never cared to see him again. Which made sense. He was nothing more than the man she was forced to marry by threat of violence.

He threw open the library door and Gill jerked his head up. "I'm going to St. Anne's Hill, if you wish to come."

Gill rose. "Where's your wife?"

"Left."

"St. Anne's Hill? You mean Elizabeth Armistead's residence? And—"

"I mean to pay a visit to the courtesan I told you about, Cressida. She's charming. You'll like her."

Gill shot him a look. But a friend of the heart knows when the moment comes to hold his tongue, and there was something in Fletch's face he'd never seen before, and he'd just as soon never see again.

If Cressida could make that look go away, Gill would happily throw her a purse himself.

Chapter 41

On the way to the Duke of Beaumont's country seat
December 15

"Are you all right, Your Grace?" Finchley asked for perhaps the five hundredth time.

Villiers ground his teeth and thought about whether pulling one of the side arms out of the carriage pocket and shooting himself would answer that question. But why bother?

He was no fool. He'd never felt worse in his life. Even lying flat during the whole damned carriage ride didn't make any difference. A gun wasn't really necessary.

"I'm dying," he snarled at Finchley. "How in the bleeding hell do you think I feel?"

"Irritable," Finchley rejoined. "You're not dying, Your Grace." His poor valet was one of the few who refused to accept the truth. "You're on your way to a Christmas house party, just as you always do at this time of year."

"More fool me," he murmured. The fever was coming on again. He knew its calling card by now. It came in as inexorably as the tide of the ocean and swept him under. He tossed about in a red haze on the brink of succumbing, as undirected as a piece of jetsam.

"Where's Miss Tatlock?"

"She'll join us at the duke's house."

"Where's Benjamin?"

There was no answer.

"Barnabe?"

"Who's Barnabe?" Finchley said. "Your Grace?"

"Dautry? My cousin?"

"He'll join us as well," Finchley said soothingly.

But he was slipping away. One of these days he'd stay under, but at that moment the carriage lurched, and jolted his side. The pain was so excruciating that he woke up again with a cry.

"I'm sorry, Your Grace." Finchley sounded close to tears and that sobered Villiers as much as the pain. "We'll be there soon, I promise. Another hour or two, that's all. I shouldn't have let you do this."

It was the right thing to do, though Villiers had no energy to explain it. He'd had two friends in his life, Benjamin and Elijah. Elijah had turned into the Duke of Beaumont, a pompous politician. Benjamin was gone.

He'd ask for Elijah's forgiveness, politician or no. For what, he didn't know. He couldn't remember their quarrel now. It happened so many years ago, but it took place at Beaumont's house, so it made sense to go there.

Say goodbye, he thought dimly. Make it all right. And then he let himself slip away again where it didn't hurt quite as much.

He didn't wake up for hours, not til he'd been slipped between linen sheets. What woke him up, finally, was the bellowing. Well, that and the fact that someone had slipped a knife under his arm pit.

"Christ," he panted. "Christ." He flailed a bit, tried to open his eyes, panted. Dimly thought that he expected to fade onto the red tide, not leave in a wash of icy pain. It didn't seem fair. The knife turned again. "Bloody hell!" And he managed to pry his eyes open.

There was a big man standing over him, a kind of rustic monster with a bushy beard. With one huge paw he was holding him down and with the other he was doing . . . something to his shoulder. Something that was so excruciatingly painful that all Villiers could do was pant. He tried to twist away and humiliatingly, couldn't even stir under the great hand holding him down.

"Hold on," the man said in a sticky Scottish brogue. "I have to get this wound cleaned out or you're done for."

Villiers would have said something, would have protested, would have—it wasn't a red tide this time; it was a black wash that covered his eyes and threw him off a cliff.

"Thank God for that," Dr. Treglown said. For the country bear was a doctor. "Ach, and this is a benighted mess, it is. Who in the bloody hell's been taking care of the duke, then?"

"The surgeon, Dr. Banderspit," Finchley said. "Is it because I wouldn't let him bleed the duke? He kept wanting to bleed him and I wouldn't allow it. Is it all my fault?"

Dr. Treglown rolled his eyes and started pouring something over the wound that smelled like acid. It even smoked a little. "You'd have killed him for sure if he'd been bled, so there's a happy thought for ye. With this infection in him, he must have the constitution of a bloody ox to have survived this long."

"What are you doing?" Finchley whispered.

"Cleaning the damn thing. Disgusting."

"We cleaned it," Finchley said anxiously. "We did clean it with lots of brandy, just as the surgeon told us to, until it finally healed over."

"Brandy! Chaw!"

Finchley wasn't sure what "chaw" meant, but he didn't mean to enquire. There was the master, lying as still as death. "Are you sure he's not gone?" he asked. "He's looking—bad. I can't see him breathing."

"He is bad," the doctor said, turning away to wash his hands. "Didn't you see what came out of that wound? It was killing him."

"But it was all mended on top," Finchley said miserably. "I didn't know . . ."

"No reason you should have," the doctor said. "Yer not calling yourself by the name of 'surgeon,' are ye?" His sneer was frightful. "This time we're keeping it open, you hear? You're going to wash that wound four times a day with spirits of turpentine." He put a black bottle down on the bureau with a clink. "Yer duke here is going to yell like the devil when he comes around enough to notice what you're doing. You'd better prepare yerself. And I'll stop by tomorrow night. If he lives til then, he might survive. Or he might not."

"Oh God," Finchley moaned. "And it's Christmas."

"Not yet," Treglown said. "There's a few days still. I expect you'll know fairly soon whether he's going to blight the ceremonies by tumbling into the grave. Wash it again in six hours. You'll have to do it during the night too."

"Yes, sir," Finchley said. "Yes, sir, I'll do that."

"When's the rest of the party coming? Beaumont himself and the duchess? We've never seen her, you know. She flit off to Paris before coming to the country. My patients are all beside themselves with excitement."

"In a few days, as I understand it."

Treglown chuckled. "It'll make an unusual house party,

I'd say. Dying duke howling off in the rafters. It sounds like one of them women's novels to me."

Finchley looked around at the gracious old bedchamber. The Duchess of Beaumont had sent orders ahead to put Villiers in the royal suite. He would like the irony of it, if he woke up long enough to see it.

"Lots of liquids, if you can get him to drink," Treglown said, taking himself out the door. "I'll try to stop back later, if I can. There's babies sprouting all over the place, and the midwife's just had one of her own. I hardly have time to deal with the handiwork of asinine London *surgeons*!" He snorted and left.

Finchley looked at his master.

He was lying on the bed, as straight as a board, as if he were ready to be measured for a coffin.

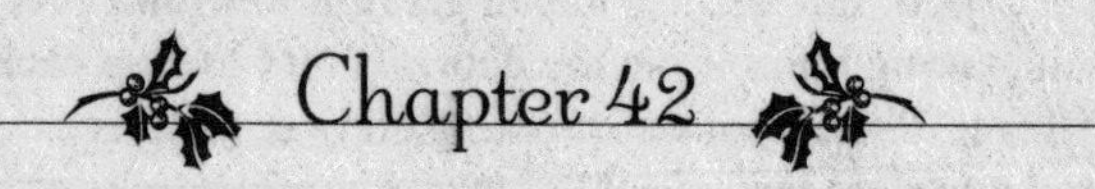

Chapter 42

December 20

Beaumont's country estate was near Sturminster Newton, in Dorset, at least three days from London. As soon as they had travel rugs tucked around them and heated bricks snuggled against their toes, Poppy blurted it out. "Do you think that Fletch will follow us?"

"That is the fourth time you've asked me that question since we sent his invitation," Jemma said. "I haven't a different answer from last time: I don't know. But I do think that repetition points to something, wouldn't you say? You're not acting like an estranged wife, happy to dance off to Paris for years."

"You said you cried for months," Poppy said weakly.

"I cried because I was broken-hearted. But you are an odd combination of anxious and cheerful."

"He says he still loves me," Poppy said with a rush.

Jemma gave her a crooked little smile. "You see? Your marriage and mine have no similarity."

"Although he doesn't desire me anymore."

"I don't believe that."

"My mother said that men are fickle and lose interest in a woman's body after a number of years. Fletch agreed."

"In my experience," Jemma said, "a man is quite happy to greet anyone who shows up ready for the business, as it were. If there's a smiling woman in his bed, he won't make a fuss about it."

"Well, Fletch said—"

"You can't listen too carefully to what men say. Perhaps he wants you to desire him," Jemma interrupted.

"But that's not—well—"

Jemma looked at her shrewdly. "Are you sure?"

"How do you know when you desire someone?"

"I feel like taking his clothes off," Jemma said bluntly. "It's easier to know when you don't feel desire. For example, when you see Lord Manning, do you feel that it would be very nice to stroke his tummy?"

"Absolutely not."

"Good. Now replace that image with one of Fletch. Would you like to stroke his . . . tummy?"

Poppy couldn't help laughing. "You are absurd, Jemma."

"Men's bodies were made to be admired. That's one thing that your mother seems to have forgotten. You are lucky: you've got a husband who seems interested in paying your body appropriate attention. Now you just have to learn how to do the same to him."

"He doesn't feel that way anymore," Poppy said, feeling a prickle of sadness.

Jemma snorted. "We'll see if he comes to the house party after the note I sent with his invitation."

"What did you say?"

"I mentioned that I was inviting naturalists and philosophers, so he would find the party remarkably tedious. By the way, a footman brought me a note this morning that Villiers has arrived before us."

"How is he?"

"I don't know. Beaumont told me that he'd trade our marriage to have Villiers live. I was furious."

"So would I be!" Poppy put in.

"But part of me agrees with him. Villiers is—"

"I've never met him. What is he like?"

"He's charming, wry, fierce, arrogant and incredibly clever. And he's a chess master," she added, as if that explained everything.

On their third day of traveling it was already dark before the carriage rocked to a halt at the Ring O'Roses inn. The innkeeper ran out gibbering with excitement over the visit of not one duchess, but two. "Your servants have everything ready for you, Your Graces," he kept saying, rubbing his hands together.

"Wonderful," Jemma said.

"His Grace has already arrived as well," the innkeeper told Jemma.

"Really? I thought Beaumont had a last session of Parliament. I was beginning to be afraid those men would never close down this year. He must have ridden like the wind to catch up with us."

But when they walked into the inn it was clear that the dukes had been confused, for Poppy glanced into the common room as they passed the open door—and stopped. There was a tall man sitting at the back of the room, leaning against the rough wooden wall. His silky hair was tied back. He was wearing all black. He looked every inch a duke.

As Poppy stood there, fixed to the ground, Fletch looked up and saw her. He lifted a tankard in greeting.

Suddenly her entire body melted with racing excitement. She lifted her hand and waved to him, as if she were a five-year-old again. He was sitting with his legs stretched out before him. And he wasn't quite as elegant as formerly. His coat hung open, and he wore a plain neck cloth.

It made her feel queer, so she almost ran down the narrow corridor after Jemma.

Jemma took one look at her, and said, "Well, I gather Beaumont is still debating the end of the civilized world."

"He came," Poppy whispered. "He's here."

"Sharing your room?" Jemma asked with a mischievous look.

"I don't know!"

"How many rooms have we for the party?" Jemma asked, turning to the innkeeper.

"There's the three of you with the best rooms in the house," he said anxiously. "And then six more for your entourage. I hope that you'll find everything to your satisfaction, Your Grace."

Poppy's heart fell a bit. She dreaded making love to Fletch. So why would she want him to share a room with her?

"I told you he was tired of me," she said to Jemma under her breath.

"Why don't you go to his room naked and see what happens? I'll bet you my best chess set that you spend the night in his room."

"It would be so embarrassing," Poppy muttered, appalled that she was even considering it.

Jemma and Fletch teased and flirted all the way through supper, while Poppy sat there tongue-tied, feeling like a stupid younger sister.

He'd brought a copy of *The Tatler.* "I didn't have time to read it," he said, "but I understand that your house party is viewed with disapprobation, Jemma."

Jemma snatched the paper from his hand. "Let me see that!" She bent over it. "This isn't about my party, but about *you*, Fletch. My goodness. I gather your recent speech in the House was a remarkable success."

He blinked. "When did *The Tatler* begin reporting on political matters?"

"Why don't I just read it?" Jemma said. "*It appears that the young Duke of Fletcher gave a short disquisition*—what on earth is a disquisition?"

"A speech," he said, looking rather embarrassed. "I gave a speech about the French trade bill."

"According to this, your speech caused the entire House of Lords to leap to their feet shouting in support. The paper maintains that any peer who dares disagree with you proves himself to be as false as he is covetous. Good work, Fletch!"

Poppy leaned forward and touched his hand. "Indeed."

Their eyes locked for a moment.

"Apparently there were calls on the floor that Fletch should be made the Secretary of State on the spot," Jemma continued. "And it says that the opposition party is shaking in their boots at the idea of the duke's rhetorical power being wielded against them."

"Foolishness," Fletch said.

Poppy just smiled at him.

Jemma turned the newspaper over. "Oh dear! Here's the bit about my party. It's really about my brother. They think that all duelers should be sent to France, given the Duke of Villiers's imminent demise. I'm sure that includes sisters as well. For, and I quote, 'the crime of base vulgarity.' Vulgarity!" she repeated. "I'm sure I'm never vulgar."

"The word only describes the actions of other people?" Fletch enquired.

"Naturally. I put a whole host of words in that category."

"Such as?"

"Virgin."

Fletch burst out laughing. He hardly even glanced at Poppy; he was so busy flirting with Jemma. And yet she couldn't take her eyes from him. He'd shed that overly precious air he used to have, though his coat still fit across his broad shoulders without a wrinkle.

"Surely you too have a group of words that you would never apply to yourself," Jemma said. "Doesn't he, Poppy? Help me. Let's see . . . limp?"

"Only applies to other men," Fletch said promptly.

Poppy hadn't the faintest idea what they were talking about, but she smiled.

"Phoenix is a good word," Fletch said. "No matter how the flames burn, it always rises again."

"What are you talking about?" Poppy asked.

Jemma was giggling, but Fletch said, "Vulgarities," and then shut his mouth.

Her mother said that a lady should never acknowledge a vulgarity but pretend the solecism didn't exist. "Could you explain it to me?" she asked.

The serving maid let out a giggle too, which made Poppy even more curious.

"You do the honors," Jemma told Fletch.

Fletch blinked. "The phoenix in question is a man's privates."

"Of course," Poppy said. "And the fire is syphilis?"

"No!" he said hastily. "I'll explain the other part of the reference later."

"I think I understand it. Shakespeare talks of castles melting away, *like the baseless vision of a dream.* Your phoenix, I gather, doesn't melt away."

In answer to Jemma's laughter and Fletch's look of shock she said, "I have been married for four years. And I spend a great deal of time working alongside beneficiaries of the

Charitable Society for the Reception of Repenting Prostitutes."

"You alarm me," Jemma said, grinning at her.

"Did you see the new print by George Townly Stubbs called *His Highness in Fitz*?" Poppy asked.

"In Fitz?" Jemma asked. "Do you mean to say, *in Mrs. Fitzherbert*?"

Poppy nodded. "He is clothed. But Mrs. Fitzherbert isn't."

Fletch chimed in with a print he'd seen of the prince called *The Morning after the Marriage,* and Poppy, feeling that she'd proved herself less than a idiotic innocent, went back to watching her husband.

He still had the little beard, just enough to cover the dimple in his chin, but she actually liked it. He looked more manly with it. Not at all pretty, as her mother used to call him.

Fletch wasn't pretty. Not a bit. His eyes were black in the center, but with a ring of odd gray-blue color around them. With his hair pulled back, and no powder, he looked as wild as the men who roam the American forests, wrestling with alligators and catching possums.

Suddenly Poppy realized that the servant bringing their dishes was sending Fletch a kind of signal. She kept brushing her bosom against his shoulder, for example, and leaning down next to him to offer a spoonful of this or that, so that even Poppy could see straight down into her bosom.

Her breasts were much bigger than Poppy's. Huge, really. And the way she kept licking her lips was absolutely revolting.

Finally the girl managed to pry herself away from Fletch long enough to come around to Poppy's side of the table and offer her a pyramid cream. The creams were shaped in mounds, and looked just as shaky as the girl's breasts, to Poppy.

She took another drink of her wine while she thought about it. Meanwhile the girl brushed some crumbs off Fletch's lap—his lap! And Fletch didn't seem to mind.

The girl came again to her to pour her some tea, her distaste barely concealed. And why? Because Poppy didn't immediately understand the phoenix joke? She bent down and Poppy looked straight into her enormous breasts.

It was the work of a moment to scoop up her pudding and drop the rounded thing straight down her bodice.

The girl shrieked and leaped in the air.

Poppy stood up and smiled sweetly. "Oh my goodness, it must have slipped right out of my hand," she cooed.

The innkeeper came to the door, took one look and grabbed the girl by the arm. They could hear him all the way up the corridor. "I've told you and told you," he was shouting. "Save those Bartholomew wares of yours for them as wants them. You've disgraced me one too many times."

Jemma was laughing again. "It's like the phoenix, hatched out right before my eyes!"

Fletch stood up and stretched. He could almost reach the ceiling. And that put his crotch level with Poppy's eyes. His breeches were tight as possible. They outlined his muscled thighs as if they'd been painted on.

"Wife," he said lazily, "you're frightening me."

Poppy stood and tossed her hair. It felt wonderful to feel her hair move with her body. She flounced down the corridor before him until a large warm hand curled around her waist.

A deep voice said in her ear, "I really should give you a scolding, Perdita."

"That girl deserved what she got!" Poppy snapped, looking over her shoulder.

He laughed down at her and the blood raced recklessly through her veins. "There's hardly room in your bodice for a pudding," he observed, looking down. "Though it would be interesting to use them as a plate."

Her gaze followed his. From this angle, her breasts didn't look meager. Oddly, she felt a prickling all over as if he might touch—

But he took her arm and started walking down the corridor as if nothing had happened.

The one thought in Poppy's head was that she was too late. She was no fool. The depraved warmth between her thighs meant desire. And she would quite like Fletch to eat pudding from her breasts.

She'd found it.

She'd found that desire for her husband that Jemma talked about, and it was only her stupidity that meant she'd found it four years too late.

Chapter 43

Poppy thought there was a chance—all right, a remote chance, but a chance—that Fletch would come to her room that night. Perhaps just to say good-night? She took out her curiosities to show him, in case he knocked on the door.

But no.

So she lay in her bed and examined the crystalline structure of her geode again. Then she picked up the little statue of Cupid and Psyche. When she bought it, she thought only of the outspread wings of the butterfly. It was a marvel, the way an insect made of stone could look so airy, as if it were on the verge of flight.

But now she looked at Cupid, kneeling before his beloved Psyche. This was no plump, pouting Cupid as is often depicted, but a lithe youth with tumbled hair and long, lean flanks. She found herself running a finger along his naked back, over the muscles in his legs. His wings were not stone lacework, but powerfully muscled, thickly feathered, ready to carry him straight from the ground to the sky.

She couldn't help thinking that in choosing the piece because of the butterfly, she had overlooked something far more interesting than a stone insect.

Even when she put the statue and the geode away, she couldn't sleep, but lay awake and had the most peculiar thoughts. It was as if she couldn't live in her own skin. Her mind kept skipping off to Fletch's room, and thinking of him without his shirt on, the way she saw him when he took a bath. And in her imagination he would stand up from the bath and shake himself, and water flew in all directions.

Poppy wiggled around in the bed, trying to get comfortable. Even thinking of Fletch made her feel most—

He would stand up and water drops would slide down his chest, down, down to that private place. In truth, she rarely looked at him, not for at least the first year of their marriage, because she was so afraid that she would throw up, the way her mother assured her she would.

But after all, what was there? An odd thing, a thing that stood out like—like a bar from his body. That looked pink and yet felt hard.

But remembering how it felt between her legs seemed utterly different now. It felt as if she were all melting there, and as if she would quite like Fletch to—

She turned over again. What was happening to her? Even licking her lips made her feel a bit feverish. And she was all damp under the covers. She pushed back all the quilts. She still felt boiling hot, so she pulled up her nightgown.

But that was all different too. For there her body lay in the moonlight. She stared down at herself. It felt almost as if a fairy had come along and exchanged her body for another, like the old stories about baby swapping. Those were definitely her breasts. Except they looked plumper, somehow.

And her nipples were a very nice color, she thought. She'd seen the kitchen maid's nipples because of the way her dress hung open and they weren't nearly as nice.

Plus her legs were long and—she sat up—they were a nice shape, as these things go. Her mind kept skittering all over the place, and now she was remembering Fletch kissing a line up the inside of her thigh. Except when he did it her head was itching so much that she felt as if it was on fire, and all she could remember was staring down at his head and thinking, *please finish, kiss faster, please kiss faster!*

Now . . . She let her leg fall open a little bit. She wished he was kissing her right now. Her hair was all loose and she'd brushed it out herself. She was developing a bit of an obsession there, and had to brush it over and over herself every night. But it wasn't bad. She liked the way her hair felt soft and silky under her fingers, not the way it used to when her maid was crimping it every day and gluing things into it, and rubbing it with tallow to make it the right shape.

If Fletch were kissing her now, he would kiss right up the pale part of her leg, and then higher, by her knee. She shivered a little bit, thinking about it and wrapped her arms around her chest. Which made her breasts start tingling. And then he'd kiss higher, one had to think, and then . . .

Of course he would kiss her breasts. She touched where he would kiss her. And then . . .

And by the end of another hour, the night was turning itself inside out, into a velvet shell in which her body was lying as she thought of Fletch doing this, and Fletch doing that. And finally she kept thinking about one night, when her hair hadn't been so terrible, and Fletch had been kissing her—there.

At the time she hadn't thought of it as kissing, but in a coarser more embarrassed sort of way. But now she remembered it as kissing, and she couldn't help remembering, again and again, what it felt like, and how she'd almost moaned once.

And then she couldn't help making little noises; after all, she was all alone and snug under the covers, in the great blackness of the inn and it felt as if she wasn't herself, not Poppy. She was some other woman, one of those women Fletch used to watch in Paris.

She had lived in Paris, after all. She knew exactly how a woman looked who wasn't a lady. The kind of purr in her voice, and the invitation in her eyes.

Poppy just never realized that she wasn't a lady either.

It made a great deal of sense to her that at the most bewilderingly lovely moment of the night, she found herself thinking in French.

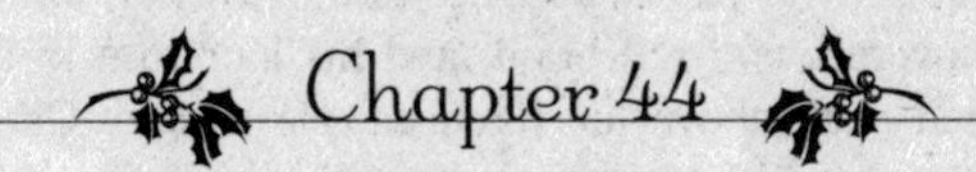

Chapter 44

Country seat of the Duke of Beaumont
December 21

Charlotte was very disconcerted to find that she had arrived before her hostess. But she knew how it happened: the duchess had undoubtedly taken her time on the road, whereas Charlotte and May had found the least expensive way for her to get to the party, which involved taking the stagecoach and then hiring someone to drive her and her maid from the coaching inn to Beaumont Manor.

The butler didn't say anything, of course. He merely bowed, and mentioned that perhaps she wouldn't mind a quiet evening, as the other guests had not yet arrived. Charlotte put her chin up and swept past him, trying to pretend that it was the duchess's fault for not arriving, not hers for being early.

The seat of the Duke of Beaumont was surrounded by

miles and miles of formal park, from what Charlotte had seen on the way in, and the house itself was just as grand. It was so large it resembled a cathedral from the outside, at least to Charlotte's mind. And inside the ceilings were so high one could hardly see them in the gloom and there were innumerable doors and corridors leading off here and there.

The butler was just as bad; he wore livery that was absolutely covered with red braid, and his hair rose in a stiff powdered peak above his forehead. He looked, Charlotte thought, rather like a bishop, but wearing his hair instead of a miter.

"I suppose the duchess has not assigned me a room?" Charlotte said meekly, half running to keep up with him. "I am sorry to put the household out."

The butler, Mr. Blount, unbent a little and said, "Her Grace sent all her instructions ahead of time. She is most organized."

They were walking along on the second-floor corridor when suddenly there was the most awful bellowing. Charlotte squeaked and dropped her knotting bag. It sounded like an animal was in pain, except that it was definitely a man.

The butler stopped as well. "I am most sorry for the disturbance, miss," he said majestically. "One of the guests is less than well."

"The Duke of Villiers?" Charlotte said, feeling her face break into a smile. "Is he here already?"

"Indeed," the butler said, disapproval showing in every twitch of his hair.

Another shout broke out and this time she realized it was from just down the hall. It was like a call to arms: she couldn't ignore it. Before the butler could stop her, Charlotte opened the door and walked in.

A horrible sight met her eyes. Villiers was bare to the waist, and being held down by two footmen while Finchley poured something that literally smoked onto a terrible wound in his side. Finchley turned and saw her; his hand wobbled and dark liquid fell on Villiers's chest.

The duke was staring straight up at the ceiling but he snarled, "For God's sake, get it over with Finchley! I can't take much more of this."

"Miss Tatlock," Finchley stuttered.

"What are you doing," she demanded, snatching the bottle out of the manservant's hand. "Just what do you think you're doing to him?"

Finchley's mouth fell open but it was Villiers who answered her. "I'd love to say that he is slaying me, but he's under doctor's orders."

"Well, what kind of doctor would suggest this!" She waved the black bottle. For some reason, she was boiling angry. She turned on the butler without a bit of the timidity she felt before. "Just who is this doctor?"

It took Villiers's laughter, weak but present, to make her stop interrogating the butler. And Finchley.

"Damn it, you have to make me stop laughing," he said, gasping a bit. "It hurts!"

"He's that much better, Miss Tatlock," Finchley said earnestly. "Truly. Dr. Treglown is a miracle, he is. He opened the wound and it was all infected there, like you wouldn't believe. We've been treating it for days."

"I might survive," Villiers remarked. "I hope you're ready to fall in love, Miss Tatlock."

The butler drew in an insulted breath and rose to his full height. "In love! Is that it? I wondered at the temerity of this young person, the way she burst into a man's bedchamber, the way—"

Villiers lifted his hand and shot him one icy look and the butler stumbled to a halt. "She's not in love with me, Blount. Nor yet will she be. But you had better prepare yourself if you're running some sort of puritan household here. You do realize that your mistress is the Duchess of Beaumont, don't you?"

The butler drew himself up again, a strange mixture of pride and dismay struggling in his face. "Her Grace is our every thought," he announced.

"Excellent. This is one of Her Grace's most highly thought-of guests, Miss Tatlock."

"I am aware," the butler said, bowing with a snap. "If I may, I shall take Miss Tatlock to her chambers. I was just escorting her there so that she could clean off her travel dirt."

I've made an enemy, Charlotte thought. She saw Villiers's eyes on her shabby traveling costume and suddenly she realized for the first time that she was, indeed, inside a duke's bedchamber—and he was unclothed.

"That mantua-maker," Villiers said suddenly. "I brought her along. Miss Tatlock must see her immediately. The plan," he said to Charlotte. "The plan!"

Oh lord. The butler was looking at her with positively virulent disapproval at this evidence that a young miss was allowing a duke to pay for her clothing. There could be no greater evidence of her status as the proverbial Whore of Babylon. "Mr. Dautry?" Charlotte ventured. "Surely his transformation is more important, Your Grace?"

"Damn, I'm tired," Villiers murmured, closing his eyes again. "I forced Dautry to see the tailor and he protested like a sheep taken for shearing. You, Miss Tatlock, will be my masterpiece. And I've made certain there will be plenty of young men here for you to choose from."

Finchley looked at her in an unmistakable signal, and she backed from the room.

The butler stalked ahead of her, every inch of his livery wiggling with indignation. Even from the back his hair could be seen cresting above his head, trembling with the shock of it.

He deposited her into a bedchamber with all the ceremony one might give a second housemaid. "I will request the mantua-maker to attend you, *if* she happens to be free at the moment," he said, staring over her shoulder.

"That would be most kind of you," Charlotte murmured.

Chapter 45

Fletch was in a state of repressed exuberance.

In the space of a few days he had fallen into a pit of despair, pulled himself out, decided to follow Poppy to the country even if she didn't love him, and would never love him . . . and now look what was happening. From the moment they got in the carriage, Poppy hadn't been able to meet his eyes. She turned pink when he touched her. In fact, he couldn't stop himself from violating his own rules and "accidentally" running his hand down her hip as he helped her into the carriage.

In the old days, Poppy wouldn't have noticed or, if she had, she would have thrown him an annoyed look, quickly covered over with a sweet smile. But this time she blinked and gave a little gasp. In fact, Fletch thought he'd never seen anything quite as pretty as the way her cheeks turned rosy. What woman blushed these days?

So Fletch spent his time in the carriage planning the next

twenty-four hours of his marriage like some sort of military campaign. Jemma, meanwhile, spent her time fretting about how long it had taken them to reach the house, due to a broken axle. "At this rate, not only my guests, but Beaumont will be there before me."

"That's a good thing," Poppy said. "The duke can welcome everyone."

Jemma opened her mouth but said, "That's not—you don't understand."

"Even the most wonderful hostess is unavoidably late sometimes," Poppy said encouragingly. "And you sent such detailed instructions beforehand. I'm sure—"

"I've never seen it," Jemma said, her words hard like little acorns. "I'm hosting a Christmas party in a house that I've never seen, with a staff whom I don't know from Adam. And now my secretary has left me."

"You still have three maids and a personal maid," Poppy said. "And I'm there, Jemma. Plus, Isidore is coming; she's likely already there."

"Everyone's coming," Jemma said, still looking flustered. "Louise will be there already, and Harriet, of course."

They said it at the same moment. "Louise!"

And then Fletch could have cut his tongue out because Poppy shrunk back in her seat and suddenly she didn't look like a rosy poppy anymore, but like a prim Englishwoman. He cursed silently, while Jemma obliviously totted up the guests who should arrive before her.

"Villiers, of course," she said. "He's been there for a few days at least; they decided to go to the country immediately. I just hope that the butler has done everything I instructed him to do for his care."

"Of course he has," Fletch said, feeling rather impatient.

"Oh, and the naturalist," Jemma said. "Dr. Loudan."

Fletch couldn't help scowling at that. He stole a look at

Poppy and thankfully the mention of Loudan's name didn't make her start smiling or anything because he'd have to stop the carriage and have a private conversation with her.

He couldn't take much more of this. He'd been hard for around two weeks without any relief. He felt as if—well—as if it was time for him and Poppy to get married, though that didn't make any sense. But she blushed when he touched her. And she kept stealing looks at him. And he could smell her wherever she was in the room, and she didn't smell like lavender powder anymore, but like the most delicious sun-warmed peach he'd ever eaten.

Which was precisely what he intended to do—tonight. He needed Jemma's help first, though.

He managed to catch her at the final stop to change horses before the carriage trundled the last hour or so to Beaumont Manor. He didn't bother with any sort of flummery; she was the kind of woman one didn't have to lie to, and he appreciated that.

"I need you to put us in the same room," he said to Jemma.

Sure enough, the corner of her mouth curled up. "I directed the butler otherwise in my letters."

"Please."

She was grinning now. She smiled like a man; you had to love that about Jemma. "Absolutely not. If you want your wife to join you, you'll have to lure her there yourself." She gave him a slow look. "I think you might be able to manage it."

"If I wasn't in love with my wife," he said, taking in the mischief dancing in her eyes, "I'd be begging for scraps at your feet."

She deliberately eyed him again from basement to attics, pausing around the front door for a good ogle. "And if you weren't married, I'd probably throw you a bone. Or two."

She was so adorable that he bent down and gave her a

kiss. And what made it all the more perfect was that Poppy came out of the inn at just the right moment to see it. He straightened up and waved to her, conscious that he hadn't kissed his wife in months. Not even a little peck. Nothing.

Of course, as far as she was concerned, he wasn't interested in his wife anymore. Not interested! There wasn't a man in seven counties who wouldn't be interested, especially now that her eyes had gone all soft and she kept kind of shivering and peeking looks.

Tonight, he promised himself.

Tonight.

When they finally arrived at the estate, an odd-looking fellow with hair like the crest of a whitecap came out to meet them. He turned out to be the butler. Then Beaumont himself appeared, followed by Miss Tatlock.

Fletch met Poppy's eyes when that happened and they shared one of those moments of private silent conversation, both of them wondering what Jemma thought of Miss Tatlock's early arrival.

It was just as if he and Poppy were living in the same household, Fletch thought, loving it.

The house was all draped in green stuff with berries and Fletch had to say that it smelled pretty good. Jemma didn't seem to like it when Miss Tatlock pointed out the mistletoe, perhaps due to the implication that Miss Tatlock and the duke had been investigating the properties of mistletoe, but Fletch memorized where every little white bunch was hanging.

Then he let Poppy go upstairs alone to freshen up, just as if he didn't have any interest in seeing her wash her face. Or change her clothes. Or take a bath. Or . . .

He swore and wandered off to stare out the window at miles of park. Snow was falling and as he stood there it started to swirl in huge curls in the air, sweeping from side to side.

Beaumont appeared at his shoulder. "Looks like a proper storm," he said.

Fletch nodded. "Have all your guests arrived?"

"All except Mr. Dautry, due this evening, if he's not held up by the weather. By the way, my butler just told me that a quantity of mail has arrived, some of which is for you. Most of it to do with that speech you gave, I expect."

He turned and looked at Fletch. "That was a damned fine performance."

"I'm honored that you think so," Fletch said. "I merely took your advice."

"Mine?"

"You told me that it was all about the story. You were right." A very pleasing memory of the majority of the House of Lords leaping to their collective feet came to mind.

"I've told that bit of wisdom to many a young man and they've paid me no mind. But you created a story that swept the House, Fletcher." He clapped him on the back. "I'm thinking you might be the savior of the party. And"—he added, leaving—"that man Higgle is lucky to have you as his landlord."

Fletch grinned out at the twilight and the snow. It *was* a good speech. And he already had the topic of his next one ready. It would tackle the question of the African slave trade, the dirty little secret that no one discussed and from which many profited. He saw the shape of the speech in his mind, its appeal to decency and sanity, its internal organization. Its rightness.

When he finally strolled upstairs and proceeded to read his mail in his bath, his letters were entirely satisfactory. So much so that when he wandered into the drawing room a while later he was smiling to himself. Of course, his smile might have had something to do with the drum beat in his head that kept saying *tonight, tonight, tonight.*

Though that didn't stop him from noticing the way the room fell silent as he entered.

Poppy leapt to her feet and flew toward him. For a moment he thought she was coming to his arms and just stopped himself from opening his own wide.

But she stopped short, waving a sheet of foolscap in the air. "Fletch, something horrible has happened to my mother!"

He raised an eyebrow. "She choked on her own venom and—"

"Fletch!"

His beloved, far-too-kind little wife frowned at him. "I'm serious. Something awful has happened to my mother. I have this letter from her." She handed it to him.

Fletch took the foolscap, noticing over Poppy's shoulder that the rest of the company was chattering with all the feverish excitement of a group of actresses after the Prince of Wales comes backstage.

"To My Daughter, Duchess of Fletcher, Countess Fulke, Baroness Ryskamp & etc." He raised an eyebrow and Poppy interjected.

"You know my mother, Fletch. She adores all those titles. Just read the note."

"I have suffered a great calamity. Though my soul is as innocent of this calumny as the purest flower, no impartial words can save me now. Truth's words, like jewels, hang in the ears of anvils. Poppy, this doesn't make any sense. An anvil is a ironmonger's block, is it not?"

"It's not anvils, Fletch, but *angels.* Truth's words hang in the ears of angels."

"What's this part about the devil—oh, I see, *his true foe.* Who is the devil's foe? Your mother?" And here I would have thought she and devil were close companions rather than enemies, he added to himself.

"I'm not sure about that," Poppy said. "Read the next

paragraph. She isn't quite so excited and it makes more sense."

"*Gossip is a subtle knave and like the plague strikes into the brain of truth and rageth in his entrails*—Um, just a guess, but could it be someone is gossiping about her?"

"Keep going!"

"*Worse than the poison of a red-haired man.* Now we're getting somewhere! A red-haired man is gossiping about her?"

"No! I'm not sure what she meant by that."

"Well, Axminster's hair has a reddish tint," Fletch suggested. "Course I didn't know he was much interested in your mother since she doesn't frequent the backstage of the Lyceum Dance Hall, but perhaps he broadened his attentions?"

"Fletch, will you be serious? Look farther down the page!"

Fletch squinted. "It looks to me as if she has retired to the country, if that's what she means by *sanctuary and impregnable defence of oppressed virtue*."

"Not the country, Fletch."

"No?" His heart sank a little. "Truly not? She's staying in London?"

"No, she went to a sanctuary. My mother has retired to a nunnery!"

"A nunnery? We don't have any of those."

"Actually there are some nunneries in Scotland I think, but she's gone to France. You see that part about the Bishop of Meaux? He always admired her. She left, Fletch. She left for France!"

"Your mother left for France." Fletch felt like this sometimes after having a deep swallow of the best brandy. Kind of a sweet, hot happiness that spread right down his body. "Your mother left for France."

Jemma called to them. "Poppy, I have a letter about it as well!"

Fletch followed Poppy back to the circle, suppressing his grin.

"Listen to this," Jemma said. "It's from Lady Smalley. I hardly know her, which means that she must have sent a copy of this to every acquaintance she has. She adds a bit in the beginning about Lady Flora's *spotless name* and how no one believes the rumors. *We were seated in the Duke of Fletcher's drawing room—now most strangely transformed with a magnificence so extreme that Lady Cooper commented that she felt she was in a royal bordello. Lady Cooper is ever humorous, of course.*"

"If one has to lose one's reputation," Mrs. Patton interjected, "it would be better not to do it in Lady Cooper's presence—a sharp-tongued virago, if there ever was one."

"Do keep reading," Fletch said, seating himself happily. "I am all anticipation."

Poppy shot him a glance. "You are discussing my mother, Fletch. Your mother-in-law."

"Precisely," he said. "Precisely."

Jemma started reading again. "*When all of a sudden a young man appeared at the door. He cut a quite attractive figure, though there was something about him that wasn't quite of the gentleman. He hailed Lady Flora in the most tender of tones, seeming to not notice at first that we were there. For when he did recognize our presence, he fell silent and indicated in a hundred ways his distress and confusion.*"

"She had a lover!" Harriet gasped. And then glanced at Poppy. "Of course, that is merely the way it looked. One can hardly believe it of such a stalwart character as Lady Flora. Why she has never shown the slightest hint of moral laxness."

"Certainly not," Fletch murmured.

Poppy turned mystified eyes back to Jemma. "It's impossible," she stated. "I know my mother. Do read on, Jemma."

"I'll just summarize it for you. The handsome young man hastily retreated, but the damage was done. Lady Flora appears to have been overtaken by a fit of nerves that rendered her incapable of logical conversation. Lady Cooper then took it upon herself to fetch smelling salts from the butler and naturally used the opportunity to question him closely."

She looked at Poppy. "It truly was very bad luck that your mother happened to invite Lady Cooper to tea."

"Lady Cooper is one of her best friends," Poppy said. "But it doesn't matter. This is—quite simply—impossible. Inconceivable."

"Not according to Lady Cooper," Jemma said. "Your own butler straight away confessed that the young man had originally visited the house in order to assist your mother in some decorating schemes and as the last months passed, he had indeed noticed that they were spending more and more time together."

"Impossible!" Poppy exclaimed.

Fletch reached forward and took her hand. "Alas, the family is always the last to know, dearest."

She shot him a look and he shut his mouth. Really, she had moments in which she quite resembled her mother.

"Does your correspondent have anything further to say?" Poppy asked Jemma.

"Only that the young man was indeed quite handsome and when confronted, maintained that he stood as a bulwark to protect Lady Flora's renown and chastity, and that she was his dearest patron and nothing more. That's a quote. Naturally, that simply inflamed everyone further, for there's nothing worse than a man defending a woman's honor. If the man had no relationship with your mother, Poppy, he would have said so, rather than talking about her honor."

"It's true," Mrs. Patton said. "Talk of honor is always the death knell to a woman's reputation."

Poppy was shaking her head. "I simply can't believe it. I just can't—I can't believe it."

Fletch kept silent.

"Since the dinner bell rang some time ago, I think we should go in or risk choking on a chilly cut of meat," Jemma said, coming to her feet. "Poppy, I know this must be most distressing for you. Would you prefer to eat in your room?"

"No," Poppy said. "Jemma, may I read that letter myself? I simply can't believe it!"

"Don't you remember when Bussy D'Ambois turned out to be having an *affaire* with the Countess of Montsurry," Jemma asked, "when everyone thought he was toying with the Duchess of Guise? I assure you that the Count of Montsurry was just as surprised as you are now."

"But that ended so unpleasantly," Fletch said. "Didn't the count go quite mad?"

"He murdered his wife," Jemma said, "insisting that he had to defend the honor of his name."

"I suppose there are those who might think that your name has been tarnished by connection with your mother," Fletch said to Poppy, who was reading Lady Smalley's letter.

"Nonsense," she replied.

"Then I suppose I needn't be as extreme as the Count of Monsurry," he said with a pang of disappointment.

Jemma gave him a sharp look.

He smiled back at her blandly. "All's well that ends well, don't you think? I feel quite certain that Lady Flora will soon rule whatever nunnery her friend the bishop places her in."

"Of course she will," Poppy said, handing the letter back to Jemma. "But—"

She talked all the way to the dining room. And through most of the meal. The sad fact was that Poppy was having as hard a time getting her mind around the truth of this story as did the Count of Monsurry. Yet by the time the pear compotes and apple tarts appeared, she was reluctantly accepting the account.

"For why would your mother retire to France unless there was truth in it?" Fletch kept repeating. "She would simply brazen it out."

Then it turned out that Beaumont, late in opening his mail, had been sent a similar account. Beaumont's letter described the young man falling to his knees and kissing Lady Flora's feet in anguish; they all agreed that the detail was likely embellished.

"But the truth of it stands," Fletch said. "Your mother was caught by a pretty face, Poppy. She's human after all."

"No, she's—" Poppy said, and caught herself.

"Human," Fletch said happily. "Nothing more than a hapless member of the human race, just like the rest of us."

Chapter 46

The idea that her mother had a lover was inconceivable. Obviously, there had been some horrendous miscarriage of justice. Poppy drank a great deal of wine at supper, trying to talk herself into feeling sorry for her mother.

But certain facts kept intervening with her attempts at sorrow. One was that Lady Flora had moved to France. Had entered a nunnery. When Poppy and Fletch returned to London, there would be no sharp letters, no accidental encounters in ballrooms leading to vitriolic comments on her hair or dress, no meetings at all.

To say that her heart lightened at the thought would underestimate the truth. She felt as if she had drunk an entire case of champagne.

When supper was over, the ladies left the gentlemen with their port and returned to the drawing room. Harriet and Mrs. Patton left to visit the nursery. Jemma seated herself on a sofa with Isidore and—gulp—Louise. Which was distinctly humiliating, because Poppy had decided to ask for marital advice. Yet Louise already knew the worst about her marriage.

So she mentally girded her loins and marched over to Jemma. The three of them were sipping toddies, looking like a fashion plate from *The Lady's Magazine*. It wasn't that Poppy didn't feel fashionable: she knew quite well that her petticoat was flounced and furbelowed. She had a beautiful lace ruff, and her hair was raised on the smallest pad—with no powdering whatsoever. She looked pretty. In fact, she thought the way her hair shone without powder was much more attractive than when it was powdered. But the important point was that she didn't look . . .

Like Louise.

Louise had a roguish, sensual look about her. It wasn't just that her gown was lower cut and a bit tighter—which it was—it was something about the way she walked, and the color of her lips, and the way she laughed, low and deep.

"Hello, darling," Jemma said, looking up. "Are you drinking these toddies? Because honestly, I think they may be a wee bit on the strong side. I'm not sure I can stand up."

"I haven't had one," Poppy said. "Perhaps I should."

"Definitely you should," Isidore said, giggling madly. Her cheeks were bright red, which looked wonderful with her jet-black hair. She looked tipsy.

Louise reached up and pulled Poppy down next to her. "Do come sit with me," she said. "How lovely your hair looks. Please take my toddy. I only sniffed it, as I can't abide strong liquor."

"I'm not sure I can either," Poppy said. But she sipped it and thought it was very nice, like cinnamon and wine and Christmas, all mixed together. "I need help," she said bluntly.

Isidore blinked at her a bit owlishly. "Do you want us to throw your husband out of the house? Jemma, you should have done better than allow that man into your party after what happened last time we were all together!"

"I invited him," Poppy said quickly.

Isidore's mouth fell open in a comical fashion. "You did?"

"I wanted—well—I've changed my mind."

"About what?" Louise wanted to know.

"About him."

Jemma was smiling. "You've decided that a bird in the hand is better than a naturalist in the bush, is that it?"

"Yes," Poppy said.

"How can we help?" Isidore said, drinking some more.

Louise narrowed her eyes. "You're going to have a fearful head tomorrow, Isidore. And—if you don't mind my saying so—your face is quite rosy."

"I always turn red as a beet when I drink spirits," Isidore said. "But honestly, who cares? My husband is away in far-off India or some such place. I could turn purple and he wouldn't care." She drank again.

"He's a wart," Jemma said bluntly. "If you want to turn red, Isidore, you go right ahead."

"One of these days," Isidore said, with only a little slur in her voice, "I'm going to do something wild."

"No doubt," Louise said briskly. "When that times comes, we'll sober you up. It's best never to be wild while inebriated."

Poppy took a huge gulp of her toddy. In her view, it was likely easier to be wild with a little inebriation. "I want to do something wild too," she said.

"What?" Isidore said, peering at her. "Is your husband going to India as well?"

Louise reached over and took Isidore's cup away. "You've had enough, darling. At this rate, you'll sleep straight through Christmas Eve and miss all the festivities."

"I'm not sure how celebratory we can be," Jemma said,

looking worried. "My butler tells me that Villiers isn't doing very well at all. I stopped up to see him, but he was asleep again. I think he slept most of the day."

"Oh dear," Isidore said, her mouth drooping instantly. "I thought perhaps I would marry him instead of my duke, but I can only do that if he survives."

"I didn't know you liked Villiers," Jemma said, looking surprised.

"I hardly know him. But he's a duke. I could just scratch out my husband's name on the wedding certificate. It seems like a fair trade for the duke I don't really have. A duke in England is worth two off in India."

"Which reminds me," Jemma said. "So how can we help, Poppy?"

Poppy had finished her toddy and was enjoying an agreeable warmth in the pit of her stomach. "Fletch says that men are never interested in women after a few years of bedding them," she said. "So he's not interested in me anymore."

"Bastardo!" Isidore hissed, taking Jemma's cup out of her hand and drinking some of it.

"I want to—to lure him back to my bed," she said.

"You're looking as red as I am," Isidore observed.

Jemma was grinning. "A *femme fatale,*" she said. "Louise, Isidore, let's go!" She grabbed Poppy's hand. "Upstairs!"

Fletch had just decided that Jemma's odd-looking butler was the person to tell him where his wife was sleeping when Beaumont gave an odd cough. They were playing cards. Fletch looked up to meet Beaumont's eyes, alive with laughter. He put down his cards.

"Yes?" Fletch asked.

"I think," Beaumont said, rising, "that this performance is likely directed at you, not me."

Fletch rose and turned around.

She was walking in the door.

At supper, her hair had been up above her head, in one of those hair styles that women liked, albeit without the powder. She'd looked sweetly pretty. Now it was all different.

Walking in the door was the courtesan to a prince. She had curls atop her head, caught up with sparkling jewels, though a few fell to her shoulders. Her eyes were lavishly lined with black and they looked twice as big and four times as powerfully blue. Her lips were crimson and curled in a small mocking smile.

Her gown was dark crimson, a color near to black. And the bodice plunged below her breasts. There was nothing but the frailest scrap of lace covering her nipples. Around her neck she wore a dramatic, exquisite necklace, with a pendant that fell just between the curves of her breasts.

The entire drawing room went silent as a stone.

Fletch walked forward, feeling as if he should fall on his knees.

Poppy stopped and her scarlet mouth curled appreciatively.

He swept into a bow. "Good evening, madam."

"*Bon soir.*" Her voice was no sweet jangle of bells. It was husky, demanding, a woman's voice. It was a French woman's voice.

Jemma swept in behind them, laughing, with other women, but Fletch didn't take his eyes from Poppy.

There wasn't an ounce of hesitation in her eyes. Not even a tremor. She was, every inch, a woman who knew exactly what she wanted.

Him.

"I am here only for the evening," she said.

"Visiting?" he managed.

"From France."

"Could I get you . . . something, *mademoiselle*?"

"Alack," she said, lowering her eyelashes. They were outrageously black and so long that his loins stirred. "I am no mademoiselle."

"Married, are you?" he said, taking her hand and bringing it to his mouth. "I am *désolé.*"

Her shoulders rose in a little shrug. "Why should you be? I find that marriage is such an interesting state."

"Truly?"

"But of course! Only a married woman can truly know what she wants."

Behind him Jemma laughed, but Fletch's heart was beating too hard for laughter. Every inch of him had turned to fierce prowling hunter, to the kind of primitive male who throws a female to a pallet and has his way with her. He wanted to toss Poppy over his shoulder and take her upstairs, every delectable inch of her. Her breasts were visible to the whole room; he could see one pink nipple peeking at him through the white lace.

"And what did marriage teach you about desire?" he asked, the huskiness in his own voice startling him. "What do you want, *madame?*"

Something changed in her eyes, went serious for a moment.

"Poppy?" he said. "What do you want?" He brought her hand to his lips again. Even touching his lips to her skin made him start shaking a bit, like a racehorse waiting at the start line.

"You."

She said it softly, and then shot him another one of those liquid dark, dangerous looks out of her beautiful eyes.

"I want you."

Fletch's only explanation was that he lost his head. Right there in a drawing room full of giggling peers, at least two or three footmen, not to mention a butler with hair like the rise of the sea . . .

The Duke of Fletcher swept up his duchess in his arms—or perhaps it was just a wild Frenchwoman paying a visit—and stalked out of the room.

And up the stairs.

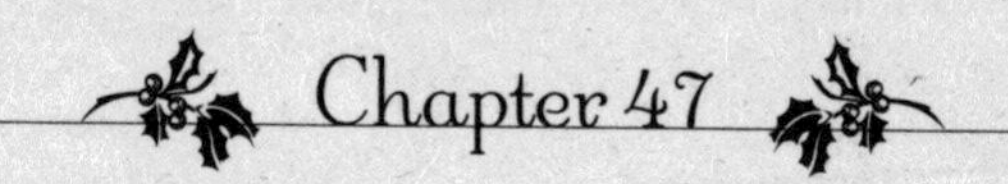

Chapter 47

Dying was not an easy business. Villiers pretty much thought he had reconciled himself to it but he wasn't enjoying the process. The Scottish doctor had stopped dropping turpentine in his wound, but the man's mouth drooped when he looked at him. Plus, Villiers could feel the bad news. The fever didn't wrench him this way and that as much, but the exhaustion was like an undertow, pulling him out to sea.

"I'm not going to live much longer," he told Charlotte. She'd suddenly appeared after supper and told him a story about Lady Flora and a young servant that he didn't believe for a moment. Now she was sitting beside him reading from one of Mr. Fielding's novels. Villiers hadn't listened for pages. He liked lying there and watching the way her mouth moved as she read, and the delicate bones in her hand as she turned the pages.

"Why aren't you down there with the philosophers?" he added. "I specifically requested philosophers."

Charlotte raised her eyes. "The duchess said that there are no philosophers in her circle of acquaintance. And you are going to live. The doctor feels the infection is gone from your wound."

Villiers smiled faintly. "You are the one who told me not to pay so much attention to my doctors."

He had been absolutely right about the house party. The so-called standards of polite society didn't operate here. Jemma had challenged him to a chess game and he even played a few pieces before he realized that he didn't care about chess anymore.

Then Jemma got a droopy look around her mouth and looked as if she might cry, so he closed his eyes and pretended to go to sleep. Except that closing his eyes was dangerous these days: he closed them and woke up to find that the light had moved straight across the room and it was night. Or the night was gone and most of the day as well.

No one cared if Charlotte sat with him, and she never looked droopy. Sure enough, she was scowling at him. "You're going to die looking like *that*?" she said pointedly.

He almost laughed but it took too much breath. "Appealing to my vanity won't do it. May I use your name, oh sage Miss Tatlock?"

She turned up that long nose of hers. "Private names are far too intimate."

"I want to be intimate," he said.

There was a moment of silence.

"Though I won't be around long enough to marry you," he added.

"You wouldn't want to marry me." She picked up the book again. "Shall I continue?"

"Yes, I would," he said, saying it because there was no reason not to. "I like you, Charlotte. I thought perhaps I could only love Jemma, but I'm fairly sure I've come to love you."

"Very foolish of you," she snapped.

"Yes." But he was watching her under his lashes, and he saw a watery gleam in her eyes. He didn't mean to make her droopy. The idea made him feel panicked. "So think about that. What a shame I'm dying. You could have inherited a fortune!"

She rallied instantly. "Don't speak too soon. I might call in a priest and marry you tonight."

"I wouldn't mind."

Now her mouth was definitely wobbling. It was a soft and pink mouth, too. Anything to do with physical intimacy was farthest from Villiers's mind, but he had noticed her mouth. She said bruising things, but with a sweet little mouth.

"Yes, you would!" she said fiercely. "I would never marry you for your fortune, and don't forget it!"

"Would you marry me for other reasons?" He watched her from under his lashes. Of course, she would say no. He was a wreck of a man, dying, stupid, foolish, alone. She was—

"And not just because you're desperate for a wedding ring?" he added. He didn't have time for social niceties, not here in the very shadow of death.

"I don't know," she said slowly. She reached out and her warm fingers curled around his.

He felt the tide of exhaustion again. He was so tired of the pain. It was all over his body now, an ache, more than one ache. "Who would think that a foolish little sword wound could come to this?" he said.

Her hand tightened on his. "Don't die." She said it quietly. "Don't."

But he didn't think he had a choice. "Do you know what I feel like, Charlotte?"

"No."

"A torch. Nothing more than a torch borne in the wind."

And then the blackness came quickly, before he had a chance to say another word.

Charlotte sat next to Villiers and watched him sleep. He was gaunt, his face as white as parchment. And yet she could still see that glorious scrap of life that makes up the soul. It wasn't hard to grasp how fragile the place was in which the soul resided.

Dautry came in quietly. He had just arrived, having missed supper.

It took her a moment to understand what had happened to him. He was no longer a slightly shabby sailor. He looked magnificent, clad in a coat of periwinkle blue that fit his shoulders like a glove. His shirt was of the finest linen. Only two things betrayed him: his hair still tumbled like a pirate, to his shoulders, and his feet wore the same scuffed, comfortable boots as before.

"Goodness," she said faintly. "You look ducal."

"I look like a blasted peacock," he said, striding around the bed. He picked up his Villiers's other hand. "Damn."

There was no point in pretending that she didn't know what he meant. Everything about the duke signaled that the time was near.

"It's Christmas Eve tomorrow," she said. "I had hoped he would be here for Christmas."

"He may surprise you yet."

"He just did," she said.

Dautry glanced at her.

"He asked me to marry him."

A look of black rage crossed his face and then it was as expressionless as ever. "Did he?" he drawled. "And did you take him up on his idea?"

She stood up and shook out her skirts. "You're an ass."

"A fine English gentlewoman using such a word!" he said, mockingly.

"Ass," she repeated, loving the sound of the word on her own lips. There was something about this trip, her acquaintance with the Duke of Villiers, that was changing her. Making her more like him, perhaps: combative, fearless. She reached out and smoothed Villiers's fingers, lying on the counterpane.

Dautry strode around the bed. "I can see that you are fond of him," he said.

She had to tip her head back: he was standing just beside her and he was so tall. "You are—"

"I know," he interrupted. "You already told me."

His eyes looked at her with such disapproval that she actually felt a thrill. As if *she*, Charlotte Tatlock, would do something immoral. It was practically a compliment. "So you think that I would seduce a dying duke into marriage in order to become a duchess?"

"Is that what you're doing?"

She loved the image of it, if only it didn't include Villiers's death.

"His name is Leopold, did you know that?"

He looked furious again. "How did you come to meet the duke?" Suddenly his hands were on her shoulders.

He's going to shake me! Charlotte thought. It was all she could do not to smile. Dautry really thought she was a fatal temptress . . . not just a plain old maid who lived in Gough Square.

"How long have you known him?"

"Long enough," she said, prolonging the deliciousness of it.

But she didn't know enough about men. Or perhaps she just didn't know enough about Dautry. He didn't shake her;

suddenly he bent his head and before she had any idea what was happening, his mouth was on hers.

On her mouth!

His lips were warm and firm, and she suddenly smelled him. He smelled like a sailor: like the clean wind and faintly of cloves. Stray thoughts whirled through her head, about temptresses who kissed strange men . . .

The idea was so delicious that she did precisely what he wanted and opened her mouth.

But then the kiss changed and she couldn't think as clearly anymore. He stopped holding her shoulders and pulled her against his body. He was warm and hard, and the spicy smell of him went to her head so she wound her arms around his neck and hung on.

They didn't stop until there was a noise on the bed. She pulled away and swung around, but Villiers was still sleeping. Her whole body was tingling. No wonder, she kept thinking. No wonder men and women . . .

She reached out and pulled up his coverlet a little, thinking about it.

"Has the local doctor anything to say?" Dautry said it quietly, in case Villiers was sleeping lightly.

The doctor had said no more than she had guessed for herself. "If he survives the night . . . but Dr. Treglown doesn't think he will. Do you?"

She saw the answer in his eyes, and it echoed the truth in her own heart.

"What will you do when he dies?" His voice sounded different. The drawl was still there, but roughened by desire.

"Nothing," she said, turning around to face him. "Weep."

"I'll come sit with him tonight," he said, turning to the door. "I need to eat. Keep me company?"

She looked at Villiers but he was sleeping in that profound way he had, as if every breath were too much and he might just slip away. It was tiring, watching a man die.

"Come sit with me," Dautry said, his voice a little softer. He held out his hand. "You can return later. We'll both come back later."

Blount disapproved. He did his butlering duty, of course. He placed the couple at a snug table in the morning room. He served them himself, because he saw the lay of the land, the way Dautry smiled at Miss Tatlock, and the way his hand lingered on her shoulder. No point in allowing that Jezebel to corrupt one of the young footmen.

But he was aware of a great uneasiness. He had identified the woman as a concubine of the Duke of Villiers, and here she was with the heir. Laughing. Talking. What sort of woman was she?

He lingered as much as he could while bringing in the courses, intent on learning her secrets. The conversation didn't seem particularly salacious. They talked of India (godforsaken place, to Blount's mind), and pirates (godforsaken people), and then about whales (he had no particular opinion, but he was suspicious).

He was pouring the second bottle of wine before he discovered what made Miss Charlotte Tatlock so irresistible. It was the way she talked back to Dautry. Talked back! Inconceivable for a young woman. Yet she did. He refreshed their wine glasses during a conversation in which she was arguing in the most lively way about smugglers. Defending them, if you please!

Blount made up his mind on the spot. They got no more wine. None! Not even if the Jezebel herself rang the bell.

So it was disappointing when they sauntered back to the Duke of Villiers's bedchamber, almost as if they didn't notice that their butler had forsaken them.

They were talking that hard.

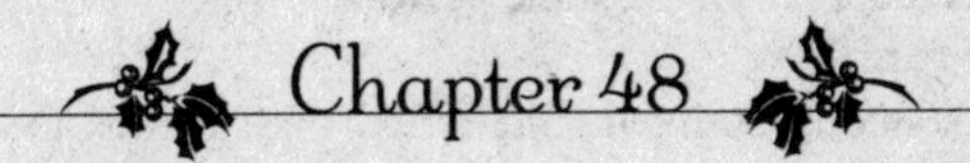

Chapter 48

Poppy wasn't herself. She wasn't the meek, silly daughter of Lady Flora. She wasn't the kind of person who could be screamed at, or told what to do.

She was more likely to scream. And tell people what to do.

She felt powerful. She let Fletch carry her into the room because it felt good to be in his arms, to be carried about. As soon as they were in the bedchamber, she pulled free. She had to control the night.

She walked away from him slowly, leaned back against the bedpost so that her breasts arched forward. Fletch was standing next to the door and what she saw in his eyes made her heart beat even faster.

It was working.

But she had a plan, a plan that Jemma and Louise had drilled into her upstairs, and she wasn't going to deviate from it now. Not after practicing it twice, even after Isidore fell on the bed and went to sleep, complaining that no man was worth all the energy.

So she let her lips curls into a sleepy, inviting smile. "I hear," she said, "that you're tired of your spouse."

"I—"

But she didn't let him answer. "*Bien*," she said. "Because as it seems, I am in the same position."

"You are?"

He sounded stunned. She lifted both hands above her head to the bedpost, feeling the deliciously free, wild sense of her breasts against the frail ruffle of her bodice. She could hear Fletch breathing. He didn't look like the sophisticated sleek duke now. His eyes were gleaming.

"Poppy . . ." he said slowly.

"Monsieur?"

She brought one hand down to trail down her throat and then across her chest, just as Jemma had showed her. "It'll drive him mad," Jemma had said. "Men love it when a woman touches her own flesh."

"Maybe I should send my husband a painting of me," Isidore had said drunkenly from the bed. "Doing that."

Poppy let herself smile at Fletch, just enough to make it clear that she was in charge.

"Why don't you come closer?" she purred.

He was before her in one bound.

"No touching!"

He held up his hands. The smile in his eyes made her shiver, and she could feel herself getting warm and shivery between her legs. "*Je n'y touche pas, madame,*" he said.

But she had to be sure he understood, be sure that he knew. "A woman like myself," she told him, "has demands."

"Yes?" He came a step closer. "Tell me."

She let her hand close over her breast and dropped her head back. She could feel her entire body tingling now, longing for the touch of his hand. In the days since she'd made her discovery in the inn, she'd explored her own body. She knew what she liked . . . and she knew just what she'd like him to do, though the very thought made her feel as pink in the face as Isidore.

"Tell me," he demanded. There was a fierce wildness in his voice that made her tremble with excitement.

It was hard to be explicit. Embarrassment momentarily strangled her, stripping away her French cover. But then she looked at Fletch, and it was Fletch, her darling Fletch, standing in front of her. The only thing she really wanted was for him to touch her. And then—for her to be able to touch him.

Looking at him made her steadier. What she wanted was just what he wanted. Just like that a whole hot flush swept over her body. "I want to touch you," she said. Her voice was quiet and steady, but she wasn't whispering.

Without taking his eyes from hers, he wrenched off his coat. She leaned back against the bedpost again. She felt all the power of desire making her taller, making her more beautiful, making her lips shine and her body voluptuous.

Fletch's shoulders were powerful and muscled. He pulled his shirt out of his breeches.

"Go on," she said. To her embarrassment it came out as a croak.

But there was a smile playing around his lips too. "But what exactly do you want me to do?"

"I want you to take your shirt off."

His smile made her shiver. He pulled up his shirt slowly, so she saw his rippled stomach, and then the golden muscles on his shoulders. It was odd how she saw it all different now. She had always thought he was pretty before. He wasn't pretty.

He was . . .

She wanted to lick him. Luckily he couldn't hear that thought, though she felt her face getting even redder.

"And now?"

But she was done. She couldn't possibly ask a man to remove his breeches. Even though . . . she could see a bulge there and she—

She shook her head.

He walked forward another step so they were almost touching. "That's all right," he whispered, reaching down and feathering a kiss across her cheekbone. "I didn't want to take my breeches off. I just want to kiss you." He was nuzzling her lips, kissing her so sweetly that her knees trembled. "There's no need to—"

"Take them off!" she barked, pushing him back. She couldn't be this close to him, not when he smelled so good. She was losing her focus. Losing her Frenchness. He wouldn't desire her if she turned back into her docile little self and just let him do things. She had to stay in control.

He stepped back, looking a little surprised, but then pleased too. "*Immédiatement!*" she added, just to get the message across.

He grinned at that and started playing with his waistband. Pulling it down a little. That was something she loved about him, the way his hips were so lean and there was a little hollow there. She wanted to lick it too. She didn't know how she knew about that hollow, because she never consciously looked at him, but she did. Fletch pulled his breeches down, and farther down.

Poppy felt a little faint. She'd seen him a hundred times at least. Especially after he started insisting that they make love with all the candles lit, and she had to lie on top of the covers. She'd seen him. She never thought he was grotesque and hairy, the way her mother had described.

But she'd never looked at him and felt her whole body start to tremble either. He was large. And smooth. And he had his hands on his hips, so it looked like his whole body was just—

That. There.

"And now?" he said, his voice all deep and teasing, as if they were talking about bits of sugar.

Her mind reeled, trying to think what to say next. How could she stay French, be French, so he wasn't bored? What would a Frenchwoman do next?

She couldn't take her eyes off him and really the only thing she wanted was for him to—

That couldn't be said. It was horribly vexing. She couldn't think of anything.

"Sweetheart?"

He started to say something and his eyes were so sweet and kind that she knew she'd already failed. He was looking at her and seeing stupid old Poppy, not a sensual Frenchwoman with kohl all around her eyes.

"No!" she snapped.

He stopped, but he didn't look quite so happy. Poppy took a breath. She had to find herself again, find the pleasure in it. She was failing, she knew she was failing—she pushed the thought away. It was probably time to go to the bed. That was what she should do.

"I would like you to lie down," she said. Thankfully, she didn't have to modulate her voice: it came out all provocative and husky on its own.

"Wouldn't you like me to undress you first?"

She froze for a moment. Would a Frenchwoman let a man undress her? She couldn't remember whether Jemma had said anything about it. At some point they had all been laughing so hard that she could hardly hear the advice.

"A Frenchwoman always undresses herself," she stated.

He grinned so that must have been the right thing to do. Then he flung himself onto the bed, as cool as a cucumber. He propped his head on his arms and crossed his legs. But Poppy had trouble looking anywhere other than his . . . his waistline. She wet her lips and his hips rose just a little bit as she watched.

She did it again and he made a curious sound.

So she let her tongue play with her bottom lip. He was watching her with the sleepiest, most delicious expression she'd ever seen. She was doing it right. She knew she was doing it right. A little rush of exhilaration swept through her.

"It's so hot in here," she said, low and sultry. That was one of the lines Jemma told her and it sounded just right, even though Isidore screamed with laughter from the bed and said Jemma sounded like a three-penny whore.

Then she just pulled her neckline wide and eased it down over her shoulders. Fletch was sitting up now. He looked like a dying man seeing a drink of water.

Poppy licked her lips again and then slipped the dress down a little further. And a little further . . .

"Oh darling, you're killing me." He said it with a half groan, and Poppy felt heat flash from the tips of her ears to her toes.

"Mmmmm," she said, pulling her sleeves a bit lower.

Her breasts were free now. He was looking, so she looked down too. They looked very nice, plump and warm. She knew what they felt like in her hands. But what she wanted was to feel his hands on her breasts.

She met his eyes and saw her own desire reflected there.

"Poppy," he said, "could you please come to the bed now?" He sounded hoarse. It sounded to her as if the Frenchwoman had conquered him, and she could probably let him take over now. Which was good because—

That was the moment when she discovered that the neckline had gone down just as far as it was going to go—to her elbows. She tried to pull out an arm and couldn't.

"You're trapped," her husband said, sounding delighted. He swung his legs off the bed.

It wasn't French to get trapped in one's clothing.

And yet—

Fletch didn't even try to get her free. He just stood in front of her without touching her—couldn't he tell what she wanted?—and kissed her. His mouth was sweet, like sin and honey and everything she'd ever wanted in life.

He didn't open his lips though, and that's what she wanted. By a moment later Poppy was feeling half-crazed. She couldn't raise her arms. But he wasn't touching her. He was just kissing her without—just rubbing his lips against hers.

So she finally had to do it herself. Like the daring Frenchwoman she was, she ran her tongue along the line of his lips. He tasted sweet, like a man. A little spicy.

Kiss me, she thought. Kiss me.

His lips softened but they didn't open. There was just a gleam of humor in his eyes, and something else, something possessive and dark that made her shiver.

"Kiss me," she finally whispered. "Fletch—"

And he did it. Just like that, one hand came to the middle of her back and pulled her towards him. Her breasts came to his chest, and his mouth opened, sweeping inside hers.

"Do you like that?" he said.

She was breathing too hard to answer, pressing against him, feeling the aching tips of her breasts.

"Yes," she breathed.

"What do you like?"

He wouldn't kiss her again until she said it, so she did. "Kiss me again, Fletch." Her voice sounded as if she was begging, and a pulse of humiliation went through her, but then he started kissing her and it didn't matter, none of it mattered . . .

He put his hand on her cheek and let it drift down, down to her neck and she was shrieking inside. Why didn't he touch her?

She would say it: touch me, but it was too bold. And he was kissing her. Then she realized she wanted to touch him and she couldn't because of the stupid dress, so she started struggling with it, wiggling while still kissing him.

He pulled back and stared down at her. There was something different in his eyes: slumberous and intent. He was looking at the Frenchwoman, Poppy thought with a little throb of anxiety. What would she do next?

But he took the decision out of her hands. "*La liberté,*" he whispered. Put his hands on her neck, drew his hands down, down over her breasts. She shivered, and he cast a trail of fire down to her waist. Then with one quick wrench he ripped the delicate fabric in half and it fell to her feet.

"Very nice," he drawled.

Poppy nearly covered her breasts with one hand and her private parts with the other—just in time she remembered that she wasn't herself. She was French. Instead, she stretched, all the way above her head. Her whole body was tingling, feeling pink and ready for—

Him.

He was smiling, so she just went by instinct, turned to the bed and climbed onto it. His hand brushed over her bottom and she thought she heard a little groan, like a curse. She lay down slowly and then turned over.

He was there, on the edge of the bed, his eyes dark. "What would you like now, *madame?*"

"Kisses," she said, stretching again. She'd discovered that if her hands were over her head her breasts looked bigger.

He crawled toward her and she couldn't take her eyes

from his. She was shivering all over. He swung a leg over hers and she was trembling so hard she was afraid he would see so she put on her French smile and said, "*Monsieur*?" Which happened to be the only word she could think of.

"Poppy," he said, and then his mouth came to hers. It was like a gift. They'd kissed hundreds of times before, years' worth of brisk kisses and longer kisses, but never like this. Never when her desire met his, when his mouth tasted like the sweetest nectar. Never when she—not he!—pulled him against her body.

"Do you want the candles snuffed?" he whispered into her neck.

Poppy wasn't listening. She'd discovered that even running her fingers over the muscles in his back made currents of desire sing in her blood.

"The candles?"

"Hush," she whispered. And then: "Kiss me again."

Finally, some time later, with a gasp: "Harder!"

There were so many discoveries. That laughter was part of it all, the way Fletch laughed when he was kissing the sweet slope of her breast and she thought he might make better use of his time.

"You told me that I should tell you what I want," she said, catching her breath. And then with a little moan, "Oh—"

Fear was part of it, too. Because Fletch was laughing and panting and afraid, all at once. Afraid it was some sort of a dream that had caught him waking, because the reality of it was so much better than all those dreams he'd had. She twisted under his hands and sobbed a little, and even screamed, but she was so *Poppy* at the same time. She told him one thing, and then forgot and started her own explorations. And when he tried to push her back into place so that he could minister to her, and drive her mad with desire as he planned, she got fierce and before he knew it, he found himself flat on his back with his little wife doing her best to drive every logical thought out of his body.

"I meant—I want to—" he gasped, his body arched at the feeling of her soft lips kissing him everywhere, even biting him, tasting him, exploring him.

"Quiet," she said, and he humored her (all right, he lost his mind for a while), until finally he flipped her over and didn't entertain any more objections. Just feasted himself on her sweet apples of breasts, memorizing the way she squealed when he used his teeth, just a little bit, the way she tasted when he kissed his way down her body.

Until neither one of them could stand it any more, when she was sobbing for his possession, and fire was raging in his legs—and yet he was afraid, afraid it wouldn't be right, she wouldn't like it—

Afraid—

She pulled him down onto her curvy velvet little body and said in her fiercest tone, "Fletch, if you don't make love to me right now—" But then she arched against him and seemed to lose track of her threat.

And just like that, he forgot his idiotic worries. By some miracle, some Christmas miracle, he had their wedding night back. It was their first time.

He rubbed against her, teasing her, kissing her.

She started scolding him again, his sweet little shrewish wife, and so he finally took her face in his and kissed her while he sank into her . . . the first time, the best time, the only time.

Poppy looked up at him and to her horror, felt tears coming to her eyes. French seductresses didn't cry while they were making love. She knew that. She sniffed and tried to think French thoughts, but then her own Fletch kissed the tears away and drove into her again and then she stopped worrying about tears and Gallic attitudes. It was all she could do to catch the rhythm and join the dance.

At first it felt like some sort of frustrating game in which she was behind on the count. Fletch was moving, deep and strong and steady, and she was twisting under him, trying to get that pressure, the pressure she wanted—

When suddenly she realized that she was doing it again. She was letting him lead the dance, bring everything to the table. A little arch in her back and a surge back at him and, oh God, the pressure was there, it was delicious, it was building. He made a low sound in his throat and his head fell back.

It was Fletch *and* Poppy. Not just Fletch, and not just her.

The tears came in earnest this time, because how could she not? Their bodies were moving in unison, hard and sweaty and real. Fletch was saying things about love too. They were hoarse, and breathless, but real.

She was moving faster, closer to him, tears in her mouth when he was kissing her no, they were kissing each other— and then faster, until she couldn't think, until with a shuddering cry, she let go and flew into perfect, perfect pieces. Sweaty, messy, dirty pieces.

Perfect.

Chapter 49

The next night

"Christmas Eve night," Villiers said. He could hardly hear his own voice, it was so low. He didn't bother to think about what that meant: he knew. Every exhausted bone in his aching body knew. And accepted it. "Will you read me that story again?"

Somehow this slight girl with the long nose, this intelligent, wrathful old maid of a virgin had become the only person he wanted to see at his bedside. Earlier that day Benjamin's widow, Harriet, had sat with him and he couldn't remember what he wanted to say. Until he finally said he was sorry.

Harriet cried, but he didn't know why and couldn't summon up the strength to care.

Charlotte insulted him, and shouted at him, and looked as

if she might cry, but she never did. "Did I tell you that I'm marrying you?" he murmured.

Her smile was so faint that he could hardly see it. "If you survive I might take you at your word, and marry you out of revenge. But I'm sure you'll back away once you come to your senses."

"You can sue for breach of promise."

"How much do you think I'll get?"

It was hard to think, like swimming in treacle, but so much fun to have a conversation with a joke to it, that he made himself concentrate. "I'm rich. I wouldn't settle for less than thirty-six thousand pounds."

"That much?"

He felt a flash of pride. "See? You should rethink your foolishness and marry me anyway."

"Too old for me," she snapped. "And look at you. Thin as a twig."

He could make a lewd joke, but he couldn't seem to think of one. They never told you that desire fled at the shadow of death. There was a lot no one told you. "Will you read me that story again?" he said.

"Which?"

"It's His birthday tonight."

"It's a magical night," she said, smiling. "My grandmother used to tell me all sorts of stories about it. Tonight is the one time all year that the animals can talk to each other."

"Shakespeare said the same," Villiers observed. And then found the words in his head, like some sort of benediction: "*The bird of dawning singeth all night long, And then, they say, no spirit dare stir abroad.*" He paused. "Something else there, I think. And then '*No fairy takes, no witch has power to charm, so hallowed and so gracious is the time.*' "

"Would you like the *Gospel of Luke* again?" she asked.

He nodded. "Just the part about the inn, and the angels. And will you hold my hand?"

So she began, with her clear intelligent voice, and he hung on to the dear old words like a lifeline, from this world to the next. "And in the sixth month the angel Gabriel was sent from God unto Galilee . . ."

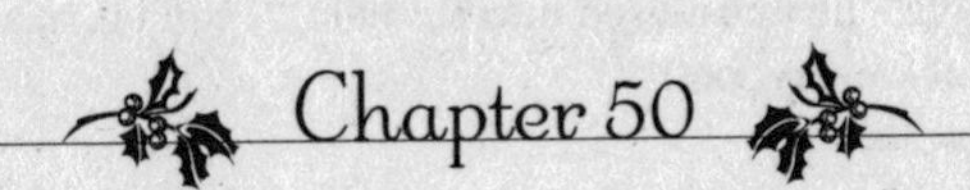

Chapter 50

It was twilight, Christmas Eve night. The snow wasn't howling around the house anymore, but it was still falling. Poppy drifted away from the party and to the window. If she stood just next to the glass, in the well of the deep window, she could peer out at the garden in the twilight. Where before had been the bare outlines of hedges in the enormous formal gardens that surrounded the house, now all was transformed into a soft and mysterious landscape of snow and shadow. Where the light fell, the snow glittered like midnight diamonds. Where the light faded, the snow looked soft, like lumpy velvet.

Somehow she knew he was standing up before he did so. It was as if they were connected by a thin, tingling wire. She knew he was walking toward her.

He stepped behind her and slipped his arms around her, dipped his head to her neck.

"Hello," she said, husky and low, her Frenchwoman's voice.

"Poppy," was all he said. But then he bumped her from behind, and the feeling of him, hard and urgent, went through her like a lightning shock.

"I love it when you don't wear panniers, but now we're in trouble," he murmured into her hair. "I can't turn around and shock everyone."

"How so?"

He held her tight against him. "I'm wearing a cut-away coat."

"Nothing would shock Jemma," Poppy pointed out.

"I don't want to drive her mad with lust," he said, a thread of laughter in his voice.

She snorted. "She's seen your like before."

"Don't count on it," he boasted.

She let her head fall back on his shoulder, even though he was a hopelessly vain and foolish creature: a male by definition, Jemma would say. He had a strong arm around her waist, so she curled her fingers around his wrist.

"You have to stop that," she said a little while later. Her voice came out with a dark edge.

"I don't think I can."

"I'm sure people can see you!"

His hand didn't stop. "I drew the curtains behind us, not that anyone was interested."

Poppy glanced back, over his shoulder, and saw that he had indeed drawn the thick velvet panels. Now they stood in a tiny room, framed by glass on one side, with the black world of snow outside, and a wall of crimson velvet on the other. She suddenly realized that the voices of the party were muffled, almost as if they came through a veil of snow as well.

"Anyone could open that curtain at any moment!" she gasped.

His hand was cupping her breast, a thumb roughly caressing her nipple until she twisted in his arms, unable to stop herself.

"They're not fools." His voice was dark as the night. He started nipping her, tiny little bites at the bottom of her ear, at her neck, at the curve of her shoulder.

"You're acting like an animal."

"I feel like an animal."

"Horses nip each other while mating, you know."

"I never examined the process."

"I read it in a book," she said, twisting again.

His other hand settled between her thighs, rubbing soft fabric over her delicate folds so that she was panting, gasping a little.

Suddenly she focused not on the dark outside the glass, but on their reflections. She, with her head thrown back on his shoulder, his dark hair falling over his cheek as he kissed her neck, his strong hands caressing her body as if it were a musical instrument by which he created a song from her gasps, her moans . . . He was rubbing a little harder and she was helpless, thrusting her hips forward, sobbing a little.

He turned her body just enough so he could take her mouth, but he didn't stop touching her.

"Fletch," she said. It was a whisper, a prayer. "You can't—" The words choked in her mouth. Her body was singing a tune she was still only coming to recognize. "People—"

"Hush. They've gone to dinner."

Sure enough, she realized that the muffled sound of laughter was gone, and the only sound she could hear was the pant of her own breath.

He was pulling up her skirts now, her pale legs reflected

in the glass until she turned all the way away from her pale image in the window, and slid her hands under his jacket, pulled out his shirt. Remembered that she was not a rag doll.

"No," he whispered. "This is my turn."

He did something with his hand and she sobbed a minute, had to catch her breath and then said, "No!"

"I can't undress in here," he said.

"But you're making me undress!" He had her gown up around her waist, and then he pushed her back against the glass. It was chilly and unexpectedly sensuous against her bottom: she felt cold and hot at the same time.

He wasn't even listening to her, just licking her neck and then kissing her chin and her cheek and the bottom of her cheekbone, and then finally taking her mouth. He was savage and soft at the same time, taking and giving, his hand keeping a rhythm that had her twisting against the cold glass, sobbing into his mouth.

Feeling the sparks fly higher and higher, until her heart was beating to a dance that no one could follow except his fingers as they drove her faster and higher, and then she was sobbing against him. He swallowed her shudders, her little scream, the way she trembled and shook in his arms.

When it was over she turned into his shoulder. "How loud was I?"

"What?" His voice sounded strained and rough.

She started to smile. "Was that my turn or yours?"

"My turn," he said.

"So when is it *my* turn?"

"Now?"

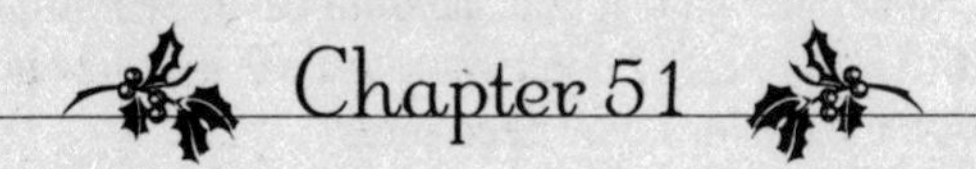

Chapter 51

Fletch was still a little red in the face, and he seemed slightly short-tempered to Poppy. She was feeling blissfully happy and couldn't stop smiling, whereas he was definitely irritable. "Wouldn't you like to go upstairs now?" he asked. "Since it's your turn?"

"Oh no," she said, smiling at him. "What I'd like . . ." She stopped and licked her lips, and then thrust out her bottom lip because she wanted to see that flare in his eyes. It was a French thing to do. "I'd like to go outside," she decided.

His face went suddenly bleak. "Outside?"

She nodded. "We can always go to bed later, Fletch."

"Do you think that you could call me by my real name?"

"Fle— What is your real name?"

"You don't know your own husband's name?"

She thought about it for a moment and refused to feel a pang of guilt. "My mother was scandalized by the mere fact that I addressed you as Fletch rather than Fletcher. If I had started calling you by your Christian name she would have fainted."

"I hate your mother." He said it flatly.

"My mother said that I shouldn't return until you had a mistress," she observed. "So I wasn't forced to service you all the time."

He grabbed her so fast that she didn't even see him move. "Forget that ugliness. I don't want to hear it; it has nothing to do with us. Besides, you need me."

She smiled into his mouth. "Why?"

"To service you. And—" He said it into her hair, and at first she didn't understand and then her heart bounded.

But there was something she had to say. "I can't be French all the time, Fletch. I'm—I'm afraid you're going to lose interest."

He looked down at her, eyes burning. "Never."

Her lips were trembling but she still wanted to say it all. Because perhaps, at the end, they could stay friends and if she didn't have that, her heart would break. That was the worst of it, the thing she realized only when she saw her own reflection in the glass. She looked—she *was*—a woman in love. The kind of love that you never got over, that was like an illness until death. "But I just want to say that if it happens, if we could stay friends, Fletch, I could—"

"Not Fletch!"

She blinked. "What is your name, then?"

"John."

"What?" It was such a simple, solid, respectable name. It seemed to have nothing to do with her exotically fashionable husband.

"You can't ever say it in public."

She stared up at him. His hair was rumpled from the way she clutched him, behind the curtain. But his coat fell in perfect seamless folds. His cravat somehow managed to make rumpled look fashionable. He looked like the most exquisite sprig of fashion in the *ton*.

"Your name is *John*?"

He looked so furious that she couldn't stop laughing.

"Didn't you say that you wanted to take your turn now?" He definitely sounded grumpy.

It was perfect for him, of course. John was the man she fell in love with: a solid, thoughtful, powerful prince of a man who loved loyally and truly. Whose exotic exterior had little do with a solid English interior.

"I love you," she said. "John." She touched his cheek.

His smile was a little crooked.

"Let's go outside. For a walk."

She had trouble getting him to stop kissing her but finally he followed her.

A man whose name is John doesn't stop loving his wife because she isn't the most beautiful in the room. Or the youngest. Or the least well-read.

A man named John loves you forever.

Chapter 52

"I don't want to go outside. It's cold. It's Christmas Eve and it's snowing. Everyone will think we're mad."

From the look on the footmen's faces, they were already certain of that fact. But Poppy, wrapping a woolen scarf around her neck and over her head, said, "You just want your turn."

"That wasn't what I meant!"

"I've never been allowed outside in a snowstorm," she said.

"The voice of reason," he groaned, accepting a pair of fur-lined gloves from the butler.

"Please do not lose yourself in the snow," the butler observed, handing Fletch a little lantern.

"That's right," Fletch said. "We could be at risk! Lost in the snow and never recovered until the spring thaw."

"It's scarcely snowing now," Poppy said, taking a lantern

for herself and nodding to a footman, who pulled open the great front door.

Light spilled from the doorway, revealing a world turned into piles of soft cakes covered with spun sugar.

Poppy danced through the door and Fletch followed.

"If Your Graces do not return in an hour, I'll send the footmen after you," the butler announced.

Fletch had the sudden idea that perhaps they could find a warm barn and test Miss Tatlock's idea that animals could talk on Christmas Eve. And a few other things he had in mind. His turn, for example.

"Two hours," he clarified.

He felt ravenous. Obsessed. Absolutely mad. What he wanted to do was drag Poppy back upstairs, throw her on the bed and plunge into her. The thought made him so hard that he hardly felt the sting of cold outside. Naturally, Poppy had pranced directly into the snow and was tracking around the side of the house.

"Wait for me," he bellowed, and then started after her, walking in her footsteps. Snow had to be up to her knees. Courtesy demanded that he break a trail, but if she were so eager that she wanted to plow through drifts, he'd allow her to be the man.

She was a fast little thing, so he tramped along in her wake, not thinking about much other than her thighs. How soft they were, and white. And how she whimpered last night when he started putting little bites there. And then when he got up a little higher, she stopped whimpering and started . . .

Well, what was it? How could it be the same woman he'd made love to for years? What happened to her?

It made him feel uneasy, as if the ground had shifted under his feet. Only last year she would lie before him like a chilled piece of molded butter, and now she was melting and shrieking. And it wasn't anything he did, either.

If he'd tried some new technique, he could have explained it to himself. He started walking slowly, thinking about it. Poppy was already around the corner of the house. He kept thinking that someone must have taught her—but he knew that wasn't true. There was no other man, except for that puny Dr. Loudan and she didn't like him that way. She liked to order the poor man about and send him fussy letters about squirrel toes and the like.

So if she wasn't melting because of another man, what was it?

It wasn't his beauty, though it was embarrassing to think of it that way, because she'd seen plenty of that in the years since they married.

Just then he heard a little shriek and sped up. He turned the corner fast to find his wife poking under a huge fir tree.

"What are you doing?" he shouted.

It was so quiet that his voice seemed swallowed up by snow. But oddly, it wasn't all that cold. The huge house reared behind them, golden light spilling out of all its windows. No one else was foolish enough to tramp around in the dark.

"Look at this," Poppy said, waving her lantern at him. "I believe some animals are living here, under the tree."

"Oh for God's sake, it's probably a bear," he groaned, plowing through the snow over to her. It was well over the top of his boots. She must be frozen, dragging skirts that had to be lined with ice.

"The tracks are much smaller than that. Look!"

He caught up with her and in a spar of light falling from his lantern, he saw the little footprints. Two tiny ones in front and two longer ones in back.

He gave a bark of laughter. "That's no bear!"

"Perhaps it's an English possum," Poppy said, giggling.

Her eyes were shining. Once he started laughing he could hardly stop.

"For a naturalist," he spluttered, "you're pretty slow, Poppy."

She narrowed her eyes at him and then looked back at the tracks. At the way the little ones were spaced, there weren't too many and . . .

"Rabbits!" she breathed. "There's a rabbit hole under this fir tree." And without a second's hesitation, she dropped to her knees and pushed her way right under the huge skirt of branches that jutted above the snow.

Fletch's mouth dropped open. For Christ's sake. "Poppy, get back out here!" he bellowed, leaning down.

No answer.

Suddenly he thought that rabbits make a good meal for a bear—who might well live under a tree. He dropped to his knees and thrashed his way under the tree so fast that he bumped right into Poppy.

She was sitting, hugging her knees, as if she were in her own bedchamber. "Fletch!" Poppy said, sounding as delighted as if he'd decided to join her for a cup of tea.

"What the hell," he growled, setting his lantern to the side. The light wavered and went out, leaving only Poppy's thin flame.

"It's like a little room," she said. "Wait a minute, Fletch. Your eyes will get accustomed."

"Are there any bears in here?"

But he took a breath.

"No rabbits and no bears. But it's a little house."

A minute later he saw what she meant. The snow had scoured around the fir tree, building little walls that came up to meet the bottom layer of fir. The ground was actually a soft mat of dried needles. The snow filtered light, somehow, so that it was a pearly gray under the tree, except for the shower of yellow light around her lantern. His head just brushed the bottom layer of fir branches.

"Very nice," he said. "Let's go, Poppy. Your skirts must be soaked through."

"I'm not cold," Poppy said. She was curled up against the fir tree, smiling at him. Her hair was escaping from a thick red wool hat the butler had given her. It was a world away from the elegant little bonnets she used to wear, tipped just so on top of elaborate nests of curls. She looked like a little girl.

Well, perhaps not so little. Not with that deep sensual lip and the way her eyes were watching him. She wasn't wearing all the face paint of last night but she didn't need it. Her lips were the dark plum color of ripe fruit.

Even as he watched her tongue stole out and wet her lips, and then she rolled out her bottom lip in that way she had and he was harder than the tree trunk.

There was hardly any room under there, so he crawled forward a bit. "Poppy," he said slowly.

"It's *your turn,*" she said.

"You'll catch your death. We can't—"

"In fact, it's warm in here," Poppy said. "This is a snow cave. I read about them in *Gentleman's Magazine.* When Captain Sybil went to the mountains of Peru, they dug snow caves and described them as quite warm."

"I am not warm," Fletch said. "My knees are wet. And my feet are frozen." He crawled forward again and stopped with his mouth just an inch from her lips. "I want my turn in a proper bed."

But she reached out one little red-mittened hand, and before he knew it, he was on his back in a soft bed of needles. She was lying on top of him, and through layers of coat he could feel the soft curves of her body. Plus, she was kissing him. Rather clumsily, it was true. She kept clicking their teeth together.

But to Fletch's mind, enthusiasm made up for everything. And when he managed to get his hands under her coat and started to rub her all over (for warmth, naturally), he found that he liked her kissing more and more.

She was kissing him and snuffling him, and licking his eyebrow and his eyelashes and then swooping down on his mouth whenever he said anything and kissing him into silence. He protested a bit when she started pulling his clothing apart, but by then they'd heated up the little cave. As she kissed her way down his chest, murmuring things about his turn, he felt his temperature go higher and higher.

"Poppy," he gasped at one point, "I don't think—"

She was playing, letting snow drift from her fingers onto his nipples and his more sensitive parts and then replacing the brief chill with her warm mouth. Being a naturalist, she accompanied her little experiments with a stream of commentary.

Fletch had never been very noisy in bed. He preferred to devote himself to his partner's pleasure . . . but now he found himself helpless in Poppy's curious hands, helpless under the ministrations of her sweet lips. Strange hoarse noises came from his lips as she played her games, laughing at him, licking him, finally driving him close to mindless pleasure—but not quite close enough.

Finally he managed to snatch her, wordlessly, wrench up her gown and hold her protesting, an inch from his body for a moment before letting her go. Her sweet wet warmth enveloped him.

She stopped protesting. Their clothes bunched up between them. He pulled his fur coat around both of them. Snow kept filtering down onto his face like a dusting of sugar . . .

It all faded away when he found the way home. The way to her.

He pulled her closer and closer until there was nothing, no end to her and no start to him, or that's how it felt.

Then he arched up, and she cried out. So he did it again, and again, and there in that perfect little room, Poppy found her voice and cried again and again.

Then she pulled back, sat up so that her head brushed the branches and sent snow all over them, but it melted the moment it struck their bodies.

She was a natural. Found a rhythm that drove him mad, too slow, too fast, he didn't know. All he knew was that pressure was building, and the pleasure was like pain, the way she kept slipping, sleek and tight and soft away from him and then coming back when the only thing he wanted was to grab her.

So finally he did that: grabbed her hips and held her where she had to be, and with a huge roar arched into her. Again and again, as fierce and as hard as he could.

She was panting and crying out, and he could feel the tension gathering in her body as if it were his own body.

And when the storm finally broke, it was the same moment for them, a shared moment, a shared tempest, a shared joy.

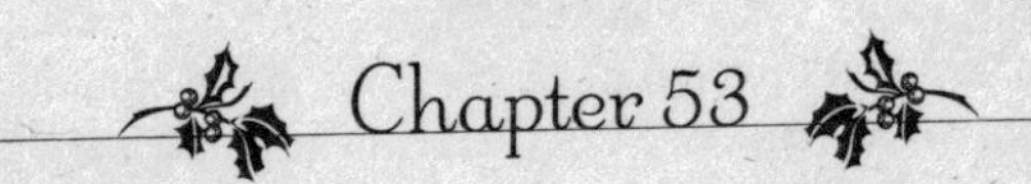

Chapter 53

When Villiers woke up, the bedroom was lit only by one candle. Charlotte was sleeping in a chair next to his bed. The Bible had fallen from her hand and lay half off his bed. He watched her for a bit. Dautry was sleeping in his chair, head awkwardly leaning against the wall.

It was later than he thought, because far away on the wind, he heard a jangle of church bells. They sounded like wild music, like the fairies that come in the night and steal souls, or children, or whoever it is that they steal.

The ringing meant that it was Christmas.

Another Christmas.

She woke up just then, like a cat from her sleep, and blinked at him.

He smiled at her.

"Leopold?" She pushed hair out of her eyes. "Oh my God, did I sleep here last night?"

"You're ruined," he said, hearing the cheer in his own

voice. "Of course, no one in Jemma's household will have noticed. I can still sue you for breach of promise if I have to."

"Breach of promise?" She sat up and stretched and then stopped. Stared at him. Froze.

He felt as weak as a kitten, but he managed to push up on his pillows.

"Oh my God," she whispered. "You—"

"You said that I put too much credence in the opinions of my doctors," he reminded her. "Treglown said that if I survived the night, I was going to live. Do you think I shouldn't believe him?"

"But he said—"

"I live to prove the man wrong. Merry Christmas, Charlotte."

"Merry Christmas," she whispered.

"Future duchess," he observed.

She leapt from her chair. "I'll be off to my own chamber now."

"Too late. You're compromised."

"In case you didn't notice," she said, "your heir is here as well. So who compromised me? Prepare your breach of promise suit, Your Grace."

"I will," he said, half under his breath. She whisked through the door and he reached out for his water glass. The water felt like a cool benediction on his tongue, sliding down his throat.

He was tired.

But he was alive.

So with his glass, he saluted the Child whose birth was about to be celebrated. "Thank you."

It sounded odd, whispered in the room. No one was there but his sleeping cousin, no one but a decrepit duke and the trace of a woman's perfume.

So he said it again, more loudly.

"Thank you."

Off in the distance the bells continued their wild jangle, and the Duke of Villiers turned on his side and fell into sleep, a clean, healing sleep.

Chapter 54

Christmas Day

Poppy woke up blinking because the bedchamber was full of light—a hard, crystal sunlight. She walked to the window to find that at some point during the night it must have sleeted, because the soft mounds of snow had transformed into a shining, sharp world of icy crystals. Light skittered along the curve of icy-looking snowbanks. Ice coated every twig of the hawthorne and fell in great icicles from the eves of the south wing.

Christmas morning.

Ever since Poppy was small, she had always welcomed Christmas. Her mother rarely lost her temper on Christmas; it was a quiet but celebratory day. They would sit about and her mother would let her skip her three hours of harpsichord practice, and the hour with the song master and the hours dancing. She even watched as Poppy played spillikins, though she always refused to play herself. And they would have gilt-topped gingerbread men to eat, a trip to church with warm bricks at their feet, and finally a roasted peacock for dinner.

There was a sound of feet and then warm arms wrapped around her waist from behind. "Come back to bed," said a sleepy voice.

"It's Christmas," she said.

"Let's celebrate."

"Not by that!"

"Why not?" He was nuzzling her neck, which was very sweet.

"Christmas is—Christmas is special," she said, pulling away.

"You are special." He reached out for her again.

"Fletch, it's morning."

He blinked at her. "So?"

She wiggled away. "It's not only morning—it's Christmas morning. All of that"—she waved at the bed—"it isn't seemly for the morning."

His expression darkened a bit. "What do you mean by seemly?"

"I couldn't—" She stopped. It almost sounded as if she'd heard herself say this before. Her mind skipped back to her-self, lecturing Fletch on the inappropriateness of open-mouthed kisses on a Christmas some years ago.

He folded his arms and raised an eyebrow.

"I can't be French all the time," she said slowly.

"I wouldn't want you to be."

"I won't always feel like making love under a tree."

"Not even behind the curtains?"

"No."

He was grinning now. "I can live with that. Because there's always the bed. Look at me, Poppy."

She met his eyes.

"No—look at me."

She started to blush. "It's morning, Fletch! My maid will be here any minute."

"She'll either knock first or learn to," he said. "Now look at me, Poppy."

She started chewing on her lower lip, but she let her eyes fall below his neck. He wasn't wearing drawers. His legs were long and very strong. It was those legs that plowed through the snow last night once he decided to carry her home. And his arms . . . she loved the way the muscles bulged in his forearms. He'd carried her all the way home as if she weighed no more than a feather. Poppy had nestled against his chest, her whole body boneless and soft and whispered things to him that she was fairly sure he couldn't hear.

Plus, she liked the way his chest came down into a hard little series of valleys. There was a little arrow of hair. And there it was. Not that it could make her blush anymore. Still, her glance lingered in an affectionate sort of way. And even looking made her feel that melting surge of heat again.

"Well," she said briskly, to cover up the fact that her knees felt a little weak, "I looked."

"What did you see?"

"Are you looking for compliments?"

"Absolutely."

She turned up her nose. "You look like a perfectly healthy male in your twenties."

He took a step toward her. "Don't I look like the person you love?"

Their eyes caught, but it was time for the truth. "Yes," she said. "Oh, yes, John."

"Like someone you married not just because your mother wanted you to?"

"I don't think"—her voice caught—"I don't think she had anything to do with it. Not really."

"Like someone who will be there, beside you, every day for the rest of your life?"

She managed a wobbly smile at that one.

"Poppy, what did you think that Christmas was for?"

"Nibbling on gingerbread men?" she whispered.

"I'm your Christmas gingerbread man," he said, just a quirk at the corner of his mouth betraying the fact he was laughing.

Poppy gathered herself together. "Are you saying that making love to one's spouse on Christmas is seemly?"

He smiled at her as if she'd won the village archery contest. "I am."

"And are you saying that making love in the morning is also seemly?"

"Yes. If not vitally important."

"And that"—and she had to say this one slowly, because it was so important—"that you won't lose interest in making love to me if I don't act like a Frenchwoman?"

"And I don't want to have to drag you out under a tree all the time either." He tilted up her face. "Don't you see, Poppy? I love you. I loved you enough to give up sex because you didn't like it. Now that you do like it . . . well, I'd like to do it anytime you'll let me. Under a tree, sure. With a French accent, *mais oui*. But snuggling in the bed with my oh-so-English wife, after she gives me a lecture on flying squirrels' toes, always. And for our whole life. So will you, please, come back to bed now?"

There were tears in her eyes. "I think," she said softly, "that I would like to marry you."

"You are married to me."

"I married a duke," she said. "I would like to marry you. My John, who happens to be a duke."

He swept her up in his arms. "Perdita, will you marry me?"

"Yes," she gasped.

"Good. Then let's seal our engagement." He swept her off toward the bed and then said, "Are you going to protest?"

She shook her head.

He deepened his voice to a silly imitation of a preacher. "It's most unseemly for unmarried people to make love."

She kissed his shoulder. He fell backwards but kept talking, the devilish laughter in his eyes as always. She kissed his neck. And then his chin, that strong chin now free of its jaunty little beard. So she kissed his dimple too.

"I love you," she said. Her voice sounded husky and seductive, except now she knew that it wasn't French but just desire. "I don't know how it happened, how I was so lucky. Because it's true that had you been some other man, some other duke, my mother would have forced me to marry you and I was such a stupid little creature that I would have. But somehow—somehow—you were the duke who appeared. I don't deserve you."

"I feel the same way. The way you respond to me while making love—"

"I listened to my mother," she said, interrupting. "I could hear her in my head all the time. I could feel her disgust—never you, Fletch. Because if I'd really felt you, if I'd really known you, it would have been different. From the very first night together. I just didn't know you were my husband, not really."

"I was always your husband," he said. "There's never been anyone for me since I saw you the first time, Poppy. Never. When you left me, I felt as if my soul had left the house. I kept walking about and pretending to be a normal person, but I was missing this vital part, this soul part—does that make sense?"

"With this kiss," she whispered, her lips against his, "I give you my soul. For keeping."

"For better, for worse," he said.

"In sickness and in health."

"'Til death do us part."

And from that moment forward, the Duke and Duchess of Fletcher fell silent. But from then onwards, they surprised their friends, and later their family, by insisting that, all evidence to the contrary, they were married on Christmas Day.

And they celebrated that day together for years, and years. And years.

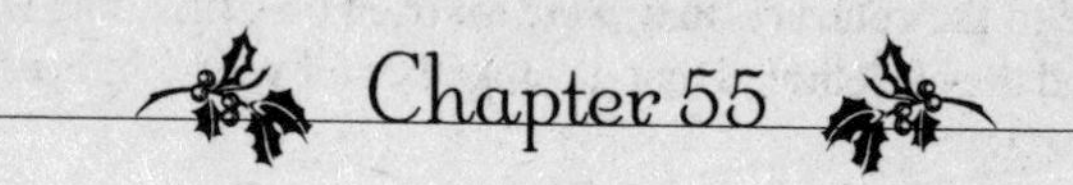

Chapter 55

A Costume Ball at the country seat of the Duke of Beaumont
January 6, Twelfth Night

"Not one of these costumes is particularly interesting," the Duke of Fletcher complained to his wife.

"I think that Mrs. Patton's costume is very imaginative. I've never seen quite such a fierce-looking Diana, and all in royal blue too. The bow and arrow is a nice touch. And I like the squire over there, the one dressed as Henry VIII."

"I know Henry VIII had a large stomach," Fletch observed. "But I think Lord Pladget took liberties in his interpretation."

"His wife told me that he tied the hearth rug around his middle with twine."

"You know, I thought that Lady Isidore was quite sedate when I first met her," Fletch said. "But look at her now!"

Isidore danced by, dressed as Zenobia, Queen of Palmyra. Her skirt was made of gold tissue and embroidered all over with peacock tails; her bodice wasn't worth mentioning because there was so little to it.

"Oh no," Poppy moaned. "That's Lord Beesby she's dancing with, isn't it?"

"He's a bit of a silly old codger," Fletch said. "Always votes—"

"That's not what I meant," Poppy said. "Just look at the way he's staring into Isidore's eyes."

"In love," Fletch said. "Hopeless case, I'd say."

"Is he married?" Poppy hissed.

"Not yet."

She relaxed and they continued dancing down the length of the room, narrowly avoiding a collision with a boisterous peer dressed, rather improbably, as the Pope. His face had turned a ripe purple and he was swaying like the sail of a tall ship. All the talk of costumes made Poppy remember something she'd been meaning to ask.

"Fletch, who was that young man you hired?" she asked.

But Fletch didn't hear; he was laughing at the way the Pope stumbled to the floor, bringing a sailor dancing with the Queen of Sheba with him.

The Queen of Sheba wasn't quite as amused. Charlotte untangled herself from the Pope's feet. Dautry pulled her to her feet as if she were a feather, and a moment later they were dancing down the floor again.

"How on earth did you learn to dance?" she said.

"Sailors dance," Dautry said. "Besides, believe it or not, Miss Tatlock, there is civilization outside the ballrooms of the *ton*."

She who had been so snappy and witty with Villiers

couldn't think of anything to say at the moment. It was as if a magic curtain had evaporated and she had returned to being a lumpy old maid. Except that . . . the old maid was dancing with a flamboyantly masculine man, the kind whom all the women in the room were watching.

"So are you going to marry him?" he asked abruptly.

"What?"

"Are you going to marry Villiers? And don't"—he added—"think that I am worried about inheriting the title. My father left me what is often called a shipping fortune. I could buy half London and sell it again, if I wished."

"Naturally, you must feel some anxiety—" she began.

He pulled her off the ballroom floor and into a small curtained alcove, and with no finesse about it either.

Suddenly she felt herself a little breathless. "Are you going to marry him?" he demanded.

Her mouth opened but no words came out.

He bent his head. His mouth wasn't soft and forgiving: it demanded and took, asked a question she wasn't ready to answer.

So she—old maid Charlotte—stepped away from him and put her hands on her hips. "I'm not sure yet," she told him.

He looked a little dazed. At least she wasn't alone feeling that wild heat when they kissed. "You're not sure of what?"

"I'm not sure who I shall marry."

"Has a choice been offered?"

She grinned, knowing that her sister May wouldn't even have recognized her. She was the Queen of Sheba tonight, a woman who commanded men's hearts. "Villiers is threatening me with a breach of promise suit if I don't marry him."

Dautry snorted.

"And I love him."

His jaw tightened.

She danced one step closer to him. "But then there's you."

"I didn't ask you to marry me."

The idiot.

"I suppose that only leaves me the duke, then. You can practice calling me Your Grace."

His eyes were fierce, but softened when he looked to the bottom of her soul, and saw a woman who wanted to stand before the wind and feel salt on her lips.

"Charlotte," he said.

She raised her chin. "I'll decide next week. Between your proposal and his. Because you did make one, didn't you? You may have forgotten to say it out loud; I have noticed a certain reticence in your nature."

There was a spark of laughter in those black eyes of his. A spark of laughter—and something else, something that made her feel a bit weak behind the knees, and as if there wasn't enough air in the room.

Which there wasn't once he started kissing her again.

"I'm sorry?" Fletch said.

"The young man you hired," Poppy repeated. "Where did you find him?"

"Which young man?"

"The one who pretended to be in love with my mother."

His face went utterly still. "Oh—"

"Yes," she said, nodding. "That young man. The one who defended my mother's reputation so bravely. He obviously had a certain amount of dramatic talent."

"Wouldn't you rather picture your mother's affection for a handsome young lad?"

Fletch smiled winningly, but Poppy just shook her head. "Is he here tonight?"

"For goodness' sake, no," Fletch said, giving in. "He was, how shall I put it, a gentleman of the night. A night-walker."

"Gentleman of the—" Poppy's eyes went round. "*Really!* Where on earth did you find him?"

"I simply asked a woman who knows about that sort of thing."

She narrowed her eyes. "And what woman might that be?"

"A young relative of Mrs. Armistead, Fox's consort."

"I wasn't even aware you were acquainted with Mrs. Armistead."

He swept her off the dance floor and then looked down at his own sweet wife. "You do realize how much I love you, don't you?"

She frowned.

"Tell me you're jealous. Her name is Cressida, and she is *very* beautiful."

"I am not jealous," she said instantly, wrinkling her nose at him. "So you have been consorting with night-walkers and day-walkers and Fox-walkers—"

"Very clever," he said, reprehensibly kissing her right in the ballroom.

But Poppy had the sense that the Duchess of Beaumont's Twelfth Night Ball would be the subject of gossip for years, and a marital kiss or two wouldn't receive much attention.

Naturally, now that the Duke of Villiers was on the mend, the Duchess of Beaumont's chess matches—with her husband, with Villiers—had flared into a wild source of gossip again.

"Did you beat him?" Mrs. Patton asked, pausing for a moment in the ladies' retiring room.

Jemma threw her a lazy wink. "Do you doubt it?"

"Not after the way you have thrashed me in the last few days."

"You took a very nice game off me last night," Jemma pointed out. "That was a very cunning move with your castle. You utterly foxed me."

"A rare victory," Mrs. Patton said. "But none the less enjoyed for that! So you won the game with your husband . . . and finished the game with Villiers as well?"

"Alas," Jemma said, frowning at herself.

"You didn't win?"

"He sacrificed and sacrificed, a whole battlefield of them. Brilliant, ruthless and cunning."

"So both matches continue to a third and final game," Mrs. Patton said. "Fascinating!"

"And the final games are to be played blind-folded," Jemma said, rubbing a bit of ruby color on her lips.

"And—or so I've heard," Mrs. Patton said, pausing delicately.

"In bed," Jemma confirmed.

"In bed with the Duke of Villiers," Mrs. Patton said, rather dreamily. "There's not a married woman in England who wouldn't consider sacrificing her queen for the chance."

"Villiers refuses to play the game until he is fully recovered. He says six months."

Mrs. Patton laughed. "Will you play your husband immediately?"

"I don't know," Jemma said, tucking in an errant curl. "I won our game a while ago and we haven't had time to discuss the topic. That's a decision for another day . . ."

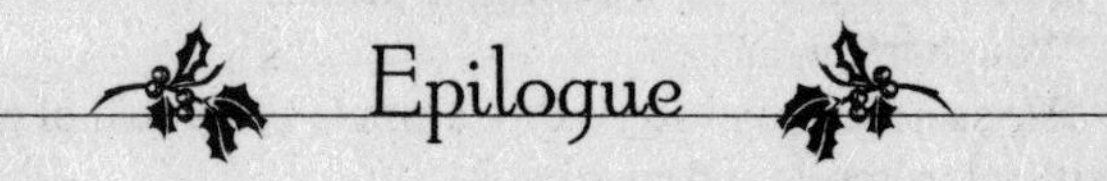

Epilogue

The Nursery, the Fletcher Estate
Seven years later
December 25

It was Christmas, and a small girl was singing rather tunelessly, the way untalented but cheerful children do: "I saw three ships come sailing in, on Christmas Day, on Christmas Day."

Her father joined her, his deep smooth voice sliding like chocolate below her piping high one. "I saw three ships come sailing in, on Christmas Day in the morning."

Then she squealed. People do that when they find themselves suddenly sailing through the air and landing on someone's shoulders. Even if they are small people, who should be used to this kind of mishandling.

"Papa!" Clementina said, clutching the Duke of Fletcher's hair. "You must stop doing that. Grandmère told me that I shouldn't shriek because I'm a young lady. But you made me shriek. It wasn't my fault."

Her father obligingly dipped her upside down until she screamed even more loudly, so much so that they attracted attention from the other person in the room.

Before Fletch realized what was happening, plump little arms wrapped around his legs and a set of five sharp teeth, two on the top and three on the bottom, clamped together. "You let Clemmie go!" screamed a voice only slightly obscured by a mouthful of silk stocking. "You let Clemmie go, bad Papa!"

"*Not* my stockings, Alexander," Fletch said, putting Clementina down on the ground so fast that her hair flew up around her shoulders like corn silk. "Oh dash it," he groaned, unwinding his son from his leg, "that's the death knell for another pair of stockings. Now what will poor Morton say?"

Alexander had no sympathy for the duke's valet. He was too busy correcting the duke himself. "You's not nice to Clemmie," he said. Then: "Assander, up!"

Fletch swung his son up on his shoulders.

"Come on, Papa," Clementina said, tugging his hand. "Let's pretend we see three ships!"

She danced her way over to the window, dragging him behind. "I saw three ships come sailing in . . ." she started over. This time he let her sing it alone, standing there with her warm little hand clutching his, and Alexander's plump knees next to his ears. Clementina swayed back and forth, obviously seeing tall sailing ships glide over the snowy lawn.

Then he turned around, because somehow he always knew when his wife was in a room. Their daughter kept singing, wildly off-key, so Fletch just smiled rather than interrupt her. Alexander made a cooing sound and started bouncing in a way that indicated either a wish to learn to fly—or a wish to be in his mother's arms.

Poppy's smile was so beautiful that Fletch felt his heart almost break from the joy of it all as he tucked her under his arm. Alexander put a hand on his mother's curls and they all looked out the window as Clementina sang on. "On Christmas day in the morning!" she carrolled, coming to a stop.

Poppy looked as if she might move, so Fletch put his son down and snatched his wife into his arms instead. "Hello," he said. She was as lovely as the moment he first saw her in Paris, and as delicious as the first time they made love under a fir tree.

The children were so used to their parents embracing that Alexander toddled away and Clementina picked up her doll and began crooning to her, a special rendition of—yes!—"Three Ships."

"It's Christmas," Fletch said, dusting Poppy's lips with a kiss. And then another one because she tasted good, and she smelled good, and she was his. "Do you remember when I first kissed you like this, on the tower of Saint Germain dés Pres?" He gave her a kiss to illustrate, a deep, possessive kiss.

"Be careful," she said a little breathlessly. "I'll smack you with my muff."

Fletch let his hands slide over his wife's derrière. "I love these new fashions," he said dreamily. "I never want to see a pannier again in my life."

"Christmas," she said, brushing a lock of hair out of his eyes, "is my favorite day of the year."

"Your day . . ." he said, leaning closer, "to nibble gingerbread men."

"Do you know what the chef made this year?" she asked, eyes wide and innocent.

"No, what?"

"Gingerbread ladies! Covered with gold and quite, quite edible."

Fletch grinned. "Are you saying that it's *my turn*?"

Poppy leaned in and gave him a kiss that suddenly turned into something sweeter and deeper, the way things did on Christmas Day. "We'll have to fight for it," she whispered, some time later.

"For what?" Fletch asked, having lost track of the situation. "Poppy, I'm—"

She craned her neck instantly. "What's he doing?" Alexander was their daredevil, but no, he was busily banging a toy carriage against the brick hearth in a manner guaranteed to destroy its wheels.

"Not Alexander," Fletch said, catching her face in his hands. "Are you sure this isn't a dream?"

Never mind the fact that women all over London sighed when they caught a glimpse of Fletch. Nor the fact that his party in the House of Lords turned as one man to the Duke of Fletcher when they needed a brilliant speech—and a clear victory. And finally the fact that his wife gave every sign of being tremendously happy in bed and out . . . her own darling husband never quite believed that he was worth it.

"John," she said, a grin curling her mouth. "Did you know that last night was Christmas Eve and that meant that donkeys were able to speak in human voices?"

He raised an eyebrow. "Is this something my wife the naturalist has noticed? Have you written a letter to poor Loudan? Maybe this fact will be the one that finally gets him the university professorship he would never deserve without all your editing of his work. Although I'm sure the university would rather hire a certain P.F., author of a recent treatise on possums."

"You may not have noticed," she said lovingly, "but I'm pretty sure there's a donkey in the room now and he's not speaking English anymore. It almost sounds as if . . . as if he didn't hear all those things I said last night."

"I think the Duchess of Fletcher just called her husband an ass," he observed. "I knew you took after your mother!" Then he ducked when she swatted at him.

"Those things I said last night . . ." She could feel herself getting a little pink, even all these years into their marriage. "Last night," she whispered, "after—"

"After supper?" His eyes were laughing at her.

Despite their years together, Poppy wasn't very good at saying things out loud, though she'd become very good indeed at doing them in private. So instead she just pulled his head down and kissed him with all her heart, with the joy that comes from being truly loved, and truly loving.

With the joy that comes from knowing one's children are utterly convinced they are lovable, and never fear a harsh word or a blow.

With the joy that comes from having a secret.

But after a while she remembered that her secret was meant to be a Christmas present, so she whispered, "Merry Christmas, John," and took his hand in hers.

There was no more than a graceful curve under Fletch's hand. "A baby?" he said, incredulous. "A baby?"

She nodded, tears prickling her eyes. "Another baby."

And then Fletch was swinging her around and around in a great laughing circle that swept Alexander into her arms, and Clementina wiggled between them, all of them shrieking and laughing and saying it over and over, "A baby! A baby!"

Which made sense. As it was a Baby's birthday, after all.

A Note on Georgian Curiosities, Including Hair

As a professor, I am constantly happening on curious bits of history that don't seem appropriate for a romance novel—and which I long to use. One of these is the state of women's hair in the Georgian period. Those towering hairstyles that we see in movies about Marie Antoinette housed all sorts of little beasts, not to mention tallow, glue, and animal fat. Poppy's allergy to hair powder and the disordered state of her hair must have been very common in the period, when hair washing was rare and styles took hours to arrange.

Curiosity cabinets are another aspect of English history that I have been longing to describe. There were few female naturalists in English history—but start looking at the historical record, and there were huge numbers of women interested in science and nature. The only way that passion could be expressed was through collection and curiosities. It was a lot of fun creating the beasts in Poppy's collection, but the truth is that there was many a curiosity cabinet with its own unicorn horn or a tooth from the Sisfreyan beast (whatever that was).

In *An Affair Before Christmas*, Poppy and Jemma collect things that speak to their natures: so Poppy buys a statue of Eros and Psyche, only to later find that the boy interests her as much as the butterfly. And Jemma buys the ferociously frowning little chess queen, which will draw her to Lord Strange's house party. But that's material for another book . . .

If you have any questions—historical or otherwise—please don't hesitate to stop by my website Bulletin Board, or send me an e-mail at *Eloisa@eloisajames.com*.

More romance from
New York Times bestselling author
ELOISA
JAMES